PERIL

AT THE

EXPOSITION

ALSO BY NEV MARCH

Murder in Old Bombay

PERIL AT THE EXPOSITION

NEV MARCH

MINOTAUR BOOKS
NEW YORK

First published in the United States by Minotaur Books, an imprint of St. Martin's Publishing Group

PERIL AT THE EXPOSITION. Copyright © 2022 by Nawaz Merchant. All rights reserved. Printed in the United States of America. For information, address St. Martin's Publishing Group, 120 Broadway, New York, NY 10271.

www.minotaurbooks.com

Library of Congress Cataloging-in-Publication Data

Names: March, Nev, 1967– author.
Title: Peril at the exposition / Nev March.
Description: First Edition. | New York : Minotaur Books, 2022. |
Identifiers: LCCN 2022010205 | ISBN 9781250855039 (hardcover) |
    ISBN 9781250855046 (ebook)
Subjects: LCGFT: Novels.
Classification: LCC PS3613.A7328 P47 2022 | DDC 813/.6—dc23
LC record available at https://lccn.loc.gov/2022010205

Our books may be purchased in bulk for promotional, educational, or business use. Please contact your local bookseller or the Macmillan Corporate and Premium Sales Department at 1-800-221-7945, extension 5442, or by email at MacmillanSpecialMarkets@macmillan.com.

First Edition: 2022

10 9 8 7 6 5 4 3 2 1

To my husband: Happy 30th Anniversary.
Thank you for these years.

PERIL AT THE EXPOSITION

CHAPTER 1

THE DAY JIM LEFT

25TH OF MARCH 1893

That evening I knew something was amiss but didn't want to admit it. To address it would make it real. We'd only just made a home here in Boston, got acquainted with the Chinese couple next door and the Welks, the Irish family below, and my husband, Jim, was learning his trade at the Dupree Detective Agency. Yet something was wrong.

A key rattled in the door, so I wiped off my hands with a flutter of excitement.

"Ah, sweetheart," Jim said, setting down a package. He took off his boots and black wool coat by the door. Seeing the seams stretch at his shoulders, the fabric thin at the elbows, I sighed. He needed a new overcoat, but always found a reason to postpone it. Instead, he'd bought a used coat because we were saving to buy a house. When I protested this parsimony, he'd just smiled.

Jim's full name is Captain James Agnihotri, but he rarely used it now. We went by O'Trey, the tail end of his name. He washed up, kissed my cheek, and sat down while I set the table. We'd been married six months, but it was still new to me. I watched him unobtrusively, his calm manner that gave an impression of contained strength. Well proportioned, one did not notice his height except by comparison. Standing beside him, even with my curly hair piled up in a Newport knot, I felt as small as a child.

I sniffed—a whiff of burning crust hovered in the air.

"Oh no!" I hurried to the stove, grabbed a towel and hauled out my tray of hot cross buns. Their healthy golden glow reassured me, but the undersides! Were they charred?

"Damn this old stove!" I wailed. Learning to cook wasn't easy—I'd put down my book only to find my sausages singed, or my soup bubbled down to a few sticky inches. Cleaning floors tired me. When I pressed clothes with the heavy box iron, its glowing embers left sooty streaks on Jim's nice clean shirts. Fortunately, Mrs. Welks downstairs took in washing.

"Ah!" Jim plucked a bun off the tray, tossing it from hand to hand to cool it. Biting into it, he closed his eyes, his body still. "Mmm."

A glow filled me then, watching him chew slowly to savor my bread. When I'd made the buns for Christmas, Jim's face shone with such enjoyment, so I baked them often, pressing a currant into each like a button on an overstuffed pillow.

An orphan, raised in a Christian mission in Poona, Jim wasn't sure exactly what year he was born but thought it might have been 1862. At fifteen "or thereabouts," he'd run away to join the British army. My poor boy had seen few luxuries in his hard life.

He loved the smell of bread. In Bombay he'd lived in a dusty warehouse behind a bakery, a far cry from Framji Mansion, where I grew up among servants and bearers, with rows of banana, citrus and papaya trees on Papa's shady estate. That gap between us shrank last September, as our liner crawled through the Suez Canal, on to Liverpool, then plowed across the Atlantic.

Finishing the bun in two bites, Jim turned to me. His grey eyes light against the dark lashes he inherited from his Indian mother, lashes so long a girl might envy them, he said, "Someday, let's have a bakery, you and I, yes?"

I smiled as our little clock dinged the half hour. Perhaps nothing was wrong, after all. And yet I knew, deep within me, today felt different. The texture of his words was careful, like someone saying goodbye.

Pushing away the odd thought, I laid out cheesed potatoes and boiled eggs on a dish, cutting slices from a loaf for our simple supper. Jim was quiet at dinner. Although he complimented the meal and flashed a smile at me, a shadow of presentiment dogged those moments. I wanted no storm to threaten my cozy apartment with Mama's soft yellow curtains at the windows, and my father's gift, a burgundy Persian rug on the floor. After all the to-do with my parents and our Parsee brethren in Bombay, we were married; surely we deserved some peace and quiet?

We washed and dried the dishes as usual, but Jim seemed distracted, barely aware of passing me the plates. His silence reminded me of an evening high in the North India hills of Simla, when he'd been lost in thought, then watched me closely. That night he left on a secret mission into enemy terrain and was gone for weeks.

Jim was fond of fictional sleuth Sherlock Holmes. He'd been teaching me to observe, to make deductions, thinking backward, as he said, to where something was, or should be, or shouldn't be. Why this was considered "backward" I had no idea. Over dinner he'd usually tell me about his day—visiting people to investigate someone or following to see where they went. He'd ask questions to see what I'd noticed on my trip to market.

Now he had his head back against the settee, eyes closed, but I wasn't deceived. His arms clenched beside him as if awaiting a blow. Was he remembering the awful things he'd seen in the army? Or something else?

"Captain Jim?" That was what we called him when my brother Adi hired him last year.

He smiled, opening his eyes. "Ah," he said, "you know."

Heartened by his calm, I tucked my skirt under me and sat. "Something's happened."

Instead of replying, he picked up the long narrow parcel by the door and handed it to me. "A present, my sweet."

"But my birthday's two weeks away," I protested, grinning, nonetheless.

He nodded at the package, so I unwound the string and peeled back newspaper to reveal a pretty blue parasol edged with ruffles. With a staff of metal, it lay heavy upon my lap.

When I reached for the handle, Jim's hand clamped my arm.

"Careful," he said, pointing it away from me and squeezing the handle. To my surprise, the tip retracted, revealing a sharp, shiny blade.

"Goodness!" I was no fragile miss, fainting in a fit of vapors. One awful night last year I'd killed a man. I had to—if I hadn't fired that shot, I'd have lost my dear Jim. The incident left him with a scar on his neck, one more gash to mark the progress of Captain Jim's life, for he was a soldier and a good one. Yet when I fired, I could not have imagined how it would change us. It had already changed Jim's notion of me.

He released the handle and passed it to me, saying, "It is a weapon, my dear. Do not forget that."

A soldier is always preparing for trouble, I supposed. Jim had given me such gifts before. I closed the parasol with care. "Thank you, Jim. It seems rather ah, excessive, to take it shopping. What with my sharpened hairpins, and hatpins, and the muff you rigged up?" I met his gaze evenly. "What's happened?"

"Diana." He covered my hand. "I have to go away for a bit. Not long."

I felt a change coming but put on a brave face. "An investigation?"

He nodded. "I must visit Chicago."

"I'll manage for a few days," I said with airy pretense. The prospect of living alone, even a short while, seemed dry and joyless but I kept up a pleasant manner.

Jim gave me a long look, then nodded. He packed very little, taking his oldest clothes in a beat-up suitcase I'd never seen before.

Sitting cross-legged on the bed, I tossed questions at him that he answered in his usual steady way. Some weeks ago, a security guard called Thomas Grewe had been killed. Jim's colleague Arnold Baldwin had gone to investigate and now requested Jim's assistance.

Chicago seemed far away. I frowned. "Why did they ask the Duprees for help?"

"The boss was in the Union army with Brennan, who runs the Chicago police."

"You'll be armed, Jim?"

He nodded, saying, "Don't think it'll come to that, sweet."

"Don't they have detectives there, who know the place?"

He grinned. "Trust you to ask that. Been some trouble where they're building the World's Fair. Baldwin wants me to take a look at the scene. Says union fellows don't much like the Pinkertons."

What was he walking into? "You won't get . . . involved in the dispute?"

"Not likely. Just question the union fellows. Could be tricky, though. I'll be back in a couple of weeks."

"Weeks? What should I do all that time?"

"Well, you've wanted to visit the Abernathys," he said, adding an old boater hat to his valise. "Tour the Art Museum—or visit the hospital with Ida. She's a benefactor, you said."

We had met George and Ida Abernathy on the *Umbria* but didn't see them often. They were society folk, and Jim saw himself as a working man. He preferred tramping about the docks in ugly, worn overalls to dressing for society dinners.

Shoulders filling the door, Jim turned and pulled me close. I wanted to demand that the Dupree Detective Agency send someone else, but I'd known this moment was coming, so I bore up. Loosening his hold, he searched me with his gaze.

My brother Adi would have said, "Let him go, Diana. He'll be back," but I fussed over him, asking, "It's so late. Can't you take the morning train?"

"No, sweet," he said, his dark hair longer than it should be, stark against his light skin. Jim had never known his English father, though we had our suspicions. When I put my hand to his cheek, Jim turned his face into my palm, lines crowding the corners of his eyes. I heard the reluctance of his slow breath. He kissed me gently, plucked his old hat off the hook and left.

I peered out from the window to wave him farewell, but he did not turn, striding down the street to catch his train. Our room was as quiet as the Towers of Silence, where my people, the ancient Persians, leave our dead.

My dark, unruly hair, amber complexion and pointed features came from a long line of Zoroastrian Persians, successful merchants and land-owners. By marrying Jim, I'd abandoned the code of my ancient tribe, refusing my duty to that bloodline. My family, my heritage, had been my identity for so long that, cut off from my kin by an entire ocean, some-times I wondered, who was I now?

I smoothed down the tablecloth that I'd embroidered with trailing roses. On the table lay a pile of books about magnets and electricity that Jim had borrowed from the Boston Public Library.

Tidying up, I glanced at the newspaper on the table and frowned at the headline: WILL THE WORLD'S FAIR OPEN ON TIME? Chicago was preparing for the Columbian Exposition—said to be the greatest fair the world had ever seen. It would celebrate the four hundredth anniver-sary of Columbus's voyage to this continent and demonstrate America's progress in industry. And Jim had gone there to investigate the murder of a man called Thomas Grewe.

People often do not value what they have until they lose it. But I did. I knew Jim's generous nature—why else would he have carried a gaggle of filthy urchins to safety in Simla; his self-restraint said he knew I was not ready to be a mother; his doggedness—God knows a man of fainter heart would have quit the hunt for my sisters' killers last year; I trea-sured him for those reasons and a hundred more.

I didn't think I could stand to lose him.

CHAPTER 2

AN UNEXPECTED VISITOR

When we are truly happy, why don't we ever know it? I'd been happy at home in Bombay and on shipboard with Jim. We'd been happy setting up our home together. Now I stared at the open drawer containing his army medal, a gold star suspended from a red-and-blue band. Around it he'd wound a thick yellow thread, an Indian ornament called a Rakhee, gifted by sisters to their brothers.

Beside the medal lay a wedding ring. I stared at it, dropped so casually into his drawer, a thick gold band, twin of my own. I'd purchased both from Gamadia Jewelers in Bombay before we sailed. Caressing the smooth gold with my fingertips, I held it to my lips. Why had he left it behind? Some part of me argued that of course Jim traveled in disguise so he could not wear it. Yet I shivered. It looked like something given to a widow.

Pulling out a sheet of letter paper, I wrote to my brother: "*Dear Adi, I'm working at the hospital now, training to be a nurse. My friend Ida Abernathy arranged it for me.*" I'd taken up work at the hospital to do something useful, because alone in our apartment, time crawled like a crippled ant. Now, seeing Jim's wedding ring, I laid down the pen, because my vision blurred and I did not want to send Adi, and Mama, a letter burdened with tearstains.

When Jim and I arrived in Boston, fall was just setting in. Our September strolls were filled with excitement—maples brilliant with orange and gold, hedgerows of crimson burning bush against low flint walls—woodlots bursting with color, stately homes, sidewalks lit by tall, yellow gaslights. We walked everywhere, Jim and I, exploring neighborhoods, quizzing each other on street names. He was lighthearted then, grinning like a schoolboy when I forgot what the Charles River was called, or Back Bay Park. After dinner, Jim usually studied the newspaper while I practiced my knitting. He read aloud, asking me to explain a classical name or reference to a Greek myth.

Mr. Lincoln's festival of Thanksgiving came and went, then winter set in, and the bitter, piercing cold. My winters in England, though damp, had been brightened by the lively company of my friend Emily-Jane, who'd lived in a grand old place in Cheshire. This entire Boston apartment could have fit inside her parents' parlor. I shivered. In sunny Bombay, it would be a hundred degrees already.

I supposed most places must seem cold compared to Bombay. Bostonians liked April, mothers shepherding children who skipped or dashed about. All Sunday an interminable wind whistled outside. Watching dreary afternoon turn to misty dusk, I thrust the window open. Outside, the Welkses' children ran about, trampling the crocuses. Bred of sturdy New England stock, they chased a cat, their high voices calling, "Come, kitty!"

Watching couples walk out under boughs festooned with pink, knobby buds, Jim's absence was an ache.

* * *

Five weeks after Jim left, a knock sounded on my door at sunset. I opened cautiously, gripping my little two-shot derringer inside my fur muff.

"Gut heav-ning," said an elderly man, gazing at me through thick glasses. He clutched a beat-up homburg in front of his chest.

"Yes?"

"I am looking for Mr. O'Trey, James O'Trey," he said, huffing so that it sounded like "Chames Oh Dray."

That low, thick accent—was he, perhaps, German? Why did he want Jim?

"I'm sorry, he's not home. Who shall I say called?"

His eyebrows jumped in an expression of panic before he smoothed down his whiskers and looked at his hat. "I can come back. Ven will he return? Tomorrow?" he asked. *Do-morrow.*

I shook my head, reluctant to reveal that Jim was away. But the near-sighted old fellow seemed harmless. His crumpled trousers dragged under his shoes and his collar was askew, one button having gone astray. He had no wife, then, to sew it back on. His lined face was lean and hungry, but so were many in Boston this past dark winter.

As he glanced about, unsure what to do, his wire-rimmed glasses told me this was no tramp. Perhaps Jim had offered him some aid? He often did that, calling his outlay an "investment in information." I had never learned what information such poor souls provided.

As the old man replaced his hat and turned to leave, I said, "Perhaps I can help?"

I expected a tale of sorrow and loss, ending with Jim's offer of a hand-out. Instead, the old man tugged his hair in quiet turmoil.

"Vere is he, your husband? His place of business—I will see him there?"

His hair stuck out over his ears like an untidy owl. Hoary eyebrows drooped into his troubled eyes. He should be snug at home with a bra-zier at his feet, I thought.

Stepping back, I said, "Come in, please."

He shuffled in reluctantly and slumped into Jim's chair.

I heated some soup and served it with a hunk of this morning's bread. While he ate, broth dripping from his whiskers to splatter his vest, I busied myself at the stove and kneaded dough for tomorrow's biscuits. They'd rise nicely overnight, and in the morning, Mrs. Welks's children would run to me for little buns and hugs. Her youngest were twins, only four years old.

Bundling up some fruit and cheese into a newspaper parcel, I placed it before my guest, saying, "Here's something for tomorrow. Now, what is your name?"

He thanked me, then said, "Professor Grimke. Rolf Grimke."

A professor. Was that a Prussian name? "What business do you have with my husband?"

"I . . . cannot say." His face squeezed shut, wrinkles crowding his eyes and forehead as he looked helplessly at me. He wanted to say something but worry deepened his frown, his lips pulled in like he'd tasted something bad. Perhaps he did not want to trouble Mr. O'Trey's wife.

His accent sounded like the German waiters who'd served us on the *Umbria*. I asked, "Would you like to leave a note for him, a letter?"

He exhaled heavily, peering at me. "You know of this? The letter he sent to me?"

A letter from Jim? Excitement coursed through me. "What letter? Please!"

His chin dropped in thought. Then he pulled out a thick envelope from his breast pocket and laid it on the table.

I cried, "That's Jim's handwriting! When did you get this?"

"Some days, a week," he said, as I extracted the pages, my heart racing, my fingers too slow. Here was proof that Jim was alive. It was dated two weeks ago.

Only the first page bore his strong, clear script: *Professor Grimke, Sir, I regret to trouble you with a matter of great urgency. Please translate the enclosed and send it to be held for me at the Chicago Post Office and Customs House. Tell no one. J. Agney.*

Jim's real name, Agnihotri, is a Hindu, Brahmin name. "Agni" is the Hindustani word for "fire," so his name meant "one who tends the temple fire." This seemed prophetic because in my Zoroastrian religion, we venerate fire as holy, that which purifies. Jim went by O'Trey, but sometimes O'Drey, Agney, or Cagney. His nonchalance over what is dear to most people, his name, often surprised me.

The two blue-inked pages he'd included were in German. One was torn lengthwise, only half remaining.

I asked, "Did you send him your translation?"

Grimke drew back, shaking his head, mouth grim. "No, Frau O'Trey, I cannot do that. It is bad if it is found. I could be jailed, even . . . hanged."

"You could be arrested?" Had he really said "hanged"? What on earth had Jim sent him?

He pushed away from the table, saying, "I cannot write it. It would look as if it was I, me, who wrote those words." He pointed to the pages as though they were filthy.

Here was a mystery, two pages in German that I could not read. They looked crumpled, as though smoothed out to fold into the mailer.

"Will you translate it for me? I'll write it down."

Pleading my case without words, I said no more. Grimke hesitated, then nodded.

Gnarled hands shaking, he picked up the pages. Taking a sheet from Jim's table, I wrote quickly. He spoke in jerky phrases, muttering under his breath, then rushed along.

Resting my pen in the inkpot, I gazed at the last words I'd written. *"Trini-troto-luene. The man in Paterson sells me wire, but not enough."*

The German letter teemed with obscure scientific terms and phrases, names of places I had never heard, dire warnings about the corrosive quality of chemicals. Since it was only a fragment of the letter, it made little sense. I'd not studied scientific philosophy—it was considered unfeminine. Now I wished I knew more. With the first pages missing, and the last one torn in half, my only clue was a puzzle.

The word *"ballistite"* followed names of other chemicals and an ominous phrase: *"suitable source located, I struck a bargain with Herr—."* The name had been torn off.

Grimke's earlier refusal, his dread unsettled me.

My clock gave a tired ding as the fire banked to a red glow.

"Ballistite . . . what is it used for?"

He winced. "It is . . . an explosive substance."

Explosives. In Chicago? Cold air touched the back of my neck.

Puffing, he struggled into his ragged coat and picked up his hat. He rubbed the brim with his thumbs, looking somber. "I hope your husband is well, madam. *Gute Nacht.*" Accepting his packet of food with an old-fashioned bow, he left.

My stomach churned as I folded the letter into my reticule. Jim expected a reply at the Post Office and Customs House. Now I had a sense of location, a picture of where he would be, to fill the void that consumed my nights. He'd written to Grimke, but hadn't found time to write to me? I scowled. His note spoke of haste and secrecy—but why didn't he seek help from his employers?

If I were in trouble, Jim would come in a trice. But the shoe was on the other foot. What should I do? We were new to this overcast land. Jim had no one else. He belonged only to me.

CHAPTER 3

REVELATIONS

I had no appetite for breakfast the next morning, but unfolded the translation on my kitchen table and examined it. What would Jim see?

The first page described the writer's travels, train rides to Philadelphia and New York, then the difficulty of locating people he'd been told to see. He'd gone to a factory in Cheswick, Pennsylvania, to find a fellow he knew, a brother of Ulf, but the brother would not help him. The writer seemed bitter about that. Then came a series of phrases from the page that had been torn lengthwise. Most of these were names of chemicals, curious scientific terms with dire warnings about burning, blisters, avoiding contact with air or water.

I stared at the line that said, *"Eight hundred pounds of fine crystalline powder ballistite . . . suitable source located . . . I struck a bargain with Herr—."*

Oh Jim, what have you got yourself mixed up in? Only silence replied.

Despite my noisy, happy childhood, I knew the voice of silence. Then, I could not wait to run next door to visit Sanober, my impish fourteen-year-old neighbor. Only a year older than me, she invented games and puzzles like Jo March of *Little Women,* climbing trees and shimmying up walls for adventure. Giggling, we decided we would marry the Wadia brothers so that we'd live together in the same house.

But then she fell ill, and I wasn't permitted to visit for days. In a whisper Mama spoke the word "cholera." Sanober's home was quarantined, a basket lowered for food and supplies each morning, into which I slipped letters crammed with my questions.

Days later I heard wailing from her home and knew.

During the four days of her funeral prayers, a weight pressed upon my chest. The ritual chanting faded as I imagined her sitting beside me, her expressive eyes telling me it was up to me now. I had to live for both of us. Silence can speak. It insists and will not be ignored.

The next week I told Papa I wanted to study in England like my brother Adi, who'd gone there the year before. It took months of persuasion and pleading until he finally agreed. Losing my sweet Sanober had shunted my life onto a new track.

A knock on the door interrupted my reverie. Who could it be on a Sunday? Puzzled, I opened to find Tobias Brown in the corridor, standing well back from the door.

He'd brought Jim's wages. "Thank you," I said evenly, accepting the envelope from the colored man. "Any word from Jim?"

I asked him that each week. He must have noticed my present malaise, for he hesitated. "No, missus."

He must not know much or was told to reveal nothing. Disturbed by the strange German letter, my composure frayed. Should I invite him in? In India it would not be appropriate, but here? His earnest, creased face and tufted silver hair reassured me. He'd always treated me with careful respect.

"Would you like some tea?" I asked.

His eyes widened, then he smiled. "That's very kind of you, ma'am . . . but I think not."

I stepped closer. "Tobias, I'm afraid for Jim. Have you heard anything about him?"

Tobias looked down. Jim needed the translated letter so I'd planned to mail him my transcription. Should I send it to the Duprees instead? Yet Jim had written, "Tell no one."

"Step inside a moment, Tobias. I must speak with you."

"Yes, missus." Scraping off his shoes on the doorstop, he came in reluctantly.

"Please. Call me Diana."

"Yes, Lady Diana." He smiled, then pulled in his lips.

He knew something, I was sure of it.

"Where *is* Jim, Tobias?" Despite my best intentions, my worries spilled out. Gathering steam, like a locomotive pulling from the station, they chugged out, each car dragging the next. Once moving, I could not contain them. "He's been injured so many times. Just six months in Boston and they sent him off alone? How can he manage? He's a good detective, God knows, but this could be beyond him. Why didn't they send someone else?"

Slowly, Tobias said, "I believe they did, ma'am."

I recalled Jim's words before he left. "Jim mentioned Mr. Arnold Baldwin?"

Tobias turned his deep, sad gaze on me. "Yes, ma'am. It was Mr. Baldwin's assignment. But—I'm afraid he's, ah, no more."

The floor seemed to tilt under my feet. "He's dead?"

"Ma'am, he was killed some weeks ago."

Murdered. Baldwin had been murdered. And no word from Jim. I steadied myself and asked, "Is it common, in your business, that an operative is gone . . . for five weeks?"

Tobias opened and closed his mouth. What wasn't he telling me?

"I'm just the porter, ma'am."

"Then you see everybody, coming and going, every day."

He blinked. "To be gone this long without word, that's not common, no."

Jim had mailed the letter to Grimke two weeks ago at most. Urgency propelled me like a hand against my back. "I must find him. But how?"

Shifting from one foot to the other, Tobias said, "You could ask the Duprees, ma'am—Mister Alfred, who built the agency, and his son, Mister Peter."

CHAPTER 4

AT THE DUPREE DETECTIVE AGENCY

Peter Dupree had a pleasing angular face, although his chin and jaw were a bit delicate. His thin mustache and wispy beard did little to age him. He'd taken my hand and held it a trifle longer than necessary. Dapper in his blue serge suit, he seemed aware of his polished appearance.

Gloved hands folded in my lap, I sat up straight as Miss Sythe-Fornett had taught me at Foley Finishing Academy for Ladies.

Young Mr. Dupree offered me coffee.

I declined, asking, "Have you any news of my husband?"

"If you'll wait a moment, ma'am, my father would like to meet you." Straightening his cuffs, he smiled to reassure. It only made me more concerned. I'd come to find out when Jim would return. I needed to know why he hadn't written to me. After the first two weeks, he'd know how I yearned for a letter, even just a short note. Why didn't he write?

As young Mr. Dupree left the room, an odd warning knotted my gut. Men constantly used one language among each other, and quite another with women. I wanted no pleasantries today, just the truth. Yet I dreaded it. I had no illusions about Jim's job. Working for my brother Adi, Jim had been terribly injured. What if Dupree Senior said Jim was . . . dead?

Adi would have said, "It hasn't happened, stop fretting." My fingers itched for a cigarette. A silly affectation I'd adopted in England, when I lit up, somehow young fellows treated me with more respect. But Jim disliked the smell of tobacco, so I'd given it up.

I swallowed, my throat dry as I glanced over the quiet office. When Jim and I explored Boston, he often pulled me aside and studied things to figure out what they meant. "Everything means something, but you must connect it to the person first," he'd said, his brief smile curving a bracket around his mouth. I must stop daydreaming about him now, I thought, and be stern.

The younger Dupree's neat desk bore a set of elegant black pens, a blotter and monogrammed paper in a wooden tray. Unlike Papa's desk in Bombay, cluttered with invoices and bills, this burgundy felt was bare. Papers were not left in the open; the Duprees were careful.

On the table stood a shiny telephone. To own such an instrument meant the agency was doing well. I saw no typewriter machine; perhaps they employed a stenographer. Framed photographs of modern steamships adorned the walls. No romantic frigates, nor portraits of whiskered ancestors like those at home in Bombay. These were modern men of business who valued their time. If Dupree Senior wished to see me, something must be amiss—or was my fear seeping into my deductions? The door swung open.

No one could mistake the man with a piercing blue gaze who stepped in. Dupree Senior was heavyset, with thick sideburns, his salt-and-pepper hair parted in the middle, his beard neatly trimmed. My friend Ida would have eyed the giant approvingly, calling him "a fine figure of a man."

Peter said, "Mrs. O'Trey, my father."

Voice gruff, the older Dupree shook hands. "Morning, miss."

In India when introduced a man would say "Your servant, madam"—as the British do—or fold his hands in greeting if he was Indian. Miss? Dupree Senior knew I was a Mrs. Perhaps he considered me very young, despite my grey dress and stylish blue hat.

He sat down, his face unreadable. Standing beside him, his son watched me closely. Politeness required that we begin with small talk, but I felt short of air.

Taking charge, Dupree Senior asked, "Is the financial arrangement all right? You continue to receive weekly wages?"

Why didn't he use Jim's name? I said, "Jim's wages, yes. Tobias brings them each week, thank you."

"It is adequate? You're well provided for?"

How clever of him to start with finances. Now I'd appear ungrateful to complain about Jim's absence. No, I decided, I wouldn't let him direct me.

Holding his gaze, I asked, "Mr. Dupree, have you heard from my husband?"

He replied without hesitation, "Ma'am, Mr. O'Trey is on assignment."

"Where is he now, sir?"

Dupree Senior tut-tutted, his mouth wary. "I cannot disclose his location."

I returned a polite smile. "When did you last see him?"

"Some weeks ago, madam."

Refusing to be daunted, I asked, "When he took this case? Six weeks ago?"

He glowered at my persistence. "Operatives return after their assignment."

Since his answer revealed nothing, I continued the rhythm of my questions, as I'd seen Jim do last year when he investigated our family's murders.

I nodded at the telephone. "Perhaps you spoke with him?"

He shook his head as though impatient. "Most operatives cannot access a telephone."

"Some correspondence, then? How do you keep in contact with his movements?"

He smiled, tight-lipped, leaning forward. "Mrs. O'Trey. Absence is . . . an occupational hazard. You are a newlywed, yes? When were you married?"

Classic diversion. Ask the little woman about the wedding. She'll talk about chiffon and flowers all morning. That was twice he'd avoided that question. When I didn't answer, his gaze sharpened.

"Do you know where Jim is?" I asked.

That was the deciding question, one I had planned carefully. Jim always paid close attention to a suspect's reaction. If the reply was quick and easy, it was likely the truth. If the suspect did something new—blinked, paused or touched his face, if Dupree waffled, or tried to distract me—it was a lie.

Alfred Dupree glanced at his son. No lie, but no truth either. As he pulled in his lips, looking to the side, I understood. The realization gave me a strange sensation, like a jolt of the carousel Jim and I had ridden in a fair.

"You don't know!" My insides plummeted. He couldn't ask Jim to return because he didn't know where he was. Alone, in a strange place, Jim was up against a murderer.

I leapt to my feet, my fingers pressed to my lips. Jim had not told them about the German letter that mentioned ballistite. Why? Wouldn't he tell them everything he learned, like when he'd worked for my brother? Was it possible that Jim didn't trust the Duprees? Baldwin had trusted them, and Baldwin was dead. Was that why Jim stayed away, without any word? My thoughts jostled me like unruly vendors in a fish market. "And Mr. Baldwin? Where is he?"

"Calm yourself, madam!" Dupree Senior said, eyes shadowed. "Peter, fetch some water."

He had not answered me. Lips tight, his grim manner reproved, as though I'd broken into hysterics. Jim was so new to this country, why had Dupree sent him after Mr. Baldwin? Was it because he *knew* it was dangerous? Did he think Jim was unconnected to anyone here, and therefore expendable? Outrage billowed in me.

"No," I said, my voice low and menacing, "No. You owe me my husband."

He frowned his surprise. I sucked in a breath, shaking my head. I would *not* faint. I stamped my foot, which turned into a step and started me pacing the width of the office. Panic rose, a flood of bile, terrifying me. What should I do?

"Won't you sit down, Mrs. O'Trey?" said Peter Dupree, cajoling.

"Oh hush!" I cried. Dupree Senior stiffened at my tone.

Damn them. They had lost track of my sweet Jim and were hiding it. Something was very wrong. They wouldn't tell me, of course, because I was only the little wife, to be pacified with soft stories and sent away. My thoughts pulsed in hammer strokes.

Jim was alone. I would make them help me. How, Jim, how? Pleading would not work. Press them, insist. No, these men ran a detective agency. Even the younger Dupree was used to dealing with hard cases. Fingers knotted, I hugged them to my waist, remembering Dupree Senior's shocked look just now. They were ill accustomed to ladies, and determined, tough ladies, even less.

Now I knew how to gain their compliance, but what did I want? To find Jim. My urgency grew as I recalled Jim's head wound in Karachi—it had wiped an entire year from his memory. He'd been unable to recognize Major Smith, his closest friend. I shuddered, dreading any repeat of such an injury. I couldn't let that happen. Someone must find him, someone who knew him well. And who knew him better than me? So, I must go there—to Chicago.

Adi would say, "That's crazy!" Jim too would be appalled. But two weeks ago, Jim had mailed that letter to Grimke, saying, "Tell no one." Something big was at stake, something to do with explosives. I drew a quick breath and turned to do battle.

Meeting Dupree Senior's brilliant blue gaze, I said, "Here's what you will do."

Father and son stood as still as carved stone. I went on. "You will tell me everything about his case. All you know, every last bit. Then I'll go there, to Chicago. And I need a helper. The colored man, Tobias—he'll come with me."

Dupree Senior grunted. "Mrs. O'Trey, that's impossible." He winced, pitying me.

He was being kind. I could ill afford to like him, not now. Stepping up, I raised my chin. "Mr. Dupree, do this, or I will close down your agency. I'll speak to the Boston Police. I'm dining this evening at the home of

Mr. Abernathy, who knows Governor Russell and Senator Henry Cabot Lodge. If you won't help me find Jim, I think they will be interested in how you conduct business."

Both Duprees stared, affronted. The older man's eyes glinted.

I said, "Don't imagine you can do away with me. You see, I've written letters to my lawyer and *The Boston Globe*. If I don't return, my friend will mail them tomorrow, telling the newspaper about you. He will report me missing to police and my attorney will file a lawsuit against you."

Little of this was true. George Abernathy was probably acquainted with the Russell, Cabot, and Lodge families; society people usually knew one another. George would want to help me, but whether he had strong connections, I'd no idea. Yet Dupree Senior didn't call my bluff. He had not played whist against me for a month aboard ship, as Jim had.

He held my gaze for three long breaths. I did not plead.

Mustache bristling, he said, "I see."

What did he see? No similarity to my husband, who was kind and decent. Did he see that I would do anything for Jim?

His jaw hard, the older Dupree asked, "Who are you, really?"

Ordinarily I'd have said, "Mrs. James O'Trey," but today I wanted more of myself in that name. I kept my chin up. "I am Mrs. Diana Framji O'Trey, of Bombay."

"From India," he said. "You sound English."

"I was educated in England."

"When did you arrive?"

How perceptive of him to gauge whether I had the means to implement my threats.

I smiled. "We sailed from Liverpool last September on Cunard's *Umbria* in the company of Colonel and Mrs. Sean Fitch and the Abernathys. They are friends of my father and Superintendent McIntyre, who heads the Bombay Constabulary. Mr. McIntyre has friends here. The Abernathys know everyone, including Governor Russell. So, you see, I have connections."

Jim had done this once, bombarded me with lies. I'd been so confident

I could discern the truth, I'd dared him, "Tell me a lie." His face soft with memory, Jim said he had a married sister who, like me, was full of questions. Although I knew he was an orphan and lacked siblings, I believed him because the truth was also there in his words—he ached for a family, someone to love. Jim showed me I could be deceived so that I would grow up a little, be less gullible. He taught me to lie and do it well. I had indeed traveled on the *Umbria* with the Abernathys, and Papa did know Superintendent McIntyre. The conviction in my voice carried the rest.

"Madam," Dupree Senior said, his deep voice curling like one who smokes a pipe. "Do you really want to do this?"

Was he talking about this assignment, or making an enemy of him? It didn't matter. The answer was the same. But his gravelly voice sounded so much like Papa's that tears salted my eyes.

Blinking, I said, "I'll do it for Jim."

He looked pained. "It's dangerous, Mrs. O'Trey. Entirely unsuitable for ladies."

"My brother is an attorney," I said.

He ran a hand over his speckled beard. That's his giveaway, I thought in sudden excitement. Playing cards with his army fellows, Jim learned that each made a different gesture, some little twitch, when under strain. Rubbing his beard meant Dupree was upset, or astonished.

Shaking his head, Dupree growled, "No. I cannot allow it. Madam, despite what you think of me, I'd rather you were safe at home."

"I'd like that too," I said, "but I must find Jim. You have no choice, sir."

"No choice, eh?" he snorted. "I could toss your fine ass out on the street, missy. Lawyers be damned. You don't want to wrangle with me!"

Jim cursed when he was afraid; surely Dupree Senior did not fear me? But I needed to show him I was in deadly earnest. Holding his gaze, I drew my small derringer from my muff. As practiced, I pulled back the hammer, flicked off the safety and pointed, straight armed, at his son.

Peter's mouth fell open, and for a long moment no one moved.

Then I lowered the weapon, reengaged the safety, and said to the goggle-eyed young man, "I wouldn't have hurt you."

Dupree Senior gave a jerking laugh. "And me, madam? Am I safe?"

I did not want to soften, so I said, "No, sir. My husband trusted you, and he's missing."

"You think I'd harm him?" he said, lip twitching in disgust.

Dupree had built this business, and one didn't do that without breaking a few bones. Jim was missing on his watch. Holding his gaze, I reverted to a conversational tone. "Why, yes. If it suited you, you'd harm me too."

When he turned away and cursed again, I sympathized. Here was a decent man in a tough business, and I had called him to account. He seemed to admire me, so perhaps it stung that I thought him a crook.

"Don't do this, madam. I like you. I truly liked your husband."

Liked! My throat ached. He thought Jim was dead, but he was doing nothing about it.

"Jim is alive until I see his body. I will go to Chicago."

His eyes narrowed, assessing me. "You wouldn't get far without us."

"That's why I need your assistance."

He barked a laugh. "You want a job? As an operative?"

I didn't, but if it was the only way to find Jim . . . "Yes."

He rubbed his beard with his knuckles. "We've never employed a female operative."

"Until now," I said, excitement rising. He was coming round! "What was Jim investigating?"

Stepping close, Dupree Senior asked, "What's Captain O'Trey's real name?"

Had Jim told him? I took a chance. "Captain James Agnihotri. The booking clerk misheard, broke it in two, and wrote James Agney O'Trey in the ship's manifest instead."

Behind the desk, Peter Dupree drew an audible breath. He had not known. If Jim didn't trust them, I wouldn't tell them about the German letter.

"And *you* would be able to find him?" Dupree Senior looked skeptical.

"Oh no," I replied. "Jim is rather good at disguising himself. I'd never spot him."

"Then why go after him? How could you do better than a detective?"

I smiled, ignoring the pulse of pain in my chest. "Because he'll come to me."

Dupree Senior gave me a long stare and leaned back in contemplation. I waited, keeping emotion from my face.

Peter said, "Pa, you can't send a woman—"

His father cut him off with a raised hand, then asked him, "He didn't wire, you're certain? No telegram."

Peter drew back. "N-no. But how can she—"

Dupree Senior turned back to me. "You've seen blood, miss? Do you faint?"

I remembered a twilit tower among the palm trees in Bombay; breathless, I'd run up the stairs to the stone gallery, to find Jim grappling with his foe, straining against a knife at his neck. I could still hear his cry—it sent a tremor through my spine. I'd squeezed the trigger, jerked with its recoil; the men fell, tangled together. Blood soaking the front of my dress, my hands slipping, my knees sliding, I tried to hold Jim to me, to keep him in my world.

I told Dupree Senior, "I work at New England Baptist Hospital, where we're quite accustomed to blood."

CHAPTER 5

DEATH OF A CLOCK

A gust shook windows and doors, taking my breath as I stepped into the crowded street. Passing carts and hansoms rattled behind an electric trolley on its tracks. Anchored by my carpetbag, I clutched my hat to my head as the wind drove me along the sidewalk.

My thin, silk sarees and fashionable English dresses would be little use for my journey to Chicago, so I'd bought two worn, serviceable grey skirts, a black jacket and stole, four shirtwaists and a neat white cloche. My skirts blew, almost upending me as I trudged from the secondhand clothing store toward our apartment, next door to the Lins.

Leaving bag, hat, and cloak in my apartment, I went to the Lins' for the last time.

"Come, come!" Pia smiled a welcome, nodding me to the table where she'd laid out our supper in various bowls. I greeted her and Xi, dispensing with muddy boots to sit in stockinged feet and wrap my chilled fingers around a bowl of hot soup.

Xi looked up from kneading dough, his aged face creased. His wispy hair and wrinkled smile sent a tug of loss into me. Soon I'd have to leave my friends, just as I'd left Mama, Papa, and Adi.

Shaking off my melancholy, I told them that I'd soon go to Chicago to find Jim. Troubled, Pia wound the dish towel in her hands. Xi peered at me with his rheumy eyes, then washed his hands and eased himself down before his bowl. We ate in solemn silence.

Unlike Jim, a soldier who drilled hard each morning to restore his shoulder and knee, I was ill-equipped to investigate, yet I must do it. He was strong, trained to observe, to question, to defend himself. I'd been educated to run a household and entertain, to be a fine hostess.

Yet when Papa agreed to send me to England, he said, "You are built for great things, child." Although women couldn't take up positions like men, Papa'd educated me. Had he hoped I'd build a school or college, or run a hospital? I feared that I'd let him down by leaving Bombay. Now Jim was in trouble, and I could not let him down too. Our life together had just begun. Somehow, I had to help him.

The hot soup soothed me. Jim and I had joined these meals with a lively sharing of stories: his youth in Poona, my adventures in England, and the Lins' tales of their fishing village. That page was turning, even now. Soon I'd board a train to Chicago's Union Station. My skin tightened with expectation. Where to stay? I'd need money for a hotel.

The Lins regarded me soberly. Bending over the grate, Pia built up the fire and asked, "Why Jim went to Chicago?"

I told them about Baldwin, then paused. If someone had murdered Baldwin, and I asked after him, mightn't they come for me too?

After dinner, I wrote out the letters with which I had threatened the Duprees. Turning my fiction to fact, I handed them to Xi, feeling as though I'd started down a road shrouded in fog. "I'll send you a telegram each week. If I don't wire you for seven days, please mail these."

Raising them to his eyes, Xi peered at the addresses: *The Boston Globe,* police commissioner, Mrs. Abernathy, and Adi Framji—Framji Mansion, Malabar Hill, Bombay, India.

"My rent is paid for six months," I said. It seemed an eternity.

Xi's face screwed up. Pia covered my hand with her own. "Why are you going, Diana?"

The touch of her hand was like Mama's, but rougher, her palm toughened by years of peeling shrimp. Yet her kindness brought tears welling up. Unbidden, the truth tumbled out.

"Pia, I found Jim's wedding ring. He left it behind. These weeks alone . . . I'm like a leaf, blown about these endless streets, tossed here and there to smack against a wall. With him, somehow, it's as though I have some weight, some reason for doing things."

Pia hummed in sympathy. Xi spoke little English because he worked in the laundry's back room. How much of that had he understood? Pia attended customers, so she'd learned more. They had no children.

A sudden tide of sorrow overtook me—I'd be expecting my own babe, if I hadn't asked Jim to wait. We'd shared a cabin on board, but he'd been so seasick . . .

My voice dropped as I said, "Jim wanted a child, but . . . it was too soon for me. This city, this place—everything was so new. I said we should wait, but now I wish I hadn't. I'd have something of his, someone to hold."

Pia's smile was a twist of her lips, without joy. "I cannot have a child."

"Oh Pia," I said. My own regrets seemed puny against her long years of sorrow. I touched her worn hand as our words faded into the silence.

Stirring, she sent her husband a soft look. "But old Xi is good to me. In Shanghai, he worked in a bakery."

I remembered Jim loved the smell of baking. "You made bread?"

"Xi can make *hún dun* so fast! Twenty in a minute!"

"Tsch," Xi said, showing his gnarled hands. "Not so fast anymore!"

Seeing my puzzled face, she said, "It is *jiaozi*. Small, round, you know? You ate it."

She went on, eyebrows high in regret. "We cannot afford a big oven. Or a place for baking. But if I have a cart, I can sell at the train station."

I remembered Papa's creased face, tears following his wrinkles like rivulets down a mountainside. His embrace enveloped me in a blanket of safety as I'd laid my head against the smooth fabric of his Chinese-silk robe. Pushing up the indigo sleeves, he'd leaned his arms on his wide teak desk as he wrote out a cheque for Jim and me to start our new life.

Papa's cheque was deposited in the Berkeley Bank on Boylston Street. Tomorrow I'd draw some for the journey, but what of the rest?

I asked Pia, "What would it cost, to start a bakery?"

We sat talking long into the night. Then, having made a decision, I went home.

Silence greeted me as I turned up the gas lamp in the empty shell of our apartment. In the soft amber light, the clock on the mantel was still. I wound it up, but the pendulum hung, the corpse of something I'd taken for granted. Had it stopped last night, innards chilled and stuck together like sausage links? A silent clock is an awful thing.

Bereft of Jim's generous body heat, I huddled, curling tight to avoid the cold sheets. Memories crept in softly, holding me against my will, twisting my heart, squeezing. Freed by a single word—Papa—it was no mean feat to chase them back into their cage. But that night, dreams of my childhood in Framji Mansion also comforted me. I drifted, clinging to the raft of that warmth.

CHAPTER 6

STRANGE ISLAND

Next morning, Sister Mary Rose listened tight-lipped to my tale about being needed by a sick relative, then opened her metal box and handed me six dollar coins, my wages.

Shedding my life of recent weeks, I left New England Baptist Hospital. Its familiar, phenol-scented pungency followed me as I stepped through oak doors onto a wet street. Since I'd obtained my position through the kindness of Ida Abernathy, manners required that I explain why I was leaving, so I trudged down to Brookline to her tall townhome.

Rounded and shapely, she rose from her ivory white couch and received me with a warm embrace. Yet when I told her of my plan, she recoiled. "Chicago! My dear, it's quite awful—a filthy, smelly place. Quite unsuitable."

"It's where Jim went. I thought I might make some . . . inquiries." Put that way, my plan sounded hopeless, but Ida was too polite to say so.

She pulled in her lips. "Chicago. Well, George has business interests there, and oh! An attorney. I quite like him. His name is . . . Payne, Harvey Payne, esquire. His sister Camelia was at Vassar with me."

The door opened to admit a broad young man, his starched collars pointing up at a sober face with large forehead and carefully groomed hair. Jim's hair would never look so neat, I thought, as George greeted his wife with a peck on her cheek.

"My dear. And the charming Mrs. Ag-nee-ho-tree. Or should I say, Mrs. O'Trey?" he asked, smiling. It was his usual joke.

His teasing reminded me of Adi and as always, emotion tugged at me. How I missed his steadfast optimism and practical good sense! Why didn't I choose the law, I wondered, with sudden fervor. Then I should know exactly what to do! But no, women weren't allowed to take the bar exam. Tired of writing legal briefs, my lawyer friend Cornelia Sorabji had taken a post with the Indian Court of Wards to investigate domestic cases.

As I strove for composure, George's eyebrow climbed his wide forehead. Abashed, he said, "Forgive me! I did not mean—"

"It's nothing," I choked. "I seem all helter-skelter these days. But it shan't be for long." My voice steadied as I ended on a promise to myself, smoothing down my narrow skirt. I needn't meddle in the ugly business of investigating murders—just give Jim the translated letter and ask him to come home. Eager to be away, I stood to take my leave.

"Stay, my dear," cried Ida, telling George in a low voice, "She's following Jim to Chicago."

George tilted his head at her and some intelligence passed between them, a glance similar to how Jim and I could communicate.

"Mrs. O'Trey, of course you shall have an introduction to Mr. Payne. But I'll do one better. We are not entirely without means in Chicago, you know. Now, I'll send a wire to Harvey," said George, and disappeared toward his study.

Ida summoned a tea tray, and we revisited pleasant shipboard memories, but each minute's delay now chafed. Only my old teacher Miss Sythe-Fornett's insistence that "good form is the backbone of civilization" anchored me to Ida's conversation. When George returned, I tucked away the address he handed me, hugged Ida goodbye and set off for my appointment at the bank. The Abernathys and the Lins came from different continents, yet each had come to my aid. Content, I patted the document we had signed last night, now folded in my reticule.

* * *

At the station, the New Haven Railroad engine huffed at the ready like a muscular, metal bull. Its whistle blast took me by surprise as I followed Tobias down the platform. A porter had my trunk and the rest of my luggage on a cart. Buoyed by anticipation, my skirts flapping, I hurried along with my parasol, passing the coal caboose and the smoking car.

"Here's your carriage, missus," said Tobias in his deep reassuring voice. Handing me my carpetbag, he helped me up the stair and pointed. "I'd best be getting over there."

I blurted, "Aren't we traveling together?"

He smiled, teeth flashing bright in the dull afternoon. "I'll ride in the colored coach, missus." He touched his hat, signaled the porter and disappeared into the bustling crowd.

Of course. He'd have to ride in a separate car. I felt foolish to not know this. I frowned, puzzled. Were people from India considered colored? A cluster of immigrant families crowded behind me, so I entered the carriage to find most seats taken. I'd asked Tobias to buy me a coach ticket, from a desire to conserve funds. Holding my carpetbag before me, I passed through the pew-like rows and slipped into a seat. Working-class men occupied most of the benches, but a few families too, which reassured me.

Across from me, two fellows in beat-up coats and caps looked surprised. "Ma'am, this ain't first," said one.

"I am quite aware," I replied.

Eyebrows high, he touched his brim.

The train lurched, rolled forward and gathered steam. Through the windows, the city gave way to countryside, blurring into an impressionist landscape of greys, fragmenting my reflection. Now my decision seemed impetuous. Why had I imagined I could find Jim in the tangled streets of Chicago? I sighed. I'd bet everything that he'd come to the Chicago post office seeking Professor Grimke's reply.

At length, only a thin path ran alongside the railroad track. Here, young men on bicycles scurried around lumbering ox wagons that clanked their milk cans to market. Boston city gave way to farmland with solid, squat barns of brick and stone, their low walls crisscrossing the landscape. Smaller farms followed, interspersed with copses of conifers like fat ladies holding fast to thick winter coats. If I'd left Bombay, I'd see acres of soaking paddy fields, women wading ankle-deep to transplant rice seedlings. Even the light shone differently here, cloudy blues instead of the bright yellow tinge of the tropics.

I'd been shut into my own worries, but now I heard my fellow passengers speaking several languages and dialects. Some spoke English, but the vowels were so broad and flattened, I could fathom little of it.

"... that uppity bird over there," said a man, leaning sideways at his friend.

His older companion glanced warily at me. "... Spankin' fine knockout!"

"Not 'aaf she ain't," said the first.

I sent them a stern look.

"Ma'am?" said the older man. "Ah, are you going to New York?"

"To Chicago," I returned, noticing his torn collar and the gaping seam of his shoulder. In India he might have been a caretaker who secured Papa's bungalow in Simla over the winter.

My placid smile encouraged him to ask, "Traveling alone, miss?"

When I straightened up at this impertinence, he said, "Don't mind us, miss, we're just chewing the rag."

"Not at all," I said, having no idea what rag he meant. "I plan to visit the World's Fair."

"I knowed you was lettered," he said, nodding.

I'd dressed to avoid attention—and had failed, it seemed. "How did you know?"

He shrugged, saying in a drawl, "It's how you sit, ma'am. Re-al straight, see?"

His friend punched his arm with a remark. It drew a round of laughter that disconcerted me. Was he being rude? But I could not fault them for my own lack of understanding.

The older man read my face. "Don't take 'im wrong. We're jus' being companiable."

Biting off something that might have been tobacco, the younger one said he was hoping to find work at the World's Fair.

His companion grimaced. "You're too late, friend. Men been getting to Chicago for months. Ain't much to do there now." He himself was going to join Buffalo Bill's Wild West show, because they'd hire anyone to play Indians.

"Rats!" grumbled the young rogue.

Horrified, I gathered my skirts and pulled my feet off the floor, looking for vermin. This brought smirks and chuckles, which I refused to acknowledge. What peculiar expressions Americans used!

Watching the fellow mimic an Indian tribal cry, patting his open mouth to break up the call, I steeled myself against the unpleasant sound. I was, in fact, a full Indian by birth. A different sort of Indian, born in India. How Adi would roll his eyes at this musing.

At New York's Grand Central, I stepped into the crowd on the platform feeling like I'd entered a beehive. Catching sight of Tobias's raised hand and broad smile, I accompanied him to a bustling station hall with ornate ceilings.

We changed trains, entering a shiny new car with dark wood paneling and crimson seats. The Exposition Flyer, operated by the Lakeshore, Michigan and Southern Railroad, cut through rocky gaps where droplets hung from icy cascades clinging to the hillside. It rumbled through Pennsylvania, where logging had left entire slopes naked and blackened with fire. We sped past a series of coal breakers—ugly grime-coated buildings sprouting chutes at impossible angles, capped with the scaffolding of mining derricks, and swept through bare hillsides. It reminded me of a line from Shakespeare's *The Tempest*: "Be not afeared. The isle is full of noises, sounds, and sweet airs, that give delight, and hurt not"—Caliban's deceptive consolation, for the fate of those travelers in the play was uncertain.

We passed small towns where women wore knit shawls over plain dark dresses—my city jacket, shirtwaist and black skirt now felt out of place. Families left the car for food or to stretch their legs, but I hesitated. A woman traveling alone was "an easy mark," Jim would say.

Returning from the water closet I nibbled a biscuit I'd brought and made do. Jim had a penchant for sniffing out trouble. Always alert, always searching for clues, he often saw what others missed. Yet I could not dismiss the feeling that he was in danger. Where had he got that peculiar German letter?

CHAPTER 7

OUR MUTUAL ADVANTAGE

The clack-clack of our wheels through the long, fitful night was interrupted with endless coughs and snores. When the wind forced us to shut windows, the stench of humanity, sweat and other odors filled the car, so I reopened the window a crack. Although I traveled economically in second class, my nose, alas, preferred the perfumed air of first!

The train's motion brought to mind my journey from Simla to Bombay. Despite the hard seat, lulled by the rocking motion I dozed. I dreamed I was in a rail carriage with my parents and baby siblings, while Jim and my brother Adi lounged in the next car. I curled against my mama's shoulder, her snore gentle, her bangles clinking softly. But why were the babies crying?

I woke, finding myself among families with wailing infants. My stomach too murmured a protest. Hearing the conductor call, "One-hour stop!" I peered out at a little town enveloped in grey mist. One could just barely see low buildings of a darker hue lining a broad clearing. The bone-white spire of a church dissolved as the cloud descended. Puffs of steam rose as the engine huffed like a tired racehorse.

Eager to find a meal, I stepped down to the open-air platform, barely more than a wooden floor beside a stationhouse. To the left, the train track ran downhill and faded into fog. Ahead, it sliced through a block of the town, bisecting roads and byways with no regard for carriages collected to either side. An awning creaked, a wooden sign swayed, telling passengers, WESTWARD TRAINS THIS WAY.

A train station in Bombay would bustle with red-coated officers and scrawny bare-chested coolies carrying loads cushioned upon their turbans. Lawyers and businessmen in dark suits would stride among women in colored sarees fluttering like butterflies in the bright sunlight. Instead, here in the soft-hued Pennsylvanian morning was a watercolor postcard come alive. I followed dark-coated men, women wearing country aprons. Workers in overalls hurried past, their aprons stained with industry, some carrying baskets.

My fellow travelers trailed toward a hotel with a wraparound porch, but I hung back, reluctant to dine alone. Hailing a uniformed porter, I said, "Morning! Would you direct me to a convenience?"

He pulled back, squinting. "Huh?"

Seeing that he had not understood, I tried again. "A loo?"

"What's that?"

That English term wasn't common either. "The facilities—a privy?"

He pointed toward the buildings in the town square beside a row of flagpoles.

As I walked toward them, I spotted Tobias looking for me and waved. Just as I would have sent off a bearer in Bombay, I called, "Tobias, would you get me something to drink—a cup of tea—and some crumpets? I'll meet you by the flags, all right?"

The ladies' privy was in a quiet old hotel that smelled of beeswax and lavender, its paneled walls and floors of dark wood a welcome respite from the noisome railcar. Returning toward the row of flagpoles, I could not see Tobias, so I lugged my bag to where a crowd had gathered around some entertainment.

"Git him! Give him good!" cried someone. Others roared their approval.

From the edge of the crowd, I caught a glimpse of two tall fellows in overalls, one of them holding someone upright. That man drooped, his head slumped onto his chest. Another youth, a bruiser, threw a punch, and the colored man's head snapped back—Tobias!

"Please!" he called out, a deep, sad sound.

Horrified, I cried, "Stop!"

No one took the slightest notice; the crowd's yells drowned out mine.

A lady never runs or raises her voice, Miss Sythe-Fornett had said decisively as she taught proper deportment.

"Unhand him!" I hollered, trying to get closer.

When no one moved out of my way, my shock turned to outrage. Tobias was taking savage blows! Pulling my derringer from my muff I pointed it skyward and fired.

The shot was deafening. The crowd stood still, then people rushed about in a panic. Some turned back, looking *past* me.

Not one person looked at me.

Tucking my pistol into its hiding place, I charged toward Tobias, brandishing my frilly parasol before me, smacking arms and shoulders blocking my way.

At last, I was visible. Descending upon the group, I demanded of the ruffian, "Let him go at once! How dare you accost my servant!"

The din died down. A constable arrived and asked, "Who're you?"

Holding myself upright, I enunciated with such tight disdain as would have brought joy to Miss Sythe-Fornett's heart. "I am Mrs. Diana Framji Agney O'Trey of Boston. What is the name of this village?"

"East Bend, ma'am," replied the policeman, subdued.

Releasing Tobias, the ruffian protested, "He was going inside the store!"

Rounding on him, I said, "To do my bidding, sir!"

Now we paused, each uncertain. I had barged into the fracas without thought, nor any plan to extricate myself. The officer scratched his chin, contemplating Tobias.

Determined not to be detained, I said, "Goodbye, sir!" and handed my carpetbag to Tobias, saying, "We've wasted enough time. Let's not miss our train."

He took it, saying, "Yes, Lady Diana."

A tall woman had been standing beside me. As I glanced about for the station, she gestured, leading the way. "This way, ma'am."

With Tobias trailing, I glided back to the train carriage—a lady never hurries—walking as I'd been trained, as though balancing a pile of books atop my head.

There, tarnation! I paused in dismay, unsure which car to enter. Handing back my carpetbag, Tobias said, "Take any carriage, missus, they are connected." The train gave two long hoots as I watched him hobble away.

Breathing hard, I plunked into an empty seat as the train jolted forward. My forehead throbbed with a sharp ache. What in God's name was wrong with these people?

"Nice performance," said the angular woman who'd accompanied me, sitting down uninvited. "I'm Abigail Martin. You're visiting from abroad?"

The woman's voice had a pleasing whispery quality. In surprise I glanced at her plain, unremarkable features, pale lips and determined chin, her hair secured under a flat black hat. Her coarse dark coat contrasted with a flourish of lace ruffles at her throat. Clear hazel eyes returned my gaze, curious at first, then disappointed by my stiff silence.

"Why'd you think so?" I asked.

If I hadn't been watching closely, I would have missed her reaction. Her eyebrows shot up before her face settled, once more, into good-natured composure.

"You really are Lady Diana?"

"That is my name," I said. I didn't tell her the prefix was unofficial.

Her shoulders relaxed. "Perhaps if you employed me . . . it could serve our mutual advantage. I was a lady's maid in New York. Since you're not from over here, I would be, well, helpful?"

Ah, I thought, here was a quick intellect.

"How'd you know I'm not American?" I asked. My dark hair was tucked under a cloche. Mama despaired over my sun-kissed complexion, but in England it had been called Mediterranean. And surely my accent was not very pronounced?

She shrugged. "Your man. You sent him to that store?"

"For something to drink. Just a bit of hot tea!"

She shook her head. "If he wanted to drink, there was a pump by the station. But tea? He'd have to ask someone for that."

A frisson ran over my skin. No American lady would send a colored man into a white store. I had blundered, and this little miss knew it. Worse, I'd sent Tobias into harm's way. I worried that he might need a physician. Already wobbly, my confidence dwindled. I did need a guide to the norms of this new place. But to trust a plucky stranger? Was that wise? On the other hand, did I really have a choice?

"You want to be helpful?" I said. "Then prove it. I'm quite famished!"

Standing up, Miss Martin said, "Follow me," and started down the aisle.

In the concession car, sipping cups of steaming tea, we ordered meals, and then I broached the matter of her wages.

"Pay me ten dollars a week," she said, with a quick glance.

Jim earned thirty dollars a week—enough to sustain us—but he was a trained detective. I'd made six dollars each week at the hospital.

"Six," I said, accustomed to bargaining in India. "Not a penny more. But I'll pay for meals and accommodation."

She agreed, then said, "Just don't ask questions, all right?"

How very curious. I asked gently, "Are you running away from something?"

"Certainly not!" she said. "This is a business arrangement, yeah? You need a maid, and I want employment. That's all."

What a forthright young woman! Her color high, she ducked her head to avoid my gaze. Sparing her more embarrassment, I inclined my head. "All right."

Despite Miss Abigail's flushed cheeks, her general calm, Quakerish demeanor puzzled me. I'd never met a woman less inclined to talk. We passed towns too small to have a stationhouse, where the train stopped beside a wooden boardwalk, took on or unloaded a passenger or two, swapped mailbags and chugged on. The high cornice of a courthouse or library swung into view. Blocks of framed houses gave way to "Red-Indian" teepees at the edge of town. I gaped at these, recognizing them from children's books, years ago. Hooting, we tore through unending fields, long sweeps where row upon row swayed with farmers' industry. Hours stretched into evening. We sped on into dusk.

Waking the next morning, I tidied myself and returned from the washroom, then I peered out, trying to gauge our location. "Where are we?"

Abigail replied without inflection, "Indiana."

Marching towers of power lines girded the rail track. At length, flat, windowed buildings crowded together marked the city's suburbs. We thundered over a viaduct. There! A blue lake sparkled, cawing gulls floating over it, while bands of color rimmed the coast—blue that bled to deep indigo.

The city thickened, crowded streets lined with two- and three-floored buildings. Streetcars abounded! We rumbled on, wheels pulsing a warning that thrilled and terrified me. Fleeting glimpses showed only white people. Were colored folks unwelcome in Chicago? Should I not have asked for Tobias?

I'd been determined to find Jim, eager for the adventure of a new city. Now anticipation turned to dread. How could I find my way in one of America's largest cities and locate a man, one single man, who might not want to be found and was impossible to spot in disguise?

CHAPTER 8

THE MASKS WE WEAR

As our train jerked to a halt at Chicago's Union Station, my fellow travelers scrambled up. Rising to my feet, I set my shoulders back. Once I found Jim, I'd hand him the letter warning that someone was buying eight hundred pounds of explosives. He'd alert the authorities, and then we'd go home. All I had to do was find him.

Abigail and I disembarked, following passengers carrying trunks and boxes. A horde of children overtook us, yelling "Newspapers!" "Shoe shines!" "Matches 'n' smokes!" and more. But what children they were! Grimy faces, filthy hands blackened with coal, bundled in tattered clothing, some with burn scars, others missing fingers, hands, arms or hopping on one leg! Had there been a fire? A disaster? Beggars were common in India, mendicants and holy men sitting under the banyan trees, troops of wandering acrobats and urchins. During the Bengal famine, hundreds of refugees had crowded into Bombay. London too had its share of poverty, but I had never seen crippled, mangled children like these.

Seeing Tobias puffing alongside a porter with my trunks, I introduced Abigail as my new maid, then asked, "Are you quite all right? Shall we seek a doctor?"

"I'll be right fine, missus. Don't worry yourself on my account." Out of breath, Tobias mopped his creased face and ran a crumpled kerchief over his snowy stubble.

We made our way out of the station and into a bustling thoroughfare, where a sign read SOUTH CANAL STREET, and hailed a large barouche. Stepping around horse droppings in the road, Abigail and I settled inside. Deflated and anxious, now that I knew I'd been the cause of his scuffle, I turned back to Tobias. Sitting behind the carriage with our luggage, he smiled. Passing streets crowded with conveyances large and small, bicycles, carts, and pedestrians, we rode through a maze of towering structures.

"Skyscrapers!" Abigail said softly. "Some have twenty floors! Look, that street leads south to Jackson Park—they've a new train station there for the World's Fair."

Here was a bonus! Pointing out streets and trolley routes, Abigail seemed to know Chicago well.

When we arrived at the hotel, a gilt awning warned it would be ridiculously grand. Dismayed, I rebuked the carriage driver, "I said decent and fashionable, not ostentatious!" Then, remembering George Abernathy's instruction, I said, "The Oriental Place Hotel, if you please."

"Sure, 'sall right," he said, clicking to his horses to continue.

With a great rotunda and gargantuan chandelier, the Oriental seemed even more opulent. However, the Abernathys had wired ahead, so I was treated to a fine welcome. Upon hearing my name, a dark-suited employee hurried from behind the counter and motioned a group of bellhops toward our trunks.

"What about you?" I asked Tobias, wondering whether he'd be allowed inside.

He shook his head, hands spread wide, so I handed him some money and sent him to find suitable lodgings.

The somber manager introduced himself, insisted that a suite was prepared for me, and led us to an ornately carved electric lift. I followed, charmed by the fashionable amenities.

"Our elevator," he said proudly. The operator, a thin boy with a thatch of red hair, closed a safety rail and the gilt doors, then moved a lever. Glad to avoid stairs, my back aching from the motion of train and carriage, we waited as the elevator box wobbled its way up. Bombay had none of these yet, but I had traveled on electric lifts aboard the steamship *Umbria*. A head taller than me, Abigail stood quietly. If she was impressed, I could not tell. The elevator boy tweaked his lever and we eased to a stop.

Patterned in Chinese silk and Japanese art, our suite radiated luxury. When I ventured a gentle query to the manager, "Mr. Fish, to whom should I address matters of payment?" he demurred, saying I must take it up with Mr. Abernathy.

"Goodness," I exclaimed, "why?"

"Mr. Abernathy is one of the Oriental's owners."

My suite offered a parlor leading onto an iron-grilled balcony. Bed-chambers opened to either side of a corridor, mine with a dressing room upholstered in ivory silk. A marble bath chamber had been fitted with the latest plumbing. Hot running water! Gold fixtures in the shape of a bamboo-themed waterfall hovered over a porcelain tub. Blue velvet draperies contrasted with yellow wallpaper. Despite the overdone fur-nishings, I felt grateful and comforted.

Pulling my carpetbag and valise from the pile deposited by the bell-boys, I sent them to my bedchamber with Abigail and reached for my hatbox. It was dented. I popped it open to push out the dent and paused. A man's bowler hat lay within—it wasn't Jim's.

Puzzled, when Abigail returned, I asked, "Yours?"

Taken aback, she said, "You opened my things?"

I frowned. "Why do you have a man's hat?"

She glanced about in a dither. "Ah—I was in the theater. I did both male and female parts." Her plain face glum, her lean shoulders hunched so that she looked all elbows. Wouldn't an actress need to be pretty? Abigail's face was too long, her forehead too bony. But, I supposed, made up colorfully it could be dramatic enough. Was this why she'd been so reticent earlier? Thinking of my friend Mary Fenton, an Irish actress in Bombay who'd married a Parsi playwright, I grinned. "The theater! How marvelous!"

"You don't mind?"

"Why would I?"

"Well." She twisted her lips, then shrugged, shamefaced. "Folks think we're fast, sometimes."

Apparently, Americans thought speed was not a good thing.

I said, "Well, I wouldn't want to be too slow."

She gave a choking laugh, quickly suppressed in her throat. Low-throated and husky, it was a pleasing sound. Perhaps we would do well together.

* * *

Midmorning, I left Abigail to iron my dresses and ventured into a nearby park to consider my first steps. Green tendrils sprouted from a gnarled old tree, a harbinger of spring, tiny leaves catching light to look like fil-igreed lace. It could not be mimosa—honey locust, perhaps? In Bombay they would be yellow jacaranda. Red gulmohar also grew frilly leaves like that, but I doubted tropical foliage would survive a Chicago winter.

I'd had a comfortable life in Bombay with Papa's wide connections, knowing how to get things done. Jim was always so confident, at ease wherever he went. How did he do it? Walking along a path toward a fountain, I decided to behave just so. In my staid dresses I didn't look so different from Americans, although I did sound different. My train car had teemed with myriad accents, so people in Chicago would be accus-tomed to all sorts.

I sat near the fountain. How should I begin? Perhaps I could leave a note for Jim at the post office, invite him to the Oriental. But I'd have to take that hotel manager aside, the one dressed like an undertaker. Could I trust him? What if Jim came in disguise? What would I say, that I might have an unusual guest?

Weighed against my fears and worries, gossiping guests hardly mattered. But if I left a message for Jim at the post office, would others not overhear? Baldwin, an experienced operative, hadn't been careful enough. I could not risk exposing Jim.

He'd surely visit the post office for a reply. If only I had someone who could watch it! Could Tobias do that? Having already caused trouble for him, I was reluctant to suggest it.

I'd told Dupree that Jim would come to me. How could I draw his attention?

I remembered my scarlet silk saree, Mama's embroidered gift. When she wrapped it, I'd touched the silvery beadwork, protesting, "Oh Mama, I can't take this. I'm not going to a coronation!"

But Mama had smiled. "Your wedding saree? If you don't need it on board, wear it to some fancy do. Make Jim proud!"

I'd certainly attract attention, but would it be enough to get myself into the papers? Should I pretend to be royalty—the Rani of Bombay? No, that wouldn't work. There were surely some Englishmen about who'd know that was nonsense.

"Want some matches, lady?" said a young voice behind me.

I turned. A dirty boy in a red cap gazed at me, a bag of wares hung around his neck. Then he grabbed my reticule and set off.

He didn't get far because my reticule was tied to my left wrist. Instead, my arm wrenched as he yanked in desperation. Matchboxes and cigarettes tumbled from his sack as he struggled. The cord of my purse dug into my skin.

"Stop!" I cried, my voice high with alarm. Letting go of my purse, he tried to make a run for it, but I had expected this and smacked him with my parasol. "Stay there, boy! Or I'll have you before a judge in no time!"

Clutching his elbow, he said, "Gawdamaidy!"

While I nursed my wrist, gasping, he squatted to scoop up his fallen wares.

"Well!" I said. "What do you have to say for yourself, you thief?"

"Ere!" he cried, his voice breaking into an adolescent pitch. "Who you calling thief? What was took from you?"

The brazen fellow! "Only because I prevented it!" I raised my parasol.

"You got no cause to hit me!" The rascal scowled, twisting and showing me his elbow. "Whacha do that for?"

He was no more than twelve—barely older than my brother Fali in Bombay. My thief's trousers were torn at the knees. Grime coated his neck and hands, and he stank of horse dung. Here was an artful chap that Jim would have set at ease with a calm word. Within moments, he'd have won friendship and loyalty from the little blighter. But I had no such expertise.

While we stood there, an odd thing happened. The boy's britches dropped clear to the ground. With a yelp he hauled them up, but his sack of wares was in the way, and it left him clutching the sack with one hand, pulling his trousers up with the other. Heavens!

I guessed what had occurred: in his rush to escape, the cord that fastened his britches had snapped. Years ago, young Fali had lost his pajamas when his drawstring broke.

I did not laugh, for the boy's wilted face told me he could not bear that. Before he could bolt, I said, "Sit down here, and don't move!" pointing at the fountain seat with my parasol.

Shrinking inward, he sat, scooting under an overhanging branch.

After a moment, I dug around in my reticule. "Voila! Just what we need." I waved my safety pin in triumph. "Now off with those pants. And pull your shirt down, for pity's sake."

He stared, dumbstruck, so I repeated, "Don't you want the string put back? Well, this magic pin can do it!"

My scolding tone worked. Wide-eyed, he glanced around, then, satisfied we were alone in the garden, wriggled out of his sagging britches. Struck dumb, he stared as I threaded the twisted drawstring through his waistband.

Some conversation was needed to set him at ease, so I mentioned the strange children at the station. "One was missing a hand, another a foot. What's happened to them, d'you know?"

"Factory don't want them. Can't work there no more." He shrugged as though it was commonplace, as I handed back his garment. Looking pale, he climbed back into his trousers, tied the knot and settled down to count his matchboxes. Poor little rascal.

I paused—didn't the famous Mr. Holmes employ a band of urchins to run errands?

After purchasing a slim pack of Cameos, I asked, "D'you want a job?"

He stopped sorting his wares. "What kind of job?"

"Smart lad like you, I'm sure you notice people. Well, I'm looking for a man."

His mouth fell open. "You on the turf?" he squeaked.

"What d'you mean?"

"A chippy, a hustler. You know, a hooker."

Goodness! "I don't know what that is, young man," I said in my best imitation of Miss Sythe-Fornett, "but I shall let it pass. The man I want to find is tall and well-built. He might be dressed well, or not so nice. He's got a slight limp, and a scar on his neck."

Seeing the boy's dazed look, I asked, "What's your name, then?" I fished in my purse for a coin, which prompted him back to life. His eyes grew enormous.

"Whatyano," he said, buffing the coin on his filthy shirt.

"Well, Wadja, pleased to meet you. I am Mrs. Diana O'Trey."

He grinned, and the suddenness of it took me by surprise.

"Hey," he replied. "Lady, you in town a few days? I'll find those yaps and macks you want. Big chaps, limp an' all. A dollar apiece, for me, see?" He set his red cap at a rakish angle, his cheeks blushing.

I sighed. Were they all bumbling idiots? This wasn't as easy as I'd expected. I scowled at him until he dropped his gaze.

"I'm afraid not, young man. It's just the one I'm looking for. But there's ten dollars in it if you find him."

He sat up tall as I explained what he was to do.

***

That evening, Abigail and I supped companionably on soup, assorted pastries I'd become partial to aboard the *Umbria,* slices of bland turkey—oh, for a spoonful of Mama's curry!—lobster salad, desserts of green apple pie and rum jelly. Comforted by the quiet meal, I told Abigail about the boy Wadja. Although the azure twilight beckoned me to the balcony, I turned in, enjoying the luxury of having a maid untie my dress and fetch my things.

Despite Abigail's tale about having been a lady's maid, she didn't know to brush out the ends of my hair first, then work upward. After directing her a few times, I began to wonder; ah well, she wouldn't be the first parlor maid to pretend experience she didn't have. Putting my hair into a loose plait, I said good night.

My featherbed was soft and wide, but I tossed around, despite the brazier warming my chamber. The moon cast shadows around the unfamiliar room, the creaks and clacks of a new place, the hum of the elevator . . . I woke to the sound of scraping.

I knew that sound—a razor. A straight razor being honed on a strap! Leaping from my bed I rushed to the bathing room, found it closed and pounded on it.

"Jim! Open, Jim!" I struggled with the handle, then threw my shoulder at it. It burst open.

A young man stood before the washbasin, a thin boy who resembled Abigail. He gripped a leather strap in one hand; a straight razor trembled in the other. Hazel eyes shocked, lips bloodless, his hair hung in disarray. He wore a smocked cotton shift, but the hair on Abigail's chest told me he was no maid.

I gaped, befuddled. Of course, Jim wasn't here; he didn't even know I was in Chicago. But to my sleep-drowned ears, the sound of his razor had filled me with hope. Instead, it was Abigail, in such state of undress! I stared at the razor, unable to breathe. The boy dropped it into the sink, started to speak, then stopped. His Adam's apple had been concealed yesterday in a profusion of ruffles.

I felt stunned. I'd thought I had someone to rely upon, but it wasn't so. Was I really as naïve as Jim believed?

"Who are you?"

The boy sucked in a breath, looking down.

"No, no lies! I won't have it. Your name!"

"Martin Gale. It's Martin A. B. Gale."

"A. B. Gale—Abigail," I repeated, unclenching my trembling fingers. "Get dressed. We need to talk."

CHAPTER 9

WHOM CAN I TRUST?

Dressing in haste, I recalled a Boston scandal about a maid who'd done away with her widowed mistress to impersonate her. She was discovered when the woman's son surprised her with a visit.

Only last month, newspapers reported that a man had packed the body of his murdered wife into a trunk. He'd sent it off to a train station while he fled on a steamer to France. With a shudder, I slipped my derringer into a pocket.

Looking subdued, Martin, alias Abigail, entered the parlor in a modest dove-grey dress and whispered, "May I ask you a question?"

He perched on the window seat, face contrite, hands knotted in his lap. Mirroring his demeanor, I lowered myself to the couch to settle things in a civil manner. I'd needed a friend, a guide who knew "the Windy City," but how could I trust him now?

"You know my secret," he said. "Please, will you keep it?"

Why did he continue this charade? I searched his wary face, sensing restraint that one might find in a governess or novitiate. Shoulders stiff, he met my puzzled gaze, slumped and ducked his head. My mind whirled as I gazed at the demure, corseted person before me. I knew I must dismiss him, but regret tugged at me.

I said, "I don't understand. You brought a man's hat. Do you dress like one sometimes?"

When he nodded, I asked, "So which one are you, Martin or Abigail?"

His glance skittered away. "Must it be one? Can't I be both?"

I felt dizzy with confusion. "Both! How can that be? I could trust a woman, but a man I don't know, a stranger?"

He snorted. "There're women that would cut your throat!"

I jerked, horrified. He grimaced. "Can't you overlook this? It was impossible to tell you."

"But what would I call you? And won't the hotel staff notice? How would I explain a man in my suite?"

"When I'm like this, call me Abigail. Otherwise, I'm Martin—you could say he's Abigail's brother. You'd need a man's escort in some parts of this town. And I need the job."

My thoughts tangled like a plate of spaghetti. Mouth tight, the corners of his eyes drooped. The loneliness of his situation moved me—a young man dressing as a woman? What had driven him to this?

Martin said, "I can help, just tell me what you need. I know Chicago—it's grown, but I know my way about. Your colored man? Some folks won't tell him much, but they'd tell me."

Could I really keep him in my employ? Her—for she was Abigail at present. I frowned, feeling at sea. "It's a mad idea, but . . ."

The sound of her breath filled the silence. Then she said, "You called me Jim—who is he?"

Should I accept her? Or was it utter folly? I gestured at her dress.

"Please explain. Why?"

She glanced away, her face contorted. "Don't ask. Please. I don't want to lie."

The candor of her tone pulled at me, but I could not just let it go. Neither Adi nor Jim would leave such a question unanswered. Gently, I asked, "What happened to you?"

She pulled in her lips, then said, "As a boy I was thin and sickly. No good at anything, really." She gave a mirthless laugh. "My parents were theater folk. We traveled. But each town was the same. They'd put up a play, send me to the local schoolhouse. But boys can see, somehow, when you're no good. I . . . didn't fit in. Just never got on with them. Don't know what made them torment me. So, I joined the stage, playing child parts at first, then female parts. It was so easy, so natural."

"Where are your parents now?"

She looked down. "A theater caught fire in Saint Louis. They didn't get out. The other players drifted away. I tried a few jobs, but it was no good . . . Tried loading, but the boxes were too heavy." Turning her clear gaze on me, she said, "I saw an advert for a parlor maid, so I dressed as a woman and applied. The missus was a nearsighted old thing. We did well together for a while. When she died, she left me her clothes. That's how it started."

"That's why your clothes are old-fashioned! You added ruffles to lengthen the skirts?"

She nodded. "A plain woman is almost invisible. I prefer it that way." She winced and said that an over-arduous butler had compromised her last position, so she'd left without collecting her pay.

"It's not the first time you've lost wages this way, is it?"

She shook her head. "The worst of it is—no one can know. I avoid homes with many servants—maids sleep together in the attic, you see. And the lads, what pests they are!"

What a lonely life she'd lived. Unable to form close ties with either gender, she'd remained friendless. I searched her pale eyes, her hands clenched in her lap.

"Are you wanted by the police?"

"No!" she said, surprised.

"How do you know Chicago?"

"We came through here often, with the troupe."

That simple explanation rang of truth, so I said, "Jim is my husband."

She stared. "Are you—leaving him? This morning you were quite, ah, disturbed." Some feeling passed over her face, a twinge of buried emotion. Alarm? No, nothing so overt, but rather a resentment, a sort of wariness. Was she concerned for me?

"Leaving him? No." I considered my options. Here in Chicago I was out of my depth. The quick-witted girl had led me from the fracas at East

Bend and put herself forward for a position. That was resourceful. But having her live in my suite?

At last, I said, "You cannot attend me as a lady's maid."

"I meant no harm, Mrs. O'Trey," she said. "Would you c-consider paying my wage for three days?"

What a sanctuary it must be to find a position where she did not need to lie. Yet she expected to be dismissed. The quiet parlor awaited my decision.

Her face small, she clenched her hands in her lap. Some suppressed emotion passed over her face, quickly quelled. How useful it might be to have such a friend, I thought. She needed a place and I—I surely needed help if I was ever to find Jim in this enormous city.

I hesitated—she had her own room, and I could lock my door at night. Papa and Mama'd be horrified, but they weren't here. And Jim? I winced to think how he'd react. But I had to find him first, and I had this creeping dread that he was in trouble. First things first, I decided. Drastic times call for drastic measures, Adi had said when he'd hired Jim as his private detective. Adi would understand why I needed Abigail.

"You can stay," I said. "On probation. See how we do together."

She looked up, her complexion blotched and pasty. "Stay as what?"

"As a companion. Help me find Jim. It's useful that you know the city."

Abigail ducked her head in thanks, folding her hands in her lap.

"Here's the trouble," I said. "Jim's a detective. He's been . . . gone for six weeks."

"Missing?"

That word solidified my fears, but I raised my chin. "I will find him."

She listened attentively as I told her about Baldwin's murder. I'd given her the barest facts when someone knocked on our door.

Abigail opened it to the manager, Mr. Fish, standing outside with a troubled expression. Behind him, Tobias hung back in the corridor.

Offering apologies for the interruption, Mr. Fish said, "Your, ah, employee. Shall I send him to Mr. O'Trey's place of business—?"

"It's quite in order, thank you," I replied, gesturing. "Come in, Tobias! Are you quite recovered?" Mr. Fish clearly wanted to remain, but I dismissed him, saying, "I have many employees. Do not send them away, yes?"

Bowing stiffly, he departed. If Jim were to come, unless he was dressed like an exotic *houri,* he'd be admitted.

"Sit down, sit down," I said, waving Tobias in.

He hovered at the door, the whites of his eyes like pale petals in a lake at night, and said that he'd found a room in a boardinghouse.

Now I laid out my plan, telling Abigail and Tobias about the task I had assigned the boy called Wadja.

"Missus, that cannot work," said Tobias carefully. "The boy cannot watch the post office all the time. He has to eat, and well, go about his business."

"Can he not sell matches by the post office?"

"Yes, but it takes three men, most often, to shadow a bloke. Each takes a turn, so he's not spotted outright by his mark, you see? And how long will the boy keep this up, day after day. He'll tire of it, might not think it's a good bet."

"We must find Captain Jim soon. What do you propose?"

Tobias grinned. "The post and telegraph office is closed at night. We'll manage with two, ma'am. Little bloke and me—we'll watch the place in turns."

My spirits lifted as though buoyed by a great balloon. Agreeing to meet the next morning, Tobias went to the park to find young Wadja.

* * *

My plan in place, with Abigail as my guide, I explored the city, taking hansom cabs, trolleys and trains to learn my way about. Feeling steadier, I proceeded to the next step.

"Abigail," I said, in the morning, "we need a spot where we'll be very visible—where Jim might notice me. Somewhere near the exposition, d'you think?" He would not miss that cerulean parasol, the color of ocean depths, his gift.

She grinned. "Thousands pass the World's Fair station. Shall we visit?"

Right away, I found the perfect spot. Visitors to the World's Fair stepped off the train onto a wide open-air platform that moved of its own accord, efficiently ushering them in. It surprised and delighted visitors, who tottered with grunts or squeals. How different from a quiet Boston street, or sunny Bombay's festive awnings and Gothic government buildings! We positioned ourselves just before the turnstiles. Here passed men all dandied up, ladies in leg-of-mutton sleeves and long skirts, corsets tightened to flatter their waists. Such excitement on their faces: housewives, husbands, boys in Sunday best, speaking myriad languages.

Inclining my head at a passing couple, I asked Abigail, "French or Swiss?"

She smiled at my game. "Creole! From New Orleans."

In India, one's name revealed one's ancestry. Here, the clues were in one's speech and accent. Often I guessed wrong. Abigail patiently demonstrated, until I could tell apart the slow drawls and wide vowels from the southern states from self-deprecating, midwestern tones.

During a pause, she asked, "Your husband, what's he look like?"

I described Jim's build, his height and limp. His penchant for disguise could let him appear younger or older. More than visitors' clothes and hats, I searched their feet for a worn pair of khaki army boots. I'd spot them anywhere, since I'd cleaned them often, scraping them off against the doorstop. Jim's disguises had stumped me before, but he would not part with those boots.

While we waited, moments from my brief married life haunted me.

One evening, as Jim lounged at the table, I'd said, "You're watching me again."

"How do you know?" he'd asked.

"Your reflection," I said, pointing at the kettle I'd set on the stove for our tea.

Jim had enveloped me in his embrace, resting his chin on the top of my head. "You're watching me while you clean?" he asked, his voice low, like rain dripping on banana leaves. His deep quiet reassured me as we'd talked each night, his steady heartbeat against my back. He always spoke with care, and he listened when I spoke. Where was he now?

The watch pinned to my dress told me an hour had passed. How on earth did operatives shadow suspects for days? This would not work. The fair had three entrances, and even if Jim were at the fairgrounds, he could be anywhere. He was chasing a cold-blooded killer, and all I'd done was hire an urchin to spot him. I had to do more, but what?

CHAPTER 10

HE'LL FIND ME

I woke to the cooing, chugging call of cardinals on my window. I'd tossed about a dozen ways to draw attention last night but discarded them. Still undecided, Abigail and I ate together in the gleaming dining salon, with its Egyptian-themed pyramids and sphinxes on the walls. It was cordial: "Strawberry preserve—delicious"; "Did you try the marzipan?"

All the while I was thinking of Baldwin, who had been shot in the forehead.

Adi would say, "Don't fuss! Jim's tough, and he always makes it back." When Jim went to Lahore and blundered into a skirmish with the tribes there, he'd walked a hundred miles to reach me. And when he'd gone off on an army mission to the Himalayan foothills, he returned exhausted, but intact. Yet I worried, because I could see what wasn't visible—Jim's guilt over an old incident in Karachi. It plagued him. If he had to kill again, could he do it? Would his reluctance keep him from defending himself?

Tobias and the boy would find him, but if I was to be of some help, I must learn all I could about the case. The Duprees had known little about Baldwin's death, and less about Grewe's. Their information came from Sergeant Long at the Chicago Police.

Dabbing her lips with a napkin, Abigail asked, "This Baldwin. You said he was investigating a murder?"

I told her about Thomas Grewe's death.

"In an architect's office? Which one?"

I frowned, trying to remember. "Aah . . . Daniel Burnham, I think."

Abigail took something from her pocket and unfolded it on the tablecloth. The title read "Official Souvenir Program—World's Columbian Exposition."

I cried, "Where did you get that?"

"There's all sorts of things to be had. The exposition's enormous! It's on playing cards, music programs, chocolate boxes, cereal, whatever you like. Even sheet music. Every big factory or invention wants a spot in the show. Here's the map—ah!" She pointed at the page. "Daniel Hudson Burnham? He's the head architect."

"Well!" I said, congratulating Abigail with a grin. Then I nibbled on my lip. Did the death of Thomas Grewe have something to do with the fair? Jim had planned to investigate a labor union, but Dupree hadn't mentioned that.

For some time, a middle-aged couple at the next table had been eyeing us. I'd paid them no mind since other diners also seemed curious about Abigail and me. Now a trim gentleman with a thin, curling mustache approached us and inclined his head. His stylish hair and manner bore a courtly, European flair.

"Lady Diana O'Trey? I'm told you are a friend of the Boston Abernathys? I had to make myself known . . . I am Enri Bellino." Spiffy in morning coat, he reached out a hand, so I offered mine. Bowing over it, he introduced his wife, an older, heavyset woman in a stylish cutaway who nodded pleasantly from her chair. I went to her, enjoying her surprise and pleasure at my attention.

Erminia Bellino was from New York City, and didn't care much for Chicago. "This cold wind. And the streets. Awful," she said, with a dismissive wave. "Now Newport! That's the place. Of course, summertime's best."

Offering an invitation to explore the city with them the next day, they departed. I returned to my seat, buoyant to have made an acquaintance. How easy it had been, how natural, returning my sense of normalcy. But why had Mr. Bellino approached me? What had caught his interest? Was it that Mr. Fish told him I was *Lady* Diana?

Nibbling a brioche, I thought what snobs Americans were—assume a title and they were pleased to be acquainted. "Use everything," Jim had once said. I wondered, how could I use this to my advantage?

Mulling it over, I went to meet Tobias in the park as we'd agreed.

"The boy watches the post and telegraph office in the morning, ma'am," said Tobias. "A right smart lad. Says he'll sell more cigarettes there than anywhere. I'm to spell him at noon."

That was progress! I asked after his health. Heartened at his slow smile and reply, I hailed a hansom to the Chicago Police Station, at City Hall, near what the cabbie called "the Hill."

Noting that the Chicago Public Library was housed on the fourth floor of the same building, I crossed the foyer. As the only woman in the room, turning heads and surprised glances pointed out that my presence was an anomaly. Rumpled fellows lining the walls grinned and whistled. Rather than push through, I skirted the puzzled policemen, headed toward a sign marked ENQUIRIES and said, "I'm here to see Sergeant Long."

The desk sergeant looked up. "What's it about?"

I said quietly, "The death of Arnold Baldwin."

Scratching his head, he asked me to wait.

Retreating to a window, I watched him make a series of phone calls. A quarter of an hour passed, during which the novelty of my appearance gradually faded. Then I was shown into a small room with a desk and two chairs.

An hour lapsed. Alone, I planned my questions. Resolved to be patient, I filled the time by reciting Walter Scott's poem "Breathes There the Man." Would my heart too burn, as I turned my footsteps home? America was now "my own, my native land." It didn't feel that way yet.

Distant murmurs outside my door brought memories of my childhood, Papa in his loose, muslin undershirt and prayer cap as his low voice hummed the ancient Zoroastrian prayers. A few phrases filtered back, almost forgotten since my *navjote* initiation as a child: *Kem na mazda, moy-te payem dadah?* Who will help me in my hour of need?

The door opened, and a sandy-haired officer entered, his dark eyes puzzled. "Mrs. Baldwin?"

I paused. Pretending to be Arnold Baldwin's wife would earn me only sympathy and sops. Noting my hesitation, the officer's eyes narrowed.

"Sergeant Long? I'm from the Dupree Agency in Boston." I handed over Alfred Dupree's letter of introduction.

His eyebrows shot up. "Dupree sent a woman?"

"We're keen to know what happened. Perhaps I can assist?"

He read the letter, then refolded it, shaking his head. "It's no matter for a woman. We found a telegram from Dupree in his pocket. You know Baldwin was traveling under a false name? Albert Bingley. No witnesses. Likely a robbery, or a brawl in a bar got out of hand."

It did not surprise me that Baldwin used an alias, like Jim. But a drunken fistfight? Holding his keen gaze, I said, "He was investigating a murder. The death of a security guard, Thomas Grewe. Killed in the architect's office?"

He pulled out a chair and folded himself into it. "Grewe was a Pinkerton. They'll sort it out. We've got our hands full here." His lips twitched. "Didn't know that, did-ja. Yeah, we've got over three hun'red Pinkertons here at the fair. Called in Dupree for this one—didn't do much good, huh?"

Had Jim started here, with him? Without inflection, I asked, "And the other operative?"

He blinked. "There's another? From Dupree?"

I shook my head. "Never mind. May I see Baldwin's belongings?"

The sergeant squinted at me in frank curiosity. "Personal effects were picked up by his brother."

"Oh." Baldwin had a brother? I asked, "Tall fellow, slight limp?"

His brows peaked. "Tall enough. Dunno 'bout the limp."

Had Jim been here? Heavens, had I given him away? I suppressed a tremor. Despite his reluctance, I persuaded the sergeant to let me see the files on both murders. A few minutes later, he returned with them.

Opening Baldwin's first, I set the photograph aside and read quickly. "Body found at the waterside, dock thirteen. On March twenty-fourth." I paused. Jim had left Boston on the twenty-fifth. Had he known of Baldwin's death? It seemed unlikely. "No witnesses, you said?"

Sergeant Long said, "Nope. Found early morning by a beat cop."

The constable's statement and the medical coroner's told no more than I already knew. Baldwin was shot twice. The bullets were .45 caliber rounds. I chewed my lip, considering. Wasn't that a large weapon? Why hadn't Baldwin noticed it and been on guard?

The photograph told me more. Baldwin lay on his back, one ankle over the other. Though his face was turned away, ribbons of blood dripped over it. One cheek was pockmarked—with powder burns? His coat was open, his shirt bloodied. He wore suspenders. With his wavy hair, he'd been a handsome man, younger than Jim. A tag hung from one wrist. In Boston, Jim had called Baldwin a canny bloke. Yet someone had surprised the experienced operative. Was there a Mrs. Baldwin? Had Dupree broken the news to her?

Thomas Grewe's file contained even less. He'd been killed on the first of March. Grease, ink and bruises were found on his neck. The photograph taken postmortem showed a young face bearing a wispy mustache. Dark splotches on his neck, he lay on a table, shoulders bare, looking barely adult.

I tapped the coroner's report. "Cause of death: strangulation."

The sergeant shifted in his seat. "A constable was summoned to a disturbance. Seems Grewe interrupted a burglary."

Two separate accounts described the search of the premises, an architect's office on the top floor of a building called the Rookery. No one claimed anything stolen.

I floundered, searching for some link to Jim's investigation. "Next of kin? Who took his belongings?"

"No one. It's still here." He ruffled through the pages, and slid one across. It listed clothing, a few coins, a key, a hair comb. I winced. Was that all the boy carried?

"Where did he live? Any leads there?"

He sighed, looking grim. "Nothing but overdue rent. He died on the job." Pre-empting me, he said, "No known family."

Feeling morose, I took my leave. Two young men dead, and for what? I'd learned hardly anything new, and nothing that seemed useful. Worse, I'd made Sergeant Long suspicious of Baldwin's brother, who might or might not be Jim.

The sergeant shook my hand and said, "You got to understand, ma'am. We have thousands coming every day. Folks are hungry. Winter's been harsh. Some go missing, some want to disappear. Stiffs . . . er . . . bodies turn up in the lake, most every day. We can't chase our tails on every stiff."

I nodded, appreciating his euphemisms. Chicago's police were inundated. No one seemed much concerned about the deaths of Grewe and Baldwin. Would it be different if Jim or I were killed? I doubted it.

As I returned to the Oriental, little Wadja drew my attention with a sharp whistle, then disappeared into the shrubbery of the park next door. Hoping for news of Jim, I followed his red cap as it retreated behind the pavilion. There, he burst out, "If the shine finds the fella you're looking for, will I get paid?"

"Who?"

"The honey. The negro guy."

He'd been running, still panting from it. I smiled. "You'll be paid. You're a part of our group now."

He stepped closer. "I 'ad him, lady, but I lost him."

I gasped. "Are you certain? Did Tobias see him? Tobias can tell if it's him."

"Ol' guy? Nah—I'd just took his spot from him, see?"

How amusing. The boy had named us: Old Guy and Lady. Had he really spotted Jim?

He gazed up, his voice hushed. "I'll git him next week. He comes on Tuesdays."

A week away! I resolved to watch Wadja from a distance that day and handed him a coin for his supper, cautioning him, "Keep watching. That may be someone else, not him."

Grinning, he said, "Ten smackers, right? If it's him, I get ten bucks!"

Smackers? Bucks? Agreeing, I sent him on his way. Would it work? If it did, soon I'd see Jim!

CHAPTER 11

THE SPINNING WHEEL

The prospect of seven days seemed like an age. That evening, I scoured the German letter and its translation again to wring additional meaning from it, with little gain. Although I strove to keep an easy, pleasant manner, I jerked at the slightest sound. Sleep eluded me until dawn.

At breakfast I told Abigail about Wadja's news, then sighed, tapping my fingers on the table. "What can we do in the meantime?"

Abigail looked thoughtful. "Everyone's here for the fair. Shall we visit it?"

Visit the fair? My nerves frayed from waiting, I welcomed the distraction. "Why not?"

Retracing our steps, we took a train filled with an excited throng. Disembarking at the World's Fair station, the moving walkway emptied into a wide pathway, which led to an open space. Now the crowd grew silent.

All around a rectangular basin, white facades gleamed, grander than Bombay's Victoria Terminus or Elphinstone College. Awed, we followed the basin's perimeter. For sheer size, neither the mansions of London or Bath nor even Buckingham Palace could compare! Here was classical grandeur, ancient solemnity made new. Tall columns. White marble. Romanesque statues.

Plumed hats fluttered in the light breeze. People stared. A woman beside me pressed a kerchief to her lips as her tears overflowed. "Heaven itself," she said, "must surely be like this."

Yet the uniformity was an illusion—each unique structure was embellished with soaring concentric doors or carvings set upon massive plinths. Wide pristine roads, without carriages, untainted by the usual horse droppings. At the opposite side of the basin towered a statue of a maiden in robes of gold.

I addressed a pair of tall women in fine hats, "Excuse me. May I ask, what is it called?"

The one with a guidebook smiled. "The Statue of the Republic."

"She's also called Big Mary," said the other.

Despite the grandeur, I found myself searching the crowd for a tall man with wide shoulders and a limp. Each time a tall figure caught my attention I tugged Abigail's elbow, then followed the stranger for a closer look. We gained only puzzled glances and aching feet.

People thronged the fairgrounds with a sense of holiday. At length we ventured toward a lagoon where the grassy Japanese Island seemed to float upon the water. Farther lay the enormous Art Gallery, furnished with European masterworks, Erminia had said, from the collections of the fabulously wealthy Mrs. Potter Palmer.

Entering between intricate sculptures we stepped into the enormous room. Visitors gazed upward. Portraits blanketed the high walls. I'd admired fine canvases in London's great galleries. Here, fairgoers gawped as though standing in a cathedral.

There was too much to see: Columbus's cannon and his displayed contract with Ferdinand and Isabella, his ships, the Columbus caravels that had sailed from Spain! I marveled, feeling like Alice in a proverbial Wonderland. The thirty-five-foot model of the battleship *Victoria* . . . the enormous Yerkes telescope, made for the University of Chicago which could see entire worlds in the deep recesses of space . . . the huge Krupp guns that could fire shells as thick as my waist . . .

On the Midway Plaisance we glimpsed the Streets of Cairo, the Irish Village, Blarney and Donegal Castles, the Moorish Palace, Laplanders, Arabs, American Indians! Fifty thousand roses bloomed on the Wooded Island.

The Manufacturers and Liberal Arts building housed rough diamonds from Africa . . . the grey canary diamond . . . a solid silver statue from Montana, eight feet high . . . Russian jades, Sèvres vases, and Japanese enamels so delicate one held one's breath near them . . . even a long-distance telephone to New York. We craned to see a mammoth cheese wheel the size of a haymow, the Cartagena church bell, sixteenth century . . . the Liberty Bell in the Pennsylvania Building with its hallowed crack.

Gasping, we dropped to the lawn outside to rest.

Our perch overlooked the spot where a pavilion was being built. Beside a trellis of wooden poles lay plaster molding to ornament the top.

I glanced toward the Court of Honor. Were those gargantuan, gleaming buildings built not of marble, but plaster and wood?

Ballistite, I thought, shocked by a sudden chill, oh God, ballistite!

It could set such structures ablaze like giant matchboxes. My breath jerked. Fire. With thousands of excited people inside! In turmoil I searched the peaceful scene. Should I tell Abigail about the explosives? What would I say? That someone planned to destroy all this? It sounded hysterical.

"Shall we go? I'd like to see the rest," she said. I led the way back to the mammoth Manufacturers Building, which drew a steady torrent of visitors. Remembering Jim's interest in electricity, I gazed at Mr. Edison's tower of light: five thousand incandescent lamps beamed from a single tall structure, blindingly bright like a pillar carved from the sun itself.

General Electric's display of Mr. Edison's lightbulb was dwarfed by the area bearing the sign WESTINGHOUSE ELECTRICITY. While Abigail went to purchase refreshments, I browsed the strange displays of metal knobs, wires, and shapes.

Moving around to better see the glass tubes, I bumped against a young man with untidy coal-black hair and bushy mustache of the same shade.

"Beg your pardon, madame!" he cried in a heavily accented voice, stepping back.

"My fault entirely," I said, then pointed. "This machine. Can you tell me what it means?"

He touched his tie, setting it further askew. "Certainly, madame. Permit me to introduce myself. Nikola Tesla, at your service."

I gave my name and shook hands, feeling a tremor in his grip. A high-strung fellow, he spoke about the exhibit at length. I understood some of it, yet his animation was so great that it seemed churlish to stop him. When he paused, I said, "It can burn people, you say?"

"It seeks a channel, madame. Like water. If you stand below a waterfall, would you not expect to get wet?"

"But how does one prevent it?"

"Wood, madame." He smiled at my confusion. "It cannot travel through wood." He said that one day the world would be illuminated with powerful alternating current. "Enormous turbines, madame. I am to build them on Niagara Falls—the force of the waterfall could power cities, entire states!"

Just then Abigail returned, so thanking him, I said goodbye. I left, shaking my head as I told Abigail, "That remarkable young man has a fanciful imagination."

We walked all day, pausing only when my feet begged relief. We sat down on the steps of the peristyle to catch my breath. Green sod filled the spaces between buildings and around the lagoon, in a picturesque, peaceful scene. Abigail perched quietly nearby, silent and watchful, like Jim.

Glancing at the scene, I shivered. This was why Jim was here. This was why he remained, weeks after the murder of his colleague, to protect this, what the papers had dubbed the "White City." And someone planned to blow up eight hundred pounds of explosive. Emotion choked me. How could one man alone prevent it? His endeavor seemed impossible—we had to tell the authorities, the mayor, the governor! Not to warn them meant disaster.

Steadying myself, I said, "If someone wanted to destroy all this, where would they strike?"

Abigail frowned in surprise. Logic, I decided—both Jim and my brother Adi would use logic. A map was of little use; instead, I needed a vantage from which to see it all. On the horizon, a large structure curved into the sky: the Ferris wheel—the highest point around.

I pushed to my feet. "Come on. We need to know how the fair is laid out." Asking the way, we rode the elevated railroad to the Midway Plaisance. This too proved full of delight, for costumed players roamed about, among natives of nations in exotic dress. A hula dancer! Arabs in robes. A band of cowboys in bright, fringed shirts.

As we neared, the wheel's sheer size awed me. Hanging from a mammoth circular frame, thirty-six glass wagons swayed high above. Two hundred and sixty-four feet high at its apex, this was America's answer to Mr. Eiffel's tower.

A line of people snaked toward it. We joined the excited visitors peering upward. A single glass wagon could seat forty, plus twenty more standing at windows. Paying fifty cents apiece—as much as one might pay for a fancy French dinner with wine—Abigail and I joined the smiling group in a glass wagon, and each grasped a pole by the window. Soon the chamber filled, doors closed, and a uniformed guard explained the wheel's mechanism. "We are quite safe," he said. "Mr. Ferris and his wife rode on the very first day."

The great wheel jolted into motion as we ascended. Cries of surprise and wonder filled the chamber. "Look! The Wooded Isle!" "The Electricity Building!"

Someone said, "My dear, it's the Horticulture Building."

"But that gold dome!"

"That's the Administration Building. The wide one, with turrets— that's the Electricity Building."

As we rose, the fairgrounds took the shape of a large T. Ahead, colorful tents along the Midway Plaisance stretched through the city. Silver pools shimmered in a profusion of waterways. Tall domes stood out over the green Wooded Isle. By comparing the view against my map, I grasped the position of the North Pond, the lagoon around the Wooded Isle that fed into the Basin. Grecian buildings formed the Court of Honor around the Basin. To the right, I spied mechanical cranes in the harbor near the South Pool, where we'd taken the elevated railroad.

Exhilarated to be up so high, I laughed. Our car swayed, but it was no worse than the gentle motion of a ship. However, a whiskered man in a coarse woolen coat clung to his rail, one hand pressed to his mouth.

Oh dear, I thought, wincing at the prospect of a vomit in the enclosed space. The eager people around him seemed oblivious to his plight. He began to moan.

"Here, what's the matter?" called the guard.

The poor man whimpered, panting in distress. People backed away from him. The wheel had paused to load a car below, and soon our ascent continued. As we lurched upward, the fellow threw himself at the window, crying, "Let me out!"

Visitors yelled, "Don't break it!" "It's glass, man!"

When people crowded to one side, the guard begged them not to unbalance the car.

The poor man now launched himself at a metal strut with such ferocity that the entire car swayed. Passengers cried out. At his wit's end, the guard tried to grab him, but the poor blighter had lost all reason. Gripping the rail, he rammed the glass with his head.

"Nooooo!" he shrieked like a terrified horse, hammering at the window.

I exchanged a look with Abigail. A flash of memory offered a solution. Mama and I had been walking near the stable when something spooked a young horse. He shrieked and reared in terror. My clever mama caught up a blanket and threw it over the beast's head. Magically, it calmed. She'd walked it back to the stable, soothing it like a baby.

I had no blanket or cloak on this sunny day. So, undoing the hooks at my side, I slipped my skirt off my petticoats. Inverting it into a tent, I cast it over the wailing, shuddering fellow.

Silence washed through the car, broken by gasps of relief.

"Sir, you are quite safe," I assured the man. "Would you care to sit down?"

Someone offered a seat, so I guided him to it. He sat without protest. Crouching by him, I continued to talk, praising the fine buildings and charming lagoon, imparting titbits I recalled. I named the architects and said that at sundown the park would be lit by ten thousand electric lamps. The man sat immobile, as I spoke.

Moments later the car landed with a bump. The doors parted, fresh air gusted in, and people scrambled out. The guard, the man comically covered in my skirt, and I, in petticoats and vest, were the last to disembark.

As we stepped out, people applauded. Astonished, I glanced behind me. The wheel had stopped. Glass cars swayed above, people peering out. My skirt was lifted off the poor man as he was led away, blushing crimson with apologies.

Where was Abigail? I glanced around at the raucous crowd.

What now? A tall young man with a short beard stood on a stool near me and made a speech. Astonished, I heard him say, "A heroine . . . remarkable presence of mind . . ."

The young man presented my skirt as though handing me a queen's cape. "What courage! To quell the madman! Remarkable!"

"No madman, sir. I believe he has acrophobia—a fear of heights," I said, blushing. Jim and I had read of its recent discovery over Christmas.

"Your name, madam!" called a newspaperman. Others took up the clamor.

Just then, Abigail waved to catch my attention. "Lady Diana!"

The young man with a fine bushy mustache said, "May I present myself, Lady Diana? George Washington Ferris Jr. You're English, yes?" He laughed.

"Goodness. No, I'm from India!" I replied, unsettled by the to-do. Several photographers' flash pans went off a few feet away, making me flinch.

As daylight dimmed, fairgoers gathered at the waterside. My skirt once more in place, Abigail and I joined them, puzzled. The twilight sky glowed turquoise.

All at once, electric lamps glittered upon each building, outlining arches, on every column, bridge and boat, turning the fountains into a fantasy of shimmering light.

"Ahhhh!" cried people around me.

What had I expected of a World's Fair? An entertaining day of music and dancers. Instead, I'd seen a gleaming city. An impossible city of light, heralding the future. We returned to the station among visitors bubbling with awe, hope and excitement. My emotions churned. I hadn't expected to find Jim at the fair, not really, but I saw now what was at stake. The very future was being written, a fragile dream of hope.

CHAPTER 12

A FLEETING GLIMPSE

An image filled next morning's front page—me, startled, standing in my petticoats under the headline: INDIAN PRINCESS SAVES THE DAY. Well, I'd got into the papers, I thought. If that did not draw Jim's attention, I wasn't sure what would.

Entering the dining room, I caught a number of amused looks and chuckles.

"Royalty?" someone said. "Really?" Titters followed.

Tightness caught my chest, and my cheeks warmed. Five years ago when I'd first joined Foley Academy, I'd made a number of faux pas, sitting down at dinner before the matronly director indicated with a flick of her wrist. I started to eat before grace. When I dropped my spoon with a splash, the entire room broke into giggles. I'd gazed about for an explanation, as the "young ladies" erupted in laughter. The same smirks surrounded me now, mocking my title in the paper. Or was it my state of undress?

"Napkin?" Abigail asked, offering one, her gaze nonchalant.

I took it gratefully. We were both outsiders here in Chicago, yet she was unconcerned. Adopting her manner, I nodded to the nearby waiter to pour my tea. Five years ago, I'd been so mortified by the girls' ridicule that I could not eat. Potatoes tasted sour, beef congealed on my plate. "Don't cry, pet. They don't matter," Emily-Jane had insisted afterward, handing me a pear she'd secreted from the senior girls' parlor. "They're not bad, really. It's just that you're not one of us yet. When you are, you'll see."

I'd never become "one of them," but she was right. As I dived into Descartes and geometry, books by Shakespeare and Mr. Dickens, their derision ceased to matter. Their excitement about clothes and parties seemed childlike. Sometimes, though, I'd wonder, what was wrong with me? My friends in Bombay had all married early. But I wanted more, to make my own way in the world. Alas, while I prepared to read literature at Somerville College, Pilloo and Adi's wife, Bacha, were killed. I hurried home because their loss devastated my sweet mama.

Ignoring the excited whispers, I thought, if it brought Jim to me, I'd parade in my petticoat on Wabash Avenue at midday!

With four days left before Jim's visit to the post office on Tuesday, I accepted the Bellinos' invitation to tour the city. A sprawling wonder, Chicago boasted many of the world's tallest buildings, a fine waterfront drive, and magnificent mansions. Yet it seemed cobbled together like a shantytown, piled with helter-skelter homes and tenements. At the wholesale market, a bustling, bazaar-like affair in a great hall, seeing wheat flour was cheap, I contracted to buy bushels for the Lins. Mr. Bellino's eyebrows climbed toward his well-groomed hair. The purchase completed, I made arrangements to pay when the flour reached Boston.

And still Tuesday hung over the distant horizon.

* * *

On the appointed day, I waited in a carriage, watching Wadja in his too-large clothes and red cap sell cigarettes at the post and telegraph office. I'd left Abigail behind because Jim would not want strangers involved.

All morning dark-suited men went in and out. How closely I examined their gait and clothing—which was Jim?

My attention wandered back to a day just after our arrival in Boston. I'd awoken while Jim was still in the midst of his exercise drill. Sweat dripped down his arms as he pumped through an impossible number of push-ups. Rising to make our tea, I'd thought, "His poor shoulder!" since he'd injured it while working for Adi. When the town hall chimed six, Jim stood at the window, breathing hard from his exertions. Across the quadrangle, the clock tower was shrouded in a mist. Light glinted off his back.

Careful to hold the kettle with a wadded cloth, I'd poured boiling water into my teapot. Jim had not moved. "All right, dear?"

His glance across the room caught me as though he'd grabbed my arms and turned me to him. But all he said was, "Mmm. Our clock's running fast." Mopping his chest with his nightshirt, he went to our cuckoo clock and nudged the minute hand with a careful finger, then drew back, satisfied. With a careful pull on the chain, he wound the clock. As he passed me on his way to bathe, he stopped and kissed my neck. Just that, no embrace, no caress down my back, just the touch of his breath and his warm lips under my ear.

I'd shivered, protesting, "Jim! Go bathe!"

Grinning, he'd disappeared into the bedroom.

Forcing my attention back to Chicago and the present, I glanced toward the post office. My heart gave a nasty jolt. Wadja was hurrying after a man in dark overcoat who loped along at an easy pace.

The boy scampered, slipping on the cobbles. He made up for it by hawking his wares—"Matches and smokes, folks!" The effect was ruined when he scurried past prospective customers. Telling the coachman to wait, I pulled my cloak closer and followed.

The filthy street was slick with mud. Grimacing, I avoided a puddle. When I looked up again, the empty road mocked me. Pulse pounding, I rushed forward. Had they turned into a lane between stores? Where? One moment the boy was there, the next, he was gone.

Training my gaze where I'd last seen him, I reached a bend in the street. A pair of men came out of a door and passed me. A pub? Too quiet for that. When I peered into the alley, the air left my lungs. A large figure stooped over Wadja's cowering form.

"Well, boy?"

Wadja must have remembered my instruction, but the man's size surely daunted him. Goggle-eyed, he said, "A bundle wants to see you."

"Who wants to see me?"

"A heifer, a ginny. A foreign dame."

"Foreign dame?"

That voice! It had an American sound to it, but . . .

"Cun-hard Umbrella," said Wadja, half remembering the words he was to say, the Cunard *Umbria*, but mangling them in his distress.

The man caught Wadja's arm. "What did you say?"

Hearing it repeated, he released the boy.

"She's here?" asked Jim, his voice hoarse.

I gasped, light-headed with relief. I wanted to call out, but my voice had dried up, my feet rooted to the ground. Later, Wadja would crow, "He nearly keeled over, he did! Then he looks at me, and says, 'Where is she?' I didn't tell him, 'course!"

Jim offered Wadja something.

The boy took it. "You're to give me a note. And if I bring a reply, you owe me a dollar."

"A note. Do you carry paper and ink?"

That stumped Wadja. We should have thought of it. Gathering my wits, I stepped into the alley.

"Jim."

He spun around, his hair unkempt. A workman's cap dangled in his hand. Wadja made a strangled sound.

"Hush, boy," I said, stepping up. "I know him."

Jim strode up fast and enveloped me in his embrace. Pressed against his rough coat, my breath whooshed, a flood of relief.

His mouth moved against my temple. "Sweet, I'm sorry," he said near my ear, breathing in, so the words sat softly against my hair. "Why are you here? My life, go back home."

"Why?" I mouthed.

His cheek against mine, his face moved in a grimace. I knew that look, his eyes squeezed shut, mouth bracketed with tight lines.

"This is no place to be. Not now." His lips touched my forehead, pulled back.

He eased away but I clung to his fingers. He glanced over his shoulder, then raised my fingers to his lips. I searched his bearded face, unfamiliar in the shadows.

"I have the German letter," I said, fumbling at my pouch.

He stopped me, his large hands covering mine. "Don't. I can't have it on me."

I said, "Where can I find you?"

He gripped my hands tightly. "No, Diana."

His look was implacable. Alarm coiled into me, as I whispered, "I'm at the Oriental. Come to me."

He slipped into the shadows without replying. What had I learned? His chin bore stubble—a three-day growth at least. He smelled of sweat and grease like a factory hand. He'd stayed in the dark—why? He wanted me to leave. Did he not need me, after all? Drat the man! Why didn't he say where I could find him?

I should be rejoicing to see him. Instead, my chest throbbed with ominous warning as Wadja and I trudged back to my carriage.

Wadja blurted out, "What's that you speaked? Wot language?"

I was about to say, "English, of course," when I realized that Jim and I had both spoken in Hindustani. Trying to smile, I said, "It's all right. I said ten dollars, yes? You've earned it."

I handed him the bill, cold seeping through my gloves. No longer close to Jim's warmth, the chill crawled up my arms. He didn't want my help, and spoke in Hindustani? Something had disturbed him. That knowledge reverberated—he didn't want to be found carrying the German letter. Had I put him at risk? I shuddered. Was his only protection a fragile disguise that my arrival now threatened? I had blundered into a tinderbox, the match ready to strike—and my sweet Jim might be caught in the flames.

CHAPTER 13

VISITORS

JIM

My God, she was here. Diana had followed me to Chicago. My pulse jumped at the sight of her dancing eyes and puckish grin, yet how I wished she'd stayed in Boston, safe. I'd found the remnants of the old steelworkers' union. Some worked at the rail yard, others found day work, if they got to the loading pier early. As I headed back to the old factory where the lads bedded down, Baldwin's letter echoed in my mind.

James, I fear I may be blown. I should leave but goddamn I never quit on a job before. Grewe had ink on his hands and round his neck. The boy was strangled face-to-face—thumb marks on his clavicle.

Went around a few printers with a story 'bout a pamphlet to print. Orrin Pierce, foreman at the station loading dock, drinks at Old Times Tavern on Wabash. Sent me to Lascar, a twisted bloke. Bad reputation with a knife. Union chaps sacked after the Carnegie Steel strike.

Jim, I snuck in to search the place. Same oily ink. Grease and piss all over. They use kegs from when the place was a tannery. Fella almost caught me—he came in quiet like, put something in his bed. When he left, I pulled it out—a letter. No time to read so

I took two pages. It looks bad. James, come soon as you get this. A place like this, most are on the take already. Tell no one. Don't trust Dupree.

A. Baldwin

That last bit had astonished me. Yet Baldwin did nothing without a purpose, so I'd sent no word to the Duprees all this time.

Baldwin. The man loved a pint, but could nurse one while he spun tale after tale. For such a young bloke he had a lot of stories, wild tales of his cases, of dodgy insurance and pretty girls married to jealous blokes. More often he sided with the wives.

I scanned the street, noting the fellows lounging at the corner. One had a peculiar beard that left his chin bare. Had I seen his massive bulk at the pier yesterday? I could not risk writing down my observations, and each day went by in a blur. It had been too long. I had to break this case soon.

When I entered the run-down factory building, a group was playing cards. Paddy Prendergast grinned a greeting, his cheekbones prominent in his skeletal face. Orrin, the redhead, sat across from a pair of Ohio farmhands. The Frenchman lying on his bedroll turned to see who'd come in.

Baldwin'd had a Colt .45, not something one carried while doing manual labor at the docks or rail yards. I'd searched for it. Whoever had it now had most likely killed him. While looking into Grewe's murder, Baldwin had blundered upon something, found that German letter, and realized what it meant—was that just coincidence? He'd been lucky, until it got him killed.

Searching for that revolver was tricky. I'd been through most of the lads' things one time or another, but a few were especially leery of thieves. And there was always the chance that the killer had the weapon on his person. Patience, friend, I told myself, slumping against a wall to watch the blokes play, listen to their talk.

Sometime later, foreman Oscar Donnelly returned. A ragtag group filed in behind him in shirtsleeves or overalls, some bearded, others clean-shaven. A few wore the bleached, hungry look of long nights in steerage. Dropping their sacks and boxes, they shook hands, taking my measure.

The bearded giant who'd been smoking on the street corner was among them. He tilted his head to one side, peering around. Indoors, most uncovered their heads. He didn't, the sides of his bent hat obscuring his eyes.

"There's space over there, Al. Help yourself," Donnelly told him.

The man called Al dropped his sack into a corner and waved the others over, saying in a thick accent, "We sleep there."

A frisson of alarm brushed my fingers. Baldwin's letter had led me to Donnelly. Now he'd invited more men into the old factory, men who knew little English and spoke with guttural accents. Why? If he'd planned an explosion, why bring around a bunch of heavies, foreign blokes, to muddy the waters? Were they all part of the plot—or did he plan to pin the blame on them?

CHAPTER 14

A MAN'S WALK

Ever since that brief glimpse of Jim, my thoughts spun in a turbulent circle. When would he come to my hotel? And how would he escape notice? Struggling to go about each day, when at any moment disaster might fall upon the poor souls at the fair, my stomach knotted in rebellion. Abigail's bland face as usual gave no indication of her thoughts, yet she'd been a steadfast companion at the fair, and her knowledge of Chicago had been useful.

Deciding to trust her, I told her about Professor Grimke's letter, and said, "Say a group of disgruntled fellows has stolen a map of the fair and bought explosives. Well, they want to cause trouble, draw attention to their plight. What would they do?"

Abigail's eyebrows rose. Carefully setting down her teacup, she said, "They'd need a plan, and a leader."

That's what Jim was doing—looking for the troublemakers, listening to the blokes' grievances. "How do we find their leader? Where do fellows gather and talk?"

She shrugged. "Where they drink. Bars and taverns?"

But in a city this size, there'd be many of those. And where were they? So, sending Abigail to buy a street map, I went to the park and searched for little Wadja in his favorite red cap.

The late May morning had drawn Chicago's residents out in couples and groups. Visitors strolled along the street, glad the rain had ceased, so I bought some matches as a pretext and put the matter to Wadja. "Say a set of fellows is upset with things, where would they gather, d'you know?"

He scratched his backside with a thoughtful expression far older than his twelve years. Tucking away my coin, he pulled out a wad of leaflets from his satchel and offered one. "Lots of working sods going. No gents, mind. Don't give 'em to posh folks, I's told."

The page was crowded with small print. At the top was an invitation to the "World Congress of Anarchists." I stared at the date—it was tomorrow.

Wadja nodded at the paper. "Cops got wind of it, so the place is changed, see?"

Anarchists, here in Chicago, right by the World's Fair! If they wanted to make a grand gesture, this was the place to do it. Did Jim know? How could I tell him? My mind spun as I folded the flyer into my glove. Throat dry, I said, "That bloke you spotted at the post office, remember him?"

"Seen him round the rail yard."

"Can you show him that page?"

Wadja tugged his lapels, then shrugged. "Mebbe."

* * *

A day later, I'd still got no word from Jim. The anarchists would convene this evening—would they dare to discuss their plans in public? It seemed impossible.

Was I willing to bet on it? To risk a half million lives? My stomach churning, I paced my room. If anarchists did indeed cause an explosion, how could I live with not having given the alarm? Wasn't I morally obliged to do so? Jim had said, "Say nothing," but that was before I learned of the anarchist meeting. I should tell the police, show them the German letter and translation, or at least the anarchist pamphlet. Let them decide what to do.

My stomach churning, I set off, finding the streets clogged with carriages of all kinds. Already teeming, the city was crammed with thousands more, arriving for the fair. Tracing my path from last week, I pushed through Randolph Street to City Hall and asked for Sergeant Long.

"Madam, he's not here," the constable at the desk said patiently.

The corridor was empty of ruffians and drunks today. The entire building seemed vacant. "Will he be back soon?"

The constable only repeated that Sergeant Long was busy.

On board the *Umbria,* Jim and I had read about the execution of the anarchist Ravachol for bombing members of the French judiciary. That affair was related to labor unrest. Were anarchists here too, in America? I needed to learn more.

In somber thought I climbed to the fourth floor to visit the public library, a wide hall where a few men sat reading at tables. A young, spectacled librarian greeted me, smiling. "Lady reporter, eh? We had one just yesterday."

So that's what he made of me! I did not disabuse him of this notion, asking instead, "Would you have recent articles on anarchists—the Frenchman Ravachol, and other radicals?"

His eyebrows shot up, but he strode off and brought me a great deal of useful material. Astonished, I read until the library closed.

One author wrote, "After France's Boulevard Saint-Germain and Rue de Clichy explosions, this April, Spain suffered a plot to blow up the Congreso and other buildings in Madrid. The arrested, Frenchman Jean Marie Delboche and a Portuguese, Manuel Ferreira, were found in possession of two very powerful bombs weighing nearly six pounds apiece."

Another piece mentioned the Walsall bomb plot. "Frederick Charles, Joseph Deakin, Victor Cailes and Jean Battola were arrested at Walsall in Staffordshire on charges of manufacturing bombs and engaging in a criminal conspiracy. Battola was sentenced to ten years penal servitude, and Deakin, to five. In February and at Easter, some bombs were exploded in Rome . . ."

I frowned, my anxiety growing. Sergeant Long had made clear his opinion that a woman was of little use in his investigation. Yet anarchists were active in France, Spain, England, as well as other countries. Those "very powerful bombs" contained just six pounds of explosives! What carnage could eight hundred pounds inflict?

I took a trolley back to the Oriental, clutching my reticule, where I'd folded the German letter. If I told the constable about it, would he even believe me? I stopped to catch my breath before braving across Wabash Street, busy with clopping mares and carts.

Entering the Oriental, I nodded and smiled to fellow guests, but tendrils of panic grew in me. Like one in a dream, I crossed the marbled foyer and stepped into the gilt-accented elevator. Foreboding grew, glittering like the crystal chandelier above me. Mostly I feared that things had gone too far to stop them. If the arsonist wasn't caught, he'd blow up the fair and all those in it. Even if Jim survived, would he blame himself for that carnage? Already, he wrestled with terrible dreams, memories of slaughter in his army days. If the explosion went off, how would he ever forgive himself?

My forehead ached. I couldn't get word to Jim, but someone must attend that meeting, learn what they planned. All I'd read about European anarchists now tolled in my mind as a warning.

My breath caught—could *I* attend? They might prevent entry to a woman, but what if I dressed as a bloke? I'd need to behave like one as well. Abigail could help.

* * *

"No, that won't do," she said, looking me over as I stood in my borrowed menswear. Abigail's trousers were too long for me, so we'd taken them in. Borrowed suspenders kept them up. To add bulk, I wore a cummerbund—a woolen scarf wound twice around me. A clever spot for my derringer, it also kept me warm.

We'd tucked my hair into Jim's hat, which dwarfed my head. Spotting myself in the glass, I yanked it off. I looked ludicrous, like someone in a vaudeville farce. Adi would have shouted with laughter.

Shaking her head, Abigail fetched a smaller bowler hat. When I had packed my hair into it, she nodded and affixed it with a hatpin, warning, "You can't doff your hat, so you'll seem quite rude. But you're a rich fella, so that'll be fine."

She thickened my eyebrows with paint, gave me sideburns and pasted a wispy mustache above my lip. I peered in the dressing room mirror. Better. I looked like a teenage version of Adi. We shared Mama's narrow features. From the glass, Adi's eyes watched me cautiously.

"Well." Abigail inclined her head. "Let's see you walk."

When I started across the room, she turned away, chuckling. "God, no. You'll never pass for a man. Not even a boy. Try this."

Dressed in trousers and dark coat, she loped across the room, her arms swinging, at ease. I, on the other hand, stepped like a chicken on a string, my collar too tight, trousers flapping strangely at my ankles. Without a corset, my tummy felt bare. Think of it as a saree, I told myself, but the narrow trousers caught at my knees. The famous playwright Oscar Wilde had written about reform in women's clothing and joined a society to promote rational dress. In England I'd worn a divided riding skirt. My sister Pilloo had worn trousers, but this was my first time.

I strutted about the chamber in Abigail's boots, imitating her walk, but nothing suited her. Too flashy—too mincing—too namby-pamby— "God, can't you just walk?" Nothing pleased her. Undoing Miss Sythe-Fornett's instructions proved an arduous task.

When at last satisfied with my gait, Abigail started on my gaze, how I looked at her. "No, look serious, but not angry. Are you itching for a fight? No, that's meek. You're money, man! Don't look shy. 'Shy' is an insult to a man, did you know? Like saying you're a coward—could get you worked over."

"How does one respond?"

She considered. Even when dressed as a man, I still thought of her as Abigail. Lifting her chin with a slight frown, she said, "What's it to you?"

It didn't sound threatening, but I wanted to step back. I practiced, bringing to mind the inflection of Jim's voice.

"And if they don't back down?"

Abigail chuckled. "Let fly and run!"

It was an hour before she was satisfied. Who'd imagine that pretending to be a man would be so difficult? Then she insisted I needed a name, and a story to go with it. She said, "You're on stage. No point doing a slipshod job."

Recalling a young steward on the *Umbria*, I suggested, "Elmore Dewey, son of a Pennsylvania factory owner."

"What factory?"

"Baking bread? How about a bakery?"

"Ha. Can't get rich baking bread."

"My father has tea and coffee estates," I offered.

"Tea? Not here he doesn't. And it needs be something they don't know much about. Else they'll catch you out."

"Hats. Ladies' hats! A milliner—with feathers and satin from Paris!"

"In the North? Or the southern states?"

When I stared at her, she said, "No, it'd have to be Boston. You don't know much about the South, do you?"

"What do you mean?"

Abigail and I spoke about the animosity after the Civil War, starting with abolitionists, the factions within the North, and President Lincoln's terrible resolve. She told me, "He preserved the union. At a high price. But some Chicago men ended the war as millionaires."

"Lincoln was from Chicago?"

She grinned. "Springfield, Illinois. It's why the Midwest votes Republican."

Industrial north and agricultural south had vastly different ways of life: factories, oil and railroads in the north, but cotton, sugar and plantations in the south. And slavery. While living in England I'd read about the American Civil War, but the 1860s seemed long ago, since I was born the decade after. In India, we'd paid it no mind, occupied with our own civil war, the Sepoy Mutiny of 1857. In both cases, the rebels lost. How different both nations would be, I thought, if they had not!

At last, she shook her head. "Can't you just be Lady Diana's son? Stepson, if you prefer."

So that night, dressed in Abigail's trousers and dark suit, I strolled toward a warehouse on Maple Street where anarchists of the world would convene their public meeting. Abigail made a believable man, angular and hunched, to be sure, but I? My theatrical suit might have passed on stage, but now I must seem a small, ridiculous dandy, a child—a rich boy pretending to be grown up. Pulling out my Cameos, I struck a match and lit up. I'd promised Jim to give them up, but my fingers shook in anticipation. It was part of my disguise, I insisted to myself.

As the familiar burn filled my lungs, Abigail said, "Remember to call me Martin."

A group of women called to us from a street corner, their low-cut bodices advertising their profession. Feeling as though I'd betrayed my gender, I flicked the match away and followed Abigail through a crowded door.

Inside the smoke-filled hall, men paid me little heed as they scrambled for a vantage point. There were no chairs. The talk opened without fuss. Successive speakers described the hardship of railroad workers, conditions in the stockyards and nearby factories. Some blamed the new immigrants taking "lousy payin' jobs" that put "good workers" out. Others faulted "Chinamen" and "Dinges" for their hardships. At the end of the evening, a bald man, evidently a popular personality, took the stage to a round of cheers.

"Who is he?" I asked someone near me who smelled of grease.

The rumpled fellow gave me an impatient look. "That's Oscar Donnelly."

"Let me see." When he gave way, I moved up to catch a glimpse of the lectern. Abigail stayed close. Six inches taller, she had no need to crane her neck.

Donnelly now launched into a tirade. "You're a bunch of fools!" he ranted. His eyes fierce, he barked out a disgusted laugh. "There is no justice! Not now, and not ever! No law, no God, no one is going to save you. That's all lies! Lies to keep you in line, keep you working day and night, working your fingers to the bone. And all for someone else to enjoy!"

Caught by his eloquence, men glanced at each other. Someone near me crossed himself.

"You watch your children starve, while the owners stuff their faces with pastry! Your wife can't afford a doctor, but their wives buy jewels. You die at thirty, coughing your lungs out—thirty-five, if you're lucky, with a broken back, a broken head! But they go dancing at sixty! Why? Because you're a 'good man' a 'good worker,' a 'good father'!" Donnelly mocked. "That's what keeps you in chains! They don't need guns or armies because they've trapped your minds! You're a bunch of trained monkeys and you don't even know it."

For a moment I imagined a world where his words were true: a cold, lonely place, a brutal place.

"What else is there?" someone blurted.

Donnelly smirked. "There is only *now*. We must take what we need!"

"Then we'll go to prison," said a large man in front. "Or hang."

Donnelly went on. "And you could fall from a girder tomorrow! What happens then, eh? If you're not dead on the pavement, you're a broken, sniveling cur begging on the thoroughfare, while horses shit on you, and you don't have a nickel for bread. Crawl, if you want, on your hungry bellies all your life. Not I! I don't have long—nor do you, but at least I know it."

Men stirred, restless, hearing his brazen words. Tilting my head toward the heavyset fellows at the doors, I whispered to Abigail. "Who are they?"

"Union heavies."

A few glanced curiously at our fashionable suits. All around us, the audience muttered and called out. Some didn't approve, but others praised Donnelly. Someone said he was crazy.

"Criminal!" someone shouted, from the far end.

On the brightly lit stage, Donnelly heard. "I? *I'm* the criminal? I don't put children to work. I don't press on girls wanting work. I don't pay men a starving wage! *They're* the criminals! We've got to see through their game, lad! Be smarter than them!"

He strode with wild, joyful energy, his voice vengeful like an angry prophet. Well, I thought. Why not stir the waters? That's what Jim would do: "shaking trees to see what falls out."

Pitching my voice low, I called out, "They're thieves!"

Abigail flinched. Men around me turned, startled. Some moved away, glancing back in suspicion. But Donnelly grinned.

"Yes! They stole from us. All of us!" He opened his arms. "Why not take back what they stole?"

"Don't answer!" Abigail whispered, catching my arm in a tight grip.

"Those young fellows have it right!" Donnelly went on, gesturing to the crowd. "Prince Kropotkin said the people will rise up! You! *You* are the people! When you've had enough, when you're done bleeding and starving, you'll fight!"

He strode about the stage, alone in the light of two tall lamps. His bald head shone. Perspiration ran down his red face. Among the gathered company I saw both admiration and doubt. This man came from a different mold, both terrifying and envied. He had shed the shackles they still wore.

"He killed a man in New Orleans," someone said behind us. "Seven years in the nick."

A man called from elsewhere, "What should we do?"

Donnelly's tone grew more compelling. No teacher ever gave more care to his students than he. First, he enumerated the ills of factories. Then, how little aid could be had from churches, courts or the law.

"Democracy is the greatest trap of all!" he cried. "It's the backbone of deceit! The common man, he has the illusion of a vote. He thinks, 'Well, if this government does not care for my concerns all I must do is wait and vote them out!' So, he bides his time. But years pass, and lo! The next is much the same! Why would a senator care for the woes of the poor man? It is the factory owner, the capitalist who pays him handsomely! That hidden purse buys goons from downriver, poor deluded sots who'll kill for him, go to the nick for him! All for a tenner!"

"Let's go," hissed Abigail, tugging at me. But now I had to hear the end of Donnelly's speech, his remedy. Many of these men had no work to strike from. Would he exhort them to violence? Or revolution! Men had been hanged for less.

On stage, Donnelly gave a sad smile, that of a pastor arriving at his sermon's end, eyes brimming with benevolence and resolve.

"I have studied the works of Karl Marx, but he does not go far enough. He asks us to exchange one set of masters for another. No, no! The answer is with Prince Kropotkin, a great mind, born of royal blood! Ever heard of him? You would not, for he's banned from newspapers! He knows what we'll do. We'll build a new world, return to the ways of nature. We'll live peaceful lives, simple lives, lives of plenty."

Donnelly seemed to laugh at us, but gently, as one indulges a curious child. He spoke of being ready, of a change that would come all at once, when we laborers would rise against our masters, grasp our rights and know our own ideas.

Men looked at each other, shaking their heads, but Donnelly chuckled. "All at once you will know, without being told! You will see the blow struck and capital blown to bits! You can seize your chance then, when the yoke is gone and no one to stop you!"

Blown to bits. *Ballistite,* I thought. I needed air but dared not leave. I had to tell Jim—was this the arsonist? As yet I had no evidence, just an odd turn of phrase. The dark room grew oppressive, smelling of sweat and grease and liquor. Here was his finale, the point of his exhortations—a philosophy of slaughter. Strange that the man who claimed to want a peaceful, simple life demanded such violence.

Those around me seemed entranced, their faces upturned to the stage. My stomach churned. Was it really that simple? Hunger made men angry, and angry men could be swayed.

Abigail caught my elbow and tugged me toward the door. Donnelly's words whirled in my mind as we left the hall.

We started down the alley, when a voice behind us called, "Sir! Please!"

A scrawny young man approached wearing ill-fitting clothes, a blue kerchief around his neck. Distress shredded his voice. "A moment!"

"Watch this," said Abigail, curling her lip. "He'll touch you for a buck. Hard luck story and all." She snorted. "Has you down for a sucker."

"Well, he won't get my cash."

I turned to leave, when a harsh voice cut in. "No, he won't. 'Coz we will!"

Three men blocked the dark alleyway. I tensed, hoping the meeting would end and the hall would empty into this street.

Their faces hard, the three spread out to contain us. The man in the middle spoke, but his mouth twisted in a grotesque shape. I could not understand.

Beside me, Abigail breathed, "Christ."

My heart began to beat like a washerwoman thrashing a washboard. I touched the derringer tucked in my cummerbund, feeling its reassuring shape. Jim had said, "If you draw, be ready to shoot." I steeled myself, remembering that stone gallery last year, high atop a clock tower. The crack of my gunshot, the stickiness of blood and gore—brains, splattered on the parapet. Please no, not again.

Could I outwit them? Jim could speak with grimy dockworkers and somehow find a kinship with them. How did he do it? Filling my voice with that quiet certainty of Jim's, I said, "We're expected home, lads."

I must have surprised them, for they glanced at each other, uncertain.

The man with the twisted lip eyed Abigail, and sneered, "What's he to you?"

"My employer!" said Abigail.

We had to get out of this. I tried a different tack. "If I don't return right away, she'll send a flock of constables here."

"Who? Your wife?" said one of them. The others grinned at his wit—I looked too young to have one.

"No, my mother."

That surprised a chuckle from them. One asked, "Yeah? Who's she?"

I frowned, reproducing Abigail's training to inflect my voice. "What's it to you?"

They leaned together to confer. I'd almost forgotten the scrawny lad in the blue kerchief when he spoke up. "C'mon Lascar, you've no quarrel with them."

"You, git!" snarled the leader, then fixed me with a glare. "Your cash," he said, the words deforming his mouth. With a start, I realized he had no teeth. What in God's name had happened to him?

I patted my trouser pockets and found only a pack of cigarettes. Heaven's sake! I'd brought no money.

As I racked my brain for some diversion, a voice spoke from behind the three men. Tobias's deep, courteous voice like warm syrup on pancakes. "Mr. Martin, sir."

The three hoodlums whipped around. At the entrance to the alley stood Tobias, holding something—a rifle? No, thicker than that, a shotgun.

"Tobias!" I cried, forgetting to disguise my voice. My breath whooshed my relief. Abigail stalked through the three hoodlums and, collecting my wits, I followed.

Eyes narrow and mean, they watched us leave. Just before we turned the corner, my gaze met the scrawny bloke's. His grimace, was that desperation? What did he want? Was he part of Lascar's gang or had he tried to help us?

Tobias led us back to the hotel in somber silence. I gazed at him, striding ahead.

"Tobias? How did you know it was me?" I asked in my normal tone.

"Ah follo'd you, ma'am, from the hotel."

"Oh! But—how d'you know that was us? You said Martin's name . . ."

Tobias sent Abigail a quick glance and said, "I met Mr. Martin, earlier. We've spoke."

Abigail nodded. "When I went to buy maps, the first time."

I felt aglow. Tobias sought me at the hotel, then waited outside the anarchists' meeting.

"I'm glad you found us, Tobias." I glanced sideways. His shotgun had disappeared. "Where is it? The—er—"

He smiled, a gash of white in the midnight of his face. "Down me pants."

A giggle bubbled out, a cascade of relief that rolled from me in gasps. Abigail's smile widened. "You're mad as a hatter, aren't you?"

CHAPTER 15

RECRUITING AN INFORMANT

I was mulling over our escapade the next morning when Mr. Fish handed me an embossed envelope. I wanted to tell Jim about Oscar Donnelly—the phrase that had seemed pregnant with meaning, "blown to bits." Was it just rhetorical? I needed to learn more about Donnelly and that thug Lascar, but how? And what of that scrawny boy's cry, "Wait! Please!" Who was he? What did he want?

Returning to the world of discreet waiters, fluted bone-china plates and lace tablecloths, I noticed my name written on the envelope.

"An invitation!" I said, surprised. After that semiclad photograph of me was published in the papers, I'd seen the arch looks thrown my way, heard mocking whispers in the dining room. In the same breath, they'd discussed a belly dancer called Miss Egypt and the "appalling morals" of the times. It should not have mattered, but I felt somewhat miffed. The other diners didn't know me, yet they had already decided I was a loose woman. The absence of a husband did not help my reputation. Yet here was an invitation!

Smoothing his cuffs, Mr. Fish said, "Mr. and Mrs. Bellino are hosting a luncheon." He glanced around, then asked, "May one enquire . . . your stepson, Lady Diana? Will he return?"

He'd confronted Abigail and me last night, but with a few well-chosen words, the privilege of rank proved adequate disguise.

My face composed, mimicking the staid Mrs. Bellino, I said, "I believe he will, Mr. Fish. The young generation. Such a scamp." It would not do to grin just then.

I returned to my wardrobe to choose a dress. Abigail was away on errands, so I chose a shirtwaist. Sighing, I pinned up my hair and went down to join Erminia's luncheon party.

As Lady Diana of Boston, it seemed that my entrée into Chicago society might be redeemed. Erminia introduced me to a well-dressed couple, saying, "My dear Mrs. O'Trey, I don't think you have met the esteemed Governor Altgeld, Mrs. Altgeld?"

"Charmed," said the governor. His close-cropped hair and neat beard reminded me of my uncle Byram. He noticed a great deal, I thought, as he introduced his companions, a thin, erudite man and his pretty daughter. His wife wore a long blue satin. They moved to the sumptuous buffet that dominated the room.

I gazed at the retreating figures in surprise. At any given time, the governor of Bombay was flanked by a dozen flunkeys—the "civil" they were called. I found it curious that American governors walked among diners and shook hands without much ado.

Drawing me toward the platter of spring canapés and the salmon soufflé, Erminia smirked. "That's why one stays at the Oriental, you see? Isn't Mrs. Altgeld charming? But my dear, it's Mrs. Potter Palmer who has the smallest waist in Chicago."

Diners served themselves from fine silver dishes piled with delicacies. The stand-up buffet allowed guests to mingle freely, yet I could not forget the mass of sweating, weary men that had been gathered at the anarchist meeting only a few blocks away.

"Oh, Mrs. O'Trey!" Mr. Bellino exclaimed, eyebrows raised at my inattention. His close chums were a pair of bankers, Messieurs Yeats, who possessed a bushy mustache and thick brown eyebrows, and Kaperski, a thin, dyspeptic man who seemed given to speaking in percentages. Though uninterested in the stock market gossip and business scandals, I had the curious impression that I was being wooed in some way. Since they rarely addressed me, it was a strange play, each striving to outdo the other, but for whose benefit?

As the ladies clustered together, Erminia nudged me. "The mayor's here. Did you know he's soon to marry an heiress, Miss Annie Howard."

"His second wife," said Mrs. Kaperski, leaning in. "She's younger than his sons!"

Rosy complexioned, Mrs. Katerina Yeats chuckled. "She's worth three million dollars!"

The mayor, an older man with deep eyes and a patrician face, had stopped to shake hands with the governor, but I got the impression the two did not like each other. Erminia whispered, "His sons do not approve! If she has a child, they'd get nothing!"

The ladies shared a knowing look. Mrs. Kaperski fanned herself. "If our mines produce as we hope they will, Mr. Kaperski and I shall take a world tour next year."

I asked Erminia, "Does Mr. Bellino also have mining interests?"

"I've no idea, Mrs. O'Trey. Men can be such bores. Mustn't let them ruin a good meal."

I returned to my chamber, realizing that I knew little about my new friends. Many Boston families were related; was the same true of Chicago? Since my glimpse of Jim, days ago, I'd seen nothing of him and chafed at the delay. How could I tell him about the anarchist meeting?

Gathering my parasol, I lifted an apple from the basket on my table and went to the park where I'd met Wadja.

Blossoms showed on the boughs now, covering the canopy with a pink tinge. The peaceful park quieted me as I walked through the calls of crickets. They sounded like temple bells rung by devotees in distant shrines as I sat on the fountain's curved seat.

A half hour later, Wadja sauntered up and dropped onto the bench beside me.

"Well, hello!" I smiled, offering the apple.

He bit into it, slobbering, licking juice off his lips, a quaint picture with the red apple against his rosy cheeks and shapeless red cap.

I asked, "Have you seen him again, that big man?"

"You mean Cap'n?"

"Yes." That name shouldn't have surprised me. Jim went by so many.

"Saw him by Union Station yard. He's unloadin' there," Wadja said, giving me a doubtful look. I hadn't explained about speaking Hindustani. How much should I tell him? And Jim was unloading boxes despite his injured shoulder?

"Why's he kicked out?" Wadja blurted, then pulled away, ducking his head into his shoulders and his too-large coat.

A heaviness weighted my chest. Wadja thought I had abandoned Jim. Was he accustomed to the loss of affection, to being "kicked out"? How could I explain, without revealing Jim's assignment? I just shook my head, tracing patterns in the grass with the point of my parasol. Wadja seemed much older than my cheerful little brother Fali, though they were the same age.

I said, "I noticed a fellow with a twisted mouth last week. D'you know him? His hands were like this." I hooked my fingers, demonstrating.

Wadja cast me a wary look. "Lascar. He's trouble."

I got the story, though. Lascar's brother had been killed in a strike at the Carnegie Steel mill last year. In the same skirmish, Lascar had been injured. The loss of his teeth had made him "ornery"—a dangerous man. He was said to have killed someone over a chicken.

"A chicken!" I said, dismayed. This was the man who, but for Tobias's arrival, might have roughed us up. Did Jim mingle with such thugs? No wonder he could not break off to send a telegram. If they discovered his ruse, he could expect no mercy. How could I tell him about Oscar Donnelly?

"Can you get a message to Captain Jim? Ask him to meet me?"

"Maybe." Wadja sucked juice off his fingers, crunched and spat out some seeds. He'd eaten the whole apple, including its core. This fact tore a hole inside me, which I struggled to hide. Pity would not help the boy, so I gave him a dime with my instructions and returned to the Oriental.

Near the foyer, Abigail was speaking to a thin young man with untidy clothes and familiar disarrayed hair. I drew to her side. "Is something amiss?"

The fellow twitched. "I mean no trouble, ma'am!"

Looking dubiously at him, Abigail said, "He asked for you."

"Do you have a message for me?"

He cringed. "N-no, ma'am. May I speak with the Mister? It's business, see?"

The mention of Jim made me cautious. Was this his informant?

"My husband is not here presently," I said. "Where did you meet him?"

"Uh . . . I spoke with your son. Kinda. Is he here?"

"My son!" Looking closer, I recognized the scrawny lad who'd followed us from the meeting last night. I said, "He has returned to school. What's this about?"

His name was Collin Box. In a flood of rushed phrases, he tried to sell me a copper mine. "In North Michigan, ma'am. A thick vein—barely worked. We own the title free 'n' clear. A real money spinner!"

I held up a hand to stem the tide and politely declined to buy his property. He flushed with disappointment. The lad's face twisted as though he might weep.

I paused. He'd been at last night's meeting. So I asked, "My son spoke of a bald man called Donnelly. Who is he?"

Collin blinked. "Oscar Donnelly? I know him."

"Where would one find him?"

"He's got a place on Canal Street. Old building. Lets blokes sleep there for a nickel."

"Where does he work?"

Collin shrugged. Remembering the tough-looking fellows in the anarchist meeting, I asked, "He's in a worker's union, isn't he? Which one?"

He pulled back. "Dunno 'bout that."

"Find out," I said, giving him a coin. Asking questions was a delicate matter, I realized. If one pushed too hard, it made people wary. Too light, and one got evasion. Since I had not established my reasons for asking, Collin would not answer. But I had misjudged the persistent youth.

"Look, talk to my pa, will ya?" he said, his voice breaking. "He thinks I'm not workin' on it, selling his mine. At least look at his papers, will ya?"

Moved by his distress, despite Abigail's sharp look, I agreed. We would visit his father next week, and I'd take the opportunity to ask him some more questions.

"What day?" he wanted to know.

"When it pleases us!" retorted Abigail, pulling me away.

When he'd gone, she laid into me with sharp words. "There is no mine! The fellow's a cheat, setting you up. It's a trick—anyone can see that!"

She was right to be wary. An appointment might easily become an ambush. But Collin surely knew more about Donnelly. If I wanted his information, I had to gain his trust.

Unrolling the map Abigail had acquired, I examined it alongside the letter I'd translated. Abigail and I spent the next hour searching the map for locations mentioned in the German letter.

Hotels and attractions, City Hall, the post office and customs house were notated, but large city blocks were left unmarked—were they factories or tenements? North of Twelfth Street, the roads were named after presidents: Taylor, Polk, Harrison, Van Buren and so on. The State Street cable car line went all the way south. One could take the Grove Avenue cable car to the World's Fair, entering at the Midway Plaisance.

At length, I rolled up the map. How did this help? Jim had been alarmed to see me in Chicago. Something more was afoot, but what? Why had he spoken in Hindustani?

CHAPTER 16

A VISITOR

On the fifth of June it rained all day, keeping people indoors. Time hung heavy upon me. I'd been in Chicago three weeks. Two men had been killed, but I could not tell if Jim had got any further in his investigation. Well after eleven, a knock sounded on our suite door—far too late for Tobias or the scamp Wadja, and Abigail had already retired.

Jim had once said the person who moves first usually wins. I slipped my pistol into a pocket of my dressing gown and opened the door.

A waiter in crisp apron pushed in a trolley bearing a wooly tea cozy and three dishes covered with engraved silver cloches. A meal this late? Was there some mistake? I raised a cover to peek inside. The kitchen had sent up a platter of cold meats and cheeses—and a pot of tea as I'd requested the previous night.

I exhaled in anticipation. "Ah! And it's piping hot!"

"Yes, ma'am," said the waiter, leaving.

"Thought you'd like that," said a voice in the corridor. Jim! Dressed in a rumpled suit, he tipped the waiter, closed the door behind him and tossed his hat on the table.

I stifled a gasp. His overgrown hair limp, his clothes hung on him. The lamplight threw gaunt shadows on his stubbled cheeks. He looked starved!

Breaking into a grin, he said, "Saw your picture in the papers. Wanted to look at you."

I rushed up, arms reaching, but he held me off. "Don't, sweet. I'm filthy."

"Can you stay? Can you rest here tonight?"

He hesitated, then nodded. "I'll leave early."

"D'you need me, ma'am?" asked Abigail from her room.

I called back to her, "It's all right, Abigail," then turned to Jim. "That's my maid. Come now. I'll run a bath. They have hot water! And you've brought food. How did you convince the kitchen to let you have it?" I was talking too much in my excitement.

"You brought a maid?" Jim chuckled, then sat and tugged off his shoes. "Just gave them your order, things you preferred on the *Umbria*. 'Mrs. O'Trey must have it right away,' I said."

I laughed, imagining the kitchen staff's astonishment. He'd got pastry and cheese, slices of luncheon meats. "Not sure what they'll think of my midnight appetite . . ." I was so glad to see him, I felt like I'd drunk Champagne as I hurried to fetch his nightshirt and pajamas.

In the dressing room, Jim hung up his frock coat, saying, "Don't wash this."

His presence filled the small chamber as he removed his cuffs. I took them, saddened to see him wince as he shrugged out of his vest. His shoulder still hurt, then. Hurrying to gather towels, I ran water for his bath.

While he bathed, I tapped on Abigail's door and found her already dressed. Instructing her to set out the maps we'd purchased, I carried a tray of food to my room. Jim was here at last. He'd surely tell me what this was all about.

Wet hair plastered to his head, he came in his nightshirt and lowered himself onto the little chair at my dressing table.

As though I'd spoken, he looked up, his gaze questioning. Something hidden behind his eyes, some darkness there disturbed me.

Even in India, I'd never been at ease with his disguises. He seemed to disappear into them so completely, as though his very thoughts merged with his guise. Shadowed by his beard, the planes of his face had grown sharper and longer somehow. The thin nightshirt clung to his musculature, so he seemed too large, too male, uncomfortably rugged as he studied me. I wanted to touch his lean cheek, but held back. We'd been together six months before he left; I'd thought I knew him. But did I really? Or was he "in disguise" with me too?

Alerted by my stillness, he did a curious thing—he closed his eyes. I smiled, relieved that he understood. Now free to examine him, I approached, taking in the scraggly, dark locks, his shoulders, the movement of his breathing. I found the familiar scar upon his neck, the clump of hair over his ear that hid a bullet wound. My poor boy had grown lean. When my hand alighted on his shoulder, he looked up.

I said, "You seem . . . different."

He absorbed that. "Same man you married."

That low timbre of his voice I knew well, but some intonation had changed. I laid my hand against his face. He smiled, his gaze searching. Then his look eased as he pulled me in.

He smelled of tooth powder, with the gingery hint of his Ivory soap. Long, slow kisses later, I remembered that he'd likely not dined, and broke from his embrace to fuss over him.

Raising the cup I'd poured, Jim breathed in deeply. "Darjeeling."

Where were you, I wanted to demand, but I'd been brought up properly, so I busied myself with assembling his plate.

"Five weeks you've been gone." I'd meant to say it calmly, but it tumbled out as an accusation.

He set down the cup. "God, Diana. I never meant . . . you couldn't think I wanted to stay away? A word, a whisper in my sleep could betray me."

"One letter, Jim! Just a wire to say you were well."

He spread his hands. "No paper or pen where I was. A rough place. Couldn't wire either. A telegram's read on both sides." He plucked a tart from the dish and ate it in two bites.

"What's this about, Jim?" I asked. "And it's no use telling me to go back, because I won't."

He rolled a slice of ham and cheese. "Sweet, it's bad. There are two hundred thousand workers in the city—hungry men, eager for work. But there's no more work at the fairgrounds. It's got to make a profit—keep costs down. The lads are desperate."

Desperate. I was going to ask him to leave this city, come home with me, but that word told me it was futile. Jim had developed a bond with the "great unwashed" of Chicago. His tone held more than pity, almost affection. "How do you know this?"

"Keep out of it, Diana. It's a mess," he mumbled, swiping a hand through the air.

"I have something you need," I said, "and you won't get it until you answer, how are you mixed up in this?"

Eating quickly, he looked amused, then shook his head. "Better this way."

"Grimke came to me."

That got his attention. Mouth full, he said, "You have the letter translated?"

"I know about the ballistite." That stopped him, so I went on. "It's dynamite, isn't it?"

"It's an explosive. An unstable one."

He held out a hand for the letter.

"Will you tell me what this is about! And don't try to hide that Arnold Baldwin was murdered." I glared at him and waited—letting silence press between us.

He winced. "Didn't want to worry you."

"I found out from Tobias. You were gone weeks, Jim!"

"Feels longer." He rubbed a hand over his beard. "This city's in trouble. I don't want you here . . . but God, I've missed you."

His slate-grey eyes smiled but worry shadowed the creases around them. Returning his look, I asked, "How did you get that letter you sent Grimke?"

His shoulders heaved with a breath. Exhaling, he leaned back. "From the heel of Baldwin's shoe. But this starts with Tom Grewe, guarding the bank next door to the Rookery. Tom might have followed someone, come over for a look. Caught them with their hand in the till. They over-powered him, could have left him trussed up. Why kill him?"

A prickle crawled over my skin. If Jim was trying to frighten me, he was doing a fine job of it. I gazed at him, appalled. "Because he could identify them."

He scoffed. "Among thousands of men walking the streets? They didn't have to strangle him. He was eighteen, barely more than a boy."

His manner was even, but I wasn't deceived. Shaken, I crossed my arms. Trying to understand how events had unfolded, I said, "So Baldwin was summoned?"

Jim nodded. "He wrote to me about workers from a steelworkers' union, a connection between Grewe's killer and their printing press. While searching the factory where they work the press, he found that German letter. Trouble is, I don't know who wrote it. The man who murdered Grewe? Or Baldwin's killer? Both?"

I told him about meeting Sergeant Long and said, "Baldwin was found on the riverfront, shot twice."

Jim's eyes grew dark. "Shot point blank, then . . . executed. I knew Baldwin well—a plucky bloke, but smart. Fellow could get by with less sleep than anyone I knew. He'd lean over, say, 'Ten minutes,' and drop off, still standing, hands in his pockets, forehead against the wall. Minutes later he'd straighten, give me clear eyes and a grin, and return to the job."

He looked at the table, and sighed.

"Was he married?"

"Dupree doesn't hire married blokes."

"But—"

"He made me the offer when I was single and stood by it. Didn't like it, though."

I bit my lip. Alfred Dupree had liked it even less when I bullied him into giving me a job.

Jim said, "When Baldwin stumbled upon the German letter, he must have guessed he was onto something, so he took pages out. I think he left the first and last, hoping it wouldn't be discovered."

While Jim polished off his food, I poured myself some tea, frowning over this.

"But Jim, why would Baldwin send it to you, instead of the Duprees?"

"Isn't that the question," Jim said, not meeting my gaze.

"If I give you what I have, you've got to tell me everything. Play fair, Jim!"

"Play fair," he repeated on a breath, closing his eyes. "I've missed your voice."

He'd been working his case for weeks, sorely awaiting Grimke's translation.

"Of course, you shall have it, Jim," I said, covering his hand. "What have you been doing all this time?"

"Infiltrated the gang. That was the job, Diana. They're dead against the Pinkertons who've been hired to secure the fair."

When I nodded, a line appeared between his eyebrows. "How'd you know that?"

I said, "Dupree told me. He had to. I—er, threatened him. He said that's why Chicago's police asked him to investigate Grewe's killing."

Jim's smile began around his eyes. It spilled to his lips, creases bracketing his mouth. He shook with soft laughter, doubling over as it poured from him in husky spurts.

"You blackmailed Peter Dupree."

"Er, the other. Dupree Senior."

When Jim's mirth dissolved into surprise, I rushed on. "He didn't want to, but I made him tell me about the guard, and how and where he was strangled. Police didn't know if anything was taken, but Jim, an architect's workshop would be full of maps, wouldn't it? Maps of the fair, while it was still being built. Sewers, pipelines, cables!" Then I remembered Jim's instructions to tell no one. "Why don't you trust Dupree?"

He looked up, gaze sharp. "Baldwin didn't. Wrote to me as some sort of insurance, I think. That word—'ballistite,' it's clear enough."

"But—Dupree?"

He shook his head. "Baldwin sent them a report each week in the mail. That morning he wired, then—nothing. When I got here, he was dead."

Baldwin had trusted Jim, who would not let him down. The set of Jim's mouth, his tight shoulders told me he would see this through. To ask him to leave now was futile.

When he'd finished his meal, I led him to the parlor where Abigail had laid out the maps. She ducked her head as I made introductions, then retreated to her room.

I handed over the German letter and its translation. Eagerly Jim set them side by side and compared them. Tapping a page, he said, "You wrote this."

"Grimke was afraid. Said he could be arrested for writing that."

He read quietly, then whispered, "Damn."

He'd seen the bit about eight hundred pounds of ballistite. Glancing at me, he asked, "The professor. Did he say anything else?"

I frowned, trying to recollect. "Don't think so. Have you found the explosives?"

He shook his head. "I've searched most of the old steelworkers, followed them. Tricky business. Most men have a secret, some more than one. Ask too many questions of a bloke, they tend to notice."

Leaning over the outspread map, I pointed. "There. It took us a while to find it. The German word is 'metallager'—which Grimke translated as 'iron warehouse.' A storage place for iron rails? A railway warehouse, perhaps."

"There could be many."

"It says 'am Fluss,' that's 'by the river,' and 'Eisenbahn,' which he translated as 'train.' The rest is cut off, so we don't know which station. Anyway, this one is both near the Chicago River and right behind Union Station."

"I know it." He tapped the map. "This gives me another angle." He pored over the letter again, then traced a finger over the rail yards along the river. I offered him paper to write them down, but he shook his head, committing them to memory.

At last, he rolled his shoulders back, stretching with a yawn. "I'm beat, let's turn in," he said, heading to the bedroom.

Beat? Puzzled at the odd term, I rolled up the maps, secured them with string, then followed him, mulling over his earlier words. "Jim, why are the workers so angry?"

He rubbed the back of his neck. "The lads make barely enough to live on—and some have families, Diana. Farmers who lost their lands to the banks. Fellows from oilfields that sacked them. Grueling work on the fair all winter. They drove pilings into Jackson's Park—it used to be a swamp, did you know? Chicago needed them, but now the work is done, they're told to go. The rest came here riding on hope. Dangerous to take that away."

The clock's ding showed it was past one o'clock! Turning down the lamp, I followed Jim to the washroom, where he found his toiletries and once again made liberal use of his tooth powder.

"Why does the union want to blow up the fair?"

He rinsed his hands. "Don't know that they do. Why would they destroy their own work? I'll tell you one thing, though. They hate the committee. Those blighters changed plans so often, making the chaps redo their work. It's hell—hanging off the roof for hours, only to be told it isn't right, and must be undone. You know about Tito's father?"

"Who?" I washed up, while Jim lounged at the door, watching.

"Tito—the boy who spotted me. His pa was working up top a girder and fell. Broke his back. They're six in the family, with the children. Bet they haven't seen three square meals since God knows when."

Jim limped to the bedroom. I frowned, puzzled. "His name is Wadja, isn't it? It sounds like Wadia, a Parsee name!" Seeing Jim raise an eyebrow, I explained, "That's what he said—Wadja-no."

He grinned, his weight depressing the bed as he sat.

"What-d'ya-know. Shared a sandwich with him yesterday. His name's Tito."

Goodness. I'd misunderstood completely, taking the boy's exclamation to be his given name. I smiled, imagining the boy's terror to find Jim next to him, his astonishment and delight to be offered a meal.

Remembering Jim's limp, I gathered my salve and a roll of bandages and tapped his knee. He raised it obediently to bare the red, swollen joint. When would he learn to take proper care of himself? I set about applying his salve. Tearing the end of the bandage to secure it, I told him about the anarchist meeting, recounting as much as I could.

As I described Donnelly, he interrupted. "You *went* there? To this anarchist congress? God, Diana. You took a chance."

"With Abigail," I said, ignoring his fixed look. "We were quite safe." A lie. Tobias had saved us. "Oh, all right. We dressed as men. She's worked on the stage, so she showed me how."

Jim pulled in a breath, leaning back on his arms to stare at me. My cheeks warmed, but I shook away the sensation. I'd done nothing wrong.

"By God." His voice was low. "You had the derringer?"

"Yes."

"No use asking you to never do that again?"

"No use at all," I said, relieved I would not have to break my word, for I'd do it again, if I must. Turning down the lamp, I laid my cheek against his shoulder. How I'd longed for his firm skin against my face. I tucked myself against him, remembering the grim fellows I'd seen from the tram. Criminals? Or hungry and driven to lawlessness?

I thought aloud, trying to make sense of our predicament. "Jim, why haven't they already used the explosives? Could it be they don't have it?"

"The letter asks for payment, so something was agreed on. But that's weeks ago," Jim said, his voice rumbling against my ear. He stiffened. "A number of European blokes just arrived. Diana, that could be what they were waiting for."

"Be careful, Jim," I whispered.

"Means I've got to get in close with the new chaps—aaah," he said, stretching out, his arm curving around me. "Good to be home."

Home? I smiled against his skin. His chest rose with a sound like waves crashing on the shore, pulling back, receding over the sand. I wondered when next I'd have him near. "Jim?"

He didn't answer. I smiled, the tide of his breath curling over my senses. I've always loved the sound of the ocean; warm and safe, sleep blanketed me completely for the first time in months.

I woke alone.

Although Jim had warned me he'd be gone, my ebullience faded. I slumped, smoothing down the bed where he'd lain. Lines around his grey eyes, his untidy beard had aged his gaunt face. He wouldn't leave Chicago, so I now had a new goal: to discover who'd purchased eight hundred pounds of explosives.

CHAPTER 17

STRIPPED

JIM

How in God's name had Diana threatened Dupree? But she knew enough to not tell him much. Thinking of her conversation with Sergeant Long, I chuckled. He'd mentioned Baldwin's brother, and she'd guessed it was me. Once my job was done, I thought, we needed some time alone. Perhaps we might visit the Catskill Mountains on a honeymoon. A real one.

She'd gone to the anarchists' meeting and heard Oscar Donnelly's call to arms. I knew their philosophy well enough. Most of it was sound: machines stripping away the dignity of labor, wealth buying men's votes and souls. Machines made workers into just another cog, something to be used and tossed aside. The old American way of life had slipped away; the new was harsh and unforgiving. In Chicago's factories, men worked twelve hours each day, swaying on their feet. Barely a day went by without an accident on the factory floors. I'd heard all this before. But had Donnelly planned an act of revolution?

They were an odd bunch, the anarchists who came to Donnelly's flop. The entire philosophy was impractical. How could a movement exist without a leader? They despised communists, since their own manifesto prohibited men from organizing. It all seemed fine, noble talk, but to what end? Diana said Donnelly had stopped short of calling for *Attentat*—propaganda of the deed, a polite term for violent revolution. But she'd removed any doubt that he knew the anarchists in Chicago.

I returned to the loading pier, realizing Donnelly didn't trust me. On the night of the congress he'd sent me out with Orrin to unload a ferry. Blast. He'd got me away on a pretext. But Diana had heard him rallying blokes for support. What I didn't know was, how much was posturing to maintain his following, and how much was real?

Four of them were waiting for me that evening, standing around like a tribunal of sorts—Donnelly, Lascar, Collier with the thick accent, and Prendergast, who ran a team of newsies selling papers. I took off my cap as I entered, saying, "Waiting for payday, huh, lads?"

Donnelly's chin went up. No one answered. Looking around, I realized I had miscalculated—no one goes drinking on a Thursday, with pockets empty.

Lascar spoke. "Where were you?"

I turned to him, surprised. "My shift isn't until morning."

A mistake—good grammar made him irate, as though I'd flaunted my learning.

"Where'd you sleep last night?"

I frowned. None of them would stand for being asked that. "Free country, last I heard."

He hissed, "Grab him."

For an instant I didn't understand, then it was too late. Two blokes hauled on my arms, while Collier plowed his fist into me. I saw it coming and tensed, taking the punch well, but played it up, letting my head droop, gasping like a dying fish. When the second blow came, I yanked up, rolling with it. It connected, but his motion was spent, and I thought I'd likely kept my teeth.

I tamped down on the rush of panic—couldn't hope to fight my way out. But I'd seen Donnelly's methods before—soon he'd ask questions. That was the real test.

More blows followed, three or four; then they released me. I fell to my knees, winded. Propping myself up on a hand, I growled, "Christ. What's that for?"

Donnelly asked, "Where'd you go?"

If he thought I was the Pinkerton ferret, why was he waiting for an answer? His closed expression told me he knew something. Had I been followed? If he was sure, I'd already be trussed up in a wagon, headed for the pier. So, he knew where I'd been but wasn't sure why. He was waiting for me to lie.

I spat out blood, then said, "Had business uptown."

"Where?"

I cursed, then shrugged, pretending to give in. "Hotel on Wabash."

Donnelly's eyebrows jumped. He'd not expected that. He'd known where I'd gone and didn't expect me to admit it.

He flicked his hand to a pair of blokes who hauled me up. I'd worked for weeks to earn his trust. Now a single night's absence could destroy it. Had Baldwin made the same mistake, believing he was safe? I had walked through enemy terrain before, but now I was living in their camp. Odd thing, though, I couldn't think of them as the enemy. Most of them were good lads, barely earning enough to eat—twenty cents an hour, hardly enough for a meal and a pint. If I was one of them, how would I react?

Wiping blood from my stinging lips, I said, "I don't have any cash."

Donnelly barked. "We're not thieves!"

"Then what the hell you playing at?"

Donnelly said, "Let him go."

I pushed my advantage, and thrust my bloodied hand at him. "Why, huh?"

Donnelly jerked his head at someone behind me. A man caught hold of Orrin, the big redhead who was my friend, and gave him much the same treatment. Dread filled me, hearing Orrin's gasp. He was older. Could he take it? They suspected one of us was a spy but weren't sure which. Orrin's legs gave way under the beating.

I swore, calling Donnelly every foul name that entered my mind. "Stop! He's an old man!" I hollered.

Donnelly flicked a hand at us. "Strip them."

I was glad I'd stashed my revolver in Baldwin's room, because the

gang would not find it on me. Then my fear spiked as I realized their in-
tent. Goddamn it. What did they want with my scars? I'd need a story to
explain them. Some dogged instinct took hold then, refusing to buckle.
I would not give them the satisfaction.

Orrin's shirt was torn from him.

"Hands off!" I snapped at the man reaching for mine. "Cost me
ninety cents!"

When the fellow backed away, I stripped off my shirt and undershirt.
Hoping they would not notice the latter was clean, I stood in filthy trousers that sagged at the knee. "What the hell you looking for?"

"Tools stolen," said Donnelly. "And this ain't the first time."

Relief pumped through me, until I realized that could be a pretext.
I masked it with a frown of confusion. "Think I've got them down my
pants?"

Donnelly laughed, jerking his head.

Lascar handed me back my undershirt. "Where'd you get those
marks . . ." Spittle sprayed the air. "On your back?"

"No business of yours," I said, keeping a civil tone.

He stopped, his head cocked. "And that? On your neck?"

I shook my head. He could take it as he liked.

"Who's the bloke you met in that posh hotel, huh?"

His knowing look troubled me. He'd followed me to Diana's hotel,
but was that all? He was fishing for a name, pretending he already knew.

"A young fella," I invented. "Got dough."

"Kid from the meeting? He's not been seen since. My dip's watching.
We'll get him."

"Unless his ma keeps tight hold o' him!" laughed Prendergast. Kid
from the meeting. Fear prickled over my skin. Diana had got to stay out
of that guise.

Grumbling, Orrin asked someone to join him in a beer, so he seemed
all right.

As I turned toward my bedroll, Donnelly asked Prendergast, "What
about your job, huh? The mayor gonna hire you to run his paper?"

Prendergast glowered. "Wrote four hundred letters for him, I did."

Donnelly shook his head at this worn complaint. Lascar slurred, "Wisse up, fool! Hisss son runs the *Chicago Times*. You run a handful of newsies!"

"I wrote letters that got him elected! Bastard acts like I don't exist. So preoccupied with his great World's Fair!"

Donnelly placed a hand on his shoulder. "You come with us now, eh?"

Dropping to my pallet, I decided to follow the group that night. I had to find those explosives soon, before Donnelly became curious about the rich kid at the Oriental.

CHAPTER 18

COLLIN'S PLEA

Late in the morning Abigail and I took a barouche to the Forquer Street tenement where Collin Box lived. I'd dressed in a modest skirt, black seal cape and bonnet. Beside me, Abigail wore a black gingham. With Tobias riding beside the coachman, we were safe enough.

As we traveled, the smell of the river had grown more pungent. Spotting a street sign, I asked Abigail, "We're on Halstead. Is it far?"

She pointed. "The Irish and Italians live on Polk and Ewing. South of that you get Russians, Poles, Turks and such. We'll turn before Plymouth Street, where the colored folks live."

Perhaps I was complacent as we approached the dilapidated two-story—I planned to administer a little charity, decline to purchase the fake mine, say some kind words and depart, my duty done. But I wanted to gain Collin's trust and get him talking. Playing the part of a charitable society matron, I would ask about Lascar, commiserate over his injuries and learn more about Oscar Donnelly's following—his friends and what places he frequented. I did not expect much, but perhaps Collin could be induced to collect information. We were running out of time. Jim wasn't having much success because he was a stranger to the local anarchists. Little Tito was useful, but I needed an informant they already knew.

Descending from the carriage, I followed Tobias through a narrow door and up a series of foul-smelling stairs. Did this tenement have no facilities? It smelled as though the stairwell served that purpose.

Tobias led the way through a dingy corridor. Apartments showed

cramped rooms, doors flung open for air. Stepping past a pair of sleep-
ing men huddled in the hallway, we rapped on a door. It was opened by
Collin Box in shirtsleeves, his suspenders hanging loose. His startled
glance shot from Tobias to me. "Mrs. O'Trey!"

Tobias pushed past to scan the room, then returned and nodded to
me that it was safe.

"Ma'am." Collin touched his forelock, looking worried. "My father,
he's not well. You won't take it amiss?"

"Not at all, Collin," I said, cringing internally as I entered the filthy
chamber. To call it a hovel would be to praise it. Soot covered everything, the floor, the walls, a single crusted pot on the plank table. A thin
woman in drab cotton dress and apron leaned over a cot, shushing an
infant. She glanced up, then returned to comforting the child.

I nodded to her, then spotted an older man muffled in a scarf, with
bulbous nose and overgrown eyebrows slumped in a low chair.

Collin approached the man cautiously. "Pa?"

The man blinked. Squinting at me, he scratched his creased neck.

"It's the lady I told you about, come to see the deed," said Collin,
speaking so fast I could barely understand him. "Remember, I said she
might buy it? I was gonna take it to her, but she's here, Pa, she's come."

"Hmph." His father jerked his head at a trunk in the corner. Collin
seemed to take heart. Pulling out a cloth bundle, he set it on the table
and carefully unwrapped the layers.

Smoothing down her apron, Collin's mother carved a half loaf of
bread. First one, then another child sat up in bed. These were each given
a crust and set to chewing it. She held a bowl between them, into which
they dunked the crust.

Collin continued his explanation while I studied a package rolled
in leather, expecting a crude reproduction of a deed or map, something
to be sold and sold again to fools willing to purchase a dream. But the
document I uncovered was indeed a claim duly registered to three men.
Under it, the wax seal of the state of Michigan shone a dull red. Osain
Box was listed as one of the names.

"This mine belongs to three men," I said.

"Phil's dead," growled Osain, speaking for the first time.

"And—Eustace Cornberry?" I asked, reading from the paper.

He snorted. "Went off 'is rocker in New Orleans. Sold me his share, he did."

"Do you have proof of that?" I asked. Although the deed appeared genuine, I had no intention of buying it. However, Bellino's constant talk of mining had triggered an idea. Could I interest him in such a venture? Then Collin would be indebted to me!

The old man's lips curled, his face a tapestry of creases. Standing up with painful slowness, he said, "Proof? Want proof Phil's dead, eh? Only his bones that I found and put in a sack and buried. That the proof you want? After the war old Stace wasn't right in 'is head."

I examined the grizzled fellow with new interest. "You were with Union troops?"

He frowned. "I look southern to you?" He thumbed a finger at Tobias, standing quietly outside the door. "Fought for them, didn't I? And he's the first one of them I seen in my house."

"If your partners are dead or gone away, why don't you run the mine?" I said. That was a question Jim would ask.

The old man raised his hand, an awful, twisted limb bearing only two digits: a thumb and index finger. What remained was shriveled and curled. Dismayed, I covered my lips, saying, "I'm so sorry."

The old man sat, accepting some bread and a bowl of soup from his wife. Picking up a spoon, he launched upon a meandering tale as his wife placed a bowl in front of a stool, offering it to me.

Dare I eat it? The watchful look, the tension in her shoulders demanded an answer. To reject the soup was to decline her hospitality. Already I must seem dreadfully stuck-up. However, yesterday's newspaper had told of children dying of cholera in Chicago's east side.

I said, "Thank you, no, I've just eaten."

She sat with a soft groan and ate the soup quietly. In the pause, Collin said he'd worked as a brake lad on trains; his mother sewed in a garment factory. Neither of them had work now.

Osain, the old man, had served in the war against the South, then been a cowhand and a prospector. His friend Eustace had found the mine but, since he could neither read nor write, needed help to stake his claim. Putting their savings together, the three men had filed their claim and begun to dig copper ore from the mine—long, backbreaking days of hauling buckets up from the cave to cart it to Telegraph city. They decided to blast some of the rock to reach a bigger vein. At first, they had some luck, but then an explosion killed Phil. Osain lost three fingers and part of his foot. Eustace was blind for a week. I thought of Osain with injured hand and foot, gathering and burying his friend's remains.

When the tale was done, Collin and his parents watched me hopefully.

"Well, you going to buy it?" the old man asked.

Placing a ten-dollar note on the table, I considered how best to decline his offer.

The old man made a choking noise, then bellowed, "Ya jokin!" He lashed out, flinging his bottle to shatter against a wall. His face crumpled, his head bowed.

Aghast, I turned to Collin, who said in a dull voice, "That ain't enough, that there."

"For the mine? Of course not," I said, astonished. "That's just to tide you over."

I'd seen destitution in India—beggared, starving children, like those Jim had brought to us in Simla. Villagers, tribesmen without proper clothing, living in mud huts with grass roofs. The Bengal famine had killed thousands, mostly children. Escaping epidemics, those who could travel came to Bombay clinging on the roofs of trains. Relatives usually took them in. They'd rent a cart to sell bananas or coconuts. Though tattered, the poor were not always miserable. From Papa's carriage, I'd watched ragged little urchins play, bathing cows and buffalo at Talav, the tiled open reservoir by the Bombay green.

But Chicago smoldered, oppressive, angry, with a sense of something broken. Men swarmed the streets, crowded on corners, desperate families crammed into tenements.

Taking Collin aside, I said, "Someone has purchased a large quantity of explosives. If you hear about it, anything at all, I want you to tell me."

He stared, then ducked his head. "Like dynamite? What's in it fer me?"

"What do you know?"

He glanced sideways. "If you buy the mine, there's something I could tell you. But only if you help, see?"

I gasped, winded. He'd been awfully quick to seek a trade.

"Why should I believe you?"

"It's stashed in crates, ain't it? Some guys unloaded 'em off a boat. One of them dropped and split. Had to scoop up the pellets, like dry powder. You help Pa, I'll find out where they took those crates."

CHAPTER 19

THE MASK DROPS

Years ago, my sister Pilloo spotted a cobra gliding across the bathroom. Her terrified scream had jerked me from my bed. I reached her before Papa, Adi or the servants thumped their way upstairs. Warned by her shaking finger, I'd tossed a towel over the snake's hood and pulled her away. Our bearers beat on that towel soundly, pulping the cobra into a length of slack rope. I'd thought it was over then, but Papa said, "Find the nest—none of us is safe until then."

Where was the anarchists' lair?

As we rode back to the hotel, I proposed a new plan. Since Tobias knew of Abigail's other identity, I no longer needed to hide it from him. I said, "We must find those explosives. A large amount like that can't be easy to hide. The incendiary last year in Paris exploded six pounds of dynamite. Someone has eight hundred pounds—perhaps Donnelly, who spoke at the anarchist meeting. Could you follow him?"

"Follow him where?" Abigail asked, her hazel eyes narrow.

"I want to know where he works, who he meets, where he sleeps. Find out where he's known and welcome."

"I could go as Martin. For how long?"

"A week, perhaps? If his cache is found—or gets damp—he achieves nothing. So he's sure to check, now and then, that it's safe. If we watch him closely, we could locate it."

Tobias and Abigail conferred. Dressed as Martin, she would follow

Donnelly by day, and Tobias would watch his flop by night. She said, "Tito will know where Donnelly lives. I'll change attire and ask him."

Agreed, we climbed down from the hack. Before he departed, Tobias asked, "Are we quite certain they mean to cause trouble, ma'am? Dynamite, well, it's used for roads, or laying track too."

I nodded. "Or to excavate mines. But yes, Tobias. If you'd heard those anarchists speak . . . I cannot sleep for worrying about it."

Collin had promised information if I could help him sell his mine. So, I decided to broach the matter with Mr. and Mrs. Bellino. Near the elevator, Mr. Fish was speaking to a workman in overalls who departed down a narrow stairwell.

Turning to me, Mr. Fish smiled, straightening his cuffs. "Lady Diana."

"Is the elevator malfunctioning?" I inquired.

"No, ma'am! Maintenance, always maintenance. It's operated on counterweights, you see, a marvelous invention! But like Icarus, one must be careful with new machines, yes?"

Smiling at his classical witticism, he pointed through the elevator's gilded trellis.

"Inside there, that's the central cable that suspends the chamber, and behind it—you see that?—there goes the counterweight."

Abigail proceeded to our suite. I went to the dining room, where, as before, the Bellinos invited me to join their table. Though the meal was lively, I struggled to suppress my impatience. "All things in their own time," Miss Sythe-Fornett would have chided. But with a band of murderers on the loose, how could I sip politely at the lemonade?

As the plates were cleared, I whispered to Erminia. "Could we talk, just us?"

Looking pleased, she invited me to her parlor. There I described the abject poverty I'd seen at the Boxes and asked for her help.

She retreated with a knowing look. "My dear Mrs. O'Trey, I don't know what we *could* do! Those people have such troubles. Vice, of course, and drink."

I protested. "They must feel the cards are stacked against them—the game is rigged." I stopped, disconcerted. Donnelly had said that at the anarchist meeting.

She shook her head, lips tight. "Sloth. That's the bane of the lower classes. Ah, this distresses you. Give them some charity, if you must, but it will all be wasted on liquor."

"Mr. Box did not want charity," I persisted. "He wants to sell a mine. I have seen his claim, and while I know little of such things, it seemed genuine."

She laughed, tossing back her head in reproof. "Mrs. O'Trey, I've no conception of such things. Ladies do not concern ourselves with money."

Ignoring her patronizing manner, I said, "Would you intercede with Mr. Bellino? As a personal favor."

"My dear. It'd be quite improper."

Puzzled, I asked, "Would you not consider the purchase, if you liked the idea of it?"

Embarrassment twitched across her face. "Mrs. O'Trey, that's best left to the gentlemen. They've the heads for it."

"You don't handle cash? Tradesmen's bills?"

She flicked a careless hand. "Certainly not! But you're newly arrived in the States. The best people do not speak of money, ever."

Following her lead, I got up to leave, but something did not seem quite aligned. Her gesture seemed put on, like someone on stage. Then I understood. Erminia had no authority in matters of finance. It was Mr. Bellino I must ask.

"You poor thing," she said, laying a dimpled hand on my arm. "I suppose, as a widow, you must manage it all yourself."

Startled, I said, "Oh! I'm no widow!" I bit my lip. I'd blurted out the truth because I could not bear that word. I went on in a calmer tone. "My husband is away on business. I manage finances on his behalf."

I returned to my room, feeling somber. Throughout my childhood, Papa had discussed business at meals. He'd quizzed Adi and me with math sums at breakfast. How we rushed to answer first! He discussed how to approach British administrators, business partners and employees. Should we sell our tea in Hong Kong? Or buy a hotel in Simla? Adi and I often took opposite sides, arguing energetically, fencing with our wit. How Papa chuckled at us, beaming with pride.

Mrs. Bellino, however, seemed content to be cared for like a child—did American women own nothing? Did my friend Ida Abernathy have any say in matters of any consequence?

With a few hours in hand, I took myself back to the public library, where I sought the librarian's counsel. He suggested I consult the land records office registrar. After sending cables to Houghton and Detroit County registrars from the telegraph office, I waited for replies and browsed newspapers of every ilk. I dusted through newspapers and trade publications put out by unions, brotherhoods, railway affiliations and oilmen's concerns.

A Terre Haute trade paper was edited by a man named Eugene Victor Debs. Liking his clear and direct prose, I read back issues to learn how the Brotherhood of Locomotive Firemen had grown. Debs had a noble optimism—labor and capital were complementary, he said, and would not just coexist but benefit each other, if each respected the other.

The *Chicago Times* said Mr. Debs had formed the American Railway Union in February, by merging the disparate brotherhoods of engineers, firemen, and other fraternities. This single largest union in the country had just won increased wages from the Great Northern Railroad. Reading this, I paused. That was good, wasn't it? Reporters called him a "progressive," determined to improve the condition of labor.

Then, buried in discussions of the brotherhood's business—better safety measures, pleas for sick pay—I read a sentence that alarmed me: *Dynamite is a tool of war. Labor is engaged in a war and has not the luxury to overlook any tools.*

I stared, wondering. Jim had embedded himself in a disgruntled group, remnants of the Carnegie Steel union. Was he looking at the wrong one?

* * *

"Lady Diana?" Mr. Bellino said that evening, pressed and sparking in white tie. "May I present Mr. William Hooker Gillette?"

How peculiar it was to be introduced and greet people, mouthing niceties, when any moment a devastating explosion might go off! I could do nothing more to prevent that, so I offered my hand in a pantomime of polite manners.

Mr. Gillette held my fingers with an engaging, puckish smile. Blessed with a noble forehead, the thin young man resembled a lamppost wearing a flamboyant blue coat, yet his orange vest paled against the brilliance of his grin.

Mr. Bellino beamed. "Don't you recognize him? The actor, the famous actor?" He waved his arm at the short bald gentleman standing beside the actor. "And Mr. Charles Froman of New York's Empire Theater!"

"Charmed," I replied, astonished. Mr. Bellino was pulling out the stops in his eagerness to impress me. What was he after?

Our luncheon passed prettily, for both men trotted out a stock of entertaining theater stories. Mrs. Bellino and the bankers' wives seemed all a-titter, but out of sorts and distracted, I often missed the punchlines.

In a lull in the conversation, I put my question to Mr. Bellino. He listened, astonished as I described the Box family's difficulties. I ended with, "Would you consider purchasing it?"

His banker friends eyed him, eyebrows raised in silent pantomime, then chuckled. Ignoring them, I added, "I sent a wire to the land records office in Detroit city, Michigan. The names registered match Mr. Box's deed. They have sixty acres. The claim is genuine."

Mr. Bellino spread his hands and then asked me some questions. "Madam, the city is full of fellows like this. It's a trickster's game. He might have a dozen copies of his claim! If he owned a mine, he'd work it, accident or not. No, madam. He's a fraud, a rogue. The proof is in the very conditions you describe!"

His condescension grated on me, but I persisted. "Do you know someone else who might consider this venture?"

"Perish the thought, madam!" he chided. "Why trouble yourself with it? Yeats here can invest your capital. Kaperski can put you in oil, coal or railroad stocks. Surefire winners!"

I'd failed to interest him in Collin's mine. Yet the man's concerted effort put me on guard. Most women would be persuaded by Mr. Bellino's air of confidence, I thought, but brought up amid constant discussion of business and bargaining, and warned by Jim's skepticism, I found Mr. Bellino's eagerness bordered on hectoring.

Then his gaze slid past me and he stiffened. He blinked rapidly with a closed-lipped smile, so I turned to see what had distressed him. Two gentlemen approached in opera hats and satin lapels. The shorter man wore a goatee; a scowl crossed on his narrow face.

Mr. Bellino bowed formally to the new arrival. The man did not reciprocate, but stalked by. Turning to his companion, he said, "Hope you don't intend to play cards. Place is full of upstarts."

Startled at his disdainful tone, I glanced at Mr. Bellino, whose cheeks had paled.

"Who was that?"

Mr. Bellino touched his perfectly knotted tie. "General Payne, ma'am."

Seething, Erminia said, "We met on a Dubuque riverboat—you spent days together in the card room!"

What could account for this? The men had met before, but the general had delivered a devastating public cut. Ah, I thought. Mr. Bellino had either lost and been unable to pay his debts or, worse, been caught cheating! So, the Bellinos were not as well accepted as Erminia had led me to believe.

Pleading a headache, I left, feeling morose. What now? How could I gain Collin's help?

* * *

The next morning I walked down Wabash to a bustling market, hearing calls of vendors touting wares. Dark-suited men streamed out of tall buildings, their steps marked with purpose. Women hurried past:

matronly women carrying the day's shopping, young spectacled typists, seamstresses and schoolteachers.

A display of colored bottles caught my attention, fanciful shapes gleaming in the perfumer's glass window like crystalline birds. Daily the city stench had assaulted me—now stepping inside, I drew in the floral aromas with delight—musk, lavender, orange blossoms, rose, jasmine, myrrh and sandalwood. The price marked near each delicate bottle gave me a twinge. But a dear little bottle reminded me of those on Mama's dressing table, so temptation won and I made my way back armed with a bottle of French civet musk.

Near the hotel, I skirted a pile of horse droppings, pausing as I recognized the muckraker. In a heavy apron, filthy from the knees down, Collin Box shoveled slop into a wheelbarrow.

He touched his cap and swallowed in agitation. "Ma'am, the mine. We sold it."

His distress puzzled me. "That's good, isn't it? Who bought it?"

"Man called Bellino. Came this morning." Words tumbled from him in a rush. "The baby cried all night. Ma tried everything. Wouldn't stop. Croup, it was. We didn't have cash fer a doctor, see?" Collin's voice was a defeated whisper. "Fifty dollars. After six years, he sells it for a lousy fifty dollars."

I said, "Is the baby all right?"

He nodded, looking glum, and returned to his work.

Riding the elevator, haunted by Collin's despair, I imagined the weight of that child's cries grinding into the huddled family. My box of French perfumes and lotions, essence of tuberose for me, French musk for Ida, had cost twenty dollars. Bellino had bought Collin's mine for fifty. I winced.

How could Enri Bellino exploit the poor family so? I was complicit, since I had persuaded him of its worth. Simmering, my remorse turned into outrage. He'd tricked me. Like a child lulled by a conjurer, I'd seen only what he wanted me to.

CHAPTER 20

DON'T KNOW WHERE

Back in my suite I sensed something amiss. An odor? A feeling that I wasn't alone. A metal toolbox stood by the door. Where had I seen it? I remembered the workman with Mr. Fish.

My derringer was still in my dressing room. I called, "Abigail?"

Jim came from the water closet, wiping his hands on a towel. He'd come as a workman. In broad daylight!

Emotion came in a storm, clogging my throat with tears. It was the sight of him, standing there, calm as you please, in fresh clothes, his mouth crooked so that he looked hopeful, like a boy waiting for an ice. I embraced him, pulled him to the sofa and curled into his lap as I used to. He held me close, his face in my hair.

For long moments I breathed, feeling the rise and fall of his chest. I'd been terrified he'd suffer the same fate as Baldwin.

Then fearing that Abigail might return and find us *en déshabillé*, I sat up and pulled out a sheet of paper. "Here's what I think. We have a puzzle."

Tucking in his shirt, Jim smiled. "You've figured out the missing piece."

I stopped. "What piece?"

He shrugged. "When you said puzzle, I thought—well, let's start with Grewe, the Pinkerton. He surprises the thief at Burnham's office and is killed there. Baldwin comes to Chicago, talks to Burnham. Let's say he realizes that a map was stolen. Construction's under way, it shows power cables, water pipes.

"Then he traces Grewe's murder to Lascar—police report mentions grease and ink, so he's snooping around printing press offices. He searches the old factory where the men sleep. Must have got deep inside to have found that letter. Daring of him to take pages. But it's in German, so he wires Dupree. Then something gives him a nasty turn."

What odd expressions Jim had learned since we'd been apart.

"Something—alerted him? But what?"

"Don't know. He mails them to me with a note about the union dispute. Tells me he's got in with the labor union chaps. But look—half the page is missing."

I frowned. "So where is it?"

His hair fell over his brow as he shook his head. "I think he sent it to someone else. Wasn't sure I'd come, so he added more insurance."

I blinked. "Or—Jim, is that what got him killed?"

Jim inhaled, his face still. "By who, Diana? Baldwin wrote, 'Don't trust the Duprees.' No way to tell, just yet. So, if that's not the puzzle you're talking about—"

"Right. I started from the other end."

I pulled forward a blank page and unscrewed my fountain pen. "To blow up something requires considerable work. Here's A—for anarchist. Let's say it's his idea—he's stolen a map from the architect's office, so he has a plan. What does he need? Well, an explosive—ballistite." I drew a line below it. "Now he needs someone to buy it and bring it here. Let's call them B."

Jim said, "Yeah, another angle. Trouble is, we don't know where to look. Where they'll strike."

Drawing another line, I asked, "Where did they get the cash? These workers don't have much to spare. So, he needs money to buy it—let's add M."

Jim nodded. "Ballistite, well, it's not easy to set off. Liable to get oneself blown up. He'd need expertise."

Agreeing, I dropped a line and added the letter E.

Chewing my lip, I said, "Baldwin found the letter, so we know B wasn't here. He may have got here now, with the explosives."

"He'd need to store it, so W for warehouse." Taking the pen, Jim added the letter W. Frowning, he said, "It's not a small container, Diana. The letter says eight hundred pounds. A barrel can take about forty pounds, so that's twenty barrels."

I shuddered to think of eight *hundred* pounds of explosives going off in one blast. "Even if the thief, A, has the map, and has got cautious because of Baldwin, we can still try to find the others. E—the explosives expert—and, well, where is the stuff kept? Did you search those warehouses, the ironworks?"

Jim sighed. "Christ, finding that warehouse is a needle in a haystack. Hundreds of ships unload at the docks, especially now. Tons of goods, machinery for the fair. All sorts of contraptions, inventions, you wouldn't believe. Produce too. Got thousands to feed. Then there are the rail yards—Grand Central depot, Union depot, Illinois Central depot and more!" He tapped the page. "But this is good. A useful way to think. Each member has a different task."

Catching my elbow, he pulled me to him, grinning. "Aren't you the detective now."

His mustache and beard brushed my cheeks. Then he flopped on the bed and stretched out. Tucking his hands under his head, he watched me apply lotion, his expression inscrutable.

Where had he been all this time? I asked, "Where do you sleep?"

"An old leather factory, shut down now. Someone used it for woodwork, once. The blokes got in, and the owner's no wiser."

On a factory floor! Not even a tenement. I gazed at him, moved.

His shoulders moved in a slow shrug. "I don't sleep much on the job. God, it's good to be here, with you."

"Jim, if I get something useful, how shall I send it to you?"

"Send Tito. He's often around the yards selling smokes."

Only later, when I was falling asleep did I wonder, why now? Why here? The anarchists could strike anywhere, at anyone. They might blow up a ship on the ocean, or in a harbor. In France they'd set explosives in restaurants, police stations, government buildings and factories, each assault driven by labor disputes. The World's Fair would bring America's elite together, but it was spread over six hundred acres. Did the anarchists have a specific enemy? If we discovered that, we could gauge when and where they would strike. But try as I might, I could not imagine who their target could be.

* * *

Despite my fitful start, I slept deeply. I woke early, stretching in bed with a sense of well-being. A newspaper rustled. Jim sat at my table, reading by lamplight. The pale glow at the window behind him warned that dawn was not far.

Catching my gaze, his eyes crinkled. "Morning, sweet. You get a morning paper under the door!"

I remembered what I'd wanted to tell him last night. "Jim, I've got Tobias watching that man Donnelly." I didn't mention Abigail, because I wasn't sure how he'd react to Abigail staying in my suite when he wasn't here.

"Watching him?" Something shifted in his face, a stiffening of his jaw.

"Following him about. To try to figure out where the stuff is, the explosives. He's got to check that it's safe, don't you think? The worry would surely eat at him."

He folded his paper. "Then what's he waiting for? I've been with them for weeks now—he seems to trust me, but they're a cagey lot."

Dressing, I called a bellboy and ordered tea, then told Jim about Collin's mine. "Mr. Bellino bought it after all. After telling me in no uncertain terms that he wasn't interested. When he asked all those questions about where they lived, I suppose I should have suspected. Jim, what should a mine cost, a copper mine?"

He buttered toast, considering it. "Depends. If it's tapped out, possibly nothing."

"Mr. Box was still mining it when he had the accident. Aren't pennies made of copper?"

"Yes. But see this?" Jim pointed to the paper. "Electricity—the fair will be lit by it. They've laid down miles of wire, Diana. The price of copper will rise when other cities do the same."

"What does copper have to do with electricity?"

"The wires, Diana. They're made of copper."

A thought slithered through my mind. "What does a pound of copper cost?"

Jim turned to the rear pages of the paper and ran a ragged fingernail down the small print. "Ah. Twelve cents a pound. That's after it's taken from the ore, sweetheart, and refined. There's transport, smelting, many other expenses."

He estimated that ore might be worth about two cents a pound. Then I wrote out the math sums like Papa had taught me. Jim watched, his eyes soft and grey as monsoon clouds.

I said, "Box said he used to make two trips to the surface. I think he could carry fifty pounds at least, don't you? He took out over a hundred pounds of ore every day. Well, that's only two dollars a day. Bellino bought the mine for fifty dollars. He'll make that back in a month."

"He'd run it for a few years, till it plays out. And he could hire twenty men to lug up the ore," Jim said, his voice without inflection. "He'd still have to cart it to a train, smelt and refine it to make wire."

A tremor quivered through me. Bellino had got himself another "fine deal" to crow about at dinner. Disgust churned my insides as I imagined his glee as he turned a nice profit or resold the mine for thousands. No wonder anarchists thought the game was rigged!

"Diana," said Jim. "This isn't your fight."

"Isn't it? I told him about it, Jim. I asked him to buy it."

"You couldn't know. Anyone could have done as he did."

Outrage pushed through me. "Take advantage of Box's need? When he had a sick child? Would you do that? Would Papa?"

Jim took a slow breath. Then he said, "My sweet, don't measure people by the yardstick of your papa. They will always fall short." Rising, he went to collect his shirt and coat from the bathroom, where I'd tried to shut out their stench.

"You won't stay?" I called.

He came back and crouched beside my chair, looking lean, but he was clean and fed. Eyes as grey as the sky over the ocean, he quoted, "I have more care to stay than will to leave."

I clung to his hand. "Shakespeare?"

"Mmm. Come, death, and welcome! Juliet wills it so." He offered the clue lightly, Romeo's teasing, making light of danger.

"Romeo and Juliet. Romantic." I touched his hair, keeping up a brave face as he departed. When he reached the door, I called out, "Captain Jim," to keep him a moment longer.

He stopped, surprised at my formal address.

Hurrying to the bathing room, I brought him my fingernail cutter. He smiled, shaking his head, then paused. "This could be useful."

I closed his hand over it. "Keep it."

Once the door shut and his footsteps receded, my cheery mask fell away. Jim's gesture in the midst of this nightmare was not lost on me. His memory often surprised me; he'd read Shakespeare in his army years, camped in the swamps of Burma or on high Himalayan slopes. But a chill touched my skin, for in the play, Romeo died at the end.

* * *

Over luncheon I confronted Mr. Bellino. "I see you bought a mine, sir?"

"Mrs. O'Trey," he smiled, spreading his hands. "I've been remiss. I do thank you for that fellow's address. I decided to do him a good turn."

His effrontery stole my breath. The soup was still being cleared from our table, but I laid into Mr. Bellino, calling him roundly to task.

He tut-tutted, fingering his mustache. "Now, now, madam. Don't worry your pretty head about this."

"Fifty dollars, sir!" My voice had risen, drawing the attention of other diners. Schooling my tone, I said, "It is worth a hundred times more!"

Mr. Bellino laughed. "Heavens! What fancies you ladies have!" Turning to his thick-eyebrowed friend Yeats, he inquired about the stock market.

Seething, I did not speak to him again. So, I was surprised, when I rose to leave, that Erminia joined me. Looking peaked, she said, "Lady Diana, may we speak?"

Wrung out from disappointment, I wanted to decline, but at her tone, I softened. She'd been wed twelve years. How did she survive the constant erosion of her very being? Did it not rankle, to be treated as a dunderhead, a fool?

We went down to the lobby, where she composed herself upon a couch, gazing at me solemnly. "Something's happened, and I would like to know what it is. Will you explain?"

The World's Fair is a tinderbox, I wanted to say. Everyone in it will burn. And it's because of men like your husband. But I only shook my head.

"Please, Mrs. O'Trey—why do they call you Lady Diana? Mrs. O'Trey is such a becoming name. I see that Enri has disappointed you. I should like to understand."

At my request, Mr. Fish brought me paper, pen and ink. I explained, writing out the numbers like a child's homework in mathematics.

When I was done, she studied the two figures at the bottom of the page: five thousand dollars—what the mine could be worth, and fifty—what Bellino had paid. Gazing at the page, she said, "I'm sorry, Mrs. O'Trey, but he won't give it back. Why does he never learn?"

My astonishment made her smile. Rising to her feet, she said, "I wouldn't be surprised if Enri loses that deed at cards this weekend. He has a workshop on Canal Street near Union depot. Number fourteen. Act soon, my dear."

What was she saying? I stared at her. "It would be all right, if he lost the deed?"

"It would serve him right if he did," she said, and left.

If Bellino lost the deed at cards, Osain Box would never get back his mine. Erminia was saying Osain should get it back. But Enri wouldn't give it.

Was she saying I should *take* it?

CHAPTER 21

WHY DON'T YOU KNOW?

JIM

The guard waved me through the rail yard gate. Over the past weeks he'd grown accustomed to seeing me about. Donnelly and some of his group worked here, so I'd joined up too. Proceeding in step with other workers, I pondered Diana's attachment to the posh couple, the Bellinos. Why was she so keen on Chicago society? To be admired? Not that she didn't deserve it—I gave her little entertainment in that regard. Her determination to uncover who'd financed this devilish business sent a flush of admiration through me. But why would a wealthy Chicago businessman destroy what his investments had built?

She'd found another lead, though. If Collin Box might know something about the powder, I'd pay him a visit. Thousands of poor blighters crowded Chicago's tenements—trust Diana to get caught up in their troubles! The thought of her had me grinning as I rolled up my coat and thrust it with my hat on the shelf beside the other men's. At the yard office I collected the ledger, my alibi, and entered the yard.

The lads were already unloading at the far end, so I sat on a carton, laid open the ledger and began to record the contents of each rail wagon. A dozen men were hired to do this as each train came in. It was slow, plodding work, but we were thorough; each sack, barrel and box was examined three times in the course of a survey. Every pallet was checked, every bale cut open. Since Donnelly's gang worked at loading the stock, he'd have ample opportunity to hide what he wanted, or avoid sheds where the explosives were stashed. I'd scrutinized his sequence for weeks, searching for a discrepancy.

We worked steadily, stopping at noon for a meal. I'd not brought any, so I stayed with the others determined to save a dime. It would be easy to forget what I was looking for and fall into the rhythm of loading and prying open boxes. At last, when the whistle sounded, I trudged outside, pretending to look for a smoke.

Crates of powder would not be piled out in the rain, so I counted the number of sheds. I'd have to break in again tonight, because Donnelly and Collier were partial to this yard.

After a twelve-hour shift, we slumped against walls, some dozing off while we waited for the wagons to carry us back. The burly redhead, Orrin Pierce, lowered himself to chew the cud, as he said. Others joined in, so it made a sociable company.

·"Here," said Orrin, around his chew of tobacco. "You come to us on Sunday, huh? Missus is expectin' us."

He had invited me to sup with his family before. Working together all day, it was inevitable that one struck up some friendships. We'd been to taverns, joints where a gent could throw some dice. But to visit a man's home?

I said, "Celebrating something?"

He chuckled at that. "Funny way you got o' saying things. Naw. No celebratin'. Wife has a sister, see? She wants I bring around a bloke that might be, ah, good for her."

The men around us chuckled, casting knowing looks.

I frowned. "Good for her?"

He sent me a look. Not quite exasperated, but close.

"C'mon. You're no kid. Time you settled down, see?"

When I glanced up, surprised, he punched my arm with a ham-like fist. "Get hitched. Raise a family."

I shook my head, smiling my regrets. "I don't think so. But thank you."

He pulled back, affronted, his voice thicker. "Whatcha matter with you? 'S my wife's sister, see? You too good fer us?"

I spread my hands. "Not what I'm saying. I can't."

He got angrier as I spoke. Face red, veins bulged in his neck. "Why not? Eh? I asked you before, you got summat to do? Got sum-un to see? Now you just tell me why."

I looked him in the eye and said, "I'm married."

That stumped him. What now? The memory of Framji Mansion was in my mind, the rustle of sarees as the women laid the table, the call of the Gurkha at the gate. Those mornings when, my plate heaped with eggs and toast, slices of chikoo fruit or mango, Adi and I would settle down to plan our next move. That was Diana's home—how much she'd given up to be with me!

All that was in my eyes, when I met Orrin's gaze.

"I'm sorry, lad," he said. "But you should wed again."

"My wife's alive," I said. He looked flummoxed, so I gave him a lie mixed with the truth, "I had to leave. You see, I married an heiress. That doesn't work too well."

I'd married her against the customs of her clan, her religion, the ancient Zoroastrians. Yet her parents did not despise me. They were the only family I'd ever known. They took me in without question; for that, and more, I held them in high regard.

Some lads looked surprised, others chuckled.

An old hand said, "No Horatio Alger story fer you, eh?" He explained that it was the dream of many a lad in his day—to impress a great man, a captain of industry, and marry his daughter.

"Captains of industry! Like Henry Frick?" enquired Donnelly, coming over to us. "Berkman should a got him, but he didn't do it right, now did he?"

Orrin scratched his chin. "I dunno. Shot him twice. And stabbed him. That should have done for him. But no, the bastard lived!"

Last year, I'd heard about this on board. A young anarchist named Alexander Berkman had shot the manager of Carnegie Steel.

"Broke the strike, did it?" I asked.

The old hand retorted, "No, the strike was off before that. Frick called in the bloody state militia! My own wife's brother was called up. Hadn't earned a day's wage in three months, so 'course he joined in."

Orrin's voice was sad. "Many of us worked there, Agney. I was a fitter four years, and a good one. But Frick wouldn't take back any union men. Those that went back took half pay. Measly fifteen cents for an hour's work! Less 'n eleven dollars a week."

I shook my head, commiserating.

"Trouble is, Agney," Donnelly broke in, staring at me. "How come you don't know?"

I glanced around at the silent men. They glanced away, unwilling to meet my gaze. Orrin's forehead wrinkled as he scratched his head. Donnelly went on, "It was in all the papers. In every city. Every kid knows 'bout the strike and Frick. How come you don't?"

I was in India then, but could not say that, since I was supposed to have been in Boston at the time. All I could do was keep my chin up when I caught Donnelly's piercing look.

"Two reasons someone might not a heard. Away at sea on a whaler six months, or . . . in the nick. You don't talk like a sailor."

"I'm not."

He thought I'd been in prison. That was useful, though I'd have to be careful not to talk about it, to hide my scanty knowledge. I let the long silence stretch out, admitting nothing, but neither did I shy away.

"So that's why you left Boston," Donnelly said, his watchful eyes narrow.

CHAPTER 22

TO CATCH A THIEF

I turned to Abigail, all dressed up for her part. "You're all right with this?"

She shrugged. "It's you that has the hard bit. I just take Mrs. Bellino to Marshall Field's, keep her there two hours. That won't be difficult. She's hard to please anyway. With me disliking this and liking that, she'll be tied up in tangles."

"Don't be too forthcoming. She doesn't like that."

"I know my part. It's the store that 'Gives the Lady what she wants,' remember? But we don't know when Mr. Bellino'll get back. If you're found there, what will you do?"

I pretended a confidence I did not feel. "I'll say Erminia invited me—and I got the day wrong. But wait! How will I get in?"

Grinning, she opened her hand. "Wrigley's chewing gum. I got the new Juicy Fruit flavor at the fair." On her palm lay flat packages in glossy paper.

Unwrapping one, she folded it into her mouth and nodded to me to do the same. "I'll pack it into the slot, so the door won't close. Here. Have a try."

It took six sticks of gum to prevent my door from locking. Handing me an empty wrapper, she tucked the wad into her palm and set off for Mrs. Bellino's suite. I clenched my hands, staring at the clock, her last words ringing in my ears. "Wait fifteen minutes after we leave, all right? She's finicky. May return for something."

I was going to steal back the deed to Box's mine. If Papa knew, he would go pale. Mama would press her fingers to her mouth, whispering, "Why? You *know* what is right." That was the trouble. I did know what was right. And Bellino's extortion of the deed wasn't. But theft? A shudder rippled through me.

Parsees don't lie. All my life I'd been taught that—it was a point of pride for us, for my parents and Adi, part of our identity—honest to a fault, upstanding, regardless of the price. That was who I thought I was.

Yet I'd lied repeatedly this last month. I'd hid information from Dupree. I'd even withheld from Jim matters that would upset him, like Abigail's secret. Now I was going to steal.

God knows I had good reason for everything, but Papa would say, "Does it matter? Aren't you making excuses?" It was easier to live in absolutes, harder to make peace with it. I was going to break the law.

Two minutes left. It wouldn't do to walk out of Erminia's apartment holding the deed in plain view. From my reticule I pulled a fifty-dollar note. On it, Mr. Franklin looked indulgent, while Lady Justice glowered. I tucked it into my glove. There! I would not steal the deed but *buy* it back. I would leave fifty dollars in its place. Bellino would suspect; but if he accused me, I'd show him astonished, wide eyes. Don't worry your little head, indeed!

Taking the stairs to avoid the elevator boy, I tapped on the Bellinos' door. No one answered. I pushed, and heaved a sigh of relief as the door swung open. Digging out the wad of gum from the slot I tucked it away in my spare wrapper and entered.

Starting with Bellino's office, I hurried to the secretary. A shiny black telephone sat by a blotter piled with letters. Pulling open drawers, I ran through the contents—letters, telegrams, bills, many unpaid, threats of legal action. Bellino was not as wealthy as he appeared.

Next, I combed their bedchamber. One bedside table held newspapers, the other religious books. In the dressing room were suits, shirts and vests—expensive stuff, and a lot of it—on hooks and in drawers. I checked the pockets. Bellino owned ten times more shirts and suits than Jim, vests of brocade, Indian silks, all manner of shoes. Where was the deed?

I heard the door of the apartment open and stiffened. Bellino had returned. I stood still, my heartbeat shouting a din in my ears.

Bellino went to his office, where I heard a soft thump. Was that him dropping into the chair? He spoke, his voice low, his words unclear through the wall.

A pause. Curious, I pressed my ear to the door.

"Yes, that's right: 7656," he said, speaking on the telephone.

The Bellinos' apartment was patterned like mine, so both bedchambers opened onto a corridor leading to the bath chamber and water closet. His office was where Abigail had her room. To get to the parlor, I had to pass his door. Surely Bellino would hear me open the bedroom door? Could I escape while he was occupied on the telephone?

While I agonized over the choice, he barked, "Yes, hello! I have it. The Cold Storage Building. It's near the station. You won't have to carry it far . . ." He listened, then interrupted. "Are you mad? Not all of them! It's a test, man! Just one." With a clang, he put up the telephone.

I had waited too long. But what was Bellino sending to the Cold Storage Building? I'd eaten the new flavored ice cream confections, soft, chilled and sweet. Was he involved in that business too? Bellino liked to buy things, I thought, but didn't like paying for them.

Minutes ticked slowly by. The rustle of paper told me Bellino was reading his letters. Biting my lip, I glanced at the watch pinned to my frock. Almost two hours had passed. Now I regretted asking Abigail to delay Erminia so long. If Bellino found me in his bedroom, he'd read only one explanation into it. Theft. He could use that against me to demand whatever he wanted. And I wasn't fool enough to let him, no sir!

His chair creaked as he stood up. As soon as his footsteps retreated to the washroom, I scurried through the corridor into the parlor. I yanked open the door, praying that Bellino would not hear. Alas! The washroom door snapped open behind me.

I turned to face it, composing myself.

"You *are* here!" I said, making a show of surprise. "Is Mrs. Bellino ill? No one answered, and she had invited me, so I asked someone to let me in. Is she all right?"

Absently wiping his hands, he frowned. "Erminia's gone shopping . . . with you, I was told." Frowning quizzically, he tossed the towel on the wash table and advanced.

I stepped back. "I had another engagement, so I loaned her my maid. Another time, then." Heart pounding, I turned to leave. If he grabbed my arm, I'd stomp his foot and dash to the door.

"A moment, madam," he said. "It's not often I find a young lady in my suite. What about your reputation, hmm?"

He was smiling. I could have responded with disdain, with one of Miss Sythe-Fornett's chilling sneers. Instead, I parried, "You're such a gentleman, you'd never do a thing like that!"

Head held high, I stalked into the parlor, leaving him nonplussed. My hands shook, but my voice had been calm and assured. As for reputation, it went both ways. One scream from me would tear his to shreds!

I reached the door to the suite just as it opened. Erminia stood there, wide eyes shocked.

"You. And Enri," she whispered, her face squeezing as though compressed by an invisible hand.

I gasped, realizing how it must seem—my maid takes Erminia off for the morning, and I'm found alone with her husband.

To reassure, I murmured, "I didn't find the deed."

She clung to the doorknob, then wobbled to a couch just as Enri Bellino came out, exclaiming over his wife's condition.

Huffing, Erminia said, "I'm all right, Mr. Bellino. The store was so crowded—and this Chicago heat. Put it there, girl," she directed Abigail, who carried a pile of boxes.

"We'll leave you to rest," I said, catching her gaze, pleading, say nothing!

She nodded. "Until dinner, then."

Abigail and I returned to our suite. My heartbeat slowed as I told her my misadventures.

"That was close." Abigail shook her head at me. "So, no deed. Well, I learned where Mr. Bellino plays cards every Sunday. A pub on Robertson, just by Buffalo Bill's show."

The memory of Collin Box's despair was stamped into my mind, his gasping regret, the hopeless slump of his shoulders. I needed his help, but also needed to set right a grievous wrong, one that I had unwittingly set in motion. I groaned. "Erminia said he'd gamble it away."

"Hmm." She perched on the couch, smoothing her skirt, an ungainly but composed young woman with freckles, a long nose and thin lips.

Feeling a spurt of affection, I said, "Abigail, I need the deed. Without it, I have no way to help Jim. Collin's my only lead. What can we do?"

She smiled. Pulling a deck of cards from her pocket, she shuffled them.

"D'you play poker?"

No longer awkward, her long, knobby fingers caressed the cards, flipped and tossed them about with ease, commanded them to slide and rearrange themselves. An idea trickled into my mind, a delicious, wild idea that spread like a bathtub overflowing.

CHAPTER 23

THE CARD GAME

The morning of the card game, sending Abigail to spell Tobias, I waited at the Lake Front Park overlooking Lake Michigan. The Sunday parade of carriages ferried people to the different churches along Wabash Avenue. These last days, Tobias had followed Oscar Donnelly all over Chicago. Where was the ballistite?

The lake had moods, like the monsoon approaching Bombay that might seem luminous with clouds one day, but soon growl deep as it advanced. Today the calm lake sent a cool breeze across to shake the boughs above me and deliver a quick shower.

It was mid-June—a month since my arrival—and spring had come to Chicago. Pale blossoms clustered in profusion. Not even the dung and mud in the rain-soaked streets could dull my spirits. Above, a thousand filigreed leaves swished. Branches bore pods resembling small tamarind fruit, but I knew they could not be. A memory assailed me—the damp earthy scent of Malabar Hill, the drip of rain drumming our verandah roof while we dined on pearly white rice, Mama's coconut curry and braised lamb vindaloo, its potatoes reddened with spice.

Tobias ambled up, touching his hat with a wide smile. "Morning, ma'am." Sunlight shone on his ebony skin, and his step was spry. Greeting him, I broached the matter of funds. Once it was squared away, I asked, "Any progress, Tobias?"

In his low singsong voice, he said, "Mister Donnelly goes from the factory with the printing press office down to the rail yard most days. He's a popular man."

"Who is he with?"

"Lots of fellows come an' go, ma'am. Captain Jim"—my heartbeat quickened as he spoke—"he sleeps at the factory too, where they print them union papers. He's pals with an Irishman—big bloke, name of Orrin Pierce. And some"—he winced—"mighty rough fellas."

So, Jim had got deep into the gang. "Rough fellows?"

"Thugs, ma'am. Fellows who can't get an honest job. Grifters, they're called."

I bit my lip. "If he's in trouble, we must be able to help."

"Don't worry yoursel', Lady Diana," Tobias reassured me. "He's very capable. Saw him down at the loadin' docks, yesterday."

Remembering Mrs. Bellino's words, I said, "Tobias, there's a place on Canal Street I'm interested in—number fourteen, a workshop owned by Mr. Bellino. Can you look it over for me?"

He blinked. "Canal Street, ma'am? Ain't I doing that?"

I stared, then understood. "*That's* Donnelly's flop, where Captain Jim sleeps?"

When he affirmed it, I sucked in a breath. "It belongs to Enri Bellino! This cannot be a coincidence."

My fingers fidgeted for a cigarette as I said goodbye and returned to the hotel, but I decided against it.

When I'd admired Abigail's prowess with cards, she'd proposed another way to retrieve Osain Box's deed—we would join the card game. I'd hesitated, but dreaded the alternative, breaking into Donnelly's flop. I could play a neat game of whist, if I must, but poker? That was beyond me.

In crisp white shirt, black pipes and suspenders, Abigail came from her room as a bony but respectable gent with a careless confidence quite unlike the sober Abigail I knew. Yet when she put on false whiskers and thick, wooly beard, a giggle escaped my lips.

"All right then," she said, offering a wooden box. "You decide."

Sifting through her collection of bits and bobs, I plucked out a narrow mustache and some elegant sideburns. I'd seen a man on the train wear this swanky style and liked it better than Jim's unkempt beard.

"Hmm." Holding Abigail's chin, I applied the sticky mustache, patted it into place, then added the trim sideburns.

Next, I frowned at her limp, ghastly hair.

"No self-respecting wife would send you out like this, Mr. Gale," I chided, fetching my brush. I brought along a pomade I'd bought for Jim, which he never remembered to use, and smoothed it onto Abigail's forelocks. Hair combed straight, with those hazel eyes, she made an interesting man.

When I leaned back to survey my handiwork, her ordinarily pallid face flushed. I had often seen Jim dress, but always maintained a proper distance from Abigail. Now I pulled back, concerned. Had I been too forward? Her wary glance darted about the room.

Dash it, Abigail was my friend. I asked, "You're sure you can do this?"

Pulling back, she scoffed. "Don't fret about me. It's you that shouldn't go."

"They won't see much of me. High rollers like Bellino will be at the table, so I can wander about as your idle pal."

"They'll want you to play," Abigail warned. "Master Elmore is Lady Diana's well-padded stepson. They'll urge you on, push you to it."

"They can try—ha, folks, not for me!" I tried out a mannish laugh.

Abigail cringed. "Stop that."

After a half hour, I could produce a passable snicker. While I'd grown accustomed to narrow trousers, the niceties of interacting with other men made me groan. Hold your ground, don't be a chump—don't push too hard, you'd get their backs up—being a man was an awful job. How in God's name did Jim manage it?

How much I'd been cosseted in Bombay! I said, "People expect less of women, don't they? But my gender usually affords me a degree of civility. It's rather scary, losing that protection." I stole a glance at Abigail, who was tugging at her collar. "Is that why you dress as a woman?"

She shook her head, packing away her things. "It's not that simple. It was a game, at first, an extension of the theater. I didn't plan it." She looked up. "I'll need some cash, to play."

I staked her forty dollars for the game—at this rate I'd soon need to visit a bank, I thought, counting my depleted nest egg. Dressed as a pair of dandies, we set off after dark, slipping out through the kitchen to avoid Mr. Fish. Abigail led the way, stepping around stinking puddles and zigzagging down a maze of streets.

We reached the gaslit tavern without incident. With scarred wainscot paneling and limp green curtains, the musty chamber smelled of liquor. At the back of the room I spotted Enri Bellino. He stood over a round table with a pair of middle-aged strangers—and Peter Dupree!

Why was he here? Ducking my head I drew Abigail's attention with a tug on her sleeve. Glad of the dim lamps, I glanced around. Men at the crowded tables seemed busy with games of chance, or their tankards of beer.

Nodding, Abigail squared her shoulders and ran a finger over her pencil mustache.

"I'll be over there." I stepped toward the bar, clenching my hands to hide my nerves. While she played for the deed, I planned to ask about Donnelly, the bloke who talked about "blowing it all up."

Slipping onto a barstool where I could catch glimpses of the card table, I raised my finger at the barkeep to order a "whiskey sour." When he slid it down the bar, I sipped at the vile beverage, suppressing a grimace. I'd have to nurse it as long as I could, because I had no head for liquor.

Bellino's card game was under way, so Abigail dawdled nearby until a man tossed his cards on the table and ceded his chair. Then she shook hands and took his place.

Flicking his cuffs, Peter Dupree shuffled. Was he also investigating Baldwin's death?

The game opened without ado. Coatless, his shirtsleeves banded by garters, Peter cut, shuffled and dealt with mechanical precision. Abigail played with a neat, quiet assurance. The others cursed and grumbled now and then, with a snort or a gibe. She rarely spoke or checked her cards, her workmanlike attention trained on the other players.

Bellino played in daring flashes. Still wearing his coat, he sweated, his face flushed as empty tankards of beer accumulated before him.

I'd planned to chat with fellows at the bar, but I'd miscalculated. My fancy togs kept them away, so I just listened to the conversations around me.

"I called! Show your hand," a voice barked. The card players gazed at Abigail. What had gone wrong? Peter Dupree glared with an odd intensity, and Bellino scowled.

My heart thumped. Should I intervene? While I was trying to gauge what had happened, a deep boom belched in the distance. Outside, a shout went up, followed by the clamor of yells. Seconds later, a man burst through the door, gasping, "Fire! The fairground's on fire!"

The tavern emptied as men ran out. Rushing up, I grabbed at Abigail's shoulder. Pushed to and fro, we joined the tide in the street.

Fire. The first warning was a smell, acrid like burning rubber, woodsmoke and something else, the sharp pungency of chemicals. Then I saw a glow in the sky.

Behind the train station, a squat tower with a conical top loomed above the adjacent buildings. It smoldered, as though the blaze wore a hat of embers.

"What's that?" I asked, forgetting to lower my voice.

"Cold Storage Building," said a man to my right. "Damned electric. It's deadly!"

Others took up this chant, heaping abuse upon the new "electric." Soon the ringing clamor of fire engines filled the air. An awful clanging announced three wagons pulled by horses. I glanced around, panic prickling as I realized there were too many people in the street. How could they get through?

Men pushed and thrust against each other. A group leapt from the water wagons to unravel hoses. When many hands reached to help, they hollered, "Give us room! Step back!"

Now it would be all right, I thought, breathing steadier. I glanced about for Abigail, but she wasn't nearby. I peered this way and that. She had disappeared. Flames lit up the block, making the street brighter than day. Heat radiated, warming my face. The crowd moved, shoving me with its momentum, as I scanned their fearful faces. Resisting the press of bodies, I tried to retreat but it was no good. I was hemmed in.

Rivulets of sweat ran down my forehead, plastering my shirt to my back. As one, the group moved. Some men tried to climb a side wall, but it proved too tall. Others took turns at the pumps, or hauled hoses from the wagons, pulling them farther.

Searching for Abigail's narrow shoulders, I elbowed my way from one group to another. Embers scattered from under that hat-like roof where the firemen climbed.

"That's a water tower, isn't it?" I asked a boy nearby. "Won't they be safe?"

He shook his head. "Cold Storage. That's electric, for the ice rink. Making ice for folks to skate on. Said they could do it, even in summer. Look!" He pointed, arm outstretched.

Something moved on the rim, above the smoldering wall.

A man. Another, and more! A dozen men clambered onto the rim encircling the structure, high above us but distant now, since we'd retreated a whole block to avoid being singed.

A shout went up. "Get a ladder to them!"

Efforts were made, but each one failed. No ladder could reach that high.

If the heat so far away burned my cheeks, what of those poor fellows? I shuddered to think of their skin roasting from the blaze.

"Where are the firemen?" I cried.

The boy's face contorted. "That's 'em on the roof!"

Cut off by the fire, they were stranded on the rim. Men groaned or crossed themselves as the firemen's plight became apparent. A hush killed all discussion. Some took off their hats and held them to their breast.

Smoke billowed as the wind turned, choking us, driving us back, our eyes stinging. When I could see again, I searched for movement against the glowing roof. The crowd stood still, like mourners at a grave site. Faces gleamed with sweat—or were they tears? On the rim, firemen shook hands, clapping each other on the shoulder, saying their farewells. A man near me prayed in a choked voice. Another sobbed, his body shaking.

One by one, the men on the rim leapt from the parapet to their deaths. That stark image seared into my mind—firemen standing on the blazing rim. Despite the heat, a shiver worked over my shoulders and down my back. There was nothing we could do.

Over the next hour the group thinned. Eyes smarting, I walked down an unfamiliar street, then retraced my steps and tried another. This took me to the waterfront, so I turned back again. I could not be lost, not today! Finally, I neared the tavern. There stood Abigail, disheveled and sooty, mustache askew, pale eyes shocked. A red glow in the sky cast a strange light over the city as we returned to the Oriental in silence. Around us, embers floated like fireflies.

In Bombay each holy day and birthday was marked by a family visit to the Zoroastrian fire temple. There, an ancient fire glimmered upon a great urn, banked with logs of sandalwood. Tended with devotion amid whispered prayers, that flame had lived a thousand years, ever since my Persian ancestors sought refuge in India. Tonight, the roaring flames were a beast unleashed.

Mr. Fish saw us in the lobby. His shoulders jerked, but he did not stop Abigail and me as we strode to the ornate elevator. Sooty and red-eyed, our gaze met in the mirrored glass.

As I stumbled toward my room, Abigail said, "Lady Diana!" holding out an envelope.

I took it and extracted a familiar threefold document. Holding it by the corners with my grimy fingers, I stared at a map embossed with a dark red seal.

"Osain Box's deed! How did you manage it?"

She brushed the back of her hand across her face, leaving a smear.

"More than one way to pluck a chicken. I pinched it from Bellino's coat."

Grinning my relief, I tucked the papers away and with heartfelt thanks, said goodnight.

I undressed, discarding sooty trousers and coat to soap my shaking hands. As I pulled pins from my hair, something hovered at the edge of my mind. Cold Storage Building. That boy's words repeated like the chant of an opium addict: Cold Storage Building—where had I heard that?

Bellino's phone call. The sharp taste of bile in my mouth, I recalled him saying, "You won't have to carry it far. A test. Are you mad, man? Just one."

Oh God, I had to tell Jim. I'd found his ballistite after all.

CHAPTER 24

RED-HANDED

JIM

On Sunday, I walked to the bathhouse with the German twins. Orrin followed out of sight, as we'd planned. Baldwin's note did not say whom he'd taken that German letter from, but I thought it was likely one of the brothers. The letter's final page would identify its author, so I'd searched the men's possessions for it. Without success. Nor had I found Baldwin's revolver or, by extension, his killer. I'd learned some of the lads' weaknesses, their secrets, but made no headway on my investigation. That weighed on me.

In the anteroom, the brothers and I stripped and rolled our clothes into bundles. A man could pay extra to have his clothes washed, but few did. Forking over a nickel to an attendant I noted where he placed our clothes and joined the line, praying that mine did not attract lice, a common infestation among blokes who slept on the factory floor.

We moved along quickly to where an old parson handed out cakes of soap and threadbare towels, urging us to attend church afterward.

Following the brothers down the hallway toward the shower baths, I let my towel slip.

"Blast it." I scowled, scooping up the muddied cloth. "I'll get another," I told them and headed back to the anteroom.

As planned, Orrin's drunken curses echoed from the hallway. He'd been puzzled when I asked him to distract the attendant, but for a half pint, agreed to help me find who was stealing tools. He'd keep the attendant occupied for a bit.

The first brother's coat contained only pamphlets. Would he keep the incriminating letter after all this time? Wouldn't he just burn it? Searching through his trousers yielded some coins, a photograph, a key and an old watch. Returning these to his pockets, I pulled down the second bundle. I'd unrolled it and extracted a wad of cloth, when a footstep sounded at the door.

Thrusting the bundle behind me, I turned. Lascar stood there, a wheeze escaping his throat.

His gaze trained on me, he unfolded a knife.

Choices. My life hung suspended by just one. My heart did a whump and began its war tattoo. Shove him away and run? It'd only postpone the confrontation. If I dared return to the factory, he'd call me a thief. I could fight, but the result was the same. If I broke cover, it would undo all my work. Nor would it succeed—it had not saved Baldwin. Lascar's narrowed eyes darted over me. He had not given the alarm.

I grimaced at his blade. "Christ's sake, put that away. It's not the other. Let's check this one."

"Not the other?" he repeated, turning his head an inch.

"The thief. Donnelly's missing tools."

He chortled, closed and slipped his knife back into a pocket. Abruptly he asked, "You knew Bingley?"

How had he connected me with my colleague Arnold Baldwin, alias Bingley? To mask my shock I frowned, patting the clothes. "Fellow at the docks? Short lad?"

"Nah."

"Works here?" I nodded toward the baths. Lascar repeated, "Nah."

Inside the second coat were swaddled a pencil, stale bread and newspaper. Rewrapping them, I asked, "Nothing here. Coming?"

"Yeah." He peeled off his clothes slowly, contorting to step out of his trousers. I went to the door to avoid looking at his scrawny haunches.

When I turned back, he was poking through my clothes, grinning. I shrugged, glad I'd left all my evidence with Diana. He counted my coins, weighing them in his mangled fist.

A pair of blokes stopped at the door, saw us and backed away.

Returning my clothes to a docket, Lascar said, "Bingley was a Pink, see. Spying on us."

I feigned confusion. "During the steel strike, last year?"

"Nah. Month ago. Friendly guy. Donnelly liked him. But he was a scab. Got him right here." Lascar poked his own contorted chest.

"You shot him?"

"Nah. Donnelly did. Asked him questions, yanked on him, beat him bad. He begged, poor fool. Blurted it all out fast. He lasted 'bout an hour."

The hair prickled on my arms. I'd seen no bruises on Baldwin's body, but he'd been clothed. I shook my head. "Tsch. Bled to death?"

"Nah. Tossed him in the river."

Baldwin had been shot in the forehead and found at the docks. Why was Lascar lying? Was this a warning or a threat? Did he know I'd met Diana? He'd followed me to her hotel, and now he was telling me about killing a spy. Did he suspect I was involved? Or Diana?

"Why are you telling me this?"

His mouth twisted in what might have been a smile.

"We liked him. Didn't make no difference. Now, what're you really after?"

I stared at him. He knew something, damn him, but what?

I started back toward the line. "After? Work, 'course."

Short answers are cleanest. Liars usually explain too much. He followed, his mouth curled to reveal grotesque gums. I held his gaze, realized he was amused.

Lascar slurred, "Didn't go sso well? At the hotel? Wit' your girl?"

Damn and blast. He knew about Diana. Shock rocked me on my heels.

"Why, eh?" asked Lascar, spitting at the wall. "Why don't s-she want you? She came here, didn't she?"

He had decided that we were estranged. I did not disabuse him of this notion. Diana's arrival had made Lascar curious.

"Wants me to go back east," I said, improvising. "Can't do that."

"Huh. Why not?"

It was my turn in line, so I took the towel offered and muttered, "Why'd you think? It'll land me in the clink! No one believed it was an accident."

He scratched his face, running a thumb over the distorted folds, then tapped his neck. "Have to do with that there scar?"

"Lay off my business," I said rudely. No Chicagoan would tolerate a man asking about his girl. To throw him off, I said, "What's your name, anyway, Lascar? Is that a given name or a surname? Where are you from?"

"Cut it out," he said, eyes narrowed. "Surname? What's that anyhow?"

"Last name? Where'd you work? Tell me one thing about you, huh?"

He moved his mouth around, then said, "Collier. You ask 'im. We was in a powder plant. In Cheswick, Pennsylvania."

"But you've got no full name, huh?" Towel over my shoulder, I headed toward the shower baths and pulled in a breath of relief.

CHAPTER 25

GO HOME

An hour had passed since Tito had gone to find Jim. My pulse jumping at every sound, I waited, alone in a carriage outside the post and telegraph office. Winding my little watch I tucked it into my vest and peered out. As shadows deepened along the avenue, a lamplighter was working the gaslights with his long pole. Chicago weather had turned balmy, so few women wore muffs now. I patted mine, finding comfort in the shape of my trusty derringer inside. At last I had a suspect. If Jim got Bellino arrested and found the ballistite, we could go home.

My carriage creaked as the coachman descended. At my window, he touched his cap. "How long, ma'am?"

"A while longer. We said twenty cents? I'll make it fifty."

He scratched his waist, nodding. "I'm about, yeah? Holler if you wanna go."

Lifting a pouch from his vest pocket, he went off to smoke.

Abigail was following Donnelly today. Tobias had gone to investigate Bellino's factory. Since his dark skin was conspicuous, I'd written out a message from a bookseller to a fictitious Mr. Cornelius Hubb—a ploy to explain his presence on the street. Jim was searching warehouses—slow plodding work, but a methodical way to find the ballistite. But it was taking him too long. Instead, I thought I had inadvertently found it.

I puzzled over Enri Bellino. Was he the head of this anarchist group? An ambitious Italian-born businessman who'd married into old money—it seemed incredible. Another troubling question was that of Peter Dupree. I could not believe his presence at the card game was a coincidence. Was he also chasing Bellino?

Minutes later, the carriage rocked, and the door swung open. A man in a crumpled sack coat climbed in and dropped onto the seat.

"Jim!"

Why did my insides jerk like a box of marbles shaken by a child when I was with him? I was no silly miss, but I reached for him, searching his expression. Despite his filthy clothes, he seemed at ease. He'd washed his face. My fretfulness softened like cheese on a griddle to know he'd cared to do that, so I leaned in and kissed him.

His arm felt dense and compact under his sleeve. All the days behind us faded, those weeks of worry. But what I had to tell him burned in my throat.

"The Cold Storage, Jim. The awful fire."

He stiffened, surprise in his liquid grey eyes. "You were there?"

I nodded. "Were you? It was such a crush."

"We had a ship to search. Bloody captain wouldn't let us board. You saw the men—?"

"Sixteen of them. Stuck on the rim of that tower. Oh, Jim. When they jumped . . ."

I remembered how they'd shaken hands and embraced, then charged off the roof at a run. The sound of it, the dreadful impacts. I shuddered. "Do they know what caused it?"

"They're saying it was wires. Electric wires caused a spark. I don't believe it, Diana. Wires are wrapped in India rubber and stuff called gutta-percha, same as the telegraph."

I grimaced. "Jim, it wasn't electricity. I think it was ballistite."

He pulled back, staring. "How do you know?"

Then I had to tell him about Bellino, searching his apartment, getting stuck in the bedroom, with Bellino speaking on the phone nearby.

"Jesus, Diana," Jim whispered, pulling me close. "What did you hear exactly?"

I tried to recall Bellino's words. "He said something about the Cold Storage Building. I thought he had stock in an ice-creamery. He said, 'only one.' I didn't understand that, but I only heard his side of the conversation. And—"

"It's not enough, sweet. He could be talking about something else."

"But he said the word 'test.' And—something about 'It's near the station. You won't have to carry it far.' He was talking about something heavy."

"Test. Sure he used that word—'test'?"

"I'm certain."

I exhaled, feeling safe as I had the night he'd rested by my side. His tumbled hair, wide forehead and dark eyebrows, his jaw encased in its soft, untidy beard, the crook in his nose from a knock he'd taken boxing, each dear to me.

He said, "Tell me again. Just how you heard it. Tell me exactly."

Sliding my hand into his, I closed my eyes, bringing to mind the cool varnish of Bellino's bedroom door pressed to my cheek. "He mentioned a number, seven six . . . can't remember the rest. He waited, then said . . ." I repeated the rest.

A horse stamped and snorted. Had the driver returned? Whispering, I went over it again, Bellino's irate tone, his insistence. Jim tucked me close. Exhaling, he said, "What were the chances, huh? To be standing there, right when he called on the telephone. A lucky break, maybe. God knows I've needed one." His chin rose in a quick movement. "He couldn't have known you were there?"

"He saw me, but I bluffed my way out. Erminia didn't give me away."

He shook his head over that. "Don't trust her, Diana."

"She told me about his workshop. Fourteen Canal Street. Tobias went there, and saw people enter. It's dark, boarded up. That's where you sleep, isn't it?"

Jim gave a start. "Bellino owns it? Diana, that's bad. What have you told him?"

"Nothing. He thinks I'm here to see the World's Fair. Jim, what'll you do?"

"Lascar knew I'd seen you, sweet. Will you do as I ask?"

I nodded, my chest tightening at his tone. His low voice carried a note I'd never heard before—fear. He held my face in his large hands, his touch warm on my cheeks.

"Leave. Go back to Boston. Take the morning train, take your maid and stay there. I'm afraid it's going to get ugly. I don't want you here when it happens. If this was a test, it means something bigger is coming. I have to find out where, and when."

"But can't you get help?" I cried. "Now you know it's Bellino, get him arrested!"

"Need more proof for that," Jim said, looking grim.

He hadn't answered my question! My temper rose. I tried to hold it in, but it was like a wriggling fish, slippery and determined to escape.

"Jim, answer me. Will you tell the authorities?"

Jim's lips were tight, his eyes fierce. "You're leaving. If I have to put you on the train myself, you're going home."

"Why? Am I a silly nit who doesn't deserve an answer?"

His gaze darted to the window.

I whispered, "Why won't you let me help?"

Jim's hand covered my mouth as he pulled me into a tight hold. "Because you compromise me," he said, his voice low. "It's a choice I cannot face. Don't you see? I'd give up anything, anyone for you. With you here, I can be bought and sold for a dime. Diana, my word, my job, my bond means nothing. You are my weakness!"

"Your Achilles' heel," I whispered, understanding at last how Jim thought of me. It didn't matter that I could shoot, or that I'd brought him Tobias and Tito to help. It didn't matter what I'd risked to help him. He had decided I was a problem.

I stiffened in his grasp, turned myself to stone, my heart bleeding as he peeled himself away inch by inch.

I said, "I'll stay out of this business. But I'm not going home without you."

"Stay away from the fair, and don't meet Bellino. Lie low. You promise?"

"All right," I agreed, feeling weary.

"You can't dress as a boy again. Hear me?"

"Yes."

He'd been furious with me once before, in Bombay, when I'd with-held things from him—the worst three days of my life. Since he insisted, I would invent an excuse, feign illness to avoid Erminia.

"You can't be seen with me, Diana. Don't summon me again." His voice was a hoarse whisper.

I nodded. He gazed at me a long time, but I didn't look up. I couldn't, because he'd see my tears, my fury, my outrage.

"Ah, sweet." He caught my hand and pressed his lips to my knuckles.

It was quiet when he eased out of the carriage and gently closed the door, leaving only the twilight and the lonely row of gaslights along the street. Spotting the bobbing light of the coachman's cigarette, I hailed him, feeling heartsick.

That night I crawled into bed, bruised and empty. Of course, Jim loved me. But I was no use to him if he didn't want my help, and I was afraid.

My fears multiplied: He was hunting desperate men. If I persisted, I could give Jim away. Taking a shaky breath, I considered our conversation. He'd refused to tell me what he was going to do.

But that jerk of surprise. What had I said to cause it?

I'd just mentioned Bellino . . . and Tobias. Tobias watching Bellino's workshop. Why should that upset Jim? It was plain that he sympathized with the workers and their troubles. He'd infiltrated the group, eaten, slept and worked among them. What if I had got it all wrong? Something turned inside my chest. Did Jim not want the group caught? But he'd never condone murder, so why didn't he want Bellino arrested?

That look on his face puzzled me. What was he thinking? When he spoke of Donnelly, had I seen admiration, even . . . affection? Jim would always be a man's man, finding friends wherever he was. Did Donnelly have some hold over him? I could no longer read him as before. This past week I had committed burglary—that Abigail actually stole the deed hardly mattered; it was done at my behest. And why? To right a wrong that the law could not address. Was Jim doing the same thing?

But fire? Explosion? Killing thousands? Jim would never agree to that, yet he was up to his neck in this. Could he get free of the anarchists? If they were caught, would he defend them, stand trial with them? Or would they fight to the finish in some futile act of courage?

Cocooned in darkness, I clutched my blanket close as the threat around Jim took on a powerful malevolence. He'd seemed at his wit's end when he'd said, "It's a choice I can't face. I'd give up anything, anyone for you." That thought chilled me. Like him, I prayed I'd never face that quandary, never have to choose between Jim and something dire, like that conflagration.

Toward morning, my thoughts turned homeward. When Jim was lost in Lahore, cut off by the tribal conflict in the north, it had seemed hopeless. But he'd come to me. He'd walked, trudging miles to Simla, and rescued a band of urchins along the way. That was Jim, the man I married, for whom I gave up my life in Bombay. He saw things through. I must think clearly too.

Starting over, I revisited the facts. The German anarchist's letter—Jim found it among Baldwin's clothing. We had part of it, but someone else held a fragment. And the man to whom it was addressed knew some pages were taken, for hadn't he'd killed Baldwin over it? I winced. So much of this was only supposition.

As morning light crept down my curtains, I considered Bellino. Was he working with Oscar Donnelly? He'd seemed partial to me when we first met in the hotel dining room. When he discovered me in his suite, he'd been astonished, then amused. Was it him, all along? Could he have planned it all?

Getting out of bed, I lit the gas lamp and considered the notations Jim and I had made. If Donnelly was A, the anarchist, then Bellino was M, the money. That left B, W and E.

Against each of these, I wrote a question: B—who brought the ballistite to Chicago? W—where is it kept? E—who will ignite it?

For these I had no answer. Although I racked my brain, I could not remember what number Bellino asked to be connected to. What did I know about him? He lived in New York yet had business interests in Chicago. He ran his business by telephone but owned a disused factory in the city. So, who was he talking to?

Well, I thought, there must be a telephone operator somewhere who'd put him through. As daylight gathered in my window, I formed a neat little plan.

CHAPTER 26

DONNELLY'S SECRET

JIM

I waited, huddled in a doorway, past midnight. Diana had said Bellino owned the factory warehouse that was Donnelly's base. She'd heard Bellino talk about a test, but he hadn't approached the flop in the weeks I'd been here. So how was Donnelly meeting him? Despite all their rhetoric, I could not connect anyone at the flop with explosives, or Baldwin's death.

Hours later, Donnelly came out, walking quickly. I followed at a distance across crisscross streets to a bar where he entered from the rear. I'd been here before, I realized, as I skirted the stinking sewer to reach the Old Times. The Railway Union fellows often met here.

I slumped against a windowsill, lurching like a drunk, and watched Donnelly shaking hands with a bald, smiling bloke who slid something across the table. Minutes later, Donnelly hurried out.

I followed again, but Donnelly had his wind up. As I turned a corner, he grabbed hold of me and shoved a hand at my chest.

"You!" He yanked back.

We stared at each other, breathing hard. Nostrils flaring, the whites of his eyes large in the gloom, he said, "You had me fooled. But why? Why kill Bingley?"

I jerked. "Me?"

It was the last thing I expected. If he suspected me, then he knew nothing about Bingley's death. But why mention Bingley? Was this a ploy to gauge what I knew? I had to get him talking.

"The anarchists? Killers? They're *your* pals."

He stiffened. "They're no killers, man! They just want a square deal."

I shook my head. "It's no use. You just met a bald man, popular fellow—Eugene Debs, runs the new Railway Union. How much did he pay?"

"Shh!" Donnelly flung a look over his shoulder. "He paid, yes. How do you think I buy coal, eh? And food, for the lads. But don't say anything, huh? It's not what it seems."

His eyes darted past me to search the alley. Rubbing a hand along his coat, he said, "You're not with them, I know that. You're not, eh?"

Was he talking about the Pinkertons? I only said, "Go on."

At my even tone, his face split into a grin. "Naw. 'Course not." He pressed a hand to his chest. "Christ, lad!"

"Hold still." I patted his clothes, searching for Baldwin's revolver. All I found was a pocketknife. Slapping it back into his hand, I stepped back. Had I been wrong? Every man at the flop had something to hide. Donnelly had met Debs, but that didn't make him the arsonist.

"What do you do for Debs?"

He said, "Damn it, Agney! I'm trying to head off another Berkman."

Was this another bluff? I frowned. "Berkman? Fellow who shot Frick?"

"Damn fool was trying to help. Instead, he turned the public against us, against the unions! Look, Debs asked me to help, quiet like. I've known him for years, and a truer man never walked. Now he hears the world's anarchists gonna meet right here in Chicago. If one of those foreign blokes killed a bigwig, it could ruin everything, discredit the new Railway Union. He wants it all legal, clean as a whistle. So, he pays me to keep the anarchists close, give them a place to stay, keep an eye on them."

I searched for signs of deceit. Either he was a damn good liar, or he was telling the truth. "Prove it."

He looked at me, puzzled. "You can't say anything, all right?"

"Sure. Tell me what you've found."

He licked his lips. "I don't know who you're working for, what your business is. How do I know you won't give me up? They're crazed men, some o' them."

So here it was, the trade. If I wanted his help, I had to give him something.

"Bingley's real name was Arnold Baldwin."

His eyes widened; then he nodded. "A Pink?"

I shook my head, no.

His face relaxed as he rubbed the back of his neck. He'd known that.

"I have a pal that's a Pinkerton," he said, "Bingley wasn't one of theirs."

I pushed my advantage, to take him by surprise. "You were seen, March twenty-third."

He stiffened. "The day Bingley died. I was with some blokes that night."

"Where?"

"A small job. Nicked some bales is all. Where'd you see me?"

When I shook my head, he cursed. "Collin. Damn wharf rat."

"Was Pierce with you? Orrin Pierce?"

He pulled back, glowering. "You a copper?"

"Tsch," I scoffed. "Not asking who you were with. Who wasn't with you?"

His voice turned flat. "I'm no rat."

I asked one last question. "The printing press, does anyone else use it?"

He'd scooped up his hat, and slapped it against his thigh. Now he stiffened, his eyes wide.

"You know, Bingley asked me the same question. I'll tell you what I told him. Someone used it in March when I was in South Bend. Finished all my paper, dropped the typeset tray on the floor, letters spread all over." That carelessness whipped his voice tight, but he shrugged. "Never learned who it was."

In the wee hours that morning I returned to my boardinghouse to change back into decent attire before going to Diana's hotel. Donnelly had not been worried about a witness, so probably had no hand in Baldwin's death. Why had Lascar lied?

I'd rented Baldwin's room, but rarely visited. Reaching into the narrow wardrobe, I pulled out my coat, then paused. I hadn't had the time to search the room!

Beginning at the bed, I rummaged under the mattress and pulled out a clump of newspapers and pamphlets. Some pages were folded to advertisements whose addresses had been circled in pencil. Laying them out on the bed, I reconstructed Baldwin's investigation. Since the smudges found on Grewe's body were printer's ink, he'd visited small press offices and newspapers. I surmised he'd reached Donnelly's factory because its old printing press churned out union pamphlets.

Baldwin had cobbled together a handwritten treatise from bits of other pamphlets, by rewording a few lines. It seemed innocuous enough, a plea to the mayor to allow common folk to attend the World's Fair without fee on the last week.

A rickety table contained only the penny I'd left there, so I scoured the filthy floorboards, then turned my attention to the wardrobe. In a shoebox, Baldwin had stuffed a fountain pen, a bottle of ink and a set of telegraph blanks. Two envelopes and a roll of lined paper matched the letter he'd sent me. He'd left two pairs of clothes and his thin black coat, underclothes and a pair of socks. Along with clothes, watch and pocketknife given me by the police, these formed Baldwin's possessions. So where was his gat? I'd combed the factory and many fellows' belongings. A weapon that size would be noticeable in a man's coat, and so far, the workmen seemed unarmed.

Reaching into the crease between the bedframe and the mattress, I pulled out my revolver. On a hunch, I slid my hand farther along the crease—to the edge. Blast. There it was, Baldwin's long Colt .45. I set it beside my .38 and contemplated the two. Too large to carry without drawing attention, we'd both elected to secrete them here.

I left seven dollars on the table so the landlord wouldn't let the room out again. Rubbing my scruffy chin, I considered my progress. Thomas Grewe had been killed by a typesetter with ink on his hands, someone among the union blokes at Donnelly's flop. Baldwin had suspected it. His own death confirmed it. Whoever used the printing press while Donnelly was away had likely left the ink stains on young Tom Grewe's neck.

CHAPTER 27

RIGHTING A WRONG

Mr. Fish escorted me down the service stairs with no less than seven apologies, saying, "This is most irregular, Lady Diana. Are you sure you won't prefer to summon her?"

I was sure. Opening a tiny room in the basement beside a door marked ELEVATOR MACHINERY, the manager cleared his throat and said to the occupant, "Lady Diana wishes to speak with you. Mind yourself now, Miss Arsenault."

A startled young woman in a dowdy apron and bonnet jumped up from her switchboard.

Dismissing the manager with a nod, I turned my smile upon the girl who looked barely seventeen. To set her at ease, I asked about the impressive array of wires at her switchboard.

When she'd stammered a reply, I broached my main inquiry. "Miss Arsenault, this is a delicate matter. What I'm going to tell you, I must ask that you not reveal to anyone. Do I have your word?"

Eyes bulging, she "promised."

I told her what I'd overheard, ending, "A few days later, that dreadful fire killed those poor firemen. Since Mr. Bellino spoke about the Cold Storage Building, it troubles me. Do you know who he was talking to?"

She closed her mouth and blinked. A ping sounded, so she picked up her instrument, said, "Certainly, ma'am," and plugged in a wire, before setting it down and turning back to me.

"Lady Diana, I don't know," she whispered. "I just plug in the wire to the room." She pointed at the numbered slots. "Only some rooms have telephones, and Mr. Fish, of course."

"And if someone wants to call outside the hotel? What do you do?"

She pointed to her board. "I call the Chicago exchange and tell them the number."

"You don't write it down?"

She shook her head, then wilted. "The fire, oh, goodness. 'Course I believe you, ma'am! But a silvertop like that!"

"Have you ever met Mr. Bellino?"

She had not. She thought him grey haired and respectable because he was a gentleman and owned businesses. Smiling, I repeated my admonition to say nothing and handed her a coin for her time. She watched me leave, her childish eyes wide like those of a porcelain doll.

I'd learned nothing from her, so I gathered my skirts and climbed back to the lobby. What a dull post she had, tucked away in the basement. At least, I thought ruefully, I'd given the poor child a bit of excitement.

With Tobias still watching Bellino's old factory, Abigail and I took a carriage to the Forquer Street tenement that afternoon, to return the deed to Osain Box's mine. There we found the family much diminished. Collin's mother was absent, but two infants crawled about the filthy floors, while their sick father slumped in his chair. An older child answered the door, face scrunched in suspicion. Abigail handed her the basket we'd brought, bread and cheese with a bottle of mild beer, and asked, "Where's your brother?"

The old man raised his head. "Collin? He's out muckrakin'."

I winced. Hauling horse droppings from city streets kept his family afloat. With his shock of grey hair over a heavily lined face and neck, Collin's father looked far older than my papa. Poverty and desperation did that, I thought.

While Abigail carved slices of bread for the children, I spoke to Osain. "Mr. Box, I've brought back something that belongs to you. You were under, ah, duress, perhaps, when you sold it?" I smiled, handing back his deed.

I expected him to rejoice. Instead, his face twisted.

"Don't want it."

Stunned, I said, "Mr. Box, I'm not trying to sell it back. It's yours. Mr. Bellino didn't pay half of what it's worth!"

He spat to one side. "Is that right? What's it worth, eh? What's it worth to you?"

How often had he been disappointed? I said, "It should be worth thousands."

He spat sideways, a rictus of despair in his face. "You buy it, then!"

Astonished, I said, "You do not expect me to manage a mining operation? I have no interest in such a thing."

Voice hoarse, he said, "That's what they all say! Been trying to sell it fer years—no one wants it."

Alas, he could find no market for his property. This realization did not help our present conundrum. How would my papa address it? When we holidayed at the North India town of Simla, he'd had no plan to buy a run-down hotel. But an old friend who needed funds had persuaded him. Papa was rebuilding it to be the finest in Simla.

Osain's bleary eyes were the saddest I had ever seen, red rimmed and creased with broken dreams. My stomach heaved at my quandary—to help him, I'd have to take matters into my own hands. Jim had been so careful with money, walking home to save the quarter on a hack, darning his own socks. He'd be shocked at what I was considering.

If I were Jim, I'd corner Collin, insist he give up his information. Could I really bully or threaten him? Was I capable of it? I chewed my lip, gauging my own resolve. I'd do it, but . . . could I live with that, the knowledge of my own cruelty? Wasn't this exactly why the working class despised the upper class? No, I'd first try to buy Collin's information.

Osain dropped his head, shrinking into himself again.

I said, "I won't leave you in such a limbo. I'll buy it from you, Mr.

Box. Properly, this time. You and I, we shall have a contract between us."
Jim and I could wait to buy that home.

Hadn't George Abernathy given me the address of a Chicago lawyer? I dug in my reticule for it. "Tomorrow morning, we shall meet at his offices to make it legal. Will that do?"

"How much?" the old man asked, his drawn face doubtful, his shaking hands gripped together over his belly. Was he ill?

"I shall ask"—I read from the paper—"Harvey Payne, esquire, to determine a fair price. Tomorrow at ten? Would you bring Collin?"

I gave Osain the address, and he agreed. Hauling himself up, he supported himself against a wall, then did a curious thing. Wiping a hand on his shirtfront, he stuck it out.

His hand lacked the last three digits. Emotion welling at this mark of trust, I shook the broken member gently, accepting his handshake agreement.

When we left, he was still gazing after us. Although having to purchase a property in Michigan held no appeal, I heaved a contented sigh. I had involved myself in the affairs of the Box family and must see it through.

Abigail was silent as we descended the filthy stairway. She'd been darting puzzled looks at me, so as we entered the hotel foyer, I asked, "You have a question, Abigail?"

She flushed. Crossing the foyer, she said, "You're really going to buy it?"

"I have to. But I will pay a fair price, if I can."

Her gaze sharpened. "And if you cannot?"

"Then," I said, half joking, "perhaps Harvey Payne, esquire, will join me in this investment!"

I returned to the looming question of the hidden explosives. When I'd told Jim that Tobias was keeping watch, he'd begged me to go home right away. Why didn't he tell the police, or involve the World's Fair Committee? Each time he refused, it sent a chill over my skin. Could he really sympathize with this crew of ruffians? It seemed impossible, yet I could barely keep still from the churning inside me.

Catching sight of Mrs. Bellino in the foyer, I sent Abigail ahead and took her aside.

"I am so sorry, Erminia," I said. "I am mortified to have caused you any concern."

She paused. Her face sagging, she confided, "Enri is my second husband, you know. I was widowed young, and, well, I met him in Cannes." She took a heavy breath. "It was just gambling debts at first . . . but now? I scarcely know what he does! We . . . live like strangers. But he's had every advantage. My uncle, Alfred Nobel, provided him with a handsome sum of capital. Perhaps you've read of him?"

I shook my head. "Someone mentioned him, in Europe."

"Mr. Nobel owns the Bofors Company," she said. "My dear, he invented dynamite."

I gasped. Bellino had access to as much explosive as he wanted! Was that how Donnelly's eight hundred pounds had been acquired? I recalled a fragment from the German letter. When the writer failed to acquire explosives in Paterson, New Jersey, he'd gone to New York—where the Bellinos lived. I'd been staring at Erminia, but now I dropped my gaze. This was it, Jim's missing link. The weight of it almost made me stagger.

* * *

Early the next morning, I confronted my husband by the simple process of swaying slowly past the factory where he slept, parading my lovely blue skirt and black seal cape. Soon, fellows were telling each other about the "knockout Jane on the street." Holding my head high, I sauntered toward a nearby train station to wait. Swirling my skirts, I sauntered near the station house, as visible as a red flag to a bull.

It took just fifteen minutes for Jim to appear, hair in disarray as though he'd just awoken. I winced. He'd asked me to leave, and I'd done the opposite.

Acutely conscious of waiting passengers, I glanced at his soiled shirt, torn collar and oil-stained hands. Half despairing, but also amused at my disobedience, he shook his head.

"Well? You got my pals' attention." Glancing at the station window, he raked a hand through his hair.

My previous doubts snaked through me. All along, he'd stopped me from investigating. At every turn, he wanted me gone. A lump lodged in my throat, making it difficult to breathe. Jim cared about the workers, about the cruel hand they were dealt. "The game" was stacked against labor, he'd said, making them powerless. But anarchists wanted to remake the world, and that was chaos. Was it possible? Could Jim really buy in to a madman's plan? Pushing away my dread, I launched into my news.

"Listen, Jim, Enri Bellino is related to Alfred Nobel. He gets a commission on every transaction. That could be how the German bought that ballistite. There's your link to Donnelly!"

Jim frowned, his gaze flicking to the train station. "Doesn't mean he's involved. How'd you learn this?"

He was defending Donnelly! Fed by my suspicions, his words resounded in me like a thunderclap. Clutching my skirts against a gust, I felt helplessly adrift.

"Jim—no. You can't believe him?" My stomach roiled. He seemed distracted, barely looking at me. "You're helping him?"

Jim's eyebrows went up as he said, "We wanted to read *War and Peace*, you recall? Tolstoy believes in anarchism, in individual rights against the industrial machine. American writers too—Emerson and Henry David Thoreau. The lads want freedom, equality and brotherhood. Doesn't seem dangerous, hmm?"

Lounging against the glass, he'd stuck a twig in the corner of his mouth. In the mountains of North India, locals use such twigs to clean their teeth. That casual gesture set me ablaze.

"Have you joined them? You bastard!" I spat out, wanting to shake that cool assurance from his eyes. My blow landed, but for the wrong reason. Jim was indeed illegitimate. Tears stung my eyes. Why had I said such a cruel thing?

His slate eyes widened and turned dark. "People always underestimate you, don't they?"

Bitter tears crowded inside me. Belittled by his chiding, I wanted to rail at him, to smash things. His next words flummoxed me.

Grabbing my arms roughly he said, "Hit me, Diana. Do it now. Then go." His hair blowing wild, his urgent look said, this is important. I need this.

Then he ducked his head and brushed his lips over mine. A kiss—in a public street!

I yanked away and slapped him, driving my anger into it. Palm stinging, I charged up to a hack, aching as though I had taken the blow.

After one alarmed look, the cabbie asked me no questions. Numbed, I slumped in the carriage seat. Jim had asked me to leave, but I'd returned, hoping to bring something useful. Did I deserve no explanation? We'd been speaking in whispers, except for my outburst. What was he playing at? I recalled his glance at the station glass and shivered. Had he spotted someone? Who?

CHAPTER 28

FROM THE FRYING PAN...

All night my head spun with new terrors. Why had Jim defended the gang? Why had he asked me to strike him? Surely he knew I was right? Donnelly and Bellino were connected, and Bellino had access to dynamite. I could not fathom Jim, now. Though it was inconceivable that he'd joined them, his loyalty seemed compromised. I felt eviscerated to even consider it.

Yet I had made a commitment to Osain, so the next morning, I put on a sober grey with white trim and prepared to visit Mr. Payne. Abigail and I were in the lobby making arrangements for a carriage when a young woman in a frumpy bonnet scurried toward us.

"Lady Diana!"

"Miss Arsenault!" I said, remembering her name. "Is everything all right?"

"I heard summin," she mumbled, blushing, casting wary glances around her.

The elevator dinged as it opened to the lobby and several men strode out. Among them was one with the clear, fresh complexion of a dairy maid. His neat derby and suit were unmistakable. Peter Dupree, here in my hotel. Had he noticed me? In a trice I sidestepped to avoid the exodus from the lift, turning so I was hidden by the brim of my hat.

Glancing with relief at the back of Dupree's head, I asked Miss Arsenault, "It is nice to see you. Have you abandoned the switchboard?"

"There's another girl does mornings."

"Then you shall join us for a cup of tea, won't you," I said, leading her to the elevator. Its gold-trimmed mirrors reflected the three of us, standing side by side as though at a wake.

In the suite we took off hats and gloves and sent word to the kitchen for tea and pastries. When they arrived, I poured, making remarks to set Miss Arsenault at ease. She sat demurely in the parlor, answering in monosyllables until Abigail sent her a sharp look and said, "Well, miss. What was it you had to say?"

Miss Arsenault took a gulp of hot tea, sputtered, and dropped the teacup, which shattered on impact. Her face crimson, she shot to her feet and bolted for the door.

"Now, now." Blocking her path, I soothed her and sent her back to her chair. Mouth like a vise, Abigail picked up the pieces of china and disappeared into the washroom.

Oddly, this seemed to be exactly what the girl wanted. Eyes wide, she whispered at me, speaking so quickly that I had to stop her.

"From the beginning, my dear?"

But when Abigail returned, the girl turned dumb. This would not do. Osain and Collin would soon arrive at Mr. Payne's.

Instructing Miss Arsenault to wait, I wrote a note begging Harvey Payne to aid Osain Box and permitting him to withdraw up to a thousand dollars from my bank to purchase Osain's deed with a legal contract. There, it was done. I hoped to buy Collin's compliance but, even more, was determined to set right a grievous wrong to his destitute family. Enclosing the deed to the mine and the registered claim, I addressed the large package to Mr. Payne.

I'd spent too much, more than I could explain to Jim, yet a pressure eased from my shoulders. Some invisible moral balance had shifted and set me right again. Whatever my reason at the start, wherever this road might lead, I had set my feet squarely upon it. Would Jim understand this compulsion to make just one thing right?

To Abigail I said, "I must give you a most serious charge. Will you take this to the lawyer right away?"

"But—"

"That is the address. Quickly, Abigail!" My urgency brooked no delay, so off she went, glancing over her shoulder with concern.

Once she left, I took a breath and turned my attention to Miss Arsenault. "Now my dear. What is it?"

She leaned forward, her previous trepidation forgotten. "Last night, ma'am, I connected Mr. Bellino. I didn't understand it all, but I heard this good. It's between Agney or Clay. They talked a lot about them. One of them's in trouble. Mr. Bellino doesn't know which one. But he said the other fella had to get rid of 'im."

My heart thumped like Mrs. Welks in Boston beating dirt from her carpet.

"Rid of him?"

"Yes, ma'am," said the little miss, tilting her head, her voice taking on a broad accent. "The other man said, 'He's gone a lot, and he went to a carriage near the post office. He was in it for a half hour. Didn't go nowhere in that carriage.' Mr. Bellino didn't approve of that. He said, 'Don't let the boss know.'"

"Agney" had to be Jim. He'd met me near the post and telegraph office. Fear brushed my skin, soft and cold. Bellino was onto him!

"The boss? Did they talk about him?"

The girl nodded. "Sounded like someone important."

"When? When did you hear this?"

Miss Arsenault leaned forward. "Last night, ma'am, past midnight. I've got mornings off, but I came and I waited for you."

She bit into a pastry, watching me pace.

Agney—I had not told the girl that name. This was real.

I questioned her again. She repeated the ominous words in a drawl. Thanking her, I sent her off. Worry tore at me. I'd drawn attention to Jim. Whose attention? It was someone close to Jim, for they knew his movements and that he was sometimes away without explanation.

My head pounded like waves crashing on a ship's hull. Jim was in trouble. I had to get word to him. Through that veil of urgency, something else tugged at the back of my mind, something that just didn't sit right. "Don't let the boss know?" What did that mean?

I paced the room, trying to grasp it, but it danced out of reach like a wraith. What was it?

Miss Arsenault had been sipping tea when Abigail spoke. Abigail's quiet voice had an unusual, whisper-like quality. Had the girl recognized it? Was Miss Arsenault afraid of Abigail?

A prickle began on my arms and trailed down my back. What nonsense to doubt poor Abigail! Yet I could not ignore this. *One must notice and understand the meaning of what one sees*—Jim's lesson. How I wished I'd asked Miss Arsenault more, but she'd already left, hurrying home. Abigail had been gone for almost an hour.

But wait—had Miss Arsenault heard Abigail speak when she was dressed as a man? Was that the source of her upset? All day long she listened to people on the telephone. But I didn't have one in my suite, so how did she know Abigail's voice?

The wraith of my suspicion had not departed, but simply slipped around a corner. A knot began to constrict my insides. For now, I would not tell Abigail what Miss Arsenault had revealed. My hollow sense of loss surprised me. I'd grown fond of Abigail.

First, I had to act on Miss Arsenault's intelligence. Dash it all, how to warn Jim? If I sent a note with Tito, it could land in the wrong hands. But a word, just one word could let Jim know the game was up and whisk him to safety.

Gathering up a dark brown stole and my cream muff, I fixed my hat with a nice, sharp hatpin and made my way to the park. The pleasant summer day had drawn a number of people to the fountain. I waited on the plaster bench for Tito.

Minutes passed. A half hour. An hour, while worry dug its nails into my middle. Should I send a note to Tobias's lodgings instead? But he was watching the printing press office . . .

Impatient for Tito's arrival, I went out the rear gate, where I'd often seen him. Spotting a diminutive newsie in ragged coat, I asked, "I'm looking for Tito. Young fellow who sells cigarettes? Red cap?"

For a penny, the lad garbled out some directions, so, following them I headed down a series of lanes. By virtue of more directions from a lanky shoeshine boy, I came down a narrow lane to a filthy stable. In front of a dilapidated archway I paused, biting my lip in indecision. I needed Tito. As I stepped through, the stench hit me—damp straw, excrement and pungent urine. Grimly I scouted the stalls empty of carriages and animals. Raised voices tangled outside, arguing.

"I ain't gonna!" cried a high, faint voice.

"Fork it over!" a man growled.

Hurrying through the slippery muck, I went around the back and spotted a familiar red cap. Tito's! A man struck him across the face.

I rushed forward, a cry escaping my lips.

Two men turned, one's hand still clenched in Tito's coat. Their surprise turned mean.

"Go away!" I hollered.

"Yell, and keep yelling," Jim had said. "If you're in danger, draw attention. If you're questioning whether to use your weapon, use it. Don't warn, don't threaten. Strike, and strike hard." He'd touched my derringer. "This does not keep you safe, Diana. It's your willingness to use it that does. Stay away from scum. But if you see danger, use it." He'd winced. "And shame on me if you ever need to."

Well, I was well and truly in it. The memory of his voice sent me flying down the alley.

A thrust of my thumb depressed the lever. Gripping my parasol, I timed my strike—I'd swish my blade across the first, then smack the second across the shoulders. That should make him release Tito. I had no time to think further, for I was upon them.

My timing was good, but I'd misjudged the space. The first bloke moved, so my blade sliced through his cudgel, then struck the stone wall, drawing sparks. It jarred me, so I spun, clutching my parasol with both hands, my back against the wall.

"It's cut through!" The man gasped, dropping the butt of his stick. "Run!"

The two scrambled away. Tito sat up, groaning, his cheek bright pink.

Gasping for breath, I crouched before him. "All right? Are you hurt?"

"Nah," he snorted, rubbing the back of his hand over his sore cheek as he got up unsteadily. "They boxed me in, see? Been trying for days, but I's too quick for them."

"Why?"

He gave me a scornful look. "Why d'you think? Made two dollars yesterday." Picking up his battered cap, he dusted it against his leg, then pulled it back on. "Wot's that you hollered? You was yelling, 'Shore! Shore!'"

What did he mean? I'd run, without thinking, shouting "Chor!" which was Hindustani for "thief." A chuckle of relief bubbled up.

We spoke for a bit, then Tito said, "Lady, you came for a carriage? They's all out today."

I checked that my cloche was still firmly on my head. "I came for you, actually."

Flummoxed, Tito blushed a dusky hue, so I said, "Need you to take a message to Captain Jim. Could you whisper a word to him? Don't tangle it up like the *Umbria*! Repeat it now, so I know you'll say it right."

Eyes bright, he grasped the task immediately, snatched up my dime and made off. I took a hack back to the hotel, pondering his nonchalance. He'd treated the assault as commonplace. Nor had he feared they would catch him again. "Just let 'em try!" he'd scoffed.

How little I knew this city. Who was "the boss"? I didn't know the lay of the land, its factions or politics. In Bombay, I'd pay a call to Mr. Byram, the newspaper editor who had his thumb on the city's pulse. I could not trust Abigail until I knew why Miss Arsenault had reacted so oddly. All I had were Tobias—new to Chicago, Tito—an urchin, and Mr. Fish.

I paused. What about Erminia? She cared little for matters of business, but took a lively interest in society and all its gossip—wouldn't she know who was who?

I found her alone in her parlor, looking like a buxom Madonna in one of the paintings on display at the fair. She patted the settee. "Sit down, my dear! Have you had luncheon?"

Kindness is ever my undoing. Struggling to frame my nebulous question, I dropped into a chair, feeling weary and wooly headed.

"I have not," I confessed. My voice thin, I said, "I cannot eat alone, not today. I have so many questions, and you were the only person I could think of."

At that, she fairly shone, summoning Mr. Fish on her telephone to request our meal.

While we waited, I searched for a way to begin. "Mrs. Bellino, I've lived in Britain and India for many years, so I do not know Chicago. Who, would you say, is the best loved man in town?"

Her voice curled in surprise. "Best loved? By whom?"

"The ordinary person. The common man."

She broke into a smile. "Why, the mayor, of course. Carter Harrison Senior. Why he's the man who put the committee together! Oh, how hard he's worked for the World's Fair—and look, it's quite astonishing, I don't mind admitting that! I wouldn't wonder if he's soon governor of Illinois! A popular man—though Enri has said some dealings weren't entirely, ah, aboveboard. Oh, you know, politics!"

She went on, earnestly describing the "useful fellows" in city government and their connection to Chicago's best families. She had met "the delightful Mrs. Ida Marie Honoré Grant, wife of Frederick Grant, who was ambassador to Austria. He's the son of the late president Ulysses Grant, did you know? You've seen the magnificent Hall of Art? Mrs. Grant and her daughter Julia visited the cities of Europe to acquire those paintings! Some must be returned, of course. The rest will form a new Chicago Art Museum."

Was this the same woman who would not discuss money? Waxing on poetic, she praised Mrs. Potter Palmer, who'd led the Lady Managers at the World's Fair. "She represents true womanhood, none of that nonsense about women's suffrage! Women's votes, what silliness. With the Palmers behind him, Mr. Carter Harrison Senior is bound to become president," said Erminia.

Though I'd paid scant attention, I knew much of this from dining room conversations. I just hadn't understood the implications. Now a picture of the factions took form.

I asked, "And who, would you say, is the least loved? The most despised?"

"Oh! I couldn't say!" She tilted her head in thought. "It may be that gentleman we met some days ago. The governor—the Honorable John Altgeld."

"Heavens! That charming man—why is he hated?"

"My dear, he released three anarchists from prison!"

A jolt ran through me. Could Governor Altgeld be the ringleader, the man who Bellino called "the boss"? "Why would he do such a thing?"

She leaned back. "Some say he sympathizes with them, because his parents are German immigrants. But I doubt that's it, my dear. Enri doesn't like me to read the papers, but that's nonsense. A woman must keep abreast of events."

She explained that in 1886 a strike at the McCormick Reaper Works had taken a nasty turn. "They were called Knights of Labor, but I can tell you, my dear, there was no chivalry about it—an ugly business, cursing, beating up scabs—fellows who work during a strike. Workers blocked the factory gates. Police fired into the crowd, killing several workers. That's what led to the Haymarket Riot. You've heard of it?"

Our meals arrived on a wide silver tray. Assembling her plate, she continued. "Armed police, Mrs. O'Trey! Confronting the workers in the Haymarket. Then someone threw dynamite, and nine policemen died! Eight people were tried for it. Found guilty."

"Sentenced to death?"

She coughed and dabbed her lips. "Hanged, my dear—four of them. Another killed himself—a suicide. The rest were sentenced to life imprisonment. Governor Altgeld pardoned them in January."

"Pardoned them! Why?"

"They weren't present! They weren't *at* the Haymarket when that dynamite was set off. They'd written things, you see? Fiery nonsense demanding that workers should take tough action, calling it a class war, violent stuff. But the governor said the trial wasn't fair and set them free. That upset a great many people."

This was curious. In the most hated man, I'd expected a target for the anarchists, but he turned out to be their friend! Or, at least, a friend to justice, no matter how unpopular it made him. Marveling at his courage to oppose an entire city, I said, "Who else is hated, do you think?"

She huffed, then said, "The poor always envy us, my dear. I know Mr. Andrew Carnegie is not liked, nor Mr. Henry Frick. You see, just last year, in Homestead, Pennsylvania, the workers went on strike. They lost, of course, went back to work at even lower wages!"

I flinched, putting down my fork. How pitiful to strike for better wages, then in desperation, accept any wage at all.

Erminia said, "After that, a man called Berkman tried to assassinate Mr. Frick."

I remembered reading this aboard the *Umbria*. "He shot him . . . in his office."

"Fortunately, Mr. Frick survived. Berkman, the anarchist, was sentenced to fourteen years' imprisonment. If Mr. Frick had died, well, that's a hanging matter."

I winced at my uneaten meal, remembering the anarchist congress. Donnelly was quite wrong. If he blew up the fair, there'd be no new world order—only destruction.

CHAPTER 29

A MEETING WITH MR. HARVEY PAYNE, ESQ.

Memories of our Boston home awakened me gently. Lying abed, I remembered my brief domestic life. One morning in December, I woke to the aroma of cooking, eggs sizzling in a pan. Reluctant to swing my feet onto the cold floor, I leaned on one elbow to peer into the kitchen.

Jim stood there in his undershirt, suspenders hanging down over his work trousers. The muscles of his back flexed as he reached for a lid and covered the pan.

Had I made a sound? I did not think so, but Jim paused and turned. His storm-grey eyes found me, held me immobile.

"Oh my," I said.

He grinned then, the sweetest smile. Holding my gaze, he tossed the dish towel over the back of a chair and knelt beside our bed. Inscrutable, he laid his chin on his hands to watch me.

Running a hand up his arm, I asked, "What did you cook? It smells like home. It smells like . . ." I stopped, in case it wasn't true.

"Mmm," he said. "Your mother's recipe for eggs. Acooree, she called it. Onion, tomato, garlic, spices. And eggs."

I gaped at him. "Mama sent you her recipe?"

He shook his head, still watching me. "She served it last year, at breakfast, told me how to make it."

My arms went around his neck so he would not see my tears. Long moments later, the ticking clock warned me that soon he'd leave. I said, "Must you go to work today?"

He tilted his head, speaking into my hair. "Ships are safe in the harbor, but that's not the purpose for which they were built."

It was so like him to give me "yes, it's my job" wrapped softly in philosophy.

But that was December, when all I worried about were the cold and learning to keep house. Now that moment seemed from another lifetime. I sat up, yesterday's fears returning—had Tito found Jim to warn him?

Jim invested so much of himself into his guises that it would not surprise me if he'd developed an affection for some of the fellows. But was he in so deep that he believed in the group's cause? No, not Jim, the soldier who traded disguises with ease. I'd hit him—jagged remorse sliced through me, sharp-edged. Why had he kissed me? Moreover, why had he asked me to strike him? It made no sense!

I completed my toilet mechanically, considering my only leads—the German letter and Collin, who'd possibly helped to load explosives on a cart. Had he found where they'd been taken? What if his bargain was just a ploy? I'd had to take the chance. Once Mr. Payne purchased his mine, I'd demand Collin tell me everything. I sighed—was it worth the enormous expense?

Last evening, I'd been so agitated over the threat to Jim, I'd turned in early. Now I called to Abigail and found her room empty. I puzzled over it, frowning. Why had she gone without a word? Had she heard from Tobias, or Tito? I paced the parlor, then dressing quickly I went to the address of George Abernathy's lawyer, Mr. Harvey Payne.

At the door of a narrow, fashionable townhome, I handed the maid my social card: MRS. DIANA AGNEY O'TREY, BOSTON. Seeing my name connected with Jim's, a flutter filled my chest, as though a pair of sparrows were trapped inside.

Moments later, a lean young man in dark jacket and stiff collar stepped smartly down the stairs. He'd be a good dancer, I thought. His quick, neat steps were echoed in trim clothing, shoes, and a composed manner. Trustworthy, but not ostentatious. Stock-in-trade for a lawyer.

Offering a well-shaped hand, he smiled. "Morning! I usually don't see clients on a Sunday, Mrs. O'Trey, but I'm glad to make an exception."

Was it Sunday? Most people would be in church. I'd been fortunate Mr. Payne was home. After the usual pleasantries, I asked, "You are acquainted with Mr. George Abernathy?"

He grinned. "He's a college chum. We were up at Princeton together," he said, inviting me through an open door to his office.

I sat and broached my question without preamble. "You received my letter? About the mine? Did the Boxes sign the contract?"

"Ah. 'Fraid not." He opened his drawer and took out my letter. "This is a very generous offer, but . . ."

"It is fair, I hope. The mine could be worth much more. I would like a contract of sale. With witnesses." When the lawyer still shook his head, I summoned Miss Sythe-Fornett's cool tone. "Why not, sir? It is my cash."

His eyebrows jerked in surprise. "Of course."

"It is right and proper to sign a contract of sale. Why wasn't it done?"

"Because, Mrs. O'Trey, the men did not come! You made an appointment by letter at ten o'clock, but no one arrived. I was available all morning. Afternoon as well."

"Oh," I said, deflated. I'd hoped this matter would be managed while I tried to warn Jim. "What could have kept them? They agreed!"

Tapping the documents, the lawyer said, "I commend your sense of fairness, madam. You already possess the deed and claim. They seem in order. What would you have me do?"

Collin would have had to work yesterday, since it was Saturday. Had he not trusted me to pay him? I could ask Mr. Payne to pay the Boxes a visit, but they'd never met him before. Poor disillusioned Osain Box would not believe him. No, I'd have to do this myself. Sighing, I said, "No, I shall have my letter back, and the documents. Did you encash my cheque?"

"I did." Pausing, he said, "Would you not prefer to bank it with me? Allow me to settle your tradesmen's bills."

"Thank you, no. I shall have it now."

I'd been too blunt. His color high, he took out some notes and handed them to me. Was he unaccustomed to women handling money? I counted them out as Papa always insisted and folded them into my reticule, pleased to have my funds replenished. "How much do I owe you?"

Holding up a hand to decline, he said, "You are from ah, India, I believe?"

"How do you know that?"

He looked bashful, but seeing the question on my face, he said, "Your messenger, perhaps he, ah, mentioned it."

Abigail would know better than to gossip. But . . . had she gone as Martin? How had she changed her clothing? Perhaps Mr. Payne had asked someone else. My letter mentioned the Abernathys. If he'd checked my reference, why hide it? Did he think I was a "merry widow" searching for a husband? "You've spoken to George, on the telephone? His wife, Ida, is very good to me."

"Yes, indeed! They're soon to arrive for the World's Fair. It seems word of our little fair has reached the great city of Boston." His smile twinkled, his soft Midwest drawl self-effacing and amused.

Relief gusted through me at this welcome news, but I had a more immediate need. Gazing at the earnest young man, hair oiled and parted in the middle, mustache neatly trimmed, I asked, "Mr. Payne, would you know who financed the World's Fair?"

"Why ma'am, the board of directors."

"The members of that board—would you have a list of them?"

Mystified, he went to his desk, rummaged in a drawer, then handed me an open booklet. "The corporation took out subscriptions of ten dollars each. I myself invested, as did many others. Five million dollars was needed, you see. These gentlemen form the forty-five directors of the board. May I ask what it's about?"

I smiled, leafing through the pages. "And each man here has invested in the fair?"

"Certainly, or they would not have been elected. Many respectable gentlemen removed their names from consideration in favor of younger men, you see?"

"Being left off this list did not mean the person did not invest?"

"Oh no! Most of Chicago did. Several thousand attended the first meeting at Battery D. What a day of festivity!"

I pondered that. "Can you think of anyone who wasn't present, or opposed to it?"

Looking mystified, he gave it some thought, then shook his head. "In this one thing you will find our citizens united. On a host of other matters, however . . ."

We spoke for some time about the lack of bathhouses, disgracefully crowded homes and the threat of cholera. Then, glancing at my pocket watch, I said goodbye and returned to the Oriental with my packet of papers. I needed a new plan.

Who wanted to destroy the World's Fair and ruin Chicago? This city had challenged New York and seemed ready to make good on its promise. Could some great New York house have a hand in this plot? I groaned internally. I was fishing without bait on my hook.

Hoping to ask Mrs. Bellino about Chicago's rivals in New York, I took the elevator to her suite. My knock on her door brought no response, yet agitated female voices clamored within.

Mrs. Kaperski opened the door, saying, "We do not wish to be . . . oh! Mrs. O'Trey." She glanced over her shoulder, then admitted me.

Huddled on the couch beside Erminia, Mrs. Yeats bent over, sobbing into her hands. "Whatever's the matter?" I hurried to the young woman, recalling her name. "Katerina?"

She shook her head, sniffing into her kerchief as she tried to compose herself.

Erminia said, "First Bank of Coonsburg has closed its doors. Mr. Yeats was rather heavily invested there."

A financial calamity. Mrs. Yeats cried, "It's all his fault. The miserable, selfish brute!"

I turned to Erminia, astonished. "Mr. Yeats?" Red cheeked and jovial, his thick eyebrows dancing, he'd often imbibed more than he should, but I could not imagine him as a brute.

"Not him—Carter Harrison Senior!" she spat, weeping. "His paper said the bank was 'wobbly and mismanaged' and that's all it took. We are ruined! They said we are overextended in South American mines. Useless mines that can't yield a copper penny! Lies, all lies."

Heavens! I felt light-headed. "And that brought down the bank?"

"It's just a little bank, but everyone in Coonsburg bought in. It helped farmers and tradespeople. Everyone in the town knows us! And now they'll think . . . that we've done something awful. Ben wouldn't buy in South America—he'd never even visit. He gets seasick!"

"So how did the newspaper know about it?"

"They don't! Because it's not true! Oh, that paper—last year they wrote about Mr. Barker's Store, and within a month no one would buy from Barker's! That, at least, was true—Barker was selling used goods as new. But this! They're just making it up! Ben wouldn't lend to the mayor—he's in hock because of the fair, you know. But Coonsburg is a small bank, so Ben said no. And now he's destroyed us! The bank has everything we own!"

Her distress moved me. "Will you keep your home, my dear?"

Mrs. Yeats shook her head, mouth twisting like a child about to cry. "The bank owns it. We'll have to give it up."

How fragile was their affluent life, to sup one day on oysters and scallops, then lose everything the next! Erminia and I consoled her as best we could.

Gradually she composed herself. "We can't go back to Coonsburg. I don't know what we'll do." She pulled on her gloves with a wobbly smile and departed.

Walking to Lake Front Park, I realized I'd been mistaken. I'd doubted those society ladies, feeling belittled and patronized for my unfamiliar manners. But there were tears behind the masks they wore, and worries, and fear. Desperate to keep up appearances, they lived one misfortune away from losing everything.

I'd envied the role of men, their place in the world. But rivalry had them tearing at each other. How could they give charity to the poor or pay a fair wage for labor, when each dollar they parted with might be needed desperately tomorrow? Was this why they lived so loud, drank so much and made such angry choices? Uncertainty led to stinginess, and fear spawned their bravado. The world they'd built had a cold, hard edge.

Tobias usually met me at the lakefront before sunset, but as the light dimmed, birds chittered away, strolling couples departed, and yet he did not come.

Walking back to my hotel, each step echoed with a warning: I wasn't certain of Jim's loyalties, but Bellino was onto him. A whole day had passed since Miss Arsenault heard Bellino's threat. It might already be too late.

CHAPTER 30

LASCAR'S CURIOSITY

JIM

Sometimes the best way to hide is to be what people stare at. The mark from Diana's hand remained on my cheek for a short while, but it drew long-lasting reactions from the fellows. Most pitied me for the tyrant I'd married. Some thought she needed "a good hiding" to cure her of her tantrums. I offered no explanation. Fellows I had not spoken to came up and smoked with me, to share their troubles. I made a show of injured pride, refusing to say her name.

It was universally accepted that I'd left her; no man was expected to return to his wife after such public humiliation. The lads would wonder about our quarrel, speculating whether I was a cuckold, or a gold digger found out. However, they'd no longer suspect I was the "stool pigeon." If Baldwin's killer doubted me, now that I'd become such a public spectacle, he'd be unsure. I hoped that would be enough to keep both Diana and me safe.

The mark on my face faded but the rift between us lingered, like a wound scabbed over which has not healed. Returning with my shift mates, I trudged into the run-down factory at Fourteen Canal Street, my arms aching, my shoulders sore. I rubbed at my sternum, but the ache felt deeper. God, I needed sleep.

A few chums lay on meager cots and pallets along the floor. My mind numb from weeks of searching, I undressed and thumped onto my bedroll. I'd planned another foray tonight. A couple of hours, I promised myself, and then I'd sneak out, see who left the flop and follow.

I'd believed Oscar Donnelly's explanation. Though he'd admitted to petty thievery in private, fellows spoke of his generosity. Who else had his reach? Orrin was preoccupied with the troubles of his large family. Warped by pain and bitterness, Lascar might partake in a plot, but I could not see him creating it, or inspiring the men needed for such conspiracy. The German brothers had neither the connections for such a purchase nor the funds for it. How could one of the new European immigrants be the typesetter who'd killed Grewe? They'd only just arrived. It had been weeks since Grewe's death, but that sort of ink didn't wash easily. If the man had used Donnelly's press again, his hands might yet be stained.

Pulling out Diana's gleaming little nail cutter, I started to trim my jagged fingernails. As expected, the invention garnered considerable interest. First Prendergast asked to use it, then a few others. I said, "Spent a quarter on that, it doesn't leave my sight."

One by one they came up, grimy hands visible as they clipped their nails, oil and grease plain on their skin. None seemed blackened with the telltale letters of printer's ink. Sighing, I slipped Diana's instrument back into a pocket. I'd get the others to have a go tomorrow.

Sometime later, Lascar clambered down to the cellar. He'd woken Paddy with a kick yesterday; I sat up in my undershirt since I had no wish to feel the toe of his boot.

Was he here to quiz me again? If the anarchists knew what I was doing, I'd be trussed up and dropped to the bottom of Lake Michigan. Had they sent Lascar to sniff around?

"You're back," Lascar sneered in his odd nasal voice. "I owe Donnelly a nickel. You an' the missus—he said it'd never work."

He'd bet Donnelly it would. I said, "You're a romantic."

He tilted his head, leering in his usual way. "Boss got a job fer you."

Pulling on my boots, I glanced at Lascar's mangled chin. What had foreshortened it, made his lip curl over his mouth like that? A blow? A fall that took off half his jaw? One effect of his injury was that every word sounded like a taunt.

I did not rise to the bait, only tied on my boots. "Donnelly? Where's he sending us?"

Two lads turned, wary. A late-night task could mean money. Or it could be a job no one would admit to.

"Us? Just you," he said, flicking his hand to exclude Al, the heavy bloke who'd sat up.

Was that twist of his mouth a smile? Threading an arm through my sweat-soured shirt, I asked, "What for?"

He shrugged. "Where'ff your lady from, eh?"

I rebuttoned my filthy vest. "Boston." He knew this already.

Lascar's eyes were alive in that distorted face. "What's her home like then?"

About to fob him off, I paused. His voice held an odd note. In another man, it would have been a shade of sadness approaching nostalgia. I met his lively gaze and understood. He was curious. He'd come for a story.

Sitting, I ran a hand through my hair by way of a comb and leaned back.

Letting memories of India wash over me, I began, "The house is large. Big as a train station. With pillars. The gardens—great, old trees wound about with vines. Wide, shady beds of ferns. More trees than I'd ever seen. And birds. What a lot of birds."

Lascar sat back, intrigued as much as his face could reflect that emotion.

"Huh. How many workers?"

"Including me? Nine."

He made a sniffling sound that I took for surprise.

"Ffff! You worked for her pa?"

"Until she said yes."

"Hah! Her father was thrilled, eh?" His peculiar voice rose at the end.

"No." I ran a hand over my face, rubbing my jaw. The memory of Burjor, Diana's father, was a sharp-edged one, for I loved that generous man. "He told me to stay away."

"When you didn't, rich bastard threw you out," said Lascar.

My throat tightened. I could not permit this stain upon Burjor, not even in my fabrication. "No—he was kind. An upstanding man."

His dark eyes glittered. I had surprised him again. Lascar tilted his head in a question.

"I . . . I'd never known a father. He was good to me."

The other lads glanced at each other. They waited, wary and watchful, a jury of my peers.

Al spoke up, his voice rough. "What went wrong? Why'd you leave?"

No man worth his salt would spill any more. "I have my reasons."

Lascar slurred, "S-sshe came for you. All iss forgiven. Going back?"

"I can't go back."

"Looks to me she wants you back," he joked. He'd seen Diana's fingermarks on my face.

"I can't return to Boston. They know about . . ." I shook my head.

"'Bout the man you killed?" Lascar guessed, his head jutting forward.

The accuracy of his words brought back a sharp memory. I'd not thought of Karachi in weeks—months. But regret and guilt had not lost their bite. Hanging my head, I beat them down.

The Frenchman spoke. "Was it an accident?"

"No," I admitted, thinking about that skirmish in the red dust of Karachi. The sound of mortar shells was a distant roar no one else could hear. But the man I'd killed, who'd come at me, who'd struck a slicing blow . . . I touched my side briefly.

"He had a knife."

"*Scheisse!*" said Lascar. "You killed him?"

In answer I tapped the scar under my ear. He craned closer, then lisped, "Closssse!"

Was it enough to persuade Lascar I could be trusted? Everything depended on it. Trying to calm the banging of my heart, I waited.

A factory siren hooted, ushering in the midnight shift. Just feet away, Al's cohorts stirred.

Lascar crooked his finger at me. Snatching up my sack coat and cap, I climbed over the resting lads. In the hallway I completed dressing, then followed Lascar to the empty workshop.

He glanced around, then pointed with a warning finger. In silent accord we raised the bar across the door, then slipped outside. At last, he had a job for me alone.

Was he taking me to the stash of ballistite? If they wanted to use it, they'd place it in the fair soon.

We set off, his pace agitated and uneven as we entered the street. Abruptly, he grabbed me, swinging us both into a recessed doorway, where he thrust me to the wall.

I stared down at him, confused. He'd grabbed my coat, shoving his ugly face close. Were we hiding to avoid being seen? Or would he try to cut my throat?

Eyes narrow, he slurred, "Baton coat. Button coat. Who's buttons?"

"What? I don't understand," I said. His broken mouth garbled his speech at the best of times. I glanced down at his hand clenching my lapel. "You mean coat button?"

He only repeated the words.

Baton coat? It sounded like something I knew. With a sense of shock, I realized what he'd said, even if he didn't. Pathankot. High up on the North India slopes, it lay deep in enemy terrain. Diana was sending me a message—how the devil had she got it to Lascar?

"Be careful. Button coat," he slurred, his face in deep shadow.

God damn it. My throat clenched in fear. "Careful of what?" Did he know where Diana was staying?

He made a clucking sound.

"So pretty," he said. "Kid likes her. She's good to him."

Kid? Realization hit like a punch to my gut.

"Tito?"

He gurgled a sound that was his laugh.

"My oldest. Hates po-lice."

Oh God, he knew. Tito had been working with Tobias. Did Lascar know what we were looking for? The game was up. When he struck, I'd fight. He saw it in my eyes.

I held back, smelling the apple-ripe stench of rotting teeth. Close up, his mangled jaw a grotesque pink, his dark eyes bore a familiar look. Coal black, a pale rim of iris, lined cheeks in a permanent grimace—he was in pain.

Some part of me weighed my life against his, my pile of grief against his mountain, my stash of joy against his empty pockets. His eyes glittered. I had killed. So had he. If he set himself against me, could I see it through? Or would my body betray me?

He gestured at his jaw. "I warn't always like thisss."

I should thrust him away with one blow, dash his head to the wall before he gave the alarm. Yet I could not.

Emotion twisted his tortured face as he wheezed out foul breaths. His eyes shifted with indecision, holding my life in the balance, and Diana's.

CHAPTER 31

...INTO THE FIRE

Where were you yesterday?" I asked Abigail the next morning. Looking embarrassed, Abigail said she'd visited a theater acquaintance who had a part in Buffalo Bill Cody's Wild West show. She seemed genuinely sorry to have alarmed me. Still puzzled by Miss Arsenault's behavior, I told her nothing of the threat to Jim. Had Tito delivered my warning? My stomach heaved, the product of sleepless nights.

My fingers wrapped around my tea, I asked, "Abigail, where would I find a telephone?"

"There's one behind the lobby, near the barber's shop. Who do you want to call?"

Surprised at the question, I invented. "My friend Ida, in Boston." Had Abigail always been so inquisitive? I had not noticed before. My thoughts twisted back and forth. All right, so she'd used the public telephone. What was I accusing her of? Did I doubt her over something as intangible as Miss Arsenault's fright?

I asked Abigail, "Have you seen Tobias lately?"

"N-no. He's at State Street. I can get him if I dress, ah, differently," she said, and went.

Tobias had called her "Mr. Martin" in the alleyway. I understood that they'd met but wasn't sure when. Why had I started to suspect everyone? Exhausted by the unanswered questions, I shivered, despite the sunlight streaming in the window.

Bellino. He was at the heart of this. I considered how to interrogate him without raising his suspicions, trying out questions and statements. Nothing seemed right.

Hours later Abigail returned, her face bleached against her stark-black coat.

Standing in the door, she said, "Tobias's landlord said he hasn't seen him for two days. But there's talk on the street that a man was killed in the stockyards. A negro man."

Her words jolted me to my feet.

"No! When was this?"

She winced. "This morning."

Was it Tobias? I felt a tremor, like a distant earthquake. Bile rose in my throat, but I clamped down on it. Abigail looked puzzled as I put on a light coat and pinned my broad hat. Despite the bright summer day, I gathered up my muff.

As I checked my reticule, she asked, "Where are you going?"

"The police station closest to the stockyards. Care to accompany me?"

She would. Casting dubious looks at me, she hailed a carriage that took us into an industrial area near the stockyards, where the air was thick with sickly, rotting odor.

"Why does it smell like a sewer?" I asked, holding my kerchief to my nose.

"Chicago sells meat," Abigail explained. "Hog butcher to the world!"

Descending in front of a building marked STATION HOUSE #17, I pasted on a polite smile and stepped in. Conversation halted as the occupants turned to stare at us.

"My employee is missing," I told the room at large. "And you have found a body. May I see . . . if I could identify him?"

Time passed in a blur—repeating my demand in clear tones to different individuals—waiting in a small office—walking down a narrow corridor into a room chilled with blocks of ice. We waited while they conferred, talking as they do to each other when they imagine women too stupid to understand their side glances and mutterings.

I translated this as: *"Can she handle this? Is she going to faint?"*

"Dunno. Who is she?"

Eyebrows raised. *"Some rich woman. Careful, we don't want to ruffle feathers."*

"Okay, you're the boss."

A gurney was brought in. I clutched my tuberose-scented kerchief to my nose and thought I'd never wear it again without recalling this rancid room.

"Ma'am?" called a young officer near the covered body. I nodded, so he folded back the cover, exposing the dead man's head.

The cause of his hesitation became plain. A brutal wound tore the man's forehead. It slashed away one eye and part of his mouth. Where half his face had been, only raw, red flesh was visible, the awful white of teeth and bone. A turban lay beside him.

Clutching Abigail's arm, I whispered, "No, thank heaven."

"Not him, then?"

"My employee is black. This man is East Indian, from Bengal."

The two men exchanged glances. "East Indian, eh? How'd you know that?"

"I lived there."

My stomach heaving, I doubled over. The constable slid a bucket below me, one so foul that it made things worse. Pressing my kerchief close, all I wanted was to return to my suite and bathe away the stench.

To the constable I blurted, "It's not him. I would like to report him missing."

The men conferred, then an officer led me to the inspector's office. The stench was weaker here, but I breathed in shallow gulps, through my mouth. Hemming and hawing, at last he began to write. "Name?"

"My employee is Tobias Brown."

"Residence?" Abigail provided it.

Last seen?—by the landlord. Where was Tobias today?—I said I did not know.

"What's his job?"

"Carrying messages, and the like." My lies multiplied, so I answered successive questions with "I don't know."

The officer leaned back. "You saw him a week ago? Why d'you think he's missing?"

Abigail pointed out that the landlord had not seen him in two days.

"Madam, he's not a slave. He may go where he pleases," the officer said tersely.

I stiffened, astonished.

"Thank you for your assistance," I said, picking up my reticule.

"Not so fast, hold up there. How'd you know that man was East Indian?"

I explained the characteristic shape of his face, the high Bengali forehead and the smear of prayer ash upon his forehead.

"Damned foreign blokes," the officer muttered, apparently unaware that I was "foreign" too. "Like we don't have enough trouble with our own. They take the lads' jobs, what do they expect?"

I let my silence answer, then took my leave. How tempted I was to garner some assistance for Jim, but I could say nothing about his quest or the Bellinos. We returned in the quiet dusk, but my mind spun with doubt and dread. In the carriage each hoofbeat echoed my worry: Where was Tobias? What had I led that poor porter into? He'd been gone two days. Men who planned to slaughter thousands would not quibble at murder. They'd killed two already, Grewe and Baldwin—and now Tobias as well? Oh God, what had I done?

I sent Abigail to ask Tito for some clue to his whereabouts. Summoning Mr. Fish, I sent a note to Tobias's boardinghouse on State Street, in case he returned.

Then I paced the floor in a fever of impatience. The clock ticked, a summer breeze tugged at the playful curtains. Jim was playing a dangerous game, befriending the anarchists. Had Tito given him my message? Had he understood? My gut wound into knots. What should I do? A single slip could mean his death.

At the enameled wash table, I splashed my face with cool water. Dark, haunted eyes gazed back from the mirror. Mama would have been aghast. And Adi, my brilliant brother, the lawyer. The memory of his cool, easy ways drew a surge of emotion that threatened to drown me. I wanted to speak with him, hear his calm sensible voice, see his narrow, intelligent face. How I yearned for the sight of Framji Mansion, to see it in the sunlight as I rode up, to be enclosed in Mama's tight embrace and hear Papa's deep, bouncing laugh. I wanted the cool, dappled morning room, to sit there with Adi and my family and explain the intricacies of this devilish business. I imagined how Adi's elegant fingers would tap the table, telling me to hurry along, while Jim listened closely.

I'd left my home and loving parents so that Jim and I could be together. Now the ground below me rippled like quicksand. I thrust myself from the mirror and paced the room.

Abigail returned, shaking her head. Tito was missing from his usual haunts. When I said goodnight, she nodded, wincing.

Alone in bed, I thought of my ancestors who'd been driven from Persia, land of mountain prophets and desert oceans. They'd left their home too. A thousand years ago, they sought refuge on the heat-seared coast of India.

My devout Papa was always so certain of what was right. He found his answers in our Zoroastrian religion, and often spoke aloud to the thin, white-bearded statue of our prophet. Draped in a long robe, pleated in the sculptor's imagination, with a curved collar, this prophet's hair was ridged with curls, his eyes deep-set. For all his snowy beard, he did not look old, or sad, or happy. His face peaceful, he pointed, gazing upward, one finger raised, looking more like a seeker of divine truth than one who has found it.

An English professor once baited Papa, saying, "If Zoroaster the Persian prophet was so wise, how is it there's so few of you left?"

Papa smiled. "He spoke for all mankind. Are there so few humans left?"

"Well, if your God Ahura Mazda were all powerful, as he said, wouldn't you have conquered the Greeks? And the Arabs, for that matter?"

Papa said, "That one God, well, he looks after them too, Greeks and Arabs."

"But they slaughtered your ancestors! And converted the rest to Islam."

"Yet here we are still," said Papa without rancor, "and whatever their faith, the Persians lived on. I'm glad of it. That old prophet's truth is embedded into their faith, and yours, whether its followers know it or not."

After that the professor said very little. With a puzzled expression, he watched Papa telling jokes and laughing his deep, booming laugh. I pitied the professor as he struggled to understand. Papa holds no grudge against anyone.

We are all descended from someone, so my bloodline does not matter. I thought perhaps someday no one would care about such things. Growing up in India, the old things seeped into one's consciousness: wells that flowed and fed generations, rivers that soaked the sun into paddy fields, farmed for centuries in the same painstaking way. I'd climbed trees older than this young United States and knelt in temples built before Christopher Columbus was weaned from his mother's breast.

Lying in the dark, I longed to speak with Jim. Only he would understand this feeling inside me, half pride, half pain. He'd see right away why it wasn't arrogance but a sense of being linked to generations before. But Jim was locked into some deep game. Turning into my pillow I tried to sleep, chased by shadows that mocked me, amid sculptures with grotesque limbs.

That night I remembered a story Mama had told from the Shahnamah, the Book of Kings. This Persian mythology told of Simurgh, a wise, magical bird who could speak. In ancient times, infants who were not expected to survive were taken to a mountaintop and abandoned there. This was the fate of a child named Zal, the old one, because he was born with white hair. He was found by Simurgh, who sheltered and raised him until he could join the world of men. In my muddled dreams, Simurgh was a dark, mammoth statue; it loomed above me, as though I was the babe abandoned on the mountain.

But to Zal was born the great warrior Rustom, and a mighty dynasty of Persian kings.

Jim had to survive. Somehow, we had to stop the anarchists from blowing up the World's Fair.

CHAPTER 32

A TELEGRAM

Our lives are made of little things. Sipping my morning tea, I realized that much of my sense of normalcy came from the comfort of my daily routine. Abandoning it made my breathing shallow and my stomach burn. Knowledge of the coming disaster weighed upon me, but each passing day also made me question the threat of an explosion. Was it real? My world was topsy-turvy. Jim was in danger. And gentle-mannered Tobias, why hadn't he sent me a message?

Abigail was away again—couldn't blame her for avoiding me, stuck at an impasse, as we were. I picked at my breakfast, when a polite knock sounded at our door. I opened it to a chipper young bellboy, smart in his red hat and uniform, who said, "Telegram, your excellency!"

Amused by his manner, I tipped him well and he left grinning.

Each Monday, I'd sent Abigail to wire the Lins and my brother. When I tore open the cover, my relief bubbled over. Adi's words embraced me as I read:

DEAR D. YOU ARE A FORCE OF NATURE. A HURRICANE. PLUG ON. JN TATA AND SWAMI VCKNANDA COMING TO POW.

A hurricane? I grinned at Adi's expensive and backhanded compliment. But the last word puzzled me. Pow? Was it a town? Why would Papa's friend Mr. Tata want to visit it?

Gathering up my purse and stole, I took a hansom to the telegraph office and cabled Adi back, sending the Lins the same brief note: AM OK JIM TOO.

As I held out my telegram forms to the attendant, I recalled Professor Grimke's pained look as he leaned over the blue writing on the German letter. He'd seemed . . . mournful. Taking a chance, I pulled out Jim's envelope, copied the professor's address and spent three dollars to send him a short wire.

Deciding a walk would do me good, I set off down Adams. At the corner of Wabash a scrawny lad hawked newspapers. The headline said: POW GALA DRAWS GREAT VISITORS.

I stopped, staring. POW? Paying a penny for the paper, I scoured the article. The Parliament of World Religions would open with a grand gala ball tomorrow. Goodness. Representatives of all the world's religions were gathering here, in Chicago? Listed among the dignitaries was an Indian sage, Swami Vivekananda, whose speech I'd attended in Bombay's Asiatic Society. Below his name was that of Papa's dear friend Mr. Jamsetji N. Tata.

Hope surged, a fountain of fond memories. I'd visit Mr. Tata—wouldn't he be astonished to see me here? The paper said that most delegates were staying at the Palmer House, so I hailed a passing buggy.

The tall, elaborate hotel stood at the intersection of Monroe and State Streets. Entering the lobby, I felt sadly underdressed. Even the footmen were buffed and shone to a gleam. Despite my Mediterranean complexion, in my flat hat, modest brown skirt and shirtwaist I looked no different from other young women.

"Excuse me," I said to the balding, officious man at the desk.

He glanced up, then continued to write, saying, "Please use the service entrance."

He thought I was looking for work! I gave him a long look, then offered my card. "Good evening, I'd like to meet Mr. J. N. Tata, recently arrived from India."

As though speaking to someone hard of hearing, he said, "Madam, he's not in. We do not know when he'll return."

His manner astonished me. While the Palmer's molded ceiling and burgundy walls dripped elegance, the desk clerk's cold dismissal stung. What appalling manners! I had ignored the ladies' giggles at my unfashionable clothes and tiny English hat. After my newspaper appearance, dining room patrons had made audible remarks about my pretensions. Now the clerk's disregard burned. Turning away to poke at his dockets, he left me with an urge to box his ears. But Miss Sythe-Fornett had taught me well, so I kept up a steely composure.

Raising my voice, I said, "Will you give him my card, or is that too much trouble?"

The prissy tyrant took it with the tips of his fingers, putting it in a docket like an unsavory piece of fish.

"Oh, do pardon me!" said a familiar voice. "What's this, young lady?"

Hearing the Indian accent, I turned to a white-haired man wearing a tall, lacquered *pagri* hat and Parsi *dugli* coat, his dark eyes beaming.

Delighted, I cried, "Mr. Tata!" His embrace swamped me, his pearly-white coat smelling pleasantly of palm oil and sandalwood. Here was Papa's friend, fresh from his travels, his clothes bringing me the scents of Bombay.

"My goodness, Diana!" Mr. Tata chortled, then introduced his traveling companion, Swami Vivekananda, who smiled at me from under an enormous turban.

"It is nice to see another Indian here," said the robust, dark-skinned sage, folding his hands. His face glowed, radiating a benevolent confidence. An orange scarf around his neck, he wore a black coat over his white kurta and traditional pleated dhoti trousers.

"My friend Mr. Tata says you are married to a detective, Mrs. Diana," he grinned. "Shall we meet him?"

The swami's clear, honest gaze instilled such trust that I blurted out, "Swamiji, he's trying to save the World's Fair. We fear there is a bomb hidden."

Mr. Tata and the swami exchanged startled looks. Then the swami extracted a note from his vest.

"I received this some hours ago. But I do not understand it. Perhaps you can?"

I read the telegram: WHEN YOU SPEAK, YOUR WORLD ENDS.

He mopped his broad forehead with a corner of his orange scarf, saying, "I am to give a speech tomorrow."

"Swamiji, could you not decline?"

Dark eyes shocked, he said, "I cannot. I've traveled across the seas to tell America about India, about Hinduism. I cannot let this prevent me!"

"This is a warning. They mean to do you harm!"

"Who? Why would they stop me?"

He looked away but seemed not to see the inlaid marble foyer. Standing under the chandelier, shoulders wide, his frame larger than most Indians, he'd come to introduce America to our homeland and Hindu tradition. He would not shirk that noble duty, even if it cost his life.

I spoke urgently. "The men who sent this are anarchists, I believe. They are giving you fair warning. When you begin your speech, it is likely the signal for a—an attack."

Did he realize he'd put the leaders of other religions at risk too?

When he only gazed at me with those soft, dark eyes, I pleaded, "A bomb, Swamiji! It will cause devastation. Any chance of friendship between continents would end. How will the world's religions ever agree to meet again?"

CHAPTER 33

A FORCE OF NATURE

Troubled and feeling helpless, hours later I returned to the Oriental. Some complex game was afoot that I did not understand. The swami's telegram pointed to a specific threat—the Parliament of World Religions, which opened with a grand gala this very night. Yet how that wire had been worded was peculiar. "When you speak, your world ends."

"Speak and your world ends" would have cost less. Was it meant to alarm the swami or alert him to a threat? Who'd sent it, anyway—Jim? He'd never deliver such an obscure warning. The swami, Mr. Tata and I had attempted to locate the parliament's organizers, but neither Chairman John Barrows nor founder Charles Bonney could be found. They'd be at the gala this evening, so at last, we decided to alert them there.

Befuddled from their long voyage, the swami's retinue could not locate an invitation. As I rode the electric lift, I pondered how to gain admittance to the gala.

"Your highness." Bowing at the waist, the elevator boy announced my floor.

I returned his shy smile. Adi had possessed the same lean angularity in his teen years.

The boy's words dropped an idea into my mind, a masquerade of sorts. Why not? I thought, amused. I'd brought that crimson saree encrusted with silver-*zari* work, and the papers had dubbed me the "Indian Princess." Outrageous, yes, but it might just work.

Entering my suite, I found Abigail in her black skirt again. She sat up on the damask settee, rubbing her smooth-shaven chin. Her hopeful glance broke through my foolish doubts.

Hadn't she been trained in the theater? Impulsively I said, "Abigail, I need your help."

"Sure. What can I do?"

I smiled. "I'm going to the gala tonight. And a princess must have an entourage. Will you come? Let's find you a costume."

Soon, wearing my midnight-blue saree as an overskirt, Abigail peered at herself in the mirror. As I tucked a switch into her hair, I told her about the threat to the parliament.

"I've never looked like this before," she said, then turned a serious look on me. "Governor Altgeld's opening the gala. It'll be invitation only."

"We have to warn them," I said, fastening my brooch into her hairdo. I gave it a pat and hurried away to put on my own togs. A well-dressed person is difficult to ignore. At the Palmer House, I'd been wearing my plain shirtwaist. Not tonight!

I pulled on a sequined blouse and white petticoat, then wound yards of crimson silk around me. Collecting a set of pleats as I'd done a thousand times before, I tucked them at my waist. Tossing one end of the saree over my shoulder, I secured it with Mama's diamond brooch. Papa's wedding present, a ruby choker, went around my neck. Then I spotted my grandmama's necklace.

In the parlor, Abigail's mouth dropped open. I held up the jewelry. "Too much? What do you think?"

All agog, she took the encrusted necklace carefully. "You weren't joking. Right. Let's have the hairbrush." She pinned the piece into place as a tiara and grinned, "Gotta have a crown, huh?" Stepping back, she said, "Gawdamaidy!"

There was Tito's word again! I smiled as I slid on satin opera gloves, then paused. God forgive me, I'd sent Tobias into danger without giving him a choice.

"Sure you want to come, Abigail? If there's an explosion . . ."

She gazed at me for what seemed a long time, so I said, "You don't have to. I could—"

"I'll come." She tugged on her black gloves and lifted her chin.

Time to make an entrance. Sending the stunned elevator boy to Mr. Fish with a request for a carriage, we rehearsed our steps. "If we don't find the reverend, alert the mayor—Carter Harrison Senior," Abigail said. "Show him the swami's telegram."

Papa would say, "Go to the top." It was worth a try.

The tall elevator operator leapt to attention, gazing steadily over my head on our ride down. In the foyer, guests stared. Mr. Fish lined up his staff and offered me the Oriental's rockaway carriage for the evening, with a pair of coachmen.

At the Palmer, Mr. Tata, the swami and a dhoti-clad companion climbed in, exclaiming. Yet my anxiety grew as we sped down Michigan Avenue toward the Auxiliary Building.

The line of carriages slowed as we neared the crowded approach. By the time we descended and climbed the wide stairway, Chicago's elite had gathered in dark tails and snowy vests, a sea of exclamation marks in white tie interspersed with colorfully clad ladies.

They gawped at our unusual attire. At the door, a sandy-haired official blocked our way, holding out his palm. Mr. Tata and the swami engaged the officer in a quiet conversation.

"I regret, gentlemen, invitations are required," said the man, asking them to step aside.

Abigail gave my name, holding out my card. The fellow puffed out his chest and peered down his nose. "Do you speak English?"

When I stared at him, he repeated, "Invitation, please."

Heat rose in my face. "Who's in charge here? I must speak with them."

"That's not possible, madam. Only the mayor's guests may enter."

My nails bit into my palms. If I did not act, disaster could strike. I couldn't let that happen. Adi's telegram came to mind. He'd written, "Dear D, you are a force of nature." So, a force of nature I would be.

Petty officials are the same all over the world. With a broad gesture, I exclaimed, "Does royalty need an invitation? I'm unaccustomed to the ways of your country."

It caused a stir. The pair of uniformed men glanced at each other. They conferred, summoned others, then turned to an older couple behind me. My ploy had failed!

The couple passed me to enter—neither the man nor his fur-clad wife carried an invitation. The official had not seemed to know them, but they were admitted—because they were white? The mayor's rules and the officials' prejudice might well lead to devastation. Should I try harder to prevent it? Or let their own arrogance bring it down upon them?

At the Ferris wheel, I'd been hailed as a hero, but I'd been dressed like them, in Western clothing. Now I must seem alien, swathed in shocking red, spilling reflections of shimmering light. At the Palmer this morning I'd been too plain, but now I must look outlandish. I suppressed a groan. "Don't let them see you flounder," Miss Sythe-Fornett's stern instruction echoed in my mind, so I gazed out like a duchess awaiting her carriage.

The swami's telegram warned him not to speak. Did that mean giving his speech, or speaking in public at all? Was the gala in danger too? We could not wait to sound the alarm.

I whispered to Abigail, "Shall I tell them?"

She shook her head. "They won't believe you." She pointed. "There's Mayor Harrison. I'll keep them busy."

"Oh! I feel faint!" she cried, reaching out. She leaned toward an officer, and in a graceful movement, dropped into his arms.

A diversion! Mr. Tata took charge, calling out, "Air, please! Move back!"

Summoned by the commotion, a man in dark, tailored coattails pushed through the crowd, his crisp voice demanding, "What is the matter?"

I swung back, recognizing Judge Altgeld's short, cropped hair and neat beard, wide forehead and deep-set eyes. "Governor Altgeld!"

His gaze locked on me, his eyebrows shot up.

"The Indian Princess! I believe we've met."

Papa always tells the truth, the unvarnished truth. I said, "Yes, at the Oriental. But I'm only Mrs. O'Trey."

"Ah." He ducked his head in acknowledgment. "Is your friend unwell?"

I winced, caught in a quandary. Governor Altgeld was a political rival of the mayor. Like the Haymarket anarchists, he was of German descent and had pardoned three of them. Should I tell him about the bomb threat? If he was a part of it, he'd not want people alerted. He'd surely mock and belittle my fears.

Pressing my palms together, I said, "It's a matter of great urgency. An impending explosion."

He jerked, then leaned toward me. "Explosion? How do you know this?"

"A bomb, at the parliament tomorrow! A telegram warned the swami."

Seeing Abigail rise to her feet, he raised a hand, summoning officials.

Moisture stung my eyes. He believed me. He was not in cahoots with the gang. In fervent tones I repeated my pleas to the larger group.

"If this is a prank, madam . . ." the stout official grated.

I said, "Are you willing to take the risk? Last year a bomb at the Carmaux Mining Company killed five policemen. It held twenty sticks of dynamite!"

The word "dynamite" caused chaos. Some officers dashed away in different directions, while others crowded closer. I explained and pleaded in turns, using every argument I could muster. Governor Altgeld's grim look gave weight to my urgency. As the hall emptied onto the stairs, the crowd near us grew dense.

The governor clamped a hand on my elbow. "That's enough, Mrs. O'Trey. I'm taking you and the—ah, swami here to Superintendent of Police Michael Brennan."

CHAPTER 34

ALL MEN DIE

Leaving Abigail to return with Mr. Tata and the swami's attendant, I accompanied Governor Altgeld and the swami to City Hall, where I had met Sergeant Long.

As I followed the governor through corridors and stairs, I asked him why, just weeks ago, Chicago had allowed the World Congress of Anarchists to meet.

Sending me a keen glance, he said, "Mrs. O'Trey, when I issued a pardon for the three surviving anarchists, Fielden, Neebe and Schwab, the *Times* called me an enemy of society. But much has changed since then. Just days ago, Lucy Parsons, the widow of one of those hanged men, inaugurated a monument to the Haymarket Martyrs at Waldheim Cemetery. Chicagoans believe it is better to let free speech have its way. Madam, we need patience and tolerance in dealing with workingmen."

So, Chicago had become a liberal city. I absorbed this as we hurried up a stairway. Rapping on a door, the governor introduced General Superintendent Brennan, an imposing gentleman with bushy white beard and mustache, who wore three stars on each lapel.

Out of breath from the brisk walk, I handed the swami's telegram to the superintendent and recognized Sergeant Long standing behind him.

The superintendent read, then turned it over. "Sent from the Chicago telegraph office," he said, with a rolling Irish accent. He tapped the telegram. "You say it's a threat?"

"It's the time and date! The swami's to give a speech tomorrow before hundreds of people."

He studied me, his gaze sharp. "What is it you think will happen?"

I drew a wary breath, reluctant to reveal anything about Jim because it could draw the police down upon him. Yet I had to warn about the impending attack, without ambivalence, else no one would believe me.

"An incendiary will explode. In a hall crowded with people."

"A bomb. How do you know?"

Fingers trembling, I extracted Jim's translated pages and handed them over.

He bent over them, glanced up, then read again.

"Eight hundred pounds of ballistite? Do you know what that is?"

I nodded. "The stuff inside dynamite."

"Who wrote this?"

"I did. But—" I stopped. To reveal more would place Jim in jeopardy.

Brennan leaned back, looking baffled. "Then you know far more than you're saying. Do you understand its importance?"

I burst out, "Of course, I do! I thrust my way into the gala to tell the governor!"

Judge Altgeld put up a hand. "That she did. Michael, if I may?" He turned to me. "Mrs. O'Trey, this is no time to waffle. Where did you get this information?"

If I told them about Professor Grimke, they'd ask how Jim got the German letter. He might well be arrested. I grimaced. "I cannot tell you."

"Enough." Brennan stood up. "Madam, you are under arrest."

My heart pounded so loud I wondered if the police chief could hear it. The swami and I exchanged an alarmed glance. I shook my head, pleading, "My information will not help you find the device. This telegram points to the parliament as the place of the attack."

"Excuse me, sir," Sergeant Long said, bending to speak into the superintendent's ear.

He nodded. "You think he could identify . . . all right. All of you, come with me."

Surprised, I followed him through a wide doorway into a group of officers clustered around tables. Conversation ceased as they turned to face us.

"Mr. Agney?" said the superintendent.

A tall man came up in long strides, a crooked smile on his face—Jim!

His hair and beard sticking out in all directions, he wore workman's overalls smelling of grease. But his soft grey eyes grinned as he took my outstretched hand and lifted it to his lips. Time paused then, as my relief overflowed.

Someone asked, "That's his informant?" Another voice said, "You dawg!"

Jim said, still looking at me, "And my wife."

He had not bought into Donnelly's rant. He was still on the job. He was working with the Chicago Police—I wanted to twirl around and dance!

Jim chuckled at my wonder. Feeling as though my limbs were as light as air, I introduced the swami. Superintendent Brennan and Jim held a rapid-fire discussion that I could not understand.

Soon we were seated around a long oval table with other officers.

Brennan nodded, filling his pipe. "Let's get started, shall we?"

Where to start? I dug in my reticule and laid the original German letter on the table.

Sitting beside me, as though he were my lawyer, Judge Altgeld took it. Reading, he muttered, "Good Lord!"

Next, I mentioned the fire at the Cold Storage Building and what I'd overheard Bellino say on the telephone.

Jim said, "You heard that before the fire, yes?"

I nodded, then said, "Bellino's an anarchist, isn't he?"

Jim shook his head. "It's not him, Diana. He's heavily invested in the fair. Took on large debts to display his machinery."

I frowned, unconvinced. "What machinery?"

"Mining equipment, pulleys, belts and winches. He's got a few booths in the Hall of Manufacturers."

I wavered, protesting. "But he said, 'It's a test'!"

"I checked that. He's got blocks of ice, stashed in a ship at the harbor. The test was to haul one to the Cold Storage, see if it melted—it's almost July. He'd hired a sculptor to carve a statue at the skating rink."

My mouth dropped open. "Ice!"

Brennan and Altgeld had followed our exchange closely.

Puzzled, I said, "Then it was coincidence that I overheard him at that exact time. Oh Jim, I'm sorry to have caused you all this work."

Jim shrugged. "That's the job, running down leads."

But what of Bellino's threat? Before I could ask, he said, "How'd you get this?" He nodded at the telegram.

Swami Vivekananda spoke up, explaining his distress at receiving the wire. He did not know who could have sent it. While he spoke, Judge Altgeld was staring at the pages on the table. I asked, "You grew up in Germany, sir?"

He started, then smiled. "No, ma'am. I was an infant when my parents came to Ohio."

Yet he could read German. Treading carefully, I asked, "You were in the Union army?"

He nodded, treating my questions as social conversation. "The Union army. President Lincoln's army. I signed up at sixteen."

Jim said, "Infantry." It was not a question. Altgeld met his glance and nodded.

Choosing my words, I asked, "Why does that letter puzzle you?"

His eyebrows shot up. Pointing to a phrase, he said, "This . . . way of writing. It's proper Hochdeutsch. Not the casual way we speak."

"Why does that matter?"

He tapped the page. "This man . . . had some education. University education. Chemical names, their characteristics . . . this is no farmhand. He writes better than I could, in German."

I sat back, astonished. "A well-educated man." Was that why Professor Grimke was so reluctant to write a translation? He'd be a likely candidate for its author. A curious picture of the gang emerged—at least one was a chemist, or a scientist!

Jim frowned. "Don't know anyone like that living at the factory. I've searched Germans, Italians . . . the new European blokes, now, they tend to stick together."

Altgeld nodded. "This style, some Austrians and Swiss use it as well."

Other officers questioned Jim, who answered methodically. Officers departed, and others arrived. Much later, Brennan pumped Jim's hand and told him to take me home.

Leading us out, Sergeant Long grinned. "Get on with you, ya pair of ducklings."

We'd given the alarm, yet a sense of relief eluded me. In the carriage, we discussed what the swami should do the next day. His face tight with worry, he said goodbye and climbed down at the Palmer Hotel.

Alone with Jim, I leaned back against the seat, my eyelids drooping. But I had a bone to pick with him first.

"Jim, I should be furious. This whole time you were with the police? You acted like you'd joined the gang!"

"Diana," he chided. "What better way to learn their plans? I've been with them for weeks, but . . . There's bluster, certainly. After the strike last year they lost their jobs, so Donnelly gave them a place to live. They're angry, sure, but I've found no trace of explosives. They're decent hardworking lads, most of them."

Tobias had called them grifters. I clutched his arm, feeling off balance, as though I teetered at the edge of a cliff.

"Jim, why are you doing this? Why take the risk?"

He winced. "Because of this country, Diana, this rough, magnificent country! It's where we can be together. Look at this new world, sweetheart. We've got to preserve it, defend it, don't you see?"

A song spilled inside me. As before, Jim was doing what he had to. He'd found something worth fighting for: not his comrades, no uniform or regiment, but these people of America. We were refugees of a sort, and America had let us in. In return, Jim was determined to protect it.

As the carriage rumbled toward my hotel, I laid my head against Jim's shoulder, his coarse linen coat rough under my cheek.

"I hate when you go back, Jim! These men are willing to kill."

"They must be stopped."

"If you go on, you could die," I whispered.

His chest lifted in a sigh. "Men die, Diana. All men die. One's life must count for something. Don't you see? This new country—it's true and precious. Not perfect, sure, but here one has a chance to make something, to live free of snide glances and sneers."

His words sent a tremor through me. This was his cause. He had loved India, loved it still, but it was no longer his home. He'd put his hopes for the future into this land, this precarious world of contradictions, of high society and desperate poverty, much like India and yet not, for it was so young. Here, people walked with heads held high. Urchins and liftboys read newspapers and talked about the nation's affairs. Jim put such stock in them. I prayed that they'd never disappoint him.

Jim stared at me, throat working. He spoke in a whisper.

"God, I want to be him."

"Who?" I caught his startled look. He had not meant to speak aloud. "Who, Jim?"

He ducked his head. "The man you see. When you look at me."

Stunned, I said, "But you are him! The finest man I know."

His breath was shallow as he eyed me.

"I want to deserve that. To earn it. Not from trust, or innocence, or your romantic notions. But because it is mine."

He needed to prove this to himself. I groaned at the paradox—to prove himself he might pay an awful price.

CHAPTER 35

TELL HER

Arm in arm, we returned to the hotel. Jim had folded away his builder's cap and straightened up, appearing taller, more military. As he smiled down at me, his workman's disguise dropped away.

Three burly bellboys jumped to their feet, then gave way as we sauntered through the entrance. Nodding to them, Jim seemed at ease. I sighed. What must they think, when I had strange men traipsing in with me? With the threat of an explosion hanging over our heads, the usual things hardly mattered.

Abigail opened the door. Noticing that she'd shed her borrowed finery, I said hello, then asked, "Jim, are we safe here? Donnelly's men could be watching."

Greeting Abigail, he tossed his cap on a table. "The hotel's secure enough."

Exhausted, I peeled off my gloves and jewelry as I explained to Abigail what had transpired. Questions crowded her face, but she retreated politely to give us the parlor.

Stripping off his coat, Jim slumped into a chair. Arms on his knees, he shook his head at me. "Damn it, Diana. I said, lie low. Don't draw attention."

I sat, fighting the urge to touch his hand. "You're upset because I went to the gala? I had to alert them, Jim! That telegram . . ."

"You put yourself at risk."

Weary, I picked at the sequins glittering on my saree. "You think I'm weak. Fragile."

Jim scoffed. "You're one of the toughest people I know!"

"You called me a weakness."

"I lied, Diana. To get you to leave."

I pulled back, remembering his desperation. "No. There was some truth there."

Jim conceded that. "The best lies contain some truth. Diana, you are . . ." He shook his head. "All this, when it's done, I just want us to go home."

Home. Where was that? Bright, sunny Bombay, where one must drench *chattai* mats over the windows to cool the breeze, where groves of banana trees crowded around dancing palms? Or pleasant Boston with the Welkses' children chattering in the courtyard, chasing cats and chickens. I remembered walks along the Charles River, a forest of tall masts creaking from sloops in the harbor.

With the next breath, I straightened up. "Jim, Tobias was watching Bellino's workshop before he went missing. Might he have found the explosives? I think . . . if we find Tobias, we may find the ballistite. Where could they take him?"

I pulled out my map of the city and unrolled it. It listed streets by the waterfront, as well as those near the exposition train station. Realizing that it lacked detail in the warehouse area, I called to Abigail to bring the rest.

She came at once and set the pile down. Jim glanced at her hands, then stiffened.

He turned, startled, a look of disbelief on his face. In one great lunge he crossed the settee and leapt at her.

With a gasp, Abigail fended him off with a crack across his forearm, but she was no match. In seconds he had her up against the wall, holding her by her neck. She struggled, then stilled. Appalled, I rushed up, confused by their rapid exchange, Jim growling, amid Abigail's desperate protestations.

"Stop, Jim!" I cried, pulling on his arm. "Don't hurt her. I know who she is."

Jim cast me a dark look. "You knew?"

"She's Martin Gale. We met on the train. I needed help, Jim! She's been on the stage as a woman. So, I hired her—she's been so helpful!"

Jim's grip relaxed but he didn't release Abigail.

Voice low, he said, "Tell her."

"I've never touched her!" Abigail wheezed, eyes locked on Jim.

He shook her, rattling her head against the wall. "Tell her!"

Abigail flinched. "Please, no."

Inches from Abigail, Jim glowered as though he would read her innermost thoughts. "About your job. Tell her, or I will."

When he released Abigail, she slumped, pleading. Jim glared, unyielding.

I stepped closer because I did not understand.

Eyes squeezed tight, Abigail whispered, "I work for Peter Dupree."

"What?"

It was the last thing I expected; then with a crack like lightning, it all made sense. "That's why Miss Arsenault heard you on the phone, you were talking to Dupree!"

The Duprees knew. What had I done? God, Jim was exposed all along, through me!

Jaw tight, Jim said, "Martin is an operative, Diana. That's the job, what we do. Follow the mark; get close. Befriend the mark, cultivate her, romance her, why not?"

Although his voice had not risen, Abigail cringed. "No. I swear!"

"She was quite proper," I said, then asked Abigail, "You were telling on me?"

She swallowed. "Cap'n Jim didn't communicate. Peter said you'd find him, so I offered to shadow you. I waited in the concession car, but you didn't come. At East Bend I was fixing to wade in, bail Tobias out, then you showed up."

Captain Jim. Who else had called him that? Tobias. Of course! It's what Alfred Dupree called Jim at the agency. It had been right in front of me; I just hadn't seen. Tobias knew Abigail as Martin, the operative. That's why he'd followed us to the anarchist meeting. That look I'd intercepted? Abigail begging Tobias to keep me in the dark, Tobias agreeing. God in heaven!

My skin prickled, sending shivers up my arms.

I glared at Abigail, breathing hard. "Did you tell Peter everything?"

Eyes wide, Abigail said, "Not everything, but enough. Peter leaves a note at the desk. I telephone him. He asked me to stay close for your own safety."

Safety, my foot! I hissed, "You used me. He knows about the German letter?"

Her voice was a thin thread. "Yes."

"And the map. You told him where Jim was searching."

"Yes."

I cried, "Jim, no wonder you couldn't find the ballistite; they've moved it!"

Jim asked Abigail, "Did you tell him Tobias was watching the old factory?"

She winced. "You can't think . . . why would Peter harm Tobias?"

Jim frowned. "Baldwin wired Peter before he was killed. And Peter knew about Tobias watching the workshop. Doesn't mean Peter's involved, but it's stacking up. Did Alfred know about this too?"

Hazel eyes bleached of color, Abigail whispered, "I don't know."

I dropped into a chair, clutching my head—the anarchist meeting, my visit to Osain Box. My interest there had puzzled Abigail. Then the card game—I cried, "You played poker with Peter! Then disappeared during the fire. It was an hour before I found you."

She sat, rubbing her neck where Jim's arm had landed. "Joining the game was a mistake. He spotted me."

"Peter's been here," I burst out. "I've seen him leaving the elevator with Enri Bellino. He didn't see us because Miss Arsenault drew us aside."

"Bellino and Peter Dupree?" Jim sat, leaning his elbows on his knees. "Bellino's a flashy sort. All bluster but no gumption."

I cast him an angry look. "He told someone to kill you!"

Abigail flinched. "Kill?"

I glared at her. "Miss Arsenault was afraid of you—that made me wonder if she'd heard your voice before. You were calling Peter, more than once—daily! Weren't my errands convenient. And you were gone all Sunday!"

Abigail licked her lips. "What did Bellino say?"

I said, "Agney or Clay—he ordered the man to 'get rid of him.' Because of you, spying on me."

Abigail swallowed, her eyes shocked. "No. It was just blackmail. Peter put the squeeze on Bellino. That's all it was."

Jim's eyes narrowed. "Blackmail? Over what?"

Abigail spread her hands in a hopeless gesture. Despite everything I wanted to believe her. She said, "I thought it had to do with a woman. Bellino's wife has the cash, see? Comes from old money. I figured Bellino did something foolish and Peter's holding it over him. Made him pay up twice."

Jim and I exchanged glances. Leaning back, he steepled his fingertips and said, "Let's play it out. Baldwin steals the German letter from someone at the flop and wires Peter Dupree. Maybe he tells him Bellino's bought the ballistite. What does Peter do? Go to his father, who's hired by his pal Superintendent Brennan? No, he comes to Chicago, blackmails Bellino and stays silent. Hmm, maybe. But why would Peter do that?"

My mind spun, imagining Peter's cold-blooded calculation. "He'd need something to hold over Bellino's head. That fragment missing from the letter—might it contain Bellino's name? Perhaps Peter asked Baldwin to send proof—the bit naming Bellino with some telling details. He saw an opportunity—and took a train to Chicago."

Jim said, "Go on."

I inhaled slowly. What would Peter do next? "When Bellino agreed to pay, Baldwin had to be silenced. Did Peter give him up to the anarchists? But Baldwin was no novice. Perhaps he got suspicious when Peter asked for the letter, and only sent part of it. Then he wrote to you as a warning and kept the letter in his shoe." I turned to Jim. "Does it fit?"

He considered it, his face drawn and weary. I wanted to put my arms around him, but now wasn't the time. "Not quite," he said. "Peter was in Boston when you left. When was that?"

"Thirteenth of May. I suppose he could have taken a train the night before, after I left the agency."

Jim shook his head. "Baldwin was killed before that, the night of March twenty-third."

Abigail spoke in a quiet, husky voice. "Peter traveled someplace at the end of March. Rumor was, he had a lady friend in New York."

A lady friend, or was it Bellino? So, we had a suspect, Peter Dupree. If we found Tobias, he might be able to confirm it. I frowned. "You asked if Alfred Dupree knew?"

Jim sighed. "He's sent me a dozen telegrams. I haven't replied. Diana, I don't know why Peter would do this. Can't see him going against his father. He might squeeze Bellino, but betray Baldwin? Conspire with anarchists to set off a bomb? Why?"

I shrugged. "For a considerable sum, perhaps? He didn't expect to get caught. Crooks never do."

"It doesn't fit, Diana. Peter's . . . proud. Stands to inherit Alfred's business. You've seen him—dresses, talks like a gentleman. The operatives grin, but they envy him too. He'd be walking away from his father, his life." He met my gaze. "Unless Alfred was in it too."

That stopped me. Alfred Dupree, who'd been hurt by my distrust, could he be at the heart of this? Jim got up with a grunt and went to the washroom.

Abigail moved to leave, so I snapped, "Sit. This conversation isn't over."

All those around me had deceived me, even courtly, gentle Tobias. But the deepest cut came from Abigail, because I'd grown close to her. I let the silence saw away at her.

She whispered, "I'm sorry."

"Sorry? You need to make amends. Where is Tobias?"

She gaped. "I don't know! God's sake, do you think I want him dead? He's my friend!"

"Get close to Peter. Find Tobias. Find out their objective."

Abigail whispered, "Or else?"

She expected a threat. Was that all we had, after accepting her, allowing her into my suite? I'd contained my emotion, cajoled it and kept it cordoned off, but now it erupted in rage.

"I trusted you! And you used me! Lied to me all along!"

She'd been my friend. Had it not been for Miss Arsenault and a broken teacup, I would have told Abigail of my plan to warn Jim. Then Bellino and Peter could have ambushed poor Tito and Jim. I trembled at how close we'd come.

Our raised voices brought Jim from the washroom, shirtless, wiping his face. Accustomed to guises, he'd accepted the turn in events, but I floundered.

I shoved a hand toward Abigail. "Make her tell us what she knows! Force her to fix this!"

Jim tilted his head. "How, Diana? Anything we compel is void the moment he leaves this room. He works for Peter. He got used. It happens." His hand dropped; the towel drooped. "People let you down, Diana. Can't let it break you."

That was Jim, an island of sanity in a treacherous world. I dove at him and was enveloped in his warmth. My worry and fear, my trepidation and blundering, my awful imaginings poured out, shaking me like a fever.

"Now, sweet," Jim sighed. "This is the job. The risk we run."

I sniffed, then mumbled, "Will someone be . . . this angry, if they find you out?"

He rubbed a large hand down my back. "Worse."

Abigail said, in a low voice, "I'm truly sorry. I'll help."

Was she genuine? I hiccupped, glancing back at her.

Abigail groaned in remorse. "I didn't know about the explosives. When you showed me that German letter, I nearly choked. Peter took me for a fool. All this time it's stuck in my craw."

I brushed my knuckles across my cheeks, frowning. How could I trust her again, when she'd nearly cost Jim's life?

Looking from Jim to me, voice rough, she said, "What I told you, most was true. That's how I came to it, from the theater. I was found out, once before. The man I was with called me 'spawn of the devil'! He hit me, cursing, kicking. Broke three ribs. Alfred Dupree hauled him off me."

That image sent a tremor through me. How little I knew of her sad life. I'd guessed at her loneliness, but the cruel reality was worse. She'd offered quiet aid and sound advice at every turn. At the turnstiles she'd taught me the intonations of different accents. We'd been so easy together, until Miss Arsenault's strange reaction.

Now she whispered, "You kept me on, even after you knew."

Her friendship had been true. Those doubtful glances—had she been conflicted? I drew a breath. If she helped, then we might yet best Bellino's gang. Reading Jim's answer in his glance, I said cautiously, "Please. Make this right. Find Tobias."

In a short while we came to an agreement. Under the guise of reporting in, Abigail would plumb Peter. Jim would return to secure the venue where the parliament was to be held.

I said, "I'll ask Tito if he's seen Peter with anyone. Resourceful little chap. Did you understand my message?"

Jim hesitated.

"Tito didn't warn you?"

When I explained my code words, a line between his brows deepened. "Diana, you cannot speak with Tito. He knows Lascar."

His words punched the air from my lungs.

"Lascar, that twisted man? Tito's a friend of his? God, Jim!"

Jim reassured me. "We've got a wide net now. You heard me ask the swami to speak last? That gives us time. We'll search the place tonight, get men around the building, in the audience." He took my hand, ran his thumb over my fingers. "This is good, Diana. Gives us a target, somewhere to focus our attention. It's been hopeless—trying to search the city, policing six hundred and ninety acres. A monstrous job."

I said, "I can help. At the parliament . . ."

"No," he said flatly. "I ask only one thing, Diana. Stay alive. As long as you live, we can go home." Turning to Abigail, he jerked his head. "A word with you?"

That night I lay awake thinking of what I'd told Abigail and when it likely reached Peter's ears. When Jim first came to me for the German letter, that's when Abigail learned about the ballistite. Jim had recognized her as Martin, jumped at her. Was it from jealousy? Or because he feared the Duprees had planted her in my company.

I quailed at the thought. That would mean that the anarchists knew who he was all along. But . . . then they'd have confronted him, perhaps even killed him, like poor Arnold Baldwin.

But . . . they hadn't caught Jim. That meant though Donnelly's group suspected a spy was among them, they didn't know who it was. With a sense of wonder, I realized that Peter must not have known that Jim was with the union gang. Even then, Abigail hadn't told him everything.

Did that mean Abigail wanted to protect Jim? She'd known him as her colleague in Boston. When I spoke of the threat to Jim, she'd been aghast—hands fisted at her sides, gripped by some strong emotion. Was she furious with Peter, or fearful for Jim?

Beside me, my husband slept the deep, soundless sleep that blesses only children and travelers returning from long voyages.

CHAPTER 36

THE SPARK

JIM

Sometime that night I left Diana asleep and returned to duty. Before dawn, Brennan's team and Sergeant Long secured the venue for the Parliament of World Religions. We explored every inch of the Auxiliary Building and posted constables at vantage points and along the way.

Returning just past eight, I thanked Sergeant Long for the ride and climbed down from his trap, a dull ache spreading from my knee. At the Oriental, the hotel detective came up fast, but I met his look evenly and he held back. The manager gave me a sharp look, then recognized me and waved him off.

Since the fair's opening, Chicago's police had grown weary, exhausted by repeated alarms, threats of fire and storms that downed electrical wires. One tore away the large, tethered balloon and threatened to topple the Ferris wheel, but it stood firm. Swamped by gargantuan crowds, twice, police barely averted a stampede. Pickpockets roamed at will, taking what they could. Three hundred Pinkertons had been hired to mingle with the crowds. Columbian guards in uniform did little more than reassure fairgoers with a visible presence—their main task was to holler out when a terrified child got separated from its mother. We had near on seven hundred acres to police.

And Diana—who'd have imagined it? Brought up in tropical splendor in the arms of a doting family, educated to be the wife of a statesman, she'd followed me into this messy business. What was it about her that lifted my spirits? Her grin, her offhand reflections, her fervor and staunch defense . . .

Diana opened the door, her eyes like brown velvet in the sun. "Goodness. You need to clean up. Come, have some breakfast."

The table bore a dozen plates, piled high. The aroma set my stomach growling. Smiling, Diana handed me a plate. While I devoured a pile of eggs and dainty sausages, she pleaded to come to the parliament.

I chewed, sighing. If I refused, she would come anyway; then I'd have even less chance of protecting her. Reluctantly, I agreed. It was goddamn insanity, but she could identify some of this vicious crowd. God knows we needed all the help we could get.

Running a hand over my stubble, I took in her black silk skirt and tiny navy-blue coat. A bit of gold sparkled in the white flounces at her throat.

"Come on," she said, heading to her bedchamber, where a row of trunks lined the windows.

On the bed, a dark morning coat and pipes were laid out—starched white shirt, collar and cuffs, silver links inserted. Burgundy vest, tie and kerchief. Black silk top hat. Fresh stockings and garters. Clean underclothes. A pair of shiny patent leather shoes on the floor. On the side table was the pocketbook I'd left in Boston. And my wedding ring.

I kissed her, putting my heart into it. When I let her go at last, cheeks rosy, she turned away, grinning. "Phew, have a bath, young man!"

Half an hour later, spruced up nicely, we rode to the parliament in fine fettle. The World's Congress Auxiliary Building on Michigan Avenue was already bustling with visitors. A tall neoclassical building, it had five arches and a Romanesque frieze on top. We descended from our carriage, catching stares, and no wonder. Peeking up at me, Diana's smile blazed. Her fingertips on my sleeve were light as the touch of a butterfly. I felt like a prince, escorting her toward a wide spread of stairs.

Diana gazed upward at imposing white columns.

"Is this also made of wood and plaster?"

I grinned. "Stone and granite, my dear. This one's built to last. What a grand effort, Diana, what achievement. Someday, every city could look like this."

We'd stationed thirty fellows around the place. If any of the gang showed up, we'd spot them. Ever since Donnelly had let me into his circle, I'd buddied up with each in turn, trying to learn their secrets. There were many I did not know well. It would take months to do that, years even.

To examine the perimeter, I led Diana down the sidewalk. Why was it that with her beside me, I wanted to share my every thought? I said, "This will attract the city's notable families."

"A good target for anarchists," she said, her mouth sour.

"This fair has changed things. Did you notice the visitors? They come in their Sunday best—could be farmers, lads I worked with, machinists, factory hands even. They're proud to come, show their wives this marvel. They'll go back and talk about it in their pubs. Maybe they'll fish out a fiver to build a library in their town."

Diana looked doubtful. "They wouldn't let me in the gala last night. Only invitees allowed—rich old men and their wives. All white. A closed club, Jim. I doubt any regular folks were there."

Her tone surprised me. Ahead, someone in a brown coat turned and disappeared behind the bandstand. Frowning, I picked up my pace, forcing Diana to run alongside.

She went on in a rush. "Certainly, it looks nice. But it's not so good on the inside. A Bengali man was killed, did you know? A laborer in the stockyards. Beaten to death, Jim! And Xi and Pia couldn't buy their store because they're Chinese. The owner insulted them and turned them out."

Diana's fierceness held a distraught note   but I dared not pause, not now. Crossing the bandstand, I found no sign of brown-coat. I turned, searching. The tree line looked clear, but he could still be nearby.

To Diana I said, "No place is perfect, but this will do, sweet. It will get better."

She was quiet as we returned to the hall. Choosing seats at the end of a row, we sat, giving Diana a chance to catch her breath. The hall filled. A constable posted at the door met my gaze and nodded. We were prepared.

"Look." Diana showed me her program. "The swami's to speak before luncheon."

I read: SWAMI VIVEKANANDA OF THE RAM KRISHNA MISSION, REPRE-SENTING THE ANCIENT HINDU TRADITION OF BRAHMO SAMAJ AND THE COUNTRY OF INDIA. I recalled the swami's telegram: *When you speak, your world ends.*

It is not easy to time an explosion. Someone must give the signal. We'd planted armed constables along the perimeter to watch who entered or left. Despite the large audience, sergeants kept the outer corridors clear. With a whispered word to Diana, I left to circle the hall.

The audience applauded as the aged president of the parliament opened the event. I paid no heed to the speeches—Diana would tell me word for word, no doubt. Instead, I leaned against a pillar and scoured the crowded scene. One man and a weapon, that was all it took.

The next speaker was an elderly rabbi, who tottered as he got up. Others hurried to his aid. During the delay, a few men headed toward the public conveniences at the rear.

As the rabbi intoned a prayer, I caught a glimpse of the hatless man in that familiar brown coat. He retreated toward the stairs at the back of the room.

I loped after him, smiling to calm the civilians. Sergeant Long, who had control of the rear section, raised his eyebrows. I flicked a finger at him, pointed upward, and increased my pace. Long was too far away.

Running up to the mezzanine floor, brown-coat flung back a look. I recognized him—Paddy Prendergast. A bony Irish bloke, he ran mes-sages for Donnelly but didn't live at the flop. He'd grumbled once about something the mayor owed him.

The mezzanine surrounded the hall, its balcony running along the perimeter, open to the audience below. Would Prendergast watch the speakers from the mezzanine? It was empty.

Ducking back into the stairwell, I hurried on. At the top, it opened onto the roof-walk. Bloody hell!

I peered out from the open hatch, but an overhang obscured my sight.

Blast. I'd have to venture out not knowing where he was. He could be alone on the roof, but I had no way to tell. Once I pulled myself through, I'd be visible. Throat dry, I listened.

From below came a shower of scattered applause. The wind blew stray notes from the distant bandstand. Which way? I searched the empty roof, where a covey of pigeons fussed.

Below me, the roof protruded to an edge, but above, its long spine ran the length of the building. I'd have to climb over that to see the opposite slope. A pigeon fluttered away as I hauled myself up, groaning from the weight on my bent knee.

I could ill afford to take in the view. Crouching, I scrambled up the slope, wind buffeting my ears. My boots clattered on the tiles—I could not help that. Speed was everything.

As I reached the pinnacle, a shout rang out. On the downslope before me, two hatless figures stooped over something. They'd seen me. The wind snatching at my clothes, I climbed over the highest point. The men bent closer. They spotted me. Blast.

Struggling against a downdraft, I hammered toward them, pain pulsing through my knee. One man turned, kneeling, and pointed a weapon.

Damn! I dropped to the roof, my hands breaking my fall. My palms stung but I could spare no time for them. The gunshot registered only after I'd crouched and lunged forward again.

Coats flapping, they backed away as I dropped beside a pair of cartons. For a second, I thought they'd shoot. My hand reached for the .38 inside my vest.

Near my knee, a short fuse sputtered. No wonder they didn't shoot.

I yanked it out and looked up. Paddy and his friend were gone.

Only then did I notice the smell, as I drew in the acrid stench of oil and burning fuse. The wind whipped at my face. I'd lost my hat.

My singed palm tingled. Breathing hard, I glanced down at myself to see whether I'd been shot. Diana would have been furious. Relieved, I checked the crates, satisfied myself they were intact, then with a groan, I limped toward the hatch where the two fellows had disappeared.

CHAPTER 37

THE SWAMI SPEAKS

During the morning's discourse, I caught occasional glimpses of Jim in the vast hall. On the dais, the swami's orange scarf and white turban stood out among the sober churchmen. However, when it was his turn to speak, he joined his hands and deferred it until later. Other speakers smiled, thinking him beset by stage fright.

I sighed in relief—he was keeping to our plan.

Jim did not return during the break for luncheon, but Sergeant Long brought me a plate of sandwiches, smiled at my gratitude and departed. Watching the speakers, I realized that I was looking at India's future. I was now in a country that had succeeded where India had failed. America had shed Britain's yoke in 1776, which had probably stiffened the crown's resolve to keep her largest colony, India.

Was that why our Sepoy Mutiny of 1857 had failed? If those revolutionaries had succeeded, would they be here among these statesmen and leaders? Already some Indians like Mr. Tata had built domestic enterprises, but to govern India today, I thought sadly, one had to be a well-connected, white male and "the right sort."

The speaker's voice droned on. My thoughts turned to Tobias. Where was he? Did he have a family? A sweet breeze slipped through the archway to caress my brow.

The chair beside me creaked with sudden weight, jolting me.

I turned, expecting Jim. Instead, a burly broad-faced man grinned at me.

"Sir," I said, "this seat is taken—"

Perspiring, his thick neck bulging around a tight collar, he interrupted. "Princess, Chicago is finished. We are the spark to set it alight!"

Alight? I gaped as his words sank in. Before I could raise an alarm, he hopped from the seat and sauntered through the archway. The brazen cheek of it, the utter gall! I scrambled up, and waved to the nearest policeman. As Sergeant Long approached, I pointed. "He knew. Stop him! Big man in a dark coat."

Drat! That described half the men in the room. As we hurried out, I repeated the anarchist's words to the astonished sergeant.

Outside, a few vendors manned their carts, serving refreshments. I peered at tradesmen and customers. The thickset man had vanished like a ghost, a figment of my daydream. I remembered a bead of sweat on his temple, the spikes of greying hair. Who was he? Why had he warned me?

The day's speeches had almost ended when I spotted Jim and made my way over.

"It's all right," he said, answering my look. I told him about the stranger in a whisper, describing his build, and features.

He listened, still searching the room. "His coat. Was it brown?"

I shook my head, trying to remember. "Dark. Black. I don't know. Jim, he seemed pleased with himself. Smiling, cock-a-hoop, sitting right beside me."

The audience crowded to either side, blocking the archways. If the hall had been full before, now almost no standing room remained. I took in Jim's shuttered, watchful look, and for a moment I did not know him. The arm that brushed my shoulder was coiled tight, as though he might leap forward in an instant. Never still, his eyes flickered over the hall.

I bit my lips as the last speaker, Swami Vivekananda, stepped forward to the podium. A broad-shouldered young man in saffron robes, his large white turban sat high on his wide forehead. A long pause followed as he faced the sea of upturned faces.

People glanced at each other. "Why doesn't he speak?" "Does he speak English?"

Spreading his arms, hands open wide, the swami's deep voice filled the hall. "Sisters and brothers of America!"

Silence. I clung to Jim's rigid arm, my body tight like a trunk packed until its hinges would split. Was this the anarchists' signal?

The hall erupted in cheers. Shouts, cries of welcome resounded. The audience, as one, rose to its feet. All afternoon they'd listened to a long line of venerable speakers and fine, erudite arguments. Many of these had been barely audible. Now the swami's deep baritone closed the distance between him and his audience.

When the din died down, he said, "It fills my heart with joy unspeakable to rise in response to the warm and cordial welcome which you have given us. I thank you in the name of the millions and millions of Hindu people of all classes and sects."

I glanced around. Nothing happened. No flash of light, no crack of thunder, no explosion. I drew a wobbly breath, noting Jim's close attention as the swami spoke.

He said, "I am proud to belong to a religion which has taught the world both tolerance and universal acceptance. We believe not only in universal toleration, but we accept all religions as true. I am proud to belong to a nation which has sheltered the persecuted and the refugees of all religions and all nations of the earth. I am proud to tell you that we have gathered in our bosom the purest remnant of the Israelites, who came to southern India and took refuge with us in the very year in which their holy temple was shattered to pieces by Roman tyranny. I am proud to belong to the religion which has sheltered and is still fostering the remnant of the grand Zoroastrian nation. The present convention, which is one of the most august assemblies ever held, is in itself a vindication, a declaration to the world, of the wonderful doctrine preached in the Gita: Whosoever comes to Me, through whatsoever form, I reach him; all men are struggling through paths which in the end lead to me."

The young monk went on, ending, "I fervently hope that the bell that tolled this morning in honor of this convention may be the death knell of all fanaticism, of all persecutions with the sword or with the pen and of all uncharitable feelings between persons wending their way to the same goal."

No one spoke, the vast audience in the grip of his rousing words. Then a volcano of applause poured forth. Lit by his openness, his brilliant smile, the audience cheered him wildly.

I glanced at Jim. His face! He turned to me, eyes shining, unashamed of his tears. "*This,* Diana!" he said, his voice thick. "This is why. Look. Listen."

The roar of the crowd went on and on. Applause cascaded across the cavernous hall; people shaking hands, smiling. Later, I'm told, they could not recall why they did so. Perhaps the swami reminded them of something, the simple joy of being human, talking without artifice to one another. I watched, astonished, and understood. This was why my Jim loved these strange, driven, yet openhearted Americans.

* * *

"We found two boxes of ballistite on the roof, with a detonator," Jim told me after the swami's speech. "It wasn't there just hours ago, but somehow they'd hauled it up. How the blazes did they get through us? We had constables everywhere."

A knot of people clustered around the swami, shaking his hand. He had introduced America to Hinduism and the wisdom of Vedanta, and they embraced him joyfully.

Grinning with pride, Mr. Tata waved me to the front. After I introduced Jim, he took my husband's hand in both of his.

"Yes, now I see," he said, smiling at me. "My dear girl, I understand it now. Poor Soli Wadia. No matter how many ships he built, he didn't have a chance, did he, Diana girl?" Mr. Tata chuckled, evidently pleased at the report he'd make to my papa.

I giggled at his nonsense, at home again for that sweet moment. The son of Papa's ship-building friend, Soli Wadia, had been a very attentive beau. But no, once I'd met Jim, there was no one else for me. Soli had business interests in Boston, so we'd spoken a few times before I left Bombay—he'd been gracious about it all, a good friend. Tucked against Jim, my hand in the crook of his arm, I was the happiest I'd been in weeks.

Watching the swami's glowing smile, how he greeted each person with such modesty and goodwill, still I worried. "Will he be all right? That telegram threatened him specifically."

Jim nodded. "We've got officers around him at all times."

"Look. That's Mr. Potter Palmer," Mr. Tata said, pointing, as he named the dignitaries on the stage. "That's Mr. Carter Harrison of the *Chicago Times*."

"Jamsetji, he's the mayor of Chicago."

"This is his son, the editor. His father, the mayor, owns the newspaper."

So much for an independent press! Staring at the handsome middle-aged man, I leaned back to tell Jim, "His father is engaged to a New Orleans heiress. His sons don't approve, so the rumor goes."

Jim frowned. "Why?"

Trying to recall Erminia's gossip, I said, "Some bad blood between them. The deal might bring capital to the Harrisons, but also a new heir."

"Huh," Jim said, a dark look crossing his face. "Is that what this is all about? Getting rid of the father?"

Eventually the dignitaries departed. We followed the crowd down Michigan Avenue toward the waiting carriages. They lined the street, three deep in places, others locked so close that coachmen yelled at each other, swearing. It would be at least an hour before the tangle moved freely.

As we walked, I told Mr. Tata about the cheeky fellow who'd surprised me.

Jim seethed. "Blast. They're sending a message. For me." He glanced over his shoulder.

"The anarchists have grandiose plans," I mused, patting his arm, "but someone had to provide capital. That brute said, 'Chicago is finished.' That's a strange way to put it. Chicago's elite have staked their reputations on the fair. Who'd want it to fail?"

"France would be quite pleased," Mr. Tata said calmly. "It hosted the previous World's Fair. You've seen the Eiffel Tower, Diana?"

"Yes, with my friend Emily-Jane and her parents in '90."

"Chicago's put up such a good show—France's fair looks puny! At the Palmer House, Diana, the French ambassador was quite dismal about it. 'Course, no government would sanction arson. Not officially."

"Hmm," Jim said, his voice quiet. "And unofficially?"

Mr. Tata shrugged. "It would have to be proven, of course."

How curious. We were playing the sort of game that Jim and I used to, aboard the *Umbria,* guessing who might benefit from a disaster.

I said, "Chicago outbid New York, remember? So, if the fair is ruined, New York or Boston could say, 'These clumsy Westerners can't do anything right.' Wouldn't that hurt Chicago's business?"

I recalled the list of directors that Harvey Payne had given me. "Most of the city's millionaires have capital in it. The exposition's forty-five members—they could go broke!"

Mr. Tata frowned. "Why would someone bankrupt them?"

Jim shrugged. "Maybe it's just one they want to break. People form grudges when they lose their livelihood. Factory owners have enemies." Smiling sweetly, he squeezed my hand. "It's a good thing we'll never be rich."

I gave his arm an irate tug, which drew a chuckle from him.

Mr. Tata said, "Capitalism requires competition. But has the competition become too intense?" His voice dropped in thought. "Is greed driving people mad?"

I asked, "If the fair's directors lose their capital, who benefits, Jim?"

He grimaced. "Competitors, I suppose. And bankers. J. Pierpont Morgan runs the East Coast banks. If midwestern states lost their capital, industry would have nowhere else to turn. Morgan would benefit."

A chill touched my back that had nothing to do with the evening breeze.

"Hoy!" Jim hailed an open-top hansom. I dropped onto the seat, grateful to be off my feet. With a relieved smile, Mr. Tata mopped his forehead with a snowy white kerchief.

"Is he here?" I asked Jim. "Mr. Morgan? If he's at the fair, then he can't be planning to destroy it."

"Yes, he's expected," Jim said, with a fond look. "The arrangements are a nightmare for Chicago's police."

Mr. Tata smiled, gazing out at the street to give us a moment together.

"My dear," said Jim, "other battles are being fought too. Mr. Edison, the inventor from New Jersey, made a bid to use direct current at this fair, but the commissioners chose his rival, Nikola Tesla, an immigrant. So, alternating current carried the day. See those lights? Every city will want to be lit with electric lamps. A phenomenal success for young Mr. Tesla."

Recalling the excitable young man who'd explained his exhibit, I said, "Jim, I met him. If there's an explosion, would he be blamed? He'd be devastated."

"He'd be ruined. But it's more than that. Edison and Morgan would be the richest men on the planet. They've invested in generating stations, monstrous great factories making electric power. Cities would use his power and nothing else. Tesla wouldn't have a chance."

Our carriage rode along a river of sparkling lamps, their white orbs glowing like a fairyland. I could scarcely breathe for staring.

I rested my head against Jim, worrying about Tobias. I'd put him at risk, hoping that if Donnelly led him to the ballistite, we'd end the threat to the World's Fair. What had he found? There were just too many suspects, each one with his own motives.

CHAPTER 38

PILLOW TALK

Saying goodbye to Mr. Tata at the Palmer, we returned to the Oriental on streets quiet except for the clacking of our horse's hooves and the distant howl of factory sirens.

Jamsetji's gentle kiss on my cheek had released a flood of memories—Mama bending over my trunks to cram in more linen, smoothing it flat, then sitting on the lid to squash it down. Papa, swiping a teardrop off his chequebook, grumbling as he dipped his pen in ink, over and over, tapped it against the bottle and grunted. Before I left Bombay, he'd sold his bungalow in Bandera to gift me five thousand rupees, my entire inheritance.

Because I married Jim, a non-Zoroastrian, Parsi law dictated that I would have nothing more. Strange that a religion founded on good thoughts, words and deeds should allow that. Yet I did not begrudge my brothers Adi and little Fali, or the sweet babies who were only three and five. My siblings' giggles would fill the void from my departure. Adi's wife, Bacha, and my sister Pilloo were gone. Whom would Mama chat with before breakfast? Who would choose her saree when she had a party to attend? She'd fuss, saying she was no beauty, why even bother? Who would insist that she wear her long gold *chera* so that Papa could put up his glasses and give a smirk of pride?

In the carriage, Jim pulled me close. Reassured by his solidness, I spilled out my worries about Tobias. Jim's careful questions and the night air revived me. By the time we reached the two great sculpted palms and the oasis of the Oriental, I felt more hopeful.

As Jim handed me down, a woman called, "Oh, I say, Diana! Mrs. O'Trey!"

The lively figure of my friend Ida Abernathy approached at full steam. In a deep purple coat, her width enveloped in a fur stole, she beamed at me, holding out her hands. Her husband, George, advanced with a languid smile to shake Jim's hand. What joy to see our friends again! I greeted them with pleasure and relief.

The Abernathys had just arrived from Boston. Feted with cocktails, we settled on the damask couches of the lounge, where George conferred with Jim, while Ida regaled me with their journey. Then, beaming, she said, "The mayor's banquet tomorrow—you will come, won't you?"

"Why, it's Lady Diana!" said Mrs. Bellino, approaching with her husband.

Jim's glance warned, say nothing; do not alert them. So, I presented them to Ida, who made a fine picture spread out in her furs on the burgundy settee. Mr. Bellino flashed a grin and bowed with a flourish, the stripe on his narrow trousers gleaming, his satin lapels aglow.

All the while I wondered, was a killer standing among us, smiling genially while planning to blast us all into bits of charred flesh? Jim didn't believe Bellino was an anarchist, but I was mired in doubt that clung like a troublesome child pointing and calling out, "Mommy, Mommy, look!"

Despite my trepidation, we had a pleasant evening, though Jim disappeared for a while. I measured every word from Enri Bellino, but could find nothing amiss. Having averted catastrophe at the parliament, I hoped for a respite, but my insides wound tight with dread.

Returning to our room, Jim dropped to the bed with a groan, his head falling back like a prizefighter who'd been knocked out. I chuckled at the relaxed line of his throat, his slack expression.

Sitting beside him in my nightdress, I smoothed lotion over my face, watching his lips tweak in an amused curve. He was listening. It never ceased to amaze me how much Jim "saw" when he listened. Could he really read my breath?

Turning down the lamp, I scooted between the sheets, happy to be warmed by Jim's body heat. Elbows bent, his arms bracketing his head on the pillow, he was not asleep. His limbs were still tense.

Pillowing my head on his arm, I whispered, "Jim, why can't you just arrest them? You've known for a while who's in this gang, haven't you?"

He sighed. "To arrest a man, there must be proof. Police cannot act until after a crime is committed. Can you imagine if they arrested just anyone on suspicion? Why even you could be hauled to the clink."

I peered at him in the muted light. "Me! What have I done?"

"You spoke of a possible attack on the gala. It didn't happen, but you knew something. People have been detained for less."

Only my connection to Jim had put me in the clear. But with so much at stake, I couldn't understand this hesitation. "So, arrest those you know and make them talk. Then nab the others."

He drew a slow breath. "We cannot alert them, Diana. If we can't find the explosives, we must nab them all at once. To miss a single one would be disastrous. It could set off the very thing we want to avoid."

"Jim, I feel awful about Tobias. Where could he be?"

His lips curved in a brief smile. "You've been worrying. While you were at dinner, I made a telephone call to Sergeant Long. No news yet from the beat. They're looking, sweet. Brennan's got hundreds of men all over the city. Six hundred policemen are here from every major city and country."

"Goodness." I cuddled close, my cheek against his neck.

It brought me to another thought, so I asked, "Jim, how does one make a bomb?"

Jim went still. "*That's* what you're thinking about?"

A chuckle began inside me and bubbled up, growing until it shook me with giggles. It was rare that I could surprise him. I enjoyed the thrill of it.

"Ah, sweet. I've missed that sound," said Jim, then went on. "Well, the explosive could be ballistite, or dynamite, or a stuff called nitroglycerin. Or something else like it. It could even be a large container of oil. Trouble is, this stuff catches fire so quickly, it could blow up the fellow setting it off. They use—"

"What is gunpowder then? Is it ballistite?"

"No, a mix of chemicals. Sulphur, charcoal and—saltpeter. Found in mines."

Mines again, I thought. "These explosives are powders? Carried in sacks?"

Jim shifted his shoulder, his arm tucking me closer. "Ballistite is. Nitro is a liquid, an oily one. Unstable, because it goes off when heated, or even under compression."

"Don't heat it or squash it."

He nodded, his jaw scraping my forehead. A sense of comfort spread through me as I reclaimed our closeness of weeks ago.

He said, "Trick is to postpone the explosion, to time it. For that, one uses a detonator, or blasting cap. A fuse—a rope soaked in chemicals— can lead the flame to the bomb. It's like a firecracker or the pin of a grenade. But there's other ways to light it—that's the point. Could be chemical, like acid, or electrical."

I considered the different ways one could set things aflame. Jim's chest rose and fell with a soothing rhythm. Recalling what he'd said earlier, I asked, "So when you said that—what were *you* thinking about?"

Jim grunted. "With my wife in my bed, what else would I be thinking of?"

I considered how to reply. "You've been in this bed before, sound asleep!"

He chuckled. "Then you ask about incendiaries, and I'm to form a sensible answer. Come, kiss me now, sweet. Thank heaven we nabbed the stuff today."

Thinking of Jim chasing a desperate man across the roof, falling on his injured knee, I quaked inside. He was paying a high price.

We could account for three boxes of explosives: two nabbed on the roof, one that blew up the Cold Storage Building. How many did that leave? The bristle of Jim's jaw scratching my cheek, our precious moment seemed unbearably fragile.

CHAPTER 39

COLLIN'S REVELATIONS

JIM

We'd lost a round to the arsonist at the Cold Storage Building, and sixteen men had lost their lives in the blaze. Now we'd saved the Parliament of World Religions only by the barest happenstance. If I'd been facing the wrong way when Prendergast set off, if his aim with a pistol had been better, if I'd reached the fuse too late . . . we'd been lucky.

No, I thought, the difference was Diana. The usual shock of fondness shot through me. When that girl wanted something, she put her heart into it. God knows, having her here was madness, but oh, how it lifted my spirits to see her.

Was it Prendergast who'd returned to sit beside her? Or Collier? The gang had noticed her and wanted me to know it. That thought pierced my side like a blade. They were warning me off.

The trolley car arrived, so I climbed aboard and swung into a seat with a groan.

Diana had said that Collin Box knew about the explosives. Donnelly'd called him a wharf rat. A week ago I'd had Tito point him out. So, I returned to Baldwin's boardinghouse to wear my working clothes. I'd told the landlord I was a traveling salesman. On the rare occasion that he saw me dressed up nice, it no longer astonished him.

Riding the cable car toward Forquer Street, I spotted Collin hauling muck on the corner of State and Randolph. Getting off, I marched over.

My brief stint with the Bombay Police had taught me the power of assuming authority. Clamping a hand on his elbow, I hauled him to a wall.

"Damn, Collin, you stink worse than this piss street," I said by way of greeting.

"Who're you?" He tried to yank his arm away, so I gripped harder.

"Never mind that. Know some blokes who work at the World's Fair pier? You loaded an unusual cart with them."

His voice wavered. "What you talking 'bout?"

"Aw, don't be like that." I sounded like Baldwin, I thought, with a twinge. He'd been younger than me, poor sod, now he'd never get to "find a gal to marry."

I crowded Collin against the wall. "You hauled stuff from a boat and loaded it on a cart. A box spilled and got the fella mad. You remember that? Did you smell powder in that box? Gunpowder?"

"I didn't spill nothing!"

"No? But you were there, weren't you? And you've been talking."

"I ain't said a word!"

So he *had* seen the powder unloaded.

"I'm the only one you're going to tell. What did you see?"

"Nothin'! I swear." He cringed, looking for a way past me.

This was no time to be squeamish. I grabbed him by the collar and shook him.

"Wouldn't want your pa hurt, would you? Where did the cart go?"

He squirmed, breathing hard, then blurted, "There was no cart. Just said so to sell Pa's mine. To a dame, a posh lady. The only time I said it."

I watched his fingers tremble. It could be true, but only the last part of that tale had sounded right. Since Collin feared the toughs from the flop, I said, "Why don't I ask Donnelly?"

His breath jerked. "You can't. He's dead."

"What?"

He tried to dart away. I gripped his collar, holding him in place.

"Dead, how?"

He choked. "Pulled from the canal."

Sergeant Long hadn't mentioned this when I called last evening. "When?"

"Last night."

"You had something to do with that?"

"No! I was home, I swear!" he cried, his voice breaking.

Damn it. The killer had silenced Oscar Donnelly. I frowned, thinking through my conversation with him. I'd asked about a typesetter—what had he said? "Bingley asked the same question." Someone else had used the printing press. Who had he suspected?

"You gonna let me go?" Collin whispered. "My pa's old. He needs me."

"If Donnelly's dead, then you need to tell me what you saw."

I released him, letting my gaze carry the weight of my words, allowing him to believe that Donnelly's killers had also heard his boast to Diana. She'd told no one else, but I rather thought *he* might have. He thrust his hair away, smearing his face with more filth.

I watched him shuffle from side to side. "What happened that night?"

Clutching his hat, he said, "The speakeasy closed at twelve, so I headed home through the docks. Two fellows was unloading at number six pier. Was late, so I hid, watched. There was a toff too, dressed mighty nice, but he left. I was gonna ask for work, but they were arguing. A box fell and broke. One cursed the other out, made him scoop it all up, every bit. His hand was in his coat pocket the whole time."

A chill ran over my skin. "And then?"

Collin rushed on. "He told the guy, get in the cart. When the fella refused, he shot him. I was jus' feet away! The man fell backward. He walked up and shot him again."

Was that how Baldwin was killed? The hair on my arms stood on end.

"When was this?"

He shook his head. "Ah . . ."

"Was there snow on the ground?"

"Yes. But . . . it was March, end of March."

"On a Sunday?"

"Saturday. Speakeasy's open late."

"You know them? Their names?"

"No!"

I quizzed him some more, then asked the one question that mattered most.

"What did he look like?"

Collin shot a look at me. He knew which one I meant.

"I ain't seen him since, I swear. But . . . he was built like a bull. Mister, if he knows I was there, I'm a goner."

CHAPTER 40

INDIGNATION

I dressed quickly the next morning. Jim had agreed to let me join his search for Tobias, now missing for five days. Leaving the Oriental, we rode a hack down the length of Madison Avenue to State Street. Tracing Tobias's steps, we started at his boardinghouse, which overlooked a foul-smelling pond.

The landlord had not seen him and wanted his week's rent. Jim paid and questioned him for some minutes.

As we left, Jim said, "You had Tobias watching us for days, but I didn't spot him. How'd he do it?"

I chewed on my lip, remembering.

"Abigail said there's a stable. The roof overlooks Bellino's factory."

Jim flung me a look. "Martin. You keep calling him Abigail. It's a ruse, sweet. His disguise."

"Jim, no." I caught his arm, threaded mine through it. "There's something so . . . stricken in her face. She hides it, but it's there. She said she first dressed as a woman from convenience, just using her stage clothes. But there's more, I'm sure of it." I recalled her manner as Martin, teaching me to walk like a man. She'd been impatient, as though wishing it was over. "She said, 'It was so easy, so natural' in feminine attire."

Jim scoffed. "That's Martin, sweetheart. Playing Abigail to land a soft spot."

Rueful admiration tinged his words. Disguises were his stock in trade, so that's what he'd see. Yet Abigail had volunteered to help Peter track me. That was puzzling.

"Jim, there's more to it. Abigail . . . I don't think it's that simple."

Refusing to let me near the factory, he left me at a produce market nearby. Browsing stalls, I bought lilies from a buxom Bohemian woman and a small pot of aloe, then observed the parade of grocers' carts. Couples laden with purchases hopped aboard one-horse traps. The scent of summer flowers mingled with the dank odor of fish as memories wafted into my mind. In India, farmers rode one-pony *ekkas* or drove their bullock carts to market. Vendors dragged vegetable-laden carts to our home on Malabar Hill, but in Simla, Mama shopped on foot each morning, two bearers following to carry her purchases.

What was taking Jim so long? Waiting, I watched a little drama unfold. A grumpy cabbie in bent sailor's cap sat atop his coach, arguing with a couple laden with packages. He refused them, saying a gent had hired him to wait. The couple departed, scowling.

An hour later Jim returned. The stable's roof had yielded no clues.

On our return we passed City Hall, that magnificent colonnaded edifice where, this evening, the mayor would felicitate the architects of the World's Fair. I glanced behind us. Was that the grumpy cabbie from the market?

"Jim!" I hissed, and told him.

He swung around to get a look. "His hat's pulled down."

Had we been spotted? I fretted—had he recognized Jim or was he following me? Or was I too wound up, seeing danger everywhere? The anarchist's bold remark at the parliament meant he knew I'd alerted the police. Did he blame me for foiling his attack? It gave me an odd sensation, like standing in an open field during a thunderstorm, my coat flapping, wind flicking my hair to sting my face.

When we descended from the coach, the strange taximan was nowhere around.

Entering the Oriental's quiet stateliness, I felt safer. Most guests would be dressing for the evening banquet, but I had no heart for it. Hoping for a quiet dinner together, I glanced at Jim's face, clean-shaven since the parliament. Had he abandoned the guise of Agney at last?

I turned to ask, then spotted a spry gentleman with grey hair, whiskers and beard step through the hotel doors. His glance caught mine. Dupree, Senior!

He gave a start, then marched up. "Mrs. O'Trey—and Captain Jim!"

We stared at each other. Jim offered his hand. "Glad to see you, sir."

The elevator pinged its arrival just then, so Jim invited him to join us. The elevator ascended slowly, Jim pleasantly formal, Dupree Senior glaring at us with piercing blue eyes.

"Dash it—" Dupree began, then huffed, glancing at the lanky elevator boy.

His lips tight, he shook his head at me in silent rebuke. Choosing a light tone, which matched his demeanor like a tiara matches a monkey, he said, "Madam, I saw your photograph in a newspaper some days ago."

I forced a smile. "The Ferris wheel incident. Is that how you found me? What luck."

"Luck indeed," he said, following us to my suite.

Jim took my key and ushered us in. Once the door closed behind him, Dupree's bonhomie evaporated.

Whiskers bristling, his chin jutted. "Seven weeks and not a word, ma'am!" he accused, his indignation broadening his Scots accent. "Is this how you treat your employer? An operative is killed and two disappear, did you think I'd do nothing?"

He turned to Jim, his arm scything through the air.

"And you sir? It has been months! Every time I called Sergeant Long, he stalled. Chicago Police know you—when Brennan described his new man, I had no doubt it was you. But you didn't wire me once!" His fingers curled back toward his chest.

Was he a part of this devious business? And calling Jim to task to deflect suspicion from himself? What audacity!

"Oh?" I returned fire. "But Martin kept you informed, sending word to Peter!"

Alfred blinked. He slumped onto a chair, gazing from me to Jim.

"Martin Gale?" He glanced at Jim. "You're certain?"

Arms crossed, Jim leaned against the door and nodded.

"Sending word to Peter? That's quite impossible, ma'am," Dupree Senior said, but the conviction had leaked from his voice. Eyebrows knotted in confusion, he drooped, tired and old.

Jim said, "Martin's been with Diana this entire time."

"But Peter," said Dupree Senior, looking up, "he's in New York!"

He had not known!

"Peter is here, in Chicago," I said, feeling sorry for Alfred. His son was part of this ugliness, although I did not know how much of the anarchists' web he'd spun, or whether he'd been ensnared.

Dupree Senior swallowed. Rubbing his mustache with his knuckles, he tried to speak but only shook his head.

"All right." Jim tossed his coat on the settee, then extracted the maps pressed under the tablecloth. He'd decided to trust Dupree Senior. Relieved that we had misjudged the old detective, I recalled bullying him into taking me on, and sighed.

Wasting no time, Jim laid out the puzzle piece by piece as he described Donnelly, Lascar and others. He tapped the map, showing where Baldwin and Grewe had been killed, and the old factory that doubled as a printing press office. Then he raised his chin at me.

Following Jim's lead, I told Alfred what I'd learned—my visit to the anarchists' congress, the card game where Peter had accosted Abigail—"I mean Martin! We've been watching Bellino's factory since then. He's a part of this."

Jim said, "You cannot accuse him because of the mine, sweet. We need proof against him."

I frowned. "If he isn't responsible, why were you at his factory?"

"I was currying up to Donnelly, not Bellino. But that's shot. Lascar thinks I'm a Pinkerton now. As Agney, I'm done."

I winced because that was my fault.

Dupree glowered. "You didn't tell me . . . about Baldwin's letter. Right from the start, you thought I was crooked."

Jim spread his hands. "I couldn't be certain. Someone gave Baldwin up. Likely the bloke he sent a piece of the letter to. I've been thinking about that. Perhaps it contained a name."

I said, "But Jim, Miss Arsenault heard Bellino. He said 'Agney or Clay.' She doesn't know you go by Agney, Jim."

"Don't know any Clay." Jim pulled in his lips. "We've searched all Bellino's properties. His ship, his booths, even the factory where the steelworkers live. If he's hidden the stuff, it's somewhere else. No sign of Tobias either."

His mouth grim, he described his conversation with Collin. "Donnelly suspected someone but didn't give me a name. Too late to ask him now. He's dead."

Silence chilled the room. Donnelly was the third person the anarchists had murdered.

Tapping the letter, Dupree said, "How is Peter involved?"

Jim replied, "I think Baldwin planned to arrest someone but delayed, because the evidence was in German, and asked Peter about it. He may have wired Peter and was instructed to hold off telling Chicago Police. We don't know. But Martin said Peter blackmailed Bellino, who paid him twice. That's evidence he must be in this already. Else why would he join the anarchists?"

Dupree mopped his forehead. "Martin saw the blackmail?"

"You didn't know he engaged Martin, did you?" Seeing Alfred's desultory shake of his head, he went on. "He needed to stop me. That means he knew what I was after. It wasn't enough that the anarchists got to Baldwin; he couldn't have me sniffing around either. He must know about the ballistite, the plot, and more. I just don't know why he'd do this."

"We had Peter late in life," Dupree said in his slow way. "My wife . . . hated living in Boston. Six years after the war, she left and went back to

Atlanta. I met Peter at her funeral. I didn't know I had a twelve-year-old son! His mother's death . . . hit him hard. What would I do with a child? I sent him to her sister, in Georgia. He had some trouble there—ran with a rough lot, and was arrested for assault. Lawyers cost me a pretty penny. But this? I need to hear this from him."

He shook his head, took a breath, then leaned over the map.

"Right. What's the plan—find the explosives? Or catch them in the act?"

Pulling out a map of the fair, Jim pointed out the Cold Storage Building close to the railroad. Tracing a line, he said, "That's the elevated train—the Intramural Railway. Goes around the perimeter of the fair. From the South Loop, near Krupp's Gun Exhibit, it swings around and turns between South Pond and the Stock Pavilion. It runs along the Railway Terminal and Transportation Building, follows Stony Island Avenue to the north end of the fairground. There it swings right to the lakeshore, ending at the North Loop. Goes right round the fair. If I had to carry seventeen crates of ballistite, a few at a time, that's how I'd do it."

Dupree Senior squinted at the map. "Where's the biggest crowd?"

Jim said, "Midway," just as I said, "The Manufacturers Building."

I smiled. "The Midway Plaisance is crowded, but it's a narrow street. The Court of Honor, now, that's wide. All the big events, the opening, for example, are held there."

The old detective frowned. "The train. How close does it get to the Court of Honor?"

Jim bent over the map. "Closest point is the South Loop, near the pier. We've got lads on it hourly, but we can't watch everywhere. The crowds are just too great." He paused, thinking. "We need to get the lynchpin," he said. "The one who captains this ship."

Dupree's eyes cleared like a summer sky. "Find him, how?"

I grinned, a bubble of devilry fizzing inside me. "Let's do what you did before, Jim. 'Shake trees and see what falls out.' Let's startle Bellino—let him think we know what he's doing. Let's go to the mayor's banquet!"

"The banquet?" Dupree asked.

Jim studied me. "Diana's right. Whoever funded all this won't stay away. They'll want to see the fireworks in person. We need access to the upper classes. Let's rattle them, ask awkward questions, hint that we know their plans, their names."

Eyes glinting, Dupree rubbed his hands. "Get them worried so they make a mistake," he said. "Watch them close. When they run, nab them. It will take some planning, lad!"

CHAPTER 41

PROMISES AND SURPRISES

Jim and Dupree Senior left for police headquarters to arrange matters with Sergeant Long. Soon after, Mr. Fish arrived at my door, blinking rapidly. "I beg your pardon, Lady Diana," he said, "a *person* wishes to speak with you."

Could it be Tobias? Had he been unwell? Or was Tito bringing me news? Pulling on my day gloves, I hurried to Mr. Fish's office.

There stood Collin Box, his filthy Wellingtons planted on outspread newspapers. I sent Mr. Fish a questioning look, since Collin was so prominently confined.

Stammering, Mr. Fish said, "The floors—they were just cleaned, ma'am!"

I greeted Collin, adding, "I did not expect to see you. I asked your father to meet Mr. Payne, but neither of you came at the appointed time."

His mouth twisting, Collin groaned something I could not hear. Such were the layers of dirt on his face that I could not read his emotions.

Gentling my voice, I asked, "Was your father ill, perhaps?"

"We went there, ma'am," choked Collin, clutching his elbows. "But the fella threw us out! Said we stunk! Da got hot with him and, well, one thing led to another."

This was not what Mr. Payne had said, quite the opposite. I frowned. Was Collin telling the truth? If so, Mr. Payne had lied, smiling all along, charming me with his shy admiration. The conniving crook! Too good for Collin, was he? A seed of anger grew within me. I'd remember this piece of nastiness.

However, now Collin was here, it presented an opportunity. Jim had implied that Collin knew his way around crooks and con men.

"I have another task for you, Collin. My employee has gone missing—Tobias, an older colored man. The first time we met"—I recalled I had been dressed as a boy and switched my words—"at your home, you recall, he was with me. I have not seen him in days. If you can bring some news of him, we'll arrange our business without Mr. Payne. Bring him here or tell me where he is. Can you do that?"

He grimaced. "I'll try. The mine, how much will you pay?"

I'd given his father my word, but now it must seem as though I had placed another condition to my purchase. To Mr. Fish's astonishment, I made Collin a pledge.

"When the contract is signed, I shall pay one thousand dollars for the mine."

* * *

Of course, Jim was not pleased about it. Reluctantly acknowledging that my reward was a clever ploy, he said he hoped it would work.

I'd been to City Hall before to see Sergeant Long. That night, however, as Jim and I entered the ornate structure in the French Revival style, it sparkled. We made a fine pair. My sleek, Parisian velvet and Jim's formals matched, drawing looks as much as Jim's trim, masculine elegance in white tie.

He handed me into the elevator, saying, "What's that perfume, sweet—tuberose?"

I smiled. On festival days, Mama hung garlands of pink roses interlaced with white tuberoses over doorways. On birthdays I'd stand on a little *patla* of wood, be garlanded with a necklace of tuberoses, showered with rice and rose petals to receive hugs and presents. Ropes of its blooms were wound around pillars. Their distinctive, delicate scent brought home so close, it was as though I could step through a doorway and be there.

With a chime, our elevator arrived at the top floor. It opened to a passage, windowed across on one side. "Look, Jim!" I cried as I went to it, gasping at the lights of the city laid out below. Streets glowed with gas lamps like strings of pearls. A hundred feet below, carriages moved in slow procession as guests disembarked. Jim chuckled at my amazement, then offered his arm to lead me to the ballroom.

Glancing back, I noticed two gentlemen step out of the elevator. Squeezing Jim's elbow, I whispered, "Company from England! Those jackets were surely cut on Bond Street."

Jim's eyebrows twitched. Without turning, he asked, "Military?"

"Civilian, I think, but the older has a fine upright bearing."

When they passed us without recognition, Jim exhaled, his arm tense under my fingers.

Preparing to act on our plan, I looked around for Alfred Dupree. Just then, a policeman claimed Jim's attention.

I smiled as George came up, beaming, with Ida in her navy-blue velvet. Exchanging greetings, his great forehead seemed to glow as he presented the two English gentlemen, "Lord Reedsbury and Mr. Lamb, his nephew."

It amused me that a gentleman is always presented to a lady, even if he's the lord chancellor, and she just a young girl. Etiquette favored women, for it was created by us! Following protocol, when Jim returned, I gave him their names. He did not usually enjoy a formal do—its ritual stiffness wore on him—but today he took it all in good humor.

Then, in just a few seconds, the tone of the evening changed. Head tossed back, the older gentleman peered at Jim. "I say, aren't you British army? India, sir?"

Eyes hooded, Jim conceded it. "Cavalry. Bombay Regiment."

"By Jove! It's Agni-ho-tree, isn't it? Captain Agnihotri?"

Chin jutting out, his myopic eyes peered up at Jim. The old gent's voice carried through the ballroom. Curious glances darted toward us, sentences abridged quickly. Why was Lord Reedsbury so excited? He licked his lips as though he'd discovered a secret.

Hearing his name, Jim stiffened. Perhaps he expected some snub at his Anglo-Indian parentage, since so many people despised mixed-race unions.

"Why, sir, your painting," the older man cried. "Mrs. Elizabeth Sutton's a famous artist! The wife of Colonel Sutton—spent many years in the tropics. Her piece hangs in the National Gallery. Ten feet high, one can hardly miss it!"

"Her . . . piece?"

"Your portrait, man!" He paused, looking from Jim to me and back again. "You didn't know? She painted you in oils. Riding a most exquisite mare. Best horseflesh I've ever seen. Arabian, she said."

"Mullicka," Jim said, his manner easing. "She was beautiful."

"Dash it, man! The piece caused a furor last year!"

Reedsbury had the room's attention. He reveled in it, casting his voice with the flourish of an orator. "Imagine a canvas that extends to a high ceiling. The lower half is dominated by a magnificent animal, coming straight on toward you, velvet coat gleaming."

"She was grand," said Jim. "I thank you."

Reedsbury went on. "The rider leans forward, gaze fixed upon some obstacle he plans to jump. A large man, shoulders of such proportions that, well, I must ask Mrs. Sutton's pardon! I had assumed he was a figment of her febrile imagination, until I met you, sir. She titled the painting *Captain James Agnihotree in Rangoon.* A fine-looking soldier on a handsome horse. Romantic, you see? It shocked people, though, because they thought the subject was English."

When he ended, the silence stretched. All eyes within hearing distance were upon us. Realizing he'd overstepped, Reedsbury patted Jim's arm. "Oh, course, you're—"

"Eurasian," said Jim, calmly. "I'm half Indian."

Reedsbury looked relieved that Jim took no offense.

"That's it. Why, many in the Commons felt that Indians should be given greater opportunities, you see, if they could, ah, do the job. But your name, now, that raised some eyebrows, I can tell you."

His nephew murmured in his ear. Reedsbury brightened. "Quite so. Here in the Americas, well, it hardly matters, what?"

"Indeed," said George. He raised a languid eyebrow, offering me his arm. "We're called to dinner, it seems. Shall we go in?"

People began to gather at the entrance to the dining hall. Jim escorted Ida and followed, still looking good-humored, but I was not deceived. The set of his head told me he had disliked being unmasked and expected more questions.

He was right. Soon, fellows collected around him. He shook hands; Ida's husky laugh punctuated the remarks. A warm glow filled me to see him so accepted.

The dining room opened to an array of tables under shimmering chandeliers. Austrian crystal, I thought. A banquet lay along one side, leaving an open space at the center. As I went in with George, I caught a glimpse of Peter Dupree. Jim would do his part among the gentlemen, and I must do mine. Mentally rehearsing the provocative remarks we'd planned, I decided to begin with the Bellinos, then try to startle Peter Dupree.

A tinkling sound called the company's attention for the master of ceremonies to open the festivities. Portly Mayor Harrison stood and raised his glass. After praising the architects, and the landscape genius Frederick Law Olmsted, who had returned to New York due to ill health, he said, "Electricity, ladies and gentlemen. Electricity will power our future. You've seen the city of light, the first city to be lit with electric lamps. Now imagine this gift offered to every city and town, every home and factory! Limitless light, limitless heat and hot water at home, limitless power to run factories.

"No more smoke from oil, no more fear of open candles. The mighty engine of industry is no longer propelled by steam but by current! Man is no longer constrained by daylight hours; light has been harnessed to his noble aims. The future, my friends! We've brought it to Chicago!"

Applause filled the room. Glancing across the entranced audience, I said, "He's running for president, isn't he?"

George chuckled. "Governor first, Mrs. O'Trey."

The mayor went on. "When the Great Fire swept over our city and laid it in ashes in twenty-four hours, then the world said: 'Chicago and its boasting is gone forever.' But Chicago said: 'We will rebuild the city better than ever,' and Chicago has done it."

Applause resounded. Watching the mayor awash in adulation, I remembered young Mrs. Yeats's distress. Mayor Harrison had ruined her husband. It gave me a queasy sensation. This man of vision possessed a dark side.

He was saying, "I intend to live for more than half a century, and at the end of that half century, London will be trembling lest Chicago shall surpass it, and New York will say, 'Let it be the metropolis of America.' In but a little while, I expect to get on a magnificent steamer at Chicago's wharf and go to a suburb, New Orleans, the Crescent City of the globe. Mr. Mayor of Omaha, we will take you in as a suburb. We are not narrow-minded. Our heart is as broad as the prairies that surround us."

The audience laughed at that gibe—New Orleans, and Omaha, suburbs of Chicago! But the mayor went on to say he wanted the World's Fair to continue for another year in Chicago.

"The day is propitious. I hope Congress will see what we have achieved this day and continue the Columbian Exposition next summer."

The man's vision was as great as his pride, I thought. If the fair ran another summer, all America would come to see it. Chicago's business would boom. The city's elite nodded at each other.

Motioning toward an elderly woman in a flashing diamond choker, I said, "How exquisite. Old money, all around?"

George grunted agreement. "And new. Railroad barons, property barons."

He said this with a sarcastic twist of his lips, so I asked, "Property?"

He snorted. "Hmph! Landlords, tenement owners. Though they won't collect rents themselves, of course. They've fellows to do that. There"—he tilted his head, indicating someone to the right—"inventor of the clasp locker, a sort of slide fastener, I'm told. Wants to put it on clothes and shoes, imagine! And the fellow with him produces musical shows. Pays the actors a pittance, 'course."

For a member of the bourgeoisie, George had strangely egalitarian views.

I nodded at a young couple. "New money?"

"Not really. Just an upstart. The money's still in oil. That tall man with the walrus mustache—that's Rockefeller. His pipeline's almost reached New York. Shut down a dozen plants in Pennsylvania just like that because it cost too much to pipe."

I frowned. "Why not just cart it on trains?"

He snorted. "The railroad wanted too much. Oil king wouldn't negotiate."

What I'd seen as a gathering of the country's elite now seemed a group of impeccably dressed hucksters. At least George and Ida did not tread upon common folk, I thought.

"Your money's in shipping, isn't it, Mr. Abernathy?"

"My father's is. I'm invested in refineries like old Rockefeller. Solid gold stock, Mrs. O'Trey, solid gold. People always need oil for heat and lamps."

Oil money. Many of these fine folk had fortunes tied to the old way of things. "What do you think of the World's Fair, proud harbinger of new innovations?"

He shrugged. "Some are interesting. Did you see the Electrotachyscope? Quite intriguing. Man called Ottomar Anschütz demonstrated a host of moving images—projected with something called a Geissler tube. Says moving pictures will replace the theater. Plays for the masses can be projected on a curtain. Of course, we'll see the real thing."

I resolved to see it on my next visit. But I still had a job to do, so tapping George's sleeve, I asked, "Is Enri Bellino here? I need to speak with him, but he was rather upset with me last week."

Eyebrows high, George gave me a sharp look. "Upset? What for?"

I shook my head, reluctant to say more. "Tell him I'd like a word, privately?"

"Intriguing. What about?"

Why did everyone doubt me? "Mr. Bellino is an agent for the Bofors Company—it's owned by Alfred Nobel, the inventor of dynamite. He has access to . . . explosives. I think he's up to no good."

With a startled glance, George said, "I've had dealings with him. Sure about this?"

Seeing I was determined, he threaded through the guests as the orchestra struck up a Viennese waltz. Mr. Lamb requested a dance, which I accepted and was swept away. Lord Reedsbury was next. On my last birthday in Bombay, I'd danced all evening, fretting that Jim did not ask me. At the end I'd confronted him, only to learn that he did not know how to dance!

A waiter approached, offering me a note on his platter. My heart did a hop as I read: *Meet by the elevator now.*

George had done it! I twisted in my seat, searching for Jim, but could not see him. I'd last seen him walk away with some uniforms. I needed to confront Bellino. Sipping my cocktail, I placed it over the note. Excitement running up my spine, I headed toward the elevator.

Jim and I had concocted a simple plan. I'd tell Bellino his investment in the fair was safe, because police had located the anarchists' secret store of ballistite. He might feign ignorance, perhaps. Either way, I'd see his eyes when I said the word "ballistite." A start, a look of awareness, that was all I needed. If he hurried off, police had placed fellows around City Hall to follow him. With luck, he'd lead them to the den like a duck to her nest.

I entered the vestibule. Here, one side led to the elevator and stairwell; the other bent around toward the cloakrooms. Ida waved me over, so I could not in good conscience turn my back on her. Worried that I'd miss my assignation, I squeezed her hand and promised to return.

The elevator lobby was empty. Drat. I was too late; Ida had delayed me too long.

I turned back to the ballroom, but an arm snaked around my neck.

A hand crushed my mouth and nose. I was propelled to the elevator. I struggled, twisting and flailing for a hairpin to defend myself. What temerity to abduct me from the mayor's dinner!

Darkness gaped between gilt doors. My blood went cold. There was no elevator before me. Hands shoved me into coal-black nothingness.

CHAPTER 42

ELECTRICITY

I snatched at the gilt doors, caught something with my fingertips, but could get no purchase. Panic choked me. I fell into darkness.

My sister Pilloo had fallen from a great height. She was found crumpled on the clock-tower green. Adi's wife, Bacha, had fallen only minutes before that and broken her neck.

I was in the elevator well. Falling.

Something brushed my face. I flailed with both hands, touched something—a rope? I caught it, scraping my fist. Was it a cable? Crying out, I clenched my hand. My weight yanked on my wrist and I swung upright. Pain, such pain! It flared from my wrist, breaking out of me in a scream. Instantly I let go.

I grabbed again, but it was no use. My skirts came up, a suffocation of layers obscuring darkness. My feet hit something, but unprepared, I fell forward. My forehead smacked down on a cold surface.

For moments I reeled from that blow, then gradually became aware of my predicament. Was I at the bottom of the shaft? How could I possibly get out?

My head throbbed; my hands burned. I smelled grease, like an oiled pistol. I shivered, limbs aching.

A buzzing permeated my body. Was that my own trembling? Pulling in my arms, I dragged my knees close; gasping, straining around, seeing darkness, the terrible blackness at the bottom of a well. Something jabbed my side, a sharp spike.

"Diana!"

I heard Jim's shout but could not reply, my chest empty of air. With each breath, pain stabbed. I pulled in small panting breaths. Little Pilloo had died, crushed to a heap on the university grounds, tossed down two hundred feet. How had I forgotten that?

No, I hadn't forgotten, just wanted something so much that I had put it out of my mind. I'd wanted Jim standing beside me on our steamship, his eyes aglow. I wanted my life back, my life with Jim.

I'd known that three men were murdered, seen those firemen killed by a ruthless hand, but I'd thought myself safe from such things. I was wrong.

"She's got to be here!" Jim's ragged voice echoed, hollow in the tormented darkness. The entire ballroom must have heard him.

"Stop the doors! No one leaves!"

Did he think I was a captive? He'd search every room! The governor was here; police were all around. I wanted to shout, "It's all right!" But someone wanted me dead, someone here at dinner. I'd got too close—what had I said? My forehead burned as I tried to raise it. I wanted to yell, "They're here, those killers. Not on Canal Street, not at the anarchists' meeting, right here, Jim. Behind you."

My chest ached. I drew a small, careful breath and said, "Jim."

It came out in a wheeze. Pain stabbed my side with the slightest movement. My wrist throbbed—my hand disjointed, as though held together by bare skin. God Almighty. Someone had tried to kill me. What brazen cheek!

Furious, I cried, "I'm here!"

The effort pierced my side, spiking fear.

Nearby, a grinding noise began. Light flickered. I turned my head to it.

An arc shot up, curving over me, a snake of iridescence joining the stump to my left. In the eerie light I saw my prison—a narrow rectangular cage. At the center, close by, was a metal ring, from which a cable rose, disappearing into the darkness. The glimmering serpent flickered, then faded as abruptly as it had appeared. Was it a product of my delirium?

Light filtered above me. Voices rumbled below. Was I lying on top of the elevator? I was still curled on my side. At the edge of my vision, something moved. A door opened, fresh air touched my skin. Oh God! Jim would come—he would come down to me now. Panic flooded me.

I sucked in air, despite the grip of pain, and let out one word, "Elec—tric!"

Movement above, footsteps pounding in the dark. A square of light opened a few feet above, outlining Jim's shape.

Desperately I cried, "Electricity, Jim! Don't. Electricity!"

He turned, spoke over his shoulder. Shouts resounded in hollow urgency. The light went out, replaced by a lantern's glow.

Only feet above, Jim peered downward. "Diana?"

The rough sound of his breath so close made me sob. Behind him slivers of light flickered. The pulse of his breath tethered me to the world of light; all else blurred. Was he trying to find me in the dark? No, he was listening. I'd forgotten how close he could listen.

"Yes, soldier," I whispered.

His breath whooshed in relief. I heard him move, clothes brushing the wall as he climbed in. I whispered, "Can I tell you something?"

"God's sake, sweet."

"My side hurts."

Crouching, he moved careful fingers over me, pushing aside flounces, then brushed my waist. I felt a slow tug at my dress. His fingers traced a path back and forth on my ribs. Something stabbed, sharp-edged.

"Jim!" I gasped. The sting receded. I tried a breath, found no pain, and drew in great gulps of precious air.

My corset. Its broken ribs had jabbed into me, but now I could breathe.

"Where does it hurt?" he asked, each time moving me a little, so it took an age to gather me into his arms. Then he got to his feet and lifted me out of the darkness.

* * *

I woke between soft layers of cotton. Remembering a dark prison, I clutched the sheet. Pain pierced my wrist, heavy with bandages, making me gasp. My head throbbed with each pulse. After a bit, it eased.

In the shadowed room I heard breathing, the slow, weary sound of deep sleep. Jim slumped against my bed, his tousled head propped on his arms. He'd been waiting for me to wake. Moving was painful—every part of me ached, but a need to touch him overtook me, as though I could not trust my sight but only the feel of him would suffice. My fingertips brushed his hair.

"Diana." His stormy grey eyes searched mine, then he held my hand to his face. We assessed each other, questions asked and answered in silence. Fingers skimming my bandages, he said, "You've hurt your wrist. The doctor said it might be broken. Can you move your feet?"

I could. His shoulders sagged in relief. "Hungry?"

I was, but I said, "Water." He brought it with a small vial of laudanum and helped me drink as though I might shatter if he held too tight.

I said, "Don't fuss; I feel fine."

Jim chuckled. "You are a terrible liar, my sweet."

His look said more, much more. Leaning against him, I closed my eyes, grateful again for this night, this safety.

Perhaps I slept. When next my eyes opened, Jim bent over me, touching my hair. "Sergeant Long is here. Can you see him?"

Groaning, I sat up, so Jim eased me back against a pile of pillows. Sergeant Long entered, his face growing solemn.

"I am not dead, officer. Sit down," I said.

His mouth twitched. Eyebrows peaked, he asked his questions.

I was no help—I'd not seen my assailant, only smelled something peculiar before he pushed me into the elevator well. His sleeve was black, like every man's in the ballroom. The elevator doors were open before I struggled with my assailant. He thanked me with surprising gentleness; then Jim walked him out.

Returning, Jim sat on my bed. His face twisted. "I should have been with you."

"God, Jim, you don't blame yourself? It was me. I was too cocksure! Going off like that."

We spoke for some time.

Looking thoughtful, he rubbed his thumb over my palm. "Sweetheart, this attack, it means you know something. It's worried our arsonist. Made him desperate enough to attempt murder." His voice softened. "So, what is it they suspect you know?"

My throbbing head against his shoulder, I said, "I don't know. How did you find me?"

"I didn't see you in the hall. It's what I feared, my life. The lift door was ajar. That's what led me to you. And your perfume. Tuberoses."

This was his nightmare, that some unknown foe would attack me. But it seemed to have freed him too. That hunted look was replaced with tight resolve.

* * *

Despite my weariness, my mind raced all night. In my agitation, I woke sharply, in the darkness. I'd dreamt of that strange spike of electricity in the elevator shaft, curved like a cobra preparing to strike.

"All right, sweet?" Jim spooned me, enveloping me with reassuring warmth. Although I was safe, my pulse still drummed. Trying to sleep would be hopeless.

Hugging Jim's arm, I asked, "How does electricity work?"

He pulled me closer, muttering something I could not hear. Then he said, "You mean the sparks from the elevator? That's akin to arc lighting, like in streetlamps. The inventor Nikola Tesla gave a public speech about it when I first got here. It's electric current, running between carbon electrodes."

"I don't understand," I whispered, feeling discouraged and small.

Jim said, "At his demonstration he poured certain chemicals in a pair of buckets and ran a wire between them. Then he wrapped the wire around an incandescent lamp and dropped the ends into the buckets. It caused quite a stir, Diana, because the lamp lit up. Right there in front of us. That's called current."

"But the elevator doesn't run on chemicals, surely?"

"No. They've got large motors now, called dynamos. Mr. Edison's built factories to make electric current—electric generators."

"And the current runs along copper wires? Copper, from Osain Box's mine."

Jim affirmed with a grunt. "Mmm. It runs through metal, but it can go through other things. Like people. Can burn them badly, even kill. The wire is a conductor—it conducts the current."

"How did you learn all this?" I whispered.

"That public speech, and some library books." He stiffened, and then exhaled. "Blast. I forgot to return them. We'll owe a fortune in fines."

I grinned. We were trying to avert a terrible disaster and Jim fretted about library fines? "Well, lucky for you, I turned them in before I left Boston."

Jim's voice smiled as he said, "Thank you for that. Now we just find the blasted ballistite before it blows up the fair."

I remembered the women at the gala snickering at me, thought of the dead Bengali workman lying in the morgue, Bellino's greed—and Peter's treacherous charm. These were the people Jim wanted to save?

I cried, "Are they worth it? Jim, you're risking so much. As am I! Is it worth it?"

"Worth it? To save lives?"

"But whose lives, Jim? These people trample each other, take what they want. They have no sense of morals, no heart! In Boston I went to church with Ida, and what a marvelous homily the pastor gave. 'Love thy neighbor,' he said, his arms spread wide. He praised women at the soup kitchen, a workman who'd fixed the school roof. But Jim, now I see it's a sham. It's grand to buy works of art. Isn't it fine to have a building bear one's name? But where did that money come from? From beating down working men, from crushing children like Tito. From grabbing people's mines, refusing to fix tenements crawling with vermin. And then, when their tenants are sick and cannot pay, from shoving them to the street! Are those who you're risking your life for?"

Jim's chest rose and fell for three long breaths. When he spoke, his voice was low. "They're people, Diana, just people. If we set ourselves up to say who is worthy and who is not, what are we, hmm? Are we not worse for making such assumptions? For judging them?"

I sat up, pulsing pain into my side. "I don't presume to judge them," I said, gazing into darkness. "But should we care so much? It's a heavy price you're asking, Jim. They dress up all fine and fancy, but their wealth is foul. Papa's never extorted people like this. You believe in fairness, decency; why can't they be like you?"

"Diana, you worry me when you speak like this. How high your standards are. Someday I'll likely disappoint you. What then, sweet?"

Jim sounded so solemn; it made my throat hurt. "How could *you* disappoint me? As for standards, isn't that the measure of civilized dealings? Not that something's illegal, but that it's fair? Why, they steal, then change the laws to suit! Ida told me about a man called Phillips. He wanted a farmer's land for a great big store, but the farmer wouldn't sell. So, the city council took it, under a law called eminent domain, to build a park. Then the council sold it to Phillips instead, for his department store. The farmer protested, but he was old and frail and couldn't fight the city's lawyers.

"And what about Collin's mine? Bellino bought it for fifty dollars. Fifty! Osain took his terms because their baby was sick, crying with croup. A lifetime's work, for fifty dollars. And it's all perfectly legal!"

"My dear," Jim said. "Someday you may fault something I do. If I wheedle a lass to charm out some information, if I lie, if I must deceive, if I—" His voice grew strained. "If I kill. Will you trust that I had a reason, that I truly had no choice?"

He drew a rough breath. "I'm a man, Diana, just a man. They're people trying to make a buck. For good or ill, my sweet, they're just people.

Should we judge them unfit, refuse them a chance to become what they could be? Best left to their maker, hmm?"

I lay back, settling my head against his shoulder. He was talking about divine judgment. Papa always spoke of God as a friend. Justice, well, it just happened, like the seasons. I'd never given it much thought. After a while, I asked, "And this God, does He care about you too?"

Jim's shoulders moved against me in a shrug.

"Don't know. But He sent me you."

I sighed. "You tell me this, and say I expect too much of *you*."

I held him close, despite my aches, and argued no more.

CHAPTER 43

THOSE NEAREST US

Sometime later, Ida Abernathy came with flowers, her arms filled with hothouse lilies. Overflowing my bedchamber with vases, the enormous blooms scented the air.

Perching on my bedside chair, she said, "You gave us the most awful turn."

I imagined the aperitifs interrupted by Jim's panic, the shock on guests' faces, and, unaccountably, I giggled. Ida's mouth curved into an O of surprise.

"Oh lordy!" I groaned. "What a to-do! 'Indian princess falls down elevator shaft!' It will be the talk of the town, won't it?"

She smiled; a chuckle bubbled up and escaped her lips. Describing what each person was doing when they learned of my predicament, she pretended to hold a spoon to her open mouth, pausing there, until I dissolved into fits of laughter. It wasn't funny, but I needed to laugh. Even though it hurt, giggles hiccupped through me, until I lay back, spent.

"Sweetheart?" Jim came from the parlor, his eyes keen and alight.

"Jim, I don't understand how my assailant knew I'd be alone," I said aloud, then remembered parts of the previous evening. I'd been dancing. Whom was I speaking to? I'd waltzed with Mr. Lamb, a smooth, easy dancer, circled the room . . .

"Oh, I told George about buying that mine, and that I wanted to speak with Mr. Bellino, to buy pullies, explosives and such."

Ida said, "Oh, my dear, what luck. That's exactly who can help you—George! He has interests in mining." I stared, as she went on. "Such a clever man. He has so many investments."

Heavens. I'd planned to examine Bellino, watch him flinch when I mentioned ballistite. Had someone overheard?

A web of suspicion grew. George had sent me to the Oriental Hotel, where Bellino introduced himself. George had directed me to the lying Mr. Payne. I'd told George that Bellino was involved in something odd. How had he reacted? If I'd been looking, would I have noticed his alarm, or at least some knowledge in his eyes?

A snippet from some classic I'd read popped into my mind: *Like jealous hearts in smiles bedecked, those nearest us, we least suspect.*

Ida was saying, "George is in oil too. My mother married Edward Van-Lysson, the oilman, you recall? He was distressed at the Columbian Exposition. It's lit not by oil, but by electricity. If cities choose electric power, why, they may not want his oil. People might even want electricity in their homes! It's quite terrifying, all that magnetism going through the walls. Why, one could get burned just leaning on the furniture!"

Jim left us, so Ida stayed an hour, sharing society gossip about who was whose mistress: actresses, some other bloke's wife. Her nose wrinkled up—thank heavens George wasn't like that.

Chicago's great and powerful elite—I wasn't awed by them anymore. All those pointed goatees and tall silk hats, pearls and sables now had a jaded look.

After Ida left, I wrote down the names of people who might want to ruin Chicago's exposition. Any one of them could be using the anarchists, including Ida's beloved husband, George.

✳ ✳ ✳

When I woke again, my limbs throbbed as though they'd been pounded between mortar and pestle. Jim's voice from the parlor murmured through my chamber door, comforting me. Whom was he speaking with?

Abigail? Seeing me hobble to the water closet, Jim capped his pen and came to help, but I needed to do this myself.

Barely able to stand, I clung to the table's edge and gazed in the mirror. My reflection stared back with wild hair, cracked lips, a purple bruise on my forehead. My pale face looked pinched, and my shoulder was mottled pink and green. Washing quickly, I tried to tidy my hair, but my brush caught, and when I pulled, the pain drew tears. Weary, I worked it away from my curls, made a simple toilet and shuffled out.

In the passage, Jim held out my dressing gown. Wincing to see my bruises, he tied my belt. "Would you like breakfast?"

"All right." Hobbling to the parlor, I collapsed into a chair. "Who was that?"

"Alfred's just left. He hopes you're soon better."

A knock at the door heralded breakfast on a series of trollies. A cheery white-hatted chef rolled in the first. Smiling broadly, he delivered a cascade of heavily accented words.

"Madame, I make a presentation for you," he said, snatching the silver cloche off a platter. His broad gesture included Jim in the sweep of his arm. Standing at attention, chin high, he recited, "Custard de caramel, smooth and soft as a silk pillow, sweet but not too sweet, a tinge of bitter orange, like the last touch of sunset."

Jim grinned at the man. "You've made it!"

"*Exactamente*, as you described."

I glanced at Jim, surprised. Was that a ruddy glow on his face? Had he given the chef that fanciful description?

He grinned. "It's for you, sweet. Happy birthday." He offered a scalloped porcelain plate that instantly looked tiny. The chef scooped a crescent of custard upon it.

It was the first of July. I'd turned twenty-two years old in April. Smiling, I popped a spoonful into my mouth.

Smooth. Silken caramel. I caught a hint of orange rind and a whiff of peppermint, garnished like my mama's custard. I was transported home, to the great teak dining table with Papa at the head and Gurung serving custard all around. The aroma of jasmine, palm trees swishing, rain drumming on leaves outside my window and Mama's face creasing in a smile as she said, "Eat, child, while it's still cold."

But I wasn't home; I was thousands of miles away. Emotion overcame me. I hurt, and I might never again see Mama's smile or feel Papa's safe embrace. Dropping my spoon, I stifled a sob and turned into Jim's clasp.

"*Alors!*" the chef cried, a tumble of apologies following. His pensive gaze searched my battered face.

What wouldn't I give for a moment, just one quiet moment back in Bombay? Pulling myself together, I dabbed my nose and raised a wobbly smile for the distraught chef.

"It's very good. Like my mother's," I managed.

Suddenly hungry, I ate the custard and handed back my plate for more. Accepting my thanks the chef gathered his trolley and fled.

When he'd gone, I had Jim fetch my list of possible culprits. One by one, I recited what I'd learned and recounted the evidence incriminating them—or, rather, the lack of it.

"My dear," said Jim, "each of these men might have some motive, but would they harm hundreds of people, thousands, to achieve it? Take Carter Harrison Junior. He might want his father dead, but why ruin the fair? Both his fortune and livelihood are tied up with his father's, in the World's Fair Corporation."

I crossed him off the list. "What about electricity—there's a fierce rivalry between the two sides. Only one can win. The Fairground Commission chose alternating current, so if it goes up in flames, wouldn't it benefit those who're invested in direct current?"

Jim looked skeptical. "But they also have a lot to lose. If there's an inferno, people may turn against electricity entirely. That's a more likely outcome."

One name remained on my list. I met Jim's gaze. "That leaves George. I sent him to bring Bellino to me. Jim, I mentioned explosives."

Jim stared. "George Abernathy?"

"He said I should stay at the Oriental, and he sent me to that awful Mr. Payne. Maybe *he* wrote the note that led me to the elevator."

"This note?" Jim pulled out a folded slip from his vest pocket. "George found it under your cocktail glass. Brought it to me, quite concerned. Diana, he helped find you. Someone said you might have left the dinner—he was downright rude. It's hard to believe . . ."

I gazed at the note. "Of course, he appeared upset! That's his alibi. I told him, Jim. Told him that I suspected Bellino."

Jim's mouth tightened into a grim line. "I'll question him. Get to the bottom of this."

He believed me—a rush of relief boosted me to my feet. "Well, I'm coming too. Let's see Ida and George—take them by surprise."

To be dressed by Jim made me feel like a china doll. Carefully, he placed my skirt over my head, settled it into place and buttoned it. Eager to go, I coiled my hair into a knot, skewering it with pins. Perhaps I'd missed George's start of surprise when I spoke of Bellino at the banquet. By God, I would not miss it again.

CHAPTER 44

ACCUSATIONS

Ida opened the door and gasped to see me there, leaning on Jim's arm. Propelling me to a settee, she said, "My dear, should you be about? Come, do sit down."

George hurried from an inner room, in shirtsleeves and brocade vest.

"Captain, good God! Surely Mrs. O'Trey should rest? What sort of chap are you to make her walk!"

Jim chuckled. "Can *anyone* make Mrs. O'Trey do something she's not of a mind to?"

They shook hands. I suspected Jim was setting George at ease so he wouldn't expect my questions, but I could not match his good humor. Ida fussed around me, bringing cushions. Ensconced against a pile of them like a small maharani, I leaned back to rest.

With a casual air, Jim said, "George—those two from India, last night? Jot down their names, will you?" Smiling, he went to the trolley and hoisted a carafe. "Shall I pour?"

That surprised me, because Jim knows better; it's always the host who pours.

"'Course!" George sat at the secretary and wrote, then handed Jim the note, asking me, "Sherry for you, Mrs. O'Trey? Ida?"

We both accepted. When the talk returned to my plunge down the elevator well, and how I'd survived it, I demurred, asking George, "Did you give Mr. Bellino my message?"

If George had attacked me, he'd be desperate to know what I recalled, I thought.

"I didn't see him, Mrs. O'Trey," said George, crestfallen. "In all the hubbub, I forgot your message."

"We spoke of meeting Mr. Bellino in private, didn't we? I told you he had access to explosives—ah—and was doing something not quite right."

George frowned, nodding. "That rather surprised me. But I didn't see him, so I couldn't arrange it."

"What d'you remember?" said Jim.

In the exchange that followed, I admired Jim's deft questions, put so casually that it seemed as though the two were simply discussing events at the banquet. Jim placed each man who was present, where they'd been and with whom, asking George where he saw them, then supplying his own observations before leading George to another bloke.

He remembered all their names. I could barely recall the women who laughed at me; of the luminaries we'd seen at the parliament, I had only the vaguest impression of their wives or where they were from.

Soon Jim's questions became more personal. "That's when you settled Diana at her table and came to fetch Ida? How long did that take?"

George shrugged. "Oh, a few minutes."

It had been more than a few. I'd finished at least two dances.

He said, "I remember. I met Candice—Ida's mother—and her new husband. We spoke before I returned to Mrs. O'Trey. That's when I saw the note."

Was that before or after I was attacked? I'd spoken to Ida moments before reaching the corridor to the elevator. A needle of suspicion pierced me. I'd met Ida there, at the vestibule—but no, that arm around my throat had been male, and smelled of chemicals. I dropped my gaze, ashamed to have doubted my friend, and turned back to the men.

Jim handed me George's written page, then took out the folded slip of paper I'd received at the banquet. This he placed near George's page. Side by side, I examined these.

George's smile fell off his face. "You don't mean—you can't. Did you think the note was from me?" His mouth twisted. "God's sake, man! Why would I want to harm your wife? What possible reason could I have?"

"George?" Ida looked from him to me, sitting there with the two bits of paper.

He cried, "They think *I* did it! *Me!*"

I repeated, "I suspected Bellino was involved in something nasty. I told you."

"But why would I do it? Tell me that."

He had not understood my suspicion that he was conspiring with Bellino! Was he faking his distress? I said, "And if I say I saw you? That it was you who grabbed my neck?"

His mouth sagged. "Mrs. O'Trey. How could it be? I was inside, talking to Ida's mother and my blasted new father-in-law!" He grimaced. "You thought it was me?"

I went over his words. If he'd said, "It couldn't be me, because you couldn't see! The man was behind you," then I would have been sure it *was* him. But seeing his astonishment, a weight shifted in my mind.

Thinking back, I said, "We spoke about landlords, if you recall. Your opinions are rather . . . egalitarian."

"And that makes me—what? A killer? A ruddy anarchist?"

Why had he used that word, "anarchist"? I searched his gaze and found hurt and offended pride. His disdain for cruel landlords had been natural, unrehearsed. I struggled to recall why I'd been so sure he was my assailant. He owned the Oriental; he had business dealings with Bellino; what else?

"Unless . . ." Ida whispered, "unless she knows something you do not want her to tell me!"

George swung to her. "You think I'd do a thing like that? Shove her into the chute?"

"Diana," Ida pleaded, the hands outstretched, her pale face shrunk small, her hairdo too large, like a Frenchman's wig. "There isn't something like—what we talked about?"

She feared that George had a mistress—that he'd harm me to prevent it getting out! How close they'd been, how carefree as they'd called to me outside the banquet hall, Ida hanging on his arm, her fur stole dangling. Now their union was unraveling.

"Ida," I said, "I don't know anything like that."

She sat down as though her feet had given way. "Thank heaven," she whispered, her voice wobbling.

George held himself stiffly. "If you believe it was me, Mrs. O'Trey . . . there's nothing more to be said."

"Diana, look," said Jim, tapping the paper in my lap. "Examine this."

I dropped my gaze and sucked in a breath. George's writing was crisp and confident, like the stroke of Adi's pen. The other note was sloppy, the letters B and A ill formed.

"They are not alike at all," I said, then remembered that the devious Mr. Payne had been present last night.

"But you could have had someone else write it. Your friend Mr. Payne, for example. He's quite adept at lying."

"Harvey Payne?" George frowned. "What's he done?"

In a few words I told him about my desire to pay a fair price for Osain Box's mine, and Mr. Payne's pretense that the Boxes hadn't arrived at the appointed time.

I ended with, "But they *did* go to his home. They were ejected. Rudely insulted and sent away. All the while, Mr. Payne told me, he was waiting patiently by his desk."

"Well," George muttered. "I'll have the answer for that. Will you come with me, Mrs. O'Trey, Captain? Ida, I suggest you come too."

Ida whispered, "Yes, George."

George arranged for a large carriage, but we climbed aboard in awkward silence. Ida and he sat across from us at either corner of the seat, holding themselves apart. My throat tightened. Had my accusation damaged their bond beyond repair?

At Mr. Harvey Payne's townhome, I took my card from my reticule. Wobbling unsteadily, I handed it to the maid. Jim gripped my arm, saying, "All right, Diana?"

The maid stared. "*You're* Lady Diana?"

"It is my name," I said, wondering what Mr. Payne had said to alarm her so.

Dressed in a well-cut morning coat and pinstriped tie, Harvey Payne appeared at the top of the stairs, saying, "A guest, Betsy?"

At her reply, he came down at once with warm smile and solicitous words, ushering us into his office. I accepted a chair with a groan of relief. Shaking hands with George and Jim, he greeted Ida and inquired after my bruised appearance with a great show of concern.

After the pleasantries, George said, "I say, Harvey, Mrs. O'Trey has a question for you. Would you mind?"

Repeating my earlier test, I asked, "May I see your appointment book, Mr. Payne? It is a matter of importance."

His eyebrows rose; then he shrugged and brought over a leather-bound diary. There, under the date marked June 19th, I read: *Draft Deed of Purchase from Osain Box for Mrs. O'Trey.*

When I laid the assassin's note beside it, the differences were plain. Mr. Payne's precise writing slanted right. His A and B were neat, and fully formed. I handed back his book and shook my head at Jim. It wasn't Harvey Payne.

Glancing around at the four of us, Mr. Payne asked, "May I ask what this is about?"

Instead of an answer, I said, "Collin Box. He said he came here with his father. You refused to see them?"

Mr. Payne's face stiffened, and his skin seemed to stretch across his cheekbones.

I said coldly, "You said he smelled of drink."

He gave a start. Striding to the door, he summoned the butler and asked, "Joe, some days ago, did two workmen come here? Messy fellows, bit off-color?"

The butler inclined his head. "Yes, sir."

I drew a breath. Well, now! Mr. Payne said, "And you asked them to leave? I specifically said I was expecting clients."

"Sir," the butler said to the floor, "perhaps if you speak with the general?"

Harvey Payne sucked in a breath. "You thought they wanted to see him?"

"No, sir. They asked for you—Mr. Payne, the lawyer. But your father was just returning from his constitutional. And—well—he called them a pair of drunks, sir, and turned them away."

Good grief! It wasn't Harvey, but his father! I felt relieved and also contrite to have misjudged him. Dismissing the butler, he apologized, looking abashed.

Wanting to be certain, I asked, "May we speak to your father, Mr. Payne?"

Harvey spread his hands. "I do not advise it. He's been unwell."

Refusing to bend to his charm, I said, "That *is* convenient, Mr. Payne."

Harvey's chin jerked up. With a bow, he said, "Excuse me. I'll see if he will have company."

A glimmer in Jim's look made me blush. This time I had not backed down. I would not relent, but neither was I harsh or unyielding. If I had mistaken Harvey, he would have my sincere apology. I rehearsed it in my mind.

The office door swung open to admit a short man with a tuft of silver hair and lively eyes over a pointed, white beard. Dapper in a pale blue vest and coat, a gold chain looped into his pocket, he made a fine portrait of a Civil War hero. I had a curious sense that I'd seen him before, perhaps in a painting somewhere.

George did the introductions. The old man shook their hands, bowed over Ida's hand and mine and drawled, "Mah pleaaaasure, gentlemen. It's a fine thing to have young ladies here, in this house again. Mr. O'Trey? Were you a soldier, sir?" His voice dropped. "What army?"

"British army," said Jim.

Looking pleased, the old man turned to me. "And where are you from, ma'am?"

"I was born in India," I replied. An aching band clenched around my heavy head. Eager to depart, I came straight to the point.

"If I may be so bold, just over a week ago, did a pair of workmen come to your door? And did you have words with them?"

The general drew back with a haughty laugh. "Have words, madam?" he asked, turning the salutation into a sneer. "With a pair of drunks? I think not. But what's this? Question *me* about who I admit into my own house? From India, eh? A hopped-up darkie, are you? All sort of mongrels dress the part these days."

Jim's eyes flashed. Mongrel. As a mixed-race man, he'd suffered many insults. How often he'd been cut, rebuffed or disparaged simply for his Indian name. An image flashed in my mind, a brute holding Tobias, while another punched him, snapping his head back. Hot emotion spiked through me.

Perhaps if I had not been so tired, my body still aching so that even to sit was painful, perhaps if I'd been rested, I might have been more circumspect. But I was all out of patience. I stood up.

In a cold, clear voice I said, "I'm as pure-blooded as they come, sir. I can trace my ancestors back twelve generations. Can you? No? That makes *you* the mongrel."

Taking Jim's arm, I stalked out. George and Ida followed, stiff and silent. Wide-eyed, Betsy backed away to let us pass. Harvey accompanied us to the carriage and handed me in, then leaned in at the window, looking pained.

"My apologies, Mrs. O'Trey. He's been, ah, more difficult, these days."

I took his hand and gave him my heartfelt regrets. Then I asked, "Are there many like him? Why do they hate colored people so?"

"He fought for the South," said Harvey, a lock of hair falling over his forehead. "Losing the war was a terrible blow—he lost everything to it. It's thirty years ago, but he won't forget. He's a tough old bird, Mrs. O'Trey. Yes, I suppose there are still a few like him."

We bid goodbye and set off, each jolt of the carriage jarring me to my bones. Remembering my duty, I said to the pair sitting across, "George, Ida, I owe you an apology too. I was terribly wrong. Do you forgive me?"

George exhaled in a gust, then smiled. "Of course. But my word, Diana! You gave the old fella back! You gave him good."

Ida laughed, repeating, "*No,* sir, that makes *you* the mongrel!"

"What an awful thing to say," I groaned, putting a hand to my throbbing forehead. "I just wanted to throw something at him!"

I stole a look at Jim. He was grinning from ear to ear.

Leaving George and Ida with heartfelt words, we rode up the elevator to find Abigail waiting in our room. Dressed as a man, she sat on a settee, legs stretched out before her.

Catching sight of my bruises, she leapt up, eyes wide. "Lord Almighty! What happened?"

As I recounted the attack and my fall, her face paled. Outrage glittered in her eyes.

That arm around my neck. So close, so tight. When I'd thrown my head back, I'd hit the man's chin. So how tall had he been? I said, "Would you help me with an experiment?"

First, I directed Jim to stand behind me and place his arm around my neck. I leaned back against his chest, but could not feel his chin. Then I did the same with Abigail.

"Tighter!" I insisted. As Abigail's elbow tightened, I snapped my head back, and bumped something.

I turned back to see her rub her nose. "The fellow was taller than Abigail!" I said with a triumphant grin. "I think I smacked his chin with the top of my head. Jim, your chin is higher than my assailant's!"

Jim glowed with a look that made me blush. "A tall fellow. Well done. Anything else?"

"His black wool sleeve smelled peculiar. Pungent, really. If I smell it again, I'll know it."

Jim's eyes went wintery.

"Enri Bellino and Peter Dupree are both fairly tall. And partial to perfume."

CHAPTER 45

A DIAMOND AMONG DROSS

Jim departed early, leaving only a brief note: *Back soon. Please rest, J.*

So, I breakfasted with Abigail. Dressed in dove grey, her hair pinned modestly, her features reserved, she poured my tea. She'd given crucial information to Peter Dupree and, through him, to Bellino. Had she held back Jim's alias, protecting him, or not known it? Then there was that look on her face when she learned of the assault on me.

Why did Miss Arsenault dislike her? I sent the bellboy to summon her.

While we waited, I scanned the morning papers. It was the second of July—a parade was planned on the fourth, with acrobats. Fairgoers would see fireworks over the lake. With festivities and speeches, Chicago would celebrate the birthday of America, a hundred and seventeen years old.

When Miss Arsenault arrived, I motioned Abigail to silence, and asked, "Tell me, why did you look so upset last time? Was it something to do with my maid?"

Pale lashes framed Mis Arsenault's round eyes. "Begging pardon, ma'am. Only, there's a lad that speaks just like her! He calls on the phone, see? Well, we chat a bit, sometimes. He's nice, ma'am. It surprised me, that's all."

Ah. Abigail's demeanor expressed only polite interest. You rascal, I thought. Not above sweet-talking the telephone girl, hmm?

Glad to have solved that conundrum, I said, "You told me you heard Mr. Bellino on the telephone. Can you repeat what he said?"

She screwed her face tight, like a child counting down a game of hide-and-seek. Eyes closed, she drawled, "Annie Oakley. Git rid of 'im."

I pulled in a breath. "Annie Oakley?" This was not what she'd told me before!

Miss Arsenault gushed. "She's a shooter, ma'am! In Buffalo Bill's Wild West Show! She's right tooting amazing!"

"You said Agney was in trouble. What about seeing him at a carriage?"

She chewed her lower lip, nodding. "I remember that. Annie was in a carriage too long, he said. A half hour. Met someone near the post office—didn't go nowhere. Mr. Bellino sounded upset about that, cussin' and all."

I puzzled over it. Perhaps she had been trying to impress me the first time, sitting upright and stiff. Even then, the words "Agney or Clay" had been garbled. She'd mentioned my meeting with Jim in the carriage by the post office just after it occurred. So, her original words must be accurate. Or . . . was Bellino speaking on the phone with Peter? I'd revealed Jim's real name to him in Boston.

"What you heard, could it have been Agnihotri?" I said it slowly, parsing out the syllables.

Miss Arsenault's mouth dropped open. "That it, ma'am! That's the one. Annie-or-tree."

There it was. So Bellino had likely been speaking with Peter. Feigning composure, I thanked Miss Arsenault and said goodbye.

When she'd gone, Abigail and I discussed her curious reversal. Then I asked, "Did you know Jim's real name?"

She shook her head. "He went by O'Trey. We used to kid him, calling him Captain."

"Indeed. That telegram to Swamiji puzzles me. What sort of killer alerts his victim? Did they want to terrify him?" Was this some strange form of chivalry? I paused. Or was someone within the anarchists' ranks on our side? After all, Jim had infiltrated them, why not someone else?

I remembered General Payne's vicious glare and frowned. "The Civil War was thirty years ago? Then the mayor, Mr. Harrison, would have fought?"

He had. So had the president, the governor and previous presidents. Most men over forty-five—many in Chicago's government and industry—had served in the Union army.

What if it wasn't oil, or direct current, or someone trying to eliminate a rival?

We had a simple luncheon, but I fidgeted with the meal, unable to eat much.

Sending it away, I tapped my fingers, wondering if I was seeing shadows where there were none. Thank heaven I had sent *Abigail* and not Tobias to that rabid General Payne's home with my letter. Then I paused, questioning that line of thought. Harvey had implied my messenger was a man.

"Abigail, that day I sent you to the lawyer, Mr. Payne—did you meet him, or someone else?"

When she pulled back, disconcerted, I said, "Please, Abigail. The truth."

Licking her lips, she said, "I didn't go. I found Tobias in the street and sent him. Peter wanted to see me, so I had Tobias take your letter. Did he not deliver it?"

"He did." Cold dread touched my spine. General Payne had been rude to me, a lady, belligerent, calling me a mongrel because I was from India. He'd snarled, despite Jim's large presence and the Abernathys.

I carefully laid down my fork. Had Tobias come across the general when he went to deliver my letter? Had he been spotted by the anarchists? Or nabbed because of his race?

I put a hand to my throbbing head, recalling the maid's startled exclamation, as I stood on Payne's stoop. "*You're* Lady Diana?"

Why would she know that name? It was a tenuous link, but I had to explore it. I would ask Jim to meet me there. When I told Abigail about the maid's reaction, her brow furrowed. "She said that—Lady Diana? That's odd."

"More than odd—Tobias calls me that. Can you let Jim know?"

Sending Abigail with a note to Jim, I began the slow process of bathing and dressing. The bruises on my side had turned purple, but a wide hat and veil masked my forehead.

When hours passed without Abigail's return, I fretted. Something flickered in my memory. After replying to Adi's telegram, I'd sent one to Professor Grimke. His answer could be waiting at the telegraph office. Anxious to waste no time, I trudged downstairs and hailed a hansom cab. My ribs protested each jolt on the short trip to Adams Street.

At the main post and telegraph office, I asked the cabbie to wait and hurried in. Grimke's reply was indeed waiting for me. It contained just a single word: ALKOLER.

I read it over again, but it made no sense. Was this a chemical? A place? Some sort of code word? Was it a German word? Jim might know, or the police detectives.

The late-summer sun was setting as I stuffed the telegram into my glove and came out.

I climbed back into the hansom, saying, "City Hall, please."

The late evening was overcast. Gaslights lined the street. A quiet pall shrouded police headquarters when I stepped from the cab. I started for the door.

"Hoy, miss!" the cabdriver called, rubbing his thumb and forefinger together.

I stared, then my surprise turned to chagrin. I'd forgotten to pay, since I was usually accompanied by a man who'd do it.

When I scrabbled in my reticule for coins, he said, "Your man in there?"

"Yes. Ten cents, you said?"

"Fifteen, but a dime'll do, if that's what you got."

His words struck me with a strange impact. A supper or breakfast cost fifteen cents, a turkey dinner was a quarter. This, here, was the real America—this stubble-faced coachman in a dented hat who didn't even know me, who made two dollars on a good day. To his midwestern ear, my London English must sound stiff and standoffish. I hadn't been polite or sociable, but he knew from the address I gave him that something was amiss, and so he was kind.

Without obtrusive questions, without pity or philosophy, his sympathy wrapped about me like a warm cloak. That nickel's worth was likely all the profit he'd make from my ride. I didn't know when he'd last eaten, what troubles he would go home to, or even if he had a home. Perhaps he slept in this very conveyance. His too-small coat was torn, his hat bent and his face grimy, but what did that matter? A moment of sweet clarity buoyed me—this was why Jim loved this country of immigrants, because one might find a shining pearl hidden anywhere, from the meanest street to the finest mansion.

I found a bill and handed it up, saying, "Keep it. You've done more than you know."

The police headquarters were deserted as I hurried in.

The aged desk sergeant frowned at me. "Emergencies only, ma'am. What's your trouble?"

I gestured at the empty hall. "Where is everyone?"

He sighed. "Past hours, ma'am. What's the nature of your business?"

"My husband, Mr. O'Trey—he's assisting an investigation. Is he here?"

He gave me a long look. "Everyone's needed today, lady. I don't know O'Trey, but you should go home. He'll be along soon enough."

Drat. I needed to show Jim what Professor Grimke had wired. It made no sense to me, but Jim might understand it. Leaving the building, my shoulders ached as though I'd hoisted a wardrobe on my back. It was too soon to be walking around after my accident. I raked the empty street for a cab, then plodded to the crossroads.

In the gloom, my foot narrowly missed a rat, which darted away with a shriek.

"Yehh!" I shuddered, running up to the sidewalk. As I turned, a thickset man in an overcoat and floppy hat ducked his head. Was he following me?

If I approached him, he could simply feign ignorance. So, I went around a corner and tucked myself to one side.

He came up fast, puffing. The grumpy cabbie from the vegetable market?

I said, "Hello," and pointed my parasol at him. "You've been following me."

"Eh? Who're you?" said the dope, feigning ignorance.

I huffed. "Left your cab, have you? You were at the State Street market."

"Huh!" he said, turning up his collar to walk away. I scowled. I needed answers! So, I jabbed my parasol between his shins to trip him.

The result was awful. The parasol yanked out of my hands. Feet entangled, the fellow gave a strangled yelp and landed in the dirt.

Astonished, I said, "I'm sorry. Hope you aren't hurt," and picked up my parasol.

Snarling, he leapt up and grabbed my elbow, hauling me toward an approaching hack. "You're coming with me."

"No!" I struggled, crying out when he grabbed my poor elbow. In the warm weather I'd forgotten my muff—and my derringer! He dragged me forward.

"Stop!" I shrieked, from the pain in my wrist.

Abigail's voice snapped out, "Let her go."

I scarcely recognized her, dressed as a man. Light glinted off the barrel of a weapon.

My assailant thrust me into her with such force that both of us tumbled to the ground. By the time I sat up, brushing off my dress, both he and the cab were gone.

Numbed by the speed of these events, I pushed my hat back on my head and nursed my wrist. Aching from tip to toe, I gasped, "Abigail, Thank heaven!"

She helped me up, grinning. "Captain Jim asked me to keep you safe. Seen that bloke around a few times, so I tailed him. Name of Prendergast—the newsies know him. He was waiting outside our hotel and followed you."

A wave of affection billowed inside me. What a strange yet loyal friend Abigail was turning out to be. Americans were curious creatures, stiff and distant when you first meet them, patronizing even. Perhaps they imagined people born elsewhere must either be deaf or stupid. Yet I'd found them to be generous and forgiving, even kindly when one did not expect it. My accusation had driven a wedge between Ida and George, but they had not held it against me. Abigail had come to my aid when most I needed it. "They're just people," Jim had said. Perhaps he was right.

I asked, "Did you give Jim my note?"

"I did. They're running raids today. All the hideouts, all at once. They expect to arrest the lot." She hailed a passing hansom. "Let's get you back to the hotel."

Climbing in cautiously, for my wrist still burned, I hesitated. Although I wanted nothing more than to put up my feet, it must wait. If there was the slightest chance of finding Tobias, I must take it.

"Abigail, we have no time to waste. We're going to visit Mr. Payne."

Calling to the hansom driver on top, I gave him the address, wincing as we clattered down the street.

CHAPTER 46

THE ENEMY WITHIN

On Dearborn Street we passed a little pharmacy touting a host of remedies, and a three-story building marked PROVIDENCE HOSPI-TAL, then turned onto Thirtieth. As we pulled up near Harvey Payne's home, its dark windows and unlit door lamps warned us no one was home. Abigail rapped the knocker, waited, then knocked again.

The door opened a few inches, and someone peeked out. Spotting Betsy, with her distinctive maid's cap, I said, "Hello?"

She opened the door wider. The corridor behind her was unlit, but candlelight flickered from the parlor. Perhaps the servants were not permitted to light gas lamps when the Paynes were out? I frowned. The true measure of a man was in how he treats those he employs.

"Please, ma'am, no one's home," Betsy whispered, her voice pleading.

Surprised, for she had not seemed timid, I said, "Why, what's the matter?"

She grimaced. "Please go!"

Abigail stepped up. "Miss, you called her Lady Diana before. Where did you hear her name?"

Betsy glanced over her shoulder. "Come, then. But God help, if they return!"

Leading us through the kitchen, she lit a candle, swung open another door and descended a set of narrow steps.

Abigail and I exchanged looks. Where was she leading us?

"Stay here," I told Abigail. Parasol clenched in one hand, the other gripping the thin indentation in the wall that passed for a rail, I followed Betsy's glimmering light as it descended.

She hurried to the bin along the wall, under the spout where coal would be shoveled in from outside. There she called, "Toby?"

To my astonishment, his deep voice said, "All right, Miss Betsy. I'll be right fine."

"Look, Toby! Someone's come for you."

The coal moved. A hand appeared, then an arm and shoulder. Tobias sat up, dropping clumps all around.

"Oh, Tobias!" I rushed forward to help him out, but he groaned, holding up a hand.

His eyes sunken and dull in the dim light, Tobias's lips spread into a wide smile. "I'm weak as a newborn hawg," he said in his slow curling voice, "but it does me good to see you, Lady Diana." Noticing my bruises, he said, "You're well, ma'am?"

"I'm not sure which of us is prettier, right now, Tobias."

He chuckled. "I told them you'd come, and sure 'nough, here you are."

Betsy said, "He can't walk, ma'am. They brought him here stone cold, told Joe to get rid of him, but he was breathing, so we jus' hid him. Joe went to get a doctor just now."

"Who, Betsy? Who did this?"

Tobias tried to lever himself from the bin, groaning, so she only said, "There's all sorts come in this house now. I jus' keep out of their way."

Between us, Betsy and I helped Tobias up. Betsy got an arm around his waist, and he leaned on my arm. Together, we reached the door.

"How'd they get you, Tobias?" I asked. Wax from the wobbling candle singed my fingers. We inched up the dusty, narrow stairwell.

"I delivered your letter, was just leaving and I came up face-to-face with two of them. Recognized me from Canal Street." He groaned as he took another step.

"Abigail!" I called, to send her for a carriage. No reply.

We made slow progress, since the stair barely allowed two abreast. Each time Tobias trod on his left foot, he moaned.

"Abigail?" I said, thrusting the cellar door open with my bandaged hand. My dress was ruined, both Betsy and I covered in soot, but Tobias was alive!

Then I saw why Abigail couldn't answer.

A man in a long overcoat stood in the door, legs planted, his blade pointed at Abigail. I gasped—it was the bloke who'd accosted me in the street, the grumpy cabbie, Prendergast.

Tobias grunted in pain, weaving on his feet.

Prendergast grinned. "Well, well! Good things come to those who wait."

A muffled hiss came from Abigail. She was staring at Prendergast's blade. What did she mean? Should I distract him so she could grab his weapon?

I asked, "You've taken a great deal of trouble to find me. What do you want?"

"What'd you tell 'em, huh? The police, what do they know?"

Trembling, I tried to think. He meant to kill us. But a man with a knife can only stab one person at a time. Tobias could barely stand. It was up to Abigail and me. "You mean, about the explosives?" I asked, stringing him along. "The ballistite?"

I'd left my parasol in the cellar. Nor could I reach for a hatpin, not holding a candle. *Use what you have,* Jim had said, *everything is a weapon.* Wax puddled at the bottom of my wick, threatening to spill. That would have to do.

"Spit it out. Or this one gets it!" Prendergast threatened Tobias.

"All right!" I cried, pretending to give up. "But don't you think . . ." Midsentence, I threw the candle at his face. This had two effects—our light blinked out, leaving us in semidarkness. And the hot wax shocked a cry from him.

Then Betsy—or was it Abigail?—was upon him. Someone fell against me, dropping me to hands and knees. Pain skewered my wrist. Shouts and cries in the dark!

Once Betsy turned up a gas lamp, I spotted Abigail.

"Thank heavens!" I cried. But where was Prendergast?

Abigail leaned, clutching her bloody forearm, grimacing. I followed her gaze to Tobias. He slumped, staring down at his chest where the white hilt of a knife protruded.

Eyes closing, he slid sideways to the floor.

The air left my body in a great gust. The next moments were a blur—rushing to the kitchen, grabbing the kitchen towel. A jumble of questions, commands; Betsy, by my side, her answers brief as she ran to turn up lamps.

Tobias stirred, his hand reaching for his chest.

"Stop!" I said. While I'd worked at Boston Baptist Hospital, a man had come in bleeding from an accident, a steel bar still protruding from his belly. If Tobias yanked out the blade, he'd bleed to death. I caught his fingers, forcing calm into my voice.

"Don't touch it."

Just then the shriek of police whistles pierced the air. The door slammed and footsteps hammered toward us. Uniformed constables burst in, weapons drawn, shouting, "Don't move! You're under arrest."

"Thank heaven!" I cried. "This man needs a doctor!"

A policeman peered down at me. "Who're you?"

I explained quickly, then remembered the hospital we'd passed on Dearborn Street.

I'd just told him what to do when Jim's voice demanded, "Diana?"

"I'm here!" I called.

Patrolmen gave way as Jim's broad form pushed past them.

I blurted, "It's Tobias. He's . . ." My shock and remorse scrambled with relief at seeing Jim. "Oh Jim, I should never have brought him!"

Army fellows don't dither. Jim grasped our predicament and rapped out orders. Making a gurney of the couch, we carried Tobias toward Chicago's Providence Hospital. I hurried alongside, murmuring words of comfort. As though making up for days without speaking, Tobias began to talk.

He said, "I just dropped and lay there, you see. They kicked me a few times, but I didn't move. 'Playing possum,' my father called it. They thought I was dead. Joe, the butler, and little Betsy, they saved me. Put me in the coal bin. I listened real careful, 'coz those hoodlums, they laugh and joke loudly. Betsy told me about POW—that's a place, ma'am? The general was gonna blow it up."

He breathed in and out in audible gasps. It was a moment before he spoke again. "Captain, I was sure you'd come. But POW was in danger, sir. So, I got Joe to send a telegram—to the fella they was talking about, at the Palmer Hotel. The Swah-mee."

Carrying a corner of the couch, Jim said, "That was well done!"

Keeping pace, I said, "We got your wire, Tobias. You saved the parliament!"

"Ahhhh." Tobias smiled his relief. "But the big one, missus, that's on the Fourth of July. It's all they ever talk about."

I drew a breath, my mind in a whirl. The big one. Tomorrow.

Tobias's words slurred. "Ain't your fault, Lady Diana. All my life I've had to watch so carefully—a single word could be taken amiss. Every look, where I lay my eyes, my shoulders too easy, my head too high. Why, anything could make a man mad. It don't take much. Like my father said, 'Be careful, son. Be watchful; don't let them see what's in your mind.'"

We turned onto Dearborn Street, hurrying in unison.

Tobias's voice thinned. "Walking careful, all my life. How long, huh? How long I got to do this? They say we free. But I ain't free. I don't know what free feels like. And what's it matter, anyhow? I am sixty years old, Lady Diana. I don't have many years left in this ole body. When Mr. Dupree said you asked for me, why it nearly knocked me over. I was so pleased, ma'am. I thank you for that. Th' others made no sense of it, asking for this old soul, no one else."

Tobias chuckled, swiping at his face as though something obstructed his eyes. Jim thrust open the hospital door. White walls. The sharp smell of carbolic soap.

A physician rushed up, a colored man with a neat mustache and intelligent eyes. "I'm Doctor Williams, what's happened?"

He bent over Tobias, drew the coat away from the protruding blade, and called a series of instructions to his staff.

"He'll live, won't he?" I choked.

"I will do all I can," he said, shooing Tobias's litter inside.

***

Slumped on a bench, we waited. When I told Jim about Prendergast, how Abigail had defended me, his jaw tightened.

"Blast. They moved quickly. We found most of the gang. Arrested nineteen. We nabbed some at the old factory. Got your friend, Bellino—he'd sold them pulleys and such. Impounded his ship. Long thinks we'll find the explosives." He went off to find a telephone.

When he returned, I asked, "They found it? The ballistite?"

He shook his head, his face grim.

"Then we're too late. The explosives are already in place. Oh Jim, this is bad!"

"There's still time."

An hour passed. I remembered Tobias's kindness each time he brought Jim's wages, how he'd inquired after my health and offered to bring me what I needed. How much I depended upon him! When my ignorance got him beat up, not once had he rebuked me, treating it with such delicacy that he had never even mentioned it again. He'd spent nights overlooking the factory, waiting in the rain, bringing me pieces of information.

Silence wrapped around us. A pair of nurses slipped by, walking softly. A prayer whispered in my mind. *Kemna Mazda* . . . who will help in this hour of need? Be fair, Lord of Wisdom, do not punish Tobias for my mistakes. Make him strong, steady his surgeon's hand. In my mind I heard a priest's baritone saying prayers at Sanober's funeral . . . or was it Papa's voice chanting a blessing? I'd woken to that sound each morning of my childhood.

Jim murmured, "I've heard your father say those words."

He'd heard me whisper. I leaned against him to drive out the shadows from his eyes. He tightened his hold against the coming tide. Footsteps neared us.

The nurse, Emma Reynolds, approached to say that Martin Gale was recovering from the slash to his arm, and presently asleep. Tobias was still in surgery.

"The knife nicked the myocardium," she said carefully, "of his heart."

A cold tremor brushed down my back. I whispered, "His heart! Then it's no use."

Her chin came up. "It's true that it's never been done. A wound to the heart is . . . usually fatal." Then her smile glowed like sunshine piercing monsoon clouds. "But Doctor Daniel Williams is the best surgeon in Chicago, perhaps best in the country."

She paused, her brown eyes concerned. "Are you injured, too?"

I smiled and assured her I was all right.

Hours later, her quick footsteps tapped back toward us. I felt Jim move and straightened, wincing. Was it over?

Her white cap stark against her midnight skin, the diminutive woman said, "Your friend survived the surgery. Doctor Williams has repaired the heart. But don't start celebratin'. It could be a while. Go on home, now."

I clutched her hand, wordless with emotion. Then, feeling wrung out, we returned to our hotel, leaving Tobias and Abigail in her care.

In my room, my legs gave way. I didn't fall, for Jim wrapped his arms around me. My feet dangled, but that was all right. "I owe Tobias a great deal," I said into his shirt.

"Hmm." His deep voice thrummed against my ear.

Long moments later, he set me down. After weeks of searching, was our task complete? My shirtwaist clung to me, sticky with Tobias's blood. Peeling it off, I stepped out of my skirt. Both were beyond repair. Aching as though I'd been riding a particularly ornery mount, I washed and put on an Indian kaftan, breathing in the scent of soft cotton, and home.

I followed Jim to the washroom, taking each item of clothing. "How did they know, Jim? How'd they know we were coming?"

Jim wiped his face, looking drawn. "It means there's an enemy within, Diana. Someone's leaking information. That's why the general and his cronies got away."

"Someone within the police force?"

"Maybe." With a groan of exhaustion, he stretched out on the bed.

I curved against Jim's side, taking comfort from his firmness, the width of him. He traced the bruise on my forehead with his fingertips. My mind whirled from one thing to another like a dervish, my heart drumming away, my mouth sour with bile.

"I feel awful, Jim; my head hurts." I groaned. "I don't feel like myself!"

His lips pressed to my temple.

"I'm scared too. And you're beat-up, sweet. Give it time. Food, rest and sleep." His chest rose and fell. "Remember when I got back to Simla?"

"You passed out on the doorstep."

Brushing hair off my forehead, he said, "Mmm. I slept—was it a day? Two? Your mother woke me for meals. Soup and food, plenty of it. And you brought my boys in from time to time."

Making his way to Simla on foot, Jim had found a starving troop of urchins and carried them back to Papa's house. I smiled, thinking of their lean faces, how they stuffed themselves with Mama's gulab jamun sweets.

Jim said, "That was the first time I knew a home, Diana, other than the barracks. The sense of shelter. Felt safe under your father's roof. That was *home*. Now it's here. With you." He raised himself on an elbow. "That's why I don't want you there tomorrow. I can't—"

This again? I cut him off. "But you'll go, yes? So how can I stay?"

His arms tightened. "God, you're so tiny. Just promise, sweet, that you'll do as I say. Promise me."

I did. Something inside me flickered like a match that caught, building to a glow. That night I prayed, repeating in my mind Persian words first uttered thousands of years ago, whose meaning had faded from my memory: *ashem vohu, vahistem asti.*

CHAPTER 47

SMALL PEOPLE

Y ou look twelve," Jim said, sitting on my bed in his undershirt. He moved a curl from my face and smiled to see me yawn. The feel of him, the gingery fresh scent of his soap felt so right, so normal after weeks apart.

"I've been thinking, sweet," he said, settling me against him. "You must know something . . . about our arsonists. It's twice they've attacked you. At the elevator, and again yesterday."

I frowned. "Prendergast asked what I'd told the police. What could he imagine I know?"

Jim's eyes flickered to the bruise on my forehead. "You've done something to alarm them. Go over it again. What did you do just before the mayor's ball?"

Considering each step I'd taken, I sat up carefully and dressed with his help. After the anarchists' meeting, I'd been pulled into Collin's troubles.

"I wired Adi, and the Lins. And Professor Grimke . . ." I grimaced. "Back in Boston, when he showed me the German letter, he seemed so upset. Why'd you send it to him—couldn't you have found someone here to translate?"

Jim's eyes crinkled. "He's a professor of chemistry. Not many of them around."

I nodded, tracing my steps. "I wired him: Was he a chemist? Received his reply yesterday, so I went to find you at City Hall— My glove! Where is it?" In all the ruckus, I'd quite forgotten it. I rummaged in the laundry hamper.

Upending the basket spread the smell of soot and hospital odors. I snatched up my sodden glove, and dug out the folded telegram.

Waving it triumphantly, I read aloud, "ALKOLER. Is that a chemical?"

Jim gazed at the telegram for long minutes. Repeating the word, he put on his shirt, vest and tie.

"You're going out?" I asked, as he buttoned on cuffs.

He nodded, wearing his coat. "I searched two German brothers, found nothing. Can't accuse them for where they were born. Some of the Haymarket eight were of German stock, but so are thousands here in the Midwest. Alkoler. Albert? No, it would be Albrecht. Al Kohler.

"I know him—goes by Al Collier. He used to hang around Donnelly, but didn't speak much. He's a chemist?"

* * *

Why did Jim let me accompany him that day? I did not ask in case he changed his mind. Perhaps after I was attacked, he no longer believed that I was safe in the hotel? I waited, out of sight in the carriage, while he stalked into a tavern.

He returned, shaking his head. "Collier's not been around in days."

At a squat, nondescript building, we met Sergeant Long. He had a word with Jim, then we took a train to the World's Fair.

The turnstiles at the station were opening for the day and the automated sidewalk did not move. Sunlight gleamed off the gold dome of the Administration Building.

Clutching Jim's arm, I hurried alongside to match his stride. We traversed the wide walkways, just now being peopled with early visitors. Now and again, he'd notice my pace and slow his steps. I'd always disliked being short, and now I swore my puny stride would not delay him. We had to find that ballistite.

By morning's end I was glad I'd worn my soft kid boots. The fairground was so vast, most visitors rode the circular Intramural Railway that ran around its perimeter. At the Transportation Building, Jim conferred with some guards. At noon, we bought sandwiches and lemonade from a vendor. Sitting on the green where the North Pool reflected perfect pillows of white cloud, we ate, then resumed our search.

Where was it, the bomb that could blow us all to kingdom come? Passing the sign for public conveniences, I said, "Jim, the water pipes? Do they run underground? Has anyone checked the public facilities?"

He nodded. "Cleared this morning."

"What about rooftops? From there, one could see most everything." I pointed to the gallery of the mammoth Machinery Building.

"Got lads posted on each of them, and inside."

In the late afternoon, pausing before the Palisade, Jim studied the scene, his gaze moving along the structures and probing the crowds. I perched on the base of a Roman statue, begged pardon of the stone giant, and tried to catch my breath.

It was a glorious day. All around, buildings reflected in the mirror-surface of the Grand Basin. Across the way, Big Mary, the Statue of the Republic, held aloft her laurel-crowned head. Burnished in gold, her uplifted face remote, she towered two hundred feet above the basin and its wreath of colonnaded buildings. Jim turned to search the arched peristyle behind us.

"That's where they'll set off fireworks." He pointed to the Water Gate, which connected to Lake Michigan. A long festive barge moved through the peristyle for the evening's entertainment. "Half a million visitors will be here this evening."

We crossed a bridge where the North Canal connected the basin to the distant lagoon. Smiling fairgoers pointed at small electric boats that sped soundlessly on the glassy canal, dimpling reflections in their wake. Some lucky visitors sat in rolling chairs pushed by enterprising young men. Grins flashed, children laughed, mothers exclaimed. My middle knotted with dread. Which of them would outlive this day?

We continued northward, joining excited fairgoers around the still lagoon. The Wooded Isle hovered on the water, willows curved like graceful maidens dipping their pots to collect water. The tops of Japanese structures peeked out among the greenery, adding a lattice of red and white. Somewhere amid that picturesque beauty a scorpion hid its sting.

Where could one stash seventeen crates? We pushed through the crowded Midway. A tout called out, "Watch Little Egypt do the hoochy koochy! Never seen in America before! The wonders of the East!" Food carts lined the walk. Tents offered acrobats and jugglers, but also snake charmers, hula dancers, lions and other attractions.

Yet the narrow streets could not contain more than a few hundred. So, we returned on the elevated train to the Court of Honor.

There, Jim swung around, frowning.

I said, "Tell me what you see?"

He flicked a look at me, then said in an undertone, "Most people enter the Court and cluster around the water. The parade starts at the street entrance near the Women's Building. It will go along the Transportation Building, there, and take the path we followed. It curves around the court to that open space near the fountain. D'you see it? The sculpture of Columbus's ship. In front of the Administration Building, the one with the gold dome."

"That's at five? Before the fireworks?" It was now three in the afternoon.

"Parade gets here at four—it will take an hour or more to reach the fountain. Music and speeches till dark. The fireworks in the harbor, that's what folks will watch . . . That gent—blue-coat. Walked down to the water and returned. What's he up to? Where will most people be? That's where it'll do the most damage . . . Ah, he's found his wife. And that short bloke's a Pinkerton—I know him.

"No point setting off the bomb in the harbor. Has to be here. But where? The Manufacturers Building is the largest. But with the parade coming, it'll be empty. How did they unload seventeen crates without drawing attention? As food supplies? But that's on the Midway, not here. Only a few vendors here. These aren't large enough."

I had a chilling thought. "Jim, what if the crates are spread around?"

He shook his head. "If the incendiaries are separated, we should have discovered at least some." Desperation threaded his voice. "Christ, Diana, they could be anywhere."

I caught his arm. "Jim, let's work backwards. Where would you put them?"

He puffed out a breath. "Somewhere central. I'd have a timing device on them and be long gone. Not too far, but where I could see it go off, and the pandemonium. I'd watch, make damned sure. I'd want to see the panic, the stampede, from high up."

Hearing his dispassionate voice, I shuddered. "A timing device?"

He jerked. "God, I hope not. A device like that exploded in Paris last year."

"Then the gang won't stay after setting it. You're searching to see them leave! Right. Let's focus on the bomb. You said someplace central to people. Where?"

Jim didn't answer, his gaze traveling along the water's edge.

"Wait here," he said, and strode over to inspect a vendor's cart. A blue-uniformed Columbian Guard in tasseled uniform and sword joined him there. They spoke, their heads close together. The vendor took off the cloth covering his cart and stood back, hands on his hips.

Collin Box stepped toward me.

"Evening," he said, his grim face pale.

I smiled. "Collin, I've found out why Mr. Payne didn't pay you. That wasn't Mr. Payne you met, but his father, General Payne. It was a mistake to send you there. But I have your money safe. Come to my hotel tomorrow, and we'll get this done. All right?"

He gazed steadily at me. "I asked lots of folks to buy the mine. No one came to our home but you." He looked away. "Doesn't matter now. Pa's dead. Died yesterday."

"No," I gasped. Osain Box was dead. He would never see the fruit of his labor. "How did it happen? Your poor ma."

I shook my head, biting my lip. To be so close to the goal, and never reach it. How unfair this was! To have worked and starved and hoped, only to be beaten away from the finish line. Had he given up, in the end?

"Oh, Collin, I'm so sorry," I whispered. Had he followed us all day to tell me? My vision blurred. I swiped at my eyes to clear the tears.

His face drained of emotion. "I'm not Collin," he blurted. "I'm Eustace."

I blinked. Where had I heard that name? Wasn't Eustace the missing miner, the one who was "not right in the head"? I'd mistaken the chalky color of Collin's hair for grime. He seemed young because of his small stature, but his worn face revealed he was older.

His voice stretched taut, he said, "Osain was my partner. After the accident I went down to Texas. Got into trouble." He cursed. "A fight, fifteen years ago. The bloke died, so I hoofed it. Osain's kid was dead, and he let me take his name. I became Collin."

Grief twisted his face, as he mourned his friend.

"Lady, go home," he said. "Get out of here."

The urgency in his voice sent my pulse racing. "Why?"

"That bloke with the broken mouth? Remember him?"

I remembered a dark street and a sneering man with a lisp. "Lascar?"

"He's bad news. Something bad's going to happen. You go back now, yeah?"

He knew. He knew about the bomb! I gaped at him. "Did he kill Osain? Is that how—?"

"Told you I'd find those crates, didn't I? So I spread it around that Pa knew 'bout dynamite, caps, that sorta thing." He choked, his words stopping and starting in spurts. "Lascar promised him five hundred for a job! I found Pa last night. Throat cut—clean through."

Oh God, if only I'd paid, Osain might not have been so desperate for cash, he might not have accepted that offer. He might yet be alive. Numbed by this torrent, now a single fact blazed in my mind. Had Osain set the explosives?

"Where? Where's the bomb?"

Collin flinched as though I'd hit him. His gaze flashed behind me, then he pulled back and fled like an arrow shot from a bow.

I searched the basin behind me. What had he seen?

Jim returned in long strides. "Who was that?"

On the water, peaceful little boats eased around on slow curves. "Collin Box. He knew, Jim. He knew what's going to happen."

"Where?"

I lifted my gaze from the boats, imitating Collin's gesture. I was looking straight at Big Mary.

"There."

Jim's breath was a hiss. A half hour remained until four o'clock, when the parade would enter the Court of Honor. If Osain had set the bomb last night, in all likelihood the anarchists had already escaped.

People clustered everywhere, filling the sidewalk around the basin. Following Jim, I pushed through visitors and hurried to the pier.

But no electric boats remained at the dock. My desperation grew.

Jim spotted something on the water, and shouted, "Hoy!"

I peered at a boat festooned with holiday flags. "Who is it?"

Taking off his hat, Jim waved it in a wide arc. Would they notice?

The boat slowed, veering toward us, showing a single occupant. It was a police boat, with Dupree Senior grinning at the helm. As we clambered aboard, he said, "Thought that was the pair of you. Found anything?"

* * *

A narrow ledge a few feet wide surrounded the Statue of the Republic, which loomed above us like a female colossus. Leaning over the gunwale, Jim stepped onto the base of Big Mary and moved toward the wooden door.

As the police boat bobbed against the statue's footing, I cried, "Wait for me!"

Jim glanced back, indecision writ large on his face, then returned. Ignoring Dupree's protests, I reached for Jim's hand and stepped across.

He tried the door. Locked. Shoving at it did no good. Grunting, he sidled around a corner of the ledge, looking for another entrance.

"Diana." He pointed upward at a narrow window, its base three feet above. Reaching, he ran his fingers along the ledge and tried to pull himself up, but dropped back and caught himself against the wall, clutching his shoulder.

"It won't do, Jim," I said. "It's too high. But I could get in, if we had something I could climb . . . ?" I looked around and saw only the lake surrounding us.

Jim's quick smile flashed. "We do," he said. "Me."

"What?"

His gaze held me; then he glanced upward to gauge the distance. "Got your gun? Keep it handy. Once you're in, open the door. Now give me your foot."

He bent at the wall, offering me cupped hands. I peered up, grasping his plan. Would it work? Water lapped at the statue's base.

I placed my boot on his crossed palms and stepped up, gasping as I rose, clutching his shoulders in fright. Jim straightened, clasping both my feet to push me upward. My hands flat to the wall, I peeked through the window and told him, "It's dark inside."

Jim raised me higher. When the window frame pressed against my waist, I leaned over, then twisted to sit on the ledge, pressing my hat to my head, feet dangling above Jim's head. "Small people are useful, aren't we?"

Gathering my skirt, I thrust a foot over the frame, then slipped inside through the narrow gap. I landed on my knees in a small, dusty anteroom, facing a flight of stairs that led downward. My bruised side throbbed as I clambered up, gasping.

The door opposite the stairs swung open.

A man halted, his mouth open—the fiend who'd stabbed Tobias. Prendergast!

What happened next was a blur. I grabbed at my muff for the gun, but Prendergast was faster. Lips pulled back in a grimace, he struck me. Pain shot through my face; the force of his blow threw me into the wall.

I heard him move. Desperate, my hat over my eyes, I tried to crawl, but my entangled skirts trapped me. Prendergast's arm snaked around my neck, hauling me up.

Osain's throat had been slit by a practiced hand. Prendergast? I gasped, swamped by the stench of turpentine. It was a mineral odor, but sharp and synthetic. I'd smelled it near the elevator chute. Oh, God. Ink? Newspaper ink?

His arm tightened, choking me. I jerked my head back but did no damage. I yanked at my muff but couldn't free my pistol. Flailing in anguish, I dragged a pin from my hair and punched it into his arm. He shrieked, releasing me.

I scrambled down the stairwell without a backward glance.

The lower room was dimly lit, but I took the stairs two at a time. At the bottom, I caught myself on the thin rail just in time. Wooden crates and boxes lay helter-skelter atop each other, a maze of debris. Somewhere in the darkness was the door.

Soon he'd come down behind me. Panic propelled me on, my skirts tearing, jagged corners scraping my shins. Climbing over crates, squeezing between them, I found the doorframe. Jim would be outside, anxious, wondering why I took so long. My fingers searched along the frame with frantic speed. Where was the handle?

I pulled on the heavy latch. It made a grinding noise but did not budge. Locked? Or was it stuck? Prendergast would be down in moments. Panic rising like floodwaters, I worked the handle up and down. Was it moving? Panting, I kept at it.

With a creak, it slid free.

Jim yanked the door open in a trice, registered my disheveled hair and clothes and stepped through, reaching for me. I gasped, "Prendergast. The elevator. Smells of turpentine and wet newspaper."

His face grim, Jim glanced at the stairs, then let the door swing shut. We'd be safer in the darkness.

CHAPTER 48

ANARCHY

I pressed close in the narrow space, terrified to make a noise. Jim touched my shoulder, then felt among the crates, carefully setting some atop others to clear a path. I nudged one with a foot. It didn't move. The musty smell of sawdust filled my nostrils. When Jim hoisted the next box, something inside rustled. Ballistite.

Oh, God, we were *inside* the bomb.

Was Prendergast preparing to set it off? I caught at Jim's sleeve in the murky light and whispered, "Upstairs."

Jim said, "Mmm." That brief beam of light from the open door had showed us a narrow flight, curving upward within the statue's base. Above us, raised voices argued distantly.

One said, "I said no, damn you!" Another, "I'm getting out!"

It wasn't just Prendergast. Who else was there? How many? Had they lit the fuse? Footsteps thumped downward.

I loosened my derringer from my twisted muff. Jim's life and mine might depend on it.

Leaning down, he breathed against my hair, "I'll distract them. Once they clear the stairs, go up." He bent and picked up a crate. "Stop the bomb. Don't wait."

How would he distract them? I could imagine only one way, and it sent tremors down my body. Footsteps approached.

Giving me no time to argue, Jim propelled me into a narrow space along the wall. Almost tripping over a wood pallet, I sank to a crouch. If I kept still, perhaps I'd be overlooked in the gloom.

The men clambered down in a rush, as I had. Like me, they hauled to a stop before the pile of debris. I clenched my shaking fingers and drew my pistol. The one in the lead moved with a peculiar gait: the twisted man, Lascar. He crabbed his way through the clutter, heading for the door. Close behind followed two more, then Prendergast, still clutching his arm where I had stabbed him.

Cursing, Lascar shoved aside crates. From the rear, a low voice said, "Told you not to throw them. Blasted fool!"

Lascar said a foul word in reply, then asked, "Your bird. Got away?"

The man snapped, "You heard the door." That voice! It was Peter Dupree.

"Didn't hear a ssplash, though."

Someone else chuckled. "Can't swim. Must be outside, dangling on the ledge."

Lascar asked, "Your man, he knowsss when to bring the boat?"

"He'll be here soon," said the low voice, as a large shape surged forward. He'd been clearing a path, tossing cartons as though they were made of paper. If he got to the door, he'd escape. Jim would act before that. I gripped my derringer, steeling myself to shoot.

Peter's narrow shape stopped close to where Jim stood, but he didn't appear to notice. Jim kept still beside a tall, untidy stack, waiting. He wanted to give me a clear path to the stairway, but Prendergast still blocked the bottom stair.

Just then an unlucky gust hit the door and thrust it open with a blast. Sunlight slashed into the room, turning dusk to day.

Instantly Jim moved, flinging something at the giant near the door. I saw this only tangentially, for I was watching Peter, disbelieving. Yanking something from his waist—a blade?—he launched himself at Jim.

Through the clutter of boxes and beams, I glimpsed someone grab Peter. They went down together. Boxes crashed, grunts, blows—someone cried out. Men heaved, shoving, crates falling in the narrow space. Who was whom? Jim could not fight them all! The frantic pace, the thump of blows, bodies straining; trembling, I struggled to see.

"Ahh!" cried a guttural voice. I glimpsed a broad face, teeth bared, twisted in fury.

The door creaked. A body—or was it two—was slumped between crates.

Jim bent over one of them. "Jesus, Lascar, why? You've six children."

Lascar wheezed, his breath bubbling. "Only Tito and me lefffft now."

He was Tito's father! My pulse drummed in my ears. Was he dying, his lifeblood spurting over his shirt? Trembling, I clutched the derringer with both hands.

Lascar coughed, his gasps tearing the air. Injury had warped his body. Seeing his family decimated by starvation and disease—how much pain could a person bear? He was our foe; yet to hear him struggle for breath twisted my gut. I glanced at the stairs. They were clear.

Lascar wheezed, "You lied to me."

Grasping Lascar's hand, Jim said, "So did you. Go easy, friend."

Lascar rasped, "My name's Vidal. Vidal Lascar, from Lombardy."

His shattered breath stopped. Jim crouched, outlined against the light, in the loud silence. Swallowing, I blinked. Each second we delayed could be our last. But as I staggered to my aching feet, another danger loomed.

Something moved in the corner. The hulking giant stepped out, rocking side to side. Jim had flung him into some crates, but he'd recovered. Now he faced Jim, grimacing only feet away, his fist red with blood. It was his knife, then, that struck Lascar. His face! If hatred could slice, my Jim would be cut to ribbons.

The burly goon cursed bitterly as he stared at the two crumpled bodies. Lascar had fought someone—was it Peter? I'd seen Peter throw back his arm, but little else. Lascar had defended Jim! Had the ragged creature changed sides at the end?

Through the open door came distant fanfare of horns and drums. The parade was approaching. The crowd roared, cheering in waves, a macabre counterpoint to the silence within as Jim and his beefy foe gauged each other. I remembered Jim staring at my telegram, mouthing the words, and realized who stood before us now. Al Collier. Albrecht Kohler, the man who'd bought the explosives.

Enough. I stood up, pointing my weapon. "You. Stop the bomb. Now."

Kohler's wild gaze snapped to me. "The woman," he said, without emphasis.

I glanced at Lascar's body, then aimed at Kohler's chest. "The device. How do we stop it?"

He straightened, his chin up like someone facing a firing squad.

Without taking his gaze from Kohler, Jim rapped out, "Don't shoot, Diana. The powder's in the air! You've got to go, turn off the bomb."

Turn it off? "I don't know how!" I cried.

Jim stepped sideways, blocking the exit. "You'll find a way. Go!"

I glanced to the stair and choked. "I can't leave you!"

"Stop the bomb, Diana!"

My breath came in puffs. Leave Jim to defend himself against Kohler? Go up to the explosives? I had promised I would obey, but how could I defuse an incendiary device? Jim might know how, but I hadn't the faintest idea.

"Go!" Jim said in Hindustani, his voice thrusting me forward like the hilt of his hand. I could not hold off Kohler, so I must go to the bomb. Kohler's ebony eyes glittered, hissing his frustration. If he escaped, he would try again until he succeeded, or died.

CHAPTER 49

THE HIDDEN FACE

JIM

God knows, I wanted to thrust Diana to the open door, not farther inside. But she was our only chance. If the bomb went off,
it would not matter where she or I stood; we'd both be rendered bone
and dust—along with countless thousands. A single crate had torn the
Cold Storage Building to smithereens. There'd be seventeen around us
now. They'd blast fragments of the burning statue into a sea of cheering
fairgoers.

Diana's neat footsteps told me she was running up the stairs. Kohler's
eyes gleamed like those of an opium eater—dark pebbles in a pale face.
We'd eaten, worked, taken our rest side by side, but I did not know this
man.

Flexing his bulky shoulders, he seemed in no hurry to leave. He was
waiting to die. He didn't need to fight me—just delay us until the blast.
All our lives were in the palm of Diana's little hand.

His wide brow knotted. "I liked you."

"Did you?" Peter and Lascar's bodies lay beside him. His friends.

"Almost asked you to join us. But you didn't squeal on Orrin. Lascar
had you down for a pacifist."

"I am." The floor above us creaked as Diana crossed it.

If I took my eyes from Kohler, he'd attack. But there'd been one more—Prendergast, who'd tried to blow up the Parliament of World Religions. God damn it, I could not look around for him. Where was he?

Kohler scoffed. "You're no pacifist. I've seen you without a shirt."

My pulse kept up that beat I knew so well. Each time I was under fire, it hammered at me like a wild thing trapped in a cage.

"More than one way to earn those scars."

Soon, he'll strike. But God knows, I did not want to kill. One day it would be my turn, but not yet, please God. I'd spent just a few scant weeks with my little wife. She'd only just stopped tensing up when I got close.

"You're a soldier," he said.

"Yes."

Head thrust forward, he peered steadily at me. I met his gaze, prepared for some last-ditch effort. He said, "You can't do it. I know you. You don't have it in you."

"I've seen men, cut to shreds . . . some by my own hand," I said.

Kohler moved closer. Something in his grip. A rod? Knife? Keep talking, I thought, lull him into it, let him gather himself. "Rather not do that again."

Long committed to this endeavor, Kohler seemed resolute. He knew when the bomb would go off, and that hour was close. He had no way out but past me.

The cheering crowd had neared us. The joyful tattoo of drums and wailing pipes carried clear across the water. There would be jugglers in the parade, and colorful floats—children, everywhere, waving flags.

Above us, alone, was Diana, standing among the incendiaries.

Forgive me, sweet. I never intended you to be here. When Lascar found me out, I feared death not for the pain, but because you'd grieve me, alone in this cold, foreign place that you don't much like. Why didn't you stay home? But if you'd obeyed me last time, in Bombay, I'd be dead. You always surprise me. Can you stop the bomb? Is it too late? Your parents, your sweet mother, will never forgive me. Your father, he gave you into my care. Adi—God, Diana! Why the hell did I let you come?

Kohler grunted. "You're young. How old's the girl?"

He wanted to talk to pass the time. This scant time, my last few moments on earth. I wanted to be with her, hold her, turn my back to the blast, but it was too late.

"Twenty-two."

"My son was nine years old, and my daughter fifteen. Lascar's wife was twenty-three."

We were talking about the dead, why he'd done this. Soon he'd strike. I tensed, waiting.

"How?"

His shoulders slumped but his eyes were alive with a plan. "Cholera. Starvation. What does it matter?"

Light flickered, and water splashed outside. Had someone jumped into the lake? A low hum told me a boat was near—the police boat?

He came at me fast. I had no time to think, or need to. My body knew what to do, and I followed its lead.

It was simple, in the end. If I won, I'd go up to the bomb and be with her. If I lost, well, I would not know it.

CHAPTER 50

QUANDARY

Against every shrieking instinct, I left Jim there.

There was no choice, after all. If I'd stayed, I might have saved him from Kohler, but the explosion would kill us all.

I sped up the stairway as fast as my feet would take me. Madness to walk into the heart of a bomb, madness to think I could stop it. I had come to Chicago for Jim. He cared about these people, these ornery, proud, yet strangely kind Americans. Now his cause was mine.

The crowd's cheers grew louder as I ran through the antechamber where I'd fought Prendergast. There I stopped, clinging to the doorframe, gasping. Daylight showed a hideous mess. Barrels, the chamber chock-full of them, some piled with barely room between. I was inside a powder keg.

I recalled Jim's voice saying, "Explosives are unstable; don't jostle them or light a match nearby."

He'd taught me to *look*. I scoured the room, the clutter inside Big Mary. Wires snaked across the floor.

A mass of wire tangled at the room's center. There, a large box squatted, an ungainly octopus. Cables ran from it to a barrel. Of course. The others would go off when the first exploded. I took a step and froze. The box hummed. That sound sent a tremor through me. Electricity.

Outside, the din grew louder. People cheered the approaching parade. Now recognizable, Sousa's march pulsed with trumpets and drums.

Holding my skirts up, I tiptoed toward the window. Anyone setting an explosive needed daylight; to light a candle here was death.

Sure enough, a heavy clock stood by the window.

Notice what is, and what should be. Notice what isn't there. I remembered Jim standing shirtless at our window in Boston, waiting for me to see footprints in the snow.

What was the clock for? *Hickory dickory dock,* I thought, hysteria bubbling in my chest. Wires connected the clock to the electric box.

The clock struck one, I thought. *Me!*

Confused by the cables tangled behind the clockface like Medusa's snake-locks, I peered around it. If Jim wasn't sure he could stop this, how could I, who knew nothing about it?

The mouse ran down . . . but how? How long did I have left? I returned to the clockface, seeing the seconds hand tick around. It jerked. I watched the arc, following its path. At the mark of four, it jerked again. A thin wire quivered, dangling out of place over the roman numerals.

It was quarter past four.

The parade got closer, trumpets no longer tinny, drums pounding.

See what is, and what shouldn't be there. A shiny notch protruded under the number IV. A wire trailed from it. A wire that should not be there. My insides jolted.

Another wire dangled from each of the clock's hands. Those threads would pass each other harmlessly until the hour and minute hands lined up with that notch.

In each turn around the clock, the long minute hand overtakes the slow hand of the hour; but it happens only *once* an hour. Kohler had clipped wires to the hands of the clock and departed, giving himself time to escape.

The hour hand twitched, coming to rest against the metal notch. A spark crackled.

Thoughts beat in my head—*ballistite explodes when heated.* The minute hand crept past three. Soon it would reach the notch. The circuit would close, flooding the explosive with current. *A fuse can be lit by electricity.*

Only seconds left. Almost time.

A hollow crack rang out from below. A barrage of gunshots answered. They faded, as I stared at the clockface. It had not blown up.

I was still alive; was Jim?

CHAPTER 51

SHOTS FIRED

JIM

I learned boxing while I was still a Sepoy in the British army—learned the hard way, taking blows until I learned to weave and block. Now I paced with Kohler, fended off his advance, turning toward his empty hand.

He'd got me talking and caught his breath. He swung, light glinting off a blade. When he stabbed with the other hand, I yanked back. Damn! He had two knives.

He charged.

Snapping a punch to his elbow, I knocked one away. The second sliced my forearm. I gasped, thrust some debris in his path, a thought flickering—relief that Diana couldn't see this.

Swapping hands, he swung fast and wide. Weaving to avoid him, I feinted. Most men protect themselves while throwing punches. Kohler didn't. It gave me an opening, but it also made him unpredictable.

He got in close, not in the rush I expected, but whirling fast. I'd not seen that before—an oriental move.

I thrust him off, but he kicked at my knee, sent me staggering. Not now, I wanted to yell, the pain shooting through me as I tottered on one foot. I recovered and rammed a fist at his jaw.

Kohler scarcely registered the blow, but followed, knocking me back with his return. In the ring one could back off, plan one's moves. Not so in this maze of broken crates. I blocked his rapid blows, barely able to keep up.

My fingers brushed a loose timber, so I rammed it at him.

While he flicked it aside, I lunged, tackling him from a low crouch, getting in close, grabbing his girth so he'd have less leverage with his blade. His slice caught my back, a quick, wicked burn.

I went down, atop him. Fearful of his knife, I pushed away, my knee screaming as it hit the ground. I rolled into something sharp and cursed.

Jarred by the movement, I struggled to rise, my foot wedged in debris. He had a chance, then, to kill me. Instead, he ran.

In the end, his need to live was stronger than his desire to kill.

It was all for naught. Firing from the police boat, Alfred Dupree shot him while he stood, bloody fisted, knife gleaming, in the doorway. He jerked, clinging to the door. Another shot cracked out, and he dropped forward into the water.

CHAPTER 52

FOR WANT OF A NAIL

I shut out the noise and shouts below, numbed myself to the meaning of it, looking only at the clock. Jim had given me a task. I'd think of nothing else; I could not bear to.

How does one stop time?

Images flashed in my mind: a clock in our Boston apartment I had forgotten to wind up, as still as a corpse on the mantel; Jim tapping our cuckoo clock, saying, "It's slow. Almost five minutes . . ." and then nudging the little hands with a fingernail.

Could I stick my finger into the clockface, catch the seconds hand and hold it? Jim's words cut into my mind. *Electricity burns. It can go through people.* So why didn't it go through the hands of the clock?

Because they were made of wood.

From my mangled topknot, I pulled a wood hairpin. Jim had sharpened it to a wicked point.

The pin's amber head felt warm. Trembling, I inserted it between the minute and hour hands. Pushing, I thrust it into the clockface. The hand that marked the seconds stopped on my pin. Trapped, it strained and twitched, but could not progress. The minute hand remained two ticks away from the hour.

Two ticks. The clock did not like to be restrained. Gears whirred in the open machinery.

Grunting, I shoved the hairpin further. It slid deeper and nicked something inside, pushing against some mechanical gear.

A clock is a finely tuned mechanism, each gear exactly aligned. I hoped I had broken some of that precious concordance. The mechanism clicked and then—nothing. Silence pooled around me.

I mentally recited my ancient Persian prayer: *ashem vohu, vahistem asti.* "Happiness is the highest, God's greatest gift."

The cheering brought Bombay to mind—a Dussehra festival to celebrate the victory of good over evil. Jugglers and street vendors, child acrobats and sadhus—a procession to where an effigy of many-headed Ravana would burn.

The parade passed, loud and joyful, oh, so close. Before me, the squat, menacing device glowered.

Breathes there the man, with soul so dead, who never to himself hath said, this is my own, my native land!

And still I clutched the hairpin's amber knob. My hand refused to release it.

To let go was death, if the pin did not hold. Could the fate of thousands, even hundreds of thousands rest upon a single hairpin? I thrust it deeper. It was stuck. And still I could not let go.

I heard a shaking breath—my own. Trembling, I loosened my grip, one finger at a time, breathing as though breath could set off the conflagration. Would my pin hold? It twitched twice and stopped. The knob was wedged in tight.

Unsteady, I backed away, still gazing at the dormant clock. The beat of drums grew faint. Numb, I stepped to the window.

The marchers crowded together in the distance, but one man stood alone. He looked up at me, ramrod straight.

The general. He strode to the basin's edge, a short, upright man. Taking out his watch, he checked the time.

He glanced up from his timepiece, stared across the water. There would be no explosion today. Tucking away his watch, he marched back toward the docked sloops.

When he stopped abruptly, I craned outward, trying to see. Someone blocked his way—a tall woman dressed in checkered western shirt and a riding skirt, narrow shoulders hunched. Annie Oakley, the markswoman? No, Abigail!

The general pointed a weapon. I gasped. A pop sounded, then another. Abigail! No!

The general crumpled to the ground.

Abigail stood over the prone figure for what seemed a long time; then her head came up. Staring straight at me, she tucked her six-shooter back into her belt and touched the brim of her hat. This was Abigail, I thought, not the person lounging on my settee, but a steady, competent operative.

Our danger had passed, had it not? In the silence of a darkened chamber, the beams roughly pounded together to hold up a shining lady. Lofty and serene, simply hewn in her inner workings. The Republic herself; a clever metaphor for a splintered nation if she'd rained down blazing fragments. We'd held her together, hadn't we?

We'd been reprieved. I searched for a sense of relief. But in the rooms of my mind I found no exultation, only a sense of cold, like touching a windowpane.

Jim had not come up to me.

I glanced toward the door, quaking. He could be lying at the foot of those steps. That image hit the wall inside me and dripped into a puddle like a pool of shimmered mercury.

Someone had fired nearby. The thought splintered against my wall.

In the rooms of my world lived Mama's loving embrace, her scent of lemon and spices; Papa's jowly smile, his voice droning prayers; Adi's puckish grin under studious glasses. I saw Abigail's cautious smile, never sure it would be returned. I heard Tobias's deep curling voice, his wide grin, lips pink in his kind, dark face. Staunch little Tito gazed up. Here was Ida and George's concern, the Lins' gentleness and that unknown cabbie, willing to forgo his nickel. But I could not see Jim.

Something rustled in the room below.

Jim? The prospect drove me to the stairs.

At the bottom, I stopped. Boxes stood askew, splintered. Sloping sunbeams reflected, drawing lattices on the walls, on the floor.

Jim stood up, oh, so carefully. "Diana." He took a large stride, coatless, his shirtsleeve soaked in blood.

The room blurred and darkened, as though an eclipse had dimmed the sun. I must have fallen, for next, I was on the floor, cradled against his chest. He knelt on one knee, holding me up, his face a grimace of relief.

The pane in my mind dissolved, bringing color and light.

Happiness is God's greatest gift. *Usta asti, usta ahmai. Yadechai vahistai ashem.* It comes to those who do good, for its own sake.

CHAPTER 53

THE PICTURE EMERGES

JIM

Police boats surrounded Big Mary as patrolmen clambered in. Officers dashed up and down the stairs, until Sergeant Long took charge. Men kept shaking my hand. Dazed, Diana barely spoke. She slumped against me as Long fired questions at us. I answered briefly, concerned by Diana's apathy. Promising him a full report, I took her back to our hotel, where she spent a fitful night, murmuring in her sleep.

I'd not had much time to dwell on yesterday's events: Lascar's strange reversal and Peter's role. Fully dressed, Diana returned from the washroom and sat at the table.

The skin under her eyes bruised and pinkish, she whispered, "What happened . . . afterwards?"

Over multiple cups of Darjeeling, I told her about the fight with Kohler, and ended with, "We retrieved their bodies—Albrecht Kohler, Vidal Lascar, Peter Dupree and General Payne. All but Prendergast. The force is looking for him."

We spoke longer, then the clock's quiet ding interrupted. Superintendent Brennan expected me at nine, so I went to dress.

Our washroom mirror showed my haggard face under a mess of hair. Glancing at Diana, neatly turned out like a Paris fashion plate as she glided between her trunks, I smoothed down my thatched mop. My forearm protested the movement, but the wound would heal. I'd collected more scars—best not to inventory them.

Keeping my tone light, I said, "Time I got a haircut, hmm? I'll have one tonight."

Diana's brown eyes were indulgent. "Why not this morning? There's a barbershop by the lobby."

"Perhaps." With difficulty, I threaded my bandaged arm through a shirt and vest.

She came and buttoned them, so I held out my tie. Was she really all right?

Winding it deftly, she sent me off with a kiss that sped up my pulse. Taking her advice, I stopped at the barbershop, where the haircut and shave were a rare treat. Mr. Fish sent the staff fussing about me and refused my payment. After months of living rough, I soaked it in.

At police headquarters, I entered a room crammed with detectives and shook hands with Dupree and Martin, both somber today. Some officers waved. A few called out insulting remarks, ribbing me about my newly trimmed look. What is it about serving together that makes such good company? I wondered whether Diana would care to live in Chicago. I'd ask, since I wasn't sure I still had a job.

Calling us to order, Superintendent Brennan addressed the events inside the Statue of the Republic. I gave a brief report, military style, that earned me curious looks.

Puffing on his pipe, Brennan asked, "So, was it Lascar that strangled the guard, Thomas Grewe?"

I shook my head. "Couldn't have. He was missing two fingers. He'd worked with Kohler at a powder plant in Cheswick, Pennsylvania, making munitions. Grewe was strangled by someone with ink on their hands. Only two people used the printing press at Canal Street—Oscar Donnelly and, in his absence, Al Collier, alias Albrecht Kohler. Donnelly was a typesetter, but he'd been hired by Debs, the Railway Union man, to prevent a fanatic like Berkman disrupting labor's cause. That leaves Kohler. Grewe surprised him stealing maps at the Rookery, so he killed him."

"And Baldwin? Who shot him?"

"That was Kohler too. Baldwin wrote to me about the Canal Street press. When he took Lascar's letter, it must have disrupted the group's plan." I glanced at Alfred Dupree, for I could not skirt this part. "He was unarmed when he was shot. Why didn't he take his revolver? I think he was meeting Peter, who told him to return to Boston. Baldwin wouldn't like that, so he followed Peter that night. Collin Box witnessed what happened next. At half past twelve, Baldwin followed a 'toff' in a fine suit to the loading pier. Another man—Collin described him as 'shaped like a bull'—forced Baldwin to load crates from a boat onto a cart, then shot him. Kohler's heavyset and muscular. The toff walked away. That had to be Peter."

Alfred Dupree seemed to shrink as I spoke. His voice cracking, he said, "I don't understand. Why?"

In the awkward pause, men avoided Dupree's tight features.

His arm in a sling, Martin leaned forward. "Perhaps I can help. I spoke to Tobias yesterday. Prendergast's blade nicked his heart, but the surgeon was able to repair it."

This caused a stir. No one survived a stab wound to the heart, until now.

Martin went on, "Tobias is weak, but he can speak. He overheard Lascar and Kohler talk with the general. Peter too. They spoke in the cellar so that the general's son, Harvey Payne, wouldn't hear. Peter joined them because of Albert Parsons, one of the Haymarket eight. He was a Confederate soldier who served under General Payne. He'd been hanged despite having no hand in the riot—"

The superintendent exploded. "The goddamn Haymarket Riot? That union scum threw dynamite at my men—injured sixty-seven! Nine good men killed!"

This drew murmurs from around the table. Reading from notepaper, Martin said, "General Payne believed that Parsons's trial was a sham. He was hot about 'stranglehold of the North.' Tobias heard him shout, 'They have perverted the Constitution!' He wanted vengeance upon this city. It seems Peter, ah, admired him."

Elbows on the table, Dupree dropped his head into his hands. Despite his detective instincts, he'd missed seeing the truth of his son.

"Alfred, I'm sorry for your loss," said the superintendent, then tapped Baldwin's incriminating German letter. "So Kohler wrote this?"

I said, "Kohler and Lascar both spoke German. They'd fought in the Confederate army, serving under General Payne. After the Civil War, Kohler went to Düsseldorf to study chemistry. That's where he learned about explosives. Then he joined Lascar in Cheswick."

Brennan's eyes narrowed. "How do you know this?"

I explained. "I needed the German letter translated, so I sent it to Professor Grimke in Boston. Unfortunately, he involved my wife. Diana suspected that Grimke recognized the handwriting and wired him. She was right. Kohler had been his student in Düsseldorf."

The superintendent tapped his pipe against the table's edge. "Mrs. O'Trey's fall into the elevator well. An accident?"

"She was pushed. She'd been rather visible at the parliament gala, alerting the governor. After we foiled their plans, Paddy Prendergast trailed her to the telegraph office. He may have heard Diana give the old professor's address and feared the jig was up. We were often together, so I presume that's why he bided his time. The mayor's gala before July Fourth was their last chance."

He'd attacked Diana while I was distracted by a clutch of excited fellows. Unclenching my fingers, I went on. "Prendergast smelled of newsprint, because he handled bales of newspaper. When he attacked her in the statue, she recognized the smell. But someone at the dinner had to know when she was alone, to lure her to the elevator. Could have been Peter or Bellino."

The superintendent compressed his lips. "They tested the ballistite at the Cold Storage Building. Killed sixteen good men. So what were they waiting for?"

I shrugged. "Independence Day, I suppose. They wanted independence from what they saw as oppression. The bomb was placed in the Statue of the Republic for that reason. To explode the old republic."

Superintendent Brennan harrumphed, then said, "So we got them all?"

I cleared my throat. "Not quite, sir. Prendergast?"

Long shook his head. "We're looking for him. May have drowned in the lake."

The superintendent ordered Prendergast's arrest, then admonished the group. "Mind, this cannot get out. If the public learns of it, they could abandon the fair. Not a word."

The door burst open, and a young policeman rushed in. "Sir! It's Mayor Harrison. He's been shot!"

CHAPTER 54

MAKING AMENDS

I felt unsettled after Jim left for City Hall. Ordinary life seemed safe, but also flat and slow. Jim's investigation had absorbed my waking moments. What now? Would we return to Boston and the Lins? The World's Fair would continue unharmed, yet some part of me had changed. Gripping my gilt-trimmed hairbrush, I gazed at the inlaid mother-of-pearl, creamy white flecked with silver, a thin layer of perfection.

How fragile was our veneer of civilization. Standing under the Statue of the Republic, I'd been prepared to shoot Kohler. I winced, recalling it. But the gang had attacked us. My blood was up; even an animal fights back.

These past weeks I'd flouted convention and pretended to be royalty. Those were means to an end, and harmed no one, really, I thought. I'd deceived Alfred Dupree so I could find Jim, and stolen Box's deed from Bellino. I'd even hidden Abigail's secret from Jim. I winced. He'd been so rough with her. If I'd told him, I could have spared her that, but it wasn't my secret to tell!

Inside the statue I'd been prepared to shoot, to kill. Again. And like before, I'd been defending Jim. I pulled in a breath of relief I hadn't had to do it. How would my parents judge my actions? Right and wrong was so clear for them. Would they be appalled? Adi would glow with pride at my adventures. But Papa always said the end does not justify the means.

So, I pinned on a creamy white hat and went to see Erminia. She was a victim too.

Dressed in black, she looked like someone living a nightmare.

"You know about Enri?" she whispered, clutching a kerchief.

I commiserated, then asked, "Now that he is arrested, can you not separate yourself from him?"

At this, tears shimmered in her eyes. She pulled in her lips, shaking her head.

Had I misread her, seeing scorn and disaffection, instead of hope and disappointment? "You were not happy as things stood, were you?"

She dabbed her lips. "It was not always so. When he courted me, I thought he could make something of himself. But . . . it was always 'my' money, you see. It hurt, constantly. The more he needed his ventures to succeed, the more rash he became in his undertakings! A patent on a new type of scissors. Bah! I saw a dozen at the fair. A machine to pop kernels of corn—as each prospect fell through, he spent more. We grew distant, the gulf so wide I do not think we have spoken honestly in years. But he is not wicked, Mrs. O'Trey. Will you not help him?"

Heaven forgive me, I thought, comforting her, then hurried back to send a message to Harvey Payne, esquire.

When Harvey arrived, he took my hand, saying, "I was so glad to receive your note. I've been most eager to apologize. Your employee, has he recovered?"

How strange it was, after yesterday, to return to polite conversation! I offered him a chair. "Thank you. Tobias is still in hospital but is doing well. Mr. Payne, I am sorry about your father."

Harvey sighed. "I had not seen him in many years. When he arrived, a few months ago, I was pleased, but . . . we just didn't see eye to eye. He could be . . . difficult. He was scornful, angry, even rough with Joe and Betsy, but I cannot believe what the police are saying."

"That he planned an attack upon the fair?"

He nodded, mouth grim. "I was brought up by my grandparents in Hoboken, a quiet town in New Jersey. My father remained in the Carolinas. He wasn't the same, after the war."

"Because the South lost?"

"It's more than that. He was wounded twice, lost three fingers. Kept going back to the field, you see? His company adored him. He lost everything to that war—his crops, slaves, plantation, his land and fortune, even his health, after my mother died."

Jim had lost his entire company in Karachi. Why did loss make some more caring, and turn others to stone? Like striking flint on iron, General Payne had tried to set the world on fire, using his own son in his vengeance.

"You didn't suspect anything?"

He flinched, looking at the floor. "I think he hated that I live in Chicago, made my home here. He sold his land for a pittance. Watching those he called *upstarts* run things and do well, while his own means crumbled . . . made him bitter. Looking back now, each conversation takes on a different meaning. He probed me for information, police connections—which I, foolishly, was happy to provide!"

"You acted out of kindness," I said, moved by his regret. I'd been wrong about him. Had I misjudged Enri Bellino too?

Coming to a decision, I said, "Mr. Payne, I need your assistance on a legal matter. I stole something from Mr. Bellino—the deed to Osain Box's mine. Can you advise me?"

Surprise registered on his open face. "You want to return it?"

"No, I wish to pay for it." My honest papa would expect no less of me. "I will pay exactly what Mr. Bellino paid Osain Box. Fifty dollars. That's what he considered its value."

Harvey frowned. "You possess it already. You do not need to pay."

"Nevertheless, I shall."

"Fascinating!" Then he sobered. "Mrs. O'Trey, Enri Bellino is a crook, a gambler. Do not put yourself within his grasp."

He was right, but was it right to cheat someone because I thought he was a cheat? I turned to him. "Mr. Bellino is in police custody. Will you come?"

Seated in his brougham, he tried again to dissuade me. "Is Mr. O'Trey aware of this?"

"No," I said, biting my lip. "I want to manage it before I tell him."

Harvey groaned, mopping his brow with a snowy white kerchief.

At police headquarters, Sergeant Long's eyebrows climbed as I explained my request. His jaw wobbled in thought; then he seated us in a room and summoned Enri Bellino.

A constable brought Bellino in rumpled shirtsleeves, hair awry, collar askew.

He stopped in the doorway, staring. "My wife Erminia—is she all right?"

Once he was seated, I said, "She is, Mr. Bellino. Now, you bought a copper mine from Osain Box."

He twitched. "So it's about that. You want it?"

The scoundrel was pretending he possessed the deed. Yet his first thought had been for his wife, so I said, "If you had the deed, would you sell it for fifty dollars?"

He stiffened, then nodded.

Instantly Harvey extracted paper and pen from his case and slid them across the table. With a gesture at Bellino, he dictated the words of an agreement. "I, Enri Bellino . . ."

Brow creased in a puzzled frown, Bellino wrote and signed as he was told.

When I counted out five ten-dollar bills and set them on the table, he stared at them without moving.

"You are an attorney?" he asked Harvey. "Will you defend me? I did not know what the explosives were for! A man called Albert Collier purchased them. My Swedish connections delivered it on my bond. But Collier's note was worthless, leaving me with a large debt. I did not know what he planned!"

Harvey glanced at me in surprise. Had Bellino too been used by the anarchists? Or was this gambler part of the plot?

To Sergeant Long's surprise, I asked Bellino, "What did you have carried to the Cold Storage Building?"

Bellino's mouth opened and closed. If he stalled, it would be a lie.

He stammered, "We, we were testing oilcloth, to protect ice. I had a block carried to the skating rink, but it melted."

I almost believed him. But the words he'd written, "I accept this remuneration of my free will and before witnesses . . ." glowed on the page. *One must understand the meaning of what one sees.*

Sighing, I said, "On the phone you spoke of someone meeting in a carriage at the post office?"

His eyes bulged as though I'd performed witchcraft. "On the phone . . ."

"You heard the name Agnihotri?"

His eyes flickered with recognition. It passed in a flash.

I winced, knowing Erminia would be heartbroken. From my glove, I extracted the note that had led me to the elevator and laid it against the contract he'd written. In both, the letters A and B were open and ill formed.

When I'd rummaged through Bellino's desk, I'd seen his writing on the blotter where he tested his pen. However, in my haste to find the deed, I paid no attention. The answer had been before me all along. I just hadn't noticed, till now.

I slid the damning pages across to Sergeant Long and said, "Look at the A in 'accept,' and the B in 'before.' Here is the note I received at the mayor's gala. This man tried to kill me."

Bellino froze. As our gaze met, his benign mask dropped away.

"An interesting interview, ma'am," said Sergeant Long as he led us out. "Now we've finally got something on him."

Poor Erminia, I thought, as I stepped into Harvey Payne's carriage. How long had greed poisoned her husband? Would she spend what remained of her fortune on defending Bellino? What contradictions I'd found in Chicago! One might do immoral things for moral reasons, as I had, or be tricked, as Harvey Payne had been. And what of those torn from the midst of their lives, pages that would never be written: Baldwin and Grewe lost in the line of duty. Oscar Donnelly. Tito had lost a father. Collin and Mrs. Box had lost Osain, a friend and a husband.

Clearing my throat, I said, "Mr. Payne, I'm going to see Collin and Mrs. Box. Will you come?"

CHAPTER 55

AN ADMISSION

JIM

At half past five, Diana came in like a dervish, skirts swirling, her cheeks fresh and blooming in the sweltering summer. Feeling grim, I put down the evening news and pulled my sweat-soaked shirt away from my back. I'd have to tell her—there was no way to shield her from this.

Unpinning her hat, her delicate brows turned up. "What is it, dear?"

I folded the newspaper, my tone somber. "Not sure how to tell you, sweet."

"Has something happened?" Her worried eyes darted over the table. "Is Mama unwell? Papa? Did Adi send a cable?"

"No telegram, no letter. Sit down, sweet." I caught her hand.

That further alarmed her. "Tobias? Oh no—Abigail!"

"No. Stop, my dear."

"Then say it! Tito? Is it Tito?"

I raised her hand and kissed the back of her fingers.

"Tell me!" she wailed.

I pulled in a breath. "You remind me of what matters. Everyone's all right. But—we're broke. Our savings, the gift from your father, they're gone." I tapped the newspaper. "Berkeley's Bank. It's gone under. They had all our cash."

She blew out a puff of air. "Is that all? You worried me."

I was glad she thought it so insignificant; perhaps women have a different conception of the import of money. Diana had grown up with plenty.

Biting her lip, she said, "Jim, dear, there's a great deal I haven't told you. I took our funds out of Berkeley's before I left Boston. I've spent it."

I stared. "All of it?"

She nodded. "'Fraid so." From her reticule, she dug out a wad of notes and counted them. "Three hundred and seventy-two dollars. That's what's left."

I teetered like I'd taken a fast turn on the Ferris wheel. She carried that vast sum in her pink satin reticule. It was all we had. She had spent over six thousand dollars.

God knows, I did not mean to take her to task; she'd come to my aid again, saved the fair, saved our lives. Yet my mind could not grasp it—six thousand?

"Spent it on what?"

She fanned herself with the newspaper. "Do you recall you said, 'One day let's buy a bakery?'" Taking out a sheet of hotel paper, she picked up my pen, saying, "The Lins wanted to buy a bakery but couldn't afford it. And they're Chinese, so the bank wouldn't give them a loan. You were gone, no word at all, and I didn't know if you . . ." She paused, frowning at the paper. Her eyes shimmered when she looked up.

I began to see. "You thought I was dead."

She bit her lip. "Feared so. And since I was going after you, I wondered if I would . . ." Another pause. I winced.

"You thought you could be killed."

She blinked. Gold flecks glimmered in her deep brown eyes like polished agate in sunlight. "Yes. And Papa's gift was just sitting there, idle."

"We were saving for a house," I reminded her.

"Yes, but that didn't seem likely, then. So, I went to the bank and bought the bakery for the Lins. The shop cost three thousand, seven hundred dollars."

She jotted down the sum, then went on. "Four hundred for expenses—ticket to Chicago, clothes, the hotel—can't have George paying for this suite. I paid Tobias and Abigail and gave some to Tito."

Her pen began another line. "A bushel of wheat flour cost seventy cents. Since we need wheat for the bakery, I bought a thousand, for seven hundred dollars. Then we needed a place to store it. I sent the Lins two hundred for that. Why buy when we could rent?"

I watched, astonished, with a sense that I would often see her like this in our married life, calmly doing her sums with the composure of a duchess.

She tapped her chin with the back of the pen. "Oh, yes. Fifty dollars to Bellino—I shall tell you about that another time, dear. And I bought Collin Box's copper mine for a thousand dollars. Well—Mr. Payne will incorporate the enterprise, and Collin and Mrs. Box will run it. They're going to ask Tito to join them."

Collin, Osain's widow and Tito? Diana had been busy!

"I see." I felt as though I was on a fast-moving train. Intrigued, I tapped her ledger. "How did you learn to do this, sweet?"

She grinned, her face rosy with a flush of pride. "Papa's bookkeeper was a sweet old Bengali. He taught me." She clutched my arm. "But it almost didn't work! Thank heavens, you gave that affidavit to the bank manager. What was it?"

At last, I had something to offer this conversation. "A legal power of attorney. Adi wrote it up based on an 1882 law, and the bank's lawyer witnessed it. He has my will too. Adi said it was the shortest will in the history of legal contracts. Four words."

She flinched. "Your last will and testament!"

"Everything to my wife, Mrs. Diana Agney O'Trey."

"That's eight words," she said softly, then continued. "Chinese people and women can't own a business, Jim! Apparently, the law believes that we are incapable of mathematics!" Her lips curled in derision; then she laughed. "So, I put it all in your name, Jim. You own a bakery. And a mining enterprise."

Astonishment gave way to pride. Though delicate, Diana was about as fragile as an India rubber ball. One moment I'd thought we were broke; the next, we owned two enterprises. Being married to Diana would certainly keep a man on his toes!

I leaned on my elbows and laughed.

CHAPTER 56

WHO ARE WE NOW?

At dinner, I told Jim about my conversation with Bellino and Harvey Payne, describing how I'd uncovered Bellino as the author of the treacherous note from the gala. He listened closely, straightening up with an intake of breath and a barrage of questions.

At last, he nodded and said, "Well done, my dear. Now perhaps you heard, we had one more casualty: last night Patrick Prendergast shot the mayor, Carter Harrison Senior."

"Prendergast? He was at the statue."

He nodded. "The fair was closed today, parade and closing festivities canceled. It's a state funeral instead."

I recalled Mayor Harrison's expansive vision for the future, his dream that one day electricity would brighten every city.

"What happened?"

"Prendergast knocked on the mayor's door last night and asked the maid for him. When he came, Prendergast shot him twice and made off. The chauffeur and Harrison Junior went after him. Seems a mob chased him down the street.

"He ran into a police station and turned himself in. But they'll try him as a criminal, no more. The governor doesn't want more talk about anarchists."

As we prepared for bed, I told him what had been twisting around in my mind so long. "Osain's murder—Jim, I'm to blame for that. I asked

Collin to find Tobias instead of just paying him what he was due. If I'd paid, Osain might not have been tempted!"

Mopping his face with a towel, Jim disagreed. "Osain Box made the choice, Diana. He set the munitions to blow up. Think he didn't know what that meant?"

I frowned. "Perhaps they killed him because he changed his mind. Thank heaven he told Collin." I rubbed my throbbing forehead. "Something I don't understand. If Peter and Bellino were on the same side, why did Peter blackmail him?"

Jim shook his head. "He didn't. When Baldwin sent him the fragment that contained Bellino's name, he realized he'd uncovered the plot, and told Collier about it."

Pulling on his nightshirt, he said, "By the way, have you seen Martin?"

I ran my brush through my hair, smiling. "He's with Tobias. They're friends. What a motley bunch we are. They'll return to Boston with us." It meant Abigail had to dress as a man, I supposed, but Tobias knew about her strange double life. I wondered what he made of it.

"Worst of it is," Jim said, sitting on the bed, "the anarchists were right. Everything's stacked against an honest man. I worked all day for under a dollar, Diana. One can't live on that, not with a family. All they wanted was a fair shake."

I put down my brush. "Governor Altgeld wants to prohibit children from working in factories. He supports an eight-hour workday. What if he ran for president?"

"Hmm." Jim lay down, elbows bracketing his head, and gazed at the ceiling.

Standing there with the bomb, I'd taken a chance with my hairpin. What if it hadn't worked? Life could be snuffed out like a candle in a gust. When I'd heard that shot, some part of me had frozen, thinking Jim could be dead. A tremor ran through me. I recalled Mama saying, "We must hold fast to what we have and treat it dear."

"Jim dear," I said, turning the lamp low, and slipping into bed. "Remember what I said, about having children? I think I've changed my mind."

He turned, his face tight as though he'd steeled himself. "You said you wanted a child, someday."

I nodded, my face warming.

His head turned an inch. "Now you don't want a child?"

"Oh no! I *do* want a baby, Jim. I'm ready."

The strain around his eyes relaxed. A smile inched over his face. "A baby, Diana, a tiny bundle. A girl."

I ran my fingers through his freshly trimmed hair, short, like the military cut he'd had in Simla.

He drew a great breath. "Diana, there's something I should tell you."

I hid a smile. My Jim was so very careful with me. At my birthday ball, I'd waited all evening for him to ask me to dance, but all he did was talk to the officers and Adi. So, when everyone had gone but family, I'd hung on his arm and demanded a dance. Of course, he led me out, but then he said he didn't know how to dance. We'd managed, though, because he hoisted me off my feet, and keeping me at a proper distance, swished me around the dance floor.

I giggled, remembering.

What he said next astonished me. "You know I'm a bastard. Well--"

"That's not your fault!" I cried. Jim's father was English, but that's all we knew.

"Wait, sweet. That's not what I'm saying. I would not want any child to grow up as I did, without feeling they had a right to be there. That's why . . . well, some of the army lads used to visit, ah . . ." He winced. "Brothels. Not me. I did not want my child born like that."

I pulled up on my elbows. What an odd conversation. Not what I'd expected at all. "Why tell me, Jim?"

Jim pulled in his lips, watching me. "I've never . . ." He tilted his head.

I understood, all at once.

"You've never . . . learned to dance?"

He absorbed that euphemism. "Exactly. And you're so tiny, my sweet. I'm terrified . . . that I'd hurt you."

"Well!" I said, lying on my forearms, on him. "Then it's a good thing I spoke with an expert. I asked her about—dancing. Will you let me lead?"

He looked stunned. "An expert?"

Someday I'd tell him about my conversations with Mama, who'd borne five children.

"Just follow my instructions."

A smile began at the corners of his eyes and spread across his face like sunshine.

* * *

I wore one satin opera glove—the other wouldn't fit over my bandaged wrist—with my blue saree to dine at the governor's mansion the next evening. Before the dinner speeches, Superintendent Brennan had a word with Jim, then stood before me.

He brought forward a small box, saying, "On behalf of the city of Chicago, I thank you, ma'am, for your efforts."

I gaped at him, then glimpsed Jim's proud smile. He'd known about this!

Inside the box nestled a familiar hairpin with an amber knob—mine! Blushing, I shook hands with him and then Governor Altgeld, speechless at the unexpected gesture.

After dinner, Ida came up, her eyes dancing with mischief. George introduced a dashing young man in a grey worsted suit, yellow-gold vest and stylish hat. "You remember my friend William Gillette, the famous actor."

I recognized the thespian's brilliant smile. Ida settled beside me, whispering, "His play *Held by the Enemy* did so well at the new London theater. But he lost his young wife, poor darling."

"Ah."

The young man sat with his back to the couples on the dance floor.

Ida tilted her head. "It was five years ago. No children. She died of a bad appendix!"

Like my brother Adi, William Gillette had lost his bride. He seemed lively, but now and again he'd look at the tablecloth for just a moment too long, then pick up his gaze and carry on. How deep the wounds of loss go, those invisible wounds no one can see.

Soon, Gillette engaged Jim in an animated discourse. Had he learned that Jim was a detective? Fellows thought it most exciting. I joined them, curling my hand around Jim's elbow.

His quick smile touched me; then he went on. "It'd make a good play. *The Sign of the Four,* now—it's based on a tale about India!"

"Fascinating. Conan Doyle, you say?"

Jim turned to me, his eyes alight.

"Can you imagine, Diana? William's never heard of Sherlock Holmes!"

AUTHOR'S NOTE

Readers often ask me, "Did it really happen?" While it is fiction, my tale intertwines research and personal accounts, so yes, many of the events in this novel did occur.

Chicago's 1893 World Fair was arguably the grandest event of modern history. Of the 63 million people that formed the population of the United States, about 29 million attended the fair. That's almost half the country's population! In 1893, Chicago was new, rebuilt from the great fire of 1871 just twenty years earlier. How the fair's inventions must have excited people's imaginations: electricity, movie camera, electric boats, and an elevated train! Grecian architecture, clean air, and horseless streets offered a breathtaking vision of what our world could be. When I learned that the World Congress of Anarchists was held in Chicago that summer, the counterpoint of two possible visions of America proved irresistible. What if Captain Jim stumbled on an anarchist plot? He'd be desperate to protect America's triumph from carnage.

Other factual events: The fair's closing pageant was canceled. On October 28, 1893, Patrick Eugene Joseph Prendergast, a disgruntled Irishman, assassinated Mayor Carter Harrison Sr., a corrupt politician and proud booster of Chicago. Harrison had bought the *Chicago Times* in 1891 and his son served as its editor. The sixty-eight-year-old Harrison was engaged to New Orleans heiress Annie Howard, whose fortune would be worth about $93 million today.

Mr. Ferris' wheel, the first such "Ferris wheel," opened late, in June, and drew great crowds. I wrote Diana's adventure, the incident on the Ferris wheel, after reading of a lady who shed her skirt and used it to cover a terrified, acrophobic man in one of its glass cars.

Admittedly, I've swapped some dates: The Cold Storage Building caught fire on July 10, not in June as in my book. The first Parliament of World Religions was held in September, not May. Indian sage Swami Vivekananda and Indian industrialist Jamshedji Tata did indeed attend the parliament and the swami is recorded as repeatedly deferring his speech, which was put down to stage fright. He spoke last and received a long ovation. Perhaps his delay had another reason, I thought, weaving it into Captain Jim's adventure.

What drew me to this story were the awful contradictions of the 1890s, many of which exist today. Enormous wealth and terrible poverty. Great strides in innovation alongside terrible deprivation, starvation, epidemics, lack of sanitation, bank failures, and the chokehold of wealth upon political and legislative change. No wonder it drove some to violence! Captain Jim's activities were based on Harry J. Wilson, one of the 1919 Seattle "Minute Men" who infiltrated the Industrial Workers of the World, Metal Trades Council, the Central Labor Council, the General Strike Committee, and the Soldier's, Sailor's and Workingmen's Council.

As to the German and Confederate connections: In the 1886 Haymarket Riot, an unknown individual threw dynamite at police attempting to quell a labor gathering. Nine patrolmen died and sixty-seven were injured. A rushed trial convicted eight innocent labor leaders, six of them German immigrants. Four were hanged, and one exploded a bomb in his mouth, killing himself. Many had German ancestry. Albert Parsons, a former Confederate soldier, was a member of the moderate Knights of Labor and the syndicalist Central Labor Union. He edited *The Alarm*, the English-language counterpart to *Arbeiter-Zeitung*. Thus, a vengeful Confederate general recruiting a pair of German-born Confederate soldiers seemed within the realm of possibility.

Actor William Hooker Gillette, who makes two appearances here, did in fact later write the play *Sherlock Holmes*, which debuted in October

1899. He played Holmes on stage a record 1,300 times, became a rock star of the times, and made Holmes a household name.

Another less-known fact: The first successful heart-repair surgery was performed by a Black surgeon, Dr. Daniel Hale Williams. The real-life open-heart surgery took place on Chicago's South Side on July 9, 1893, saving the life of young James Cornish from a knife wound to the chest during a barroom brawl. In my book, Dr. Williams saves the life of Tobias South, Diana's Black friend and guide, on July 3, 1893.

Three books were invaluable to my research: Erik Larson's *Devil in the White City* provided a rich background to the exposition. Mark Sullivan's *Our Time* described everyday life and the colossal change at the turn of the twentieth century. *Chicago: The History of its Reputation* by Lloyd Lewis and Henry Justin Smith taught me about the places, personalities, and history of Chicago. *The Bending Cross*, Ray Ginger's biography of Eugene Victor Debs, shed light on labor's struggles and the union movement, and that astonishing statement about the use of dynamite as a weapon of the labor war.

Abigail's character posed interesting questions. The word "transvestite" originated in 1910 with German sexologist Magnus Hirschfeld, who founded the Berlin Institute. So in 1893, resourceful, conflicted Abigail would not know that she might be transgender.

America had long been intrigued by Indian maharajas. Newspapers portrayed their ostentatious lifestyles, including the 1947 wedding of Jagaddipendra Narayan, the dashing, erudite maharaja of Cooch Behar, to Hollywood actress Nancy Valentine. In the 1960s, my friend Roshan Hakim visited from India with her sister and cousin, to study in New York. The three Parsi girls traveled by train and bus across the States, drawing a great deal of attention in their fine silk sarees, an unusual sight in those days. Funds running low, the three girls were in St. Louis when one of them joked, "What a fine city! How our father the king will be amazed to hear about it!" This was overheard and passed on. Alerted to the arrival of "Indian princesses," the mayor's office held a banquet in their honor and presented each of them with a key to the city. I heard this story at Roshan's wake in 2019 and was so taken with the puckish girls' audacity that I wrote it into Diana's story.

The immigrant's journey of Diana mirrors mine and those of many friends. At first, enamored of all things American, she's disheartened as she discovers the flaws inherent in society. The land of the free wasn't just or free for minorities. Since 1854, Chinese, African Americans, and Native Americans could not testify in US courts, making it effectively impossible for them to seek legal justice. The 1892 Chinese Exclusion Act banned immigration for ten more years and required Chinese immigrants to carry IRS-issued certificates of residence. Only when Diana witnesses kindness and generosity from some Americans does she esteem her new compatriots and feel kinship with them. To the Wack and Tata families of Chicagoland, and Bob and Sharon Jones, thank you for hosting this lonely foreign student in 1991.

I am indebted to my agent, Jill Grosjean, who shepherded me through the first draft. My editors, Kelley Ragland and Madeline Houpt, offered detailed suggestions and sage guidance. Thank you. Thanks, Lesley Martin of Chicago Public Library, for the research on bathhouses. A heartfelt thank-you to Jay Langley who reviewed three early drafts and suggested story twists. My family gave me the space, time, and quiet to write and ensured I went on daily walks: You are my rock. And to readers who asked, "Will we see Captain Jim again?" You will, if you tell your friends about this series!

Enjoy each journey. Thank you for being a part of mine.